Requiem for a Glass Heart

David Lindsey

Requiem for a Glass Heart

DOUBLEDAY

New York London Toronto Sydney Auckland

PUBLISHED BY DOUBLEDAY
a division of Bantam Doubleday Dell Publishing Group, Inc.
1540 Broadway, New York, New York 10036

DOUBLEDAY and the portrayal of an anchor with a dolphin
are trademarks of Doubleday, a division of
Bantam Doubleday Dell Publishing Group, Inc.

Library of Congress Cataloging-in-Publication Data

Lindsey, David L.
Requiem for a glass heart/David Lindsey.—1st ed.
   p.   cm.
I. Title.
PS3562.I51193R47   1996
813'.54—dc20   95-45464
CIP

ISBN 0-385-42312-8
Copyright © 1996 by David L. Lindsey
Printed in the United States of America
First Edition
June 1996

10   9   8   7   6   5   4   3   2   1

For Joyce,

who faithfully shares with me,
and enriches,
the abundant idea of
we

Requiem for a Glass Heart

One

St. Petersburg, Russia

IT WAS NEARLY TEN-THIRTY in the evening when she emerged from deep within the metro station at the Griboedova Canal entrance on Nevsky Prospekt. Normally night would have swallowed the grand Nevsky boulevard at this hour, but it was late June and the White Nights had arrived, a few weeks when the sun never sank more than several degrees below the horizon, precluding darkness, transforming the night hours into an eerie, endless twilight. They also introduced a season of festivities, and throughout the city there were concerts and ballets and parties.

Irina Ismaylova stood momentarily on the sidewalk at the metro entrance and let the hordes of revelers flow around and past her—tourists, hucksters, pickpockets, and students, Gypsy urchins sniffing glue and snatching purses, drug dealers, militiamen, young lovers, and peddlers of every commonplace and oddity. New Russia. In so many ways like the old Russia. Hope in bed with Despair.

She turned toward the Admiralty building, which loomed at the head of the boulevard, its golden dome and spire glowing softly in the rosy light of a static dusk, and allowed herself to be dragged along with the throng as they passed over the broad Kazansky bridge. On the canal below, water taxis filled with carousers dawdled on the dark stream beneath the dull beads of streetlamps strung along the embankment. At the far end, before the canal met the Moika River, she could just see the glint of the harlequin domes of the Church of the Savior on the Spilled Blood.

The crowd moved on, past artists displaying their canvases in half-lighted porticoes alongside prostitutes—night butterflies—lingering in the tea-rose glow of doorways. They passed cafés open late in this nightless season, and Irina longed to be one of the lucky people in the happy light of these friendly interiors.

She caught a crowded trolleybus near the Narodny bridge and stood in the opening of the broken door, lost in thought, the breeze of the late spring twilight tugging at the hem of her cotton dress. As the trolley hobbled across the Palace bridge, she stared down at the leaden water of the Neva and imagined that all the things that had gone wrong with her life were drifting by like flotsam on the swirling eddies of the current.

At the Strelka stop, on the northern tip of Vasilievsky Island, Irina stepped off the trolley and, ignoring the milling strollers who lingered along the water's edge in Pushkin Square, headed toward the tree-lined University Embankment across the intersection. Keeping to a well-planned course, she hurried past the classical and baroque buildings that faced the Neva until she drew opposite Rumyantsev Square, where she paused to watch a military vessel plow the river toward the Gulf of Finland. She dreaded crossing to the park, because it was there she would see the face, or perhaps the faces, that would set in motion the final scenes of a drama in which she had a leading and decisive role. As for the faces, she never knew their names. Krupatin only showed her the photographs of the men who would work behind her, and that was all. He was a fanatically cautious man.

Knowing they were already watching her, she turned away from the embankment and crossed the street. She didn't go into the park but entered 2-3 liniya, an adjacent street. The neighborhoods of Vasilievsky Island were among the city's oldest, their sidewalks sheltered by ancient maples and elms, which the season's anemic light had turned into inky silhouettes.

Walking on the park side of the street, she kept her eyes straight ahead as she entered the deepening shadows. The pale green undersides of the dense leaves were dimly lighted by the streetlamps, and Irina could smell the chlorophyll exuding from the moist, fresh foliage.

Someone began walking parallel to her on the murky paths of the park, and just as she got to the corner, where there was a streetlamp, he emerged from the hedges and crossed the sidewalk in front of her. With perfect timing, his face was caught for an instant in the feeble light, and then he was gone.

To her left now was the Repin Institute of Painting, Sculpture, and Architecture, where she had contrived her first meeting with Vera Vikulova. An art student at the prestigious institute, Vera was a promising painter in the realist style and lived just down the street on Bolshoy Prospekt. Like many women, especially students, who were only marginally self-supporting before the collapse of communism, Vera had turned to prostitution to help support herself after the disintegration of the economy.

She was a pretty dark-haired girl of twenty-four who had had the good fortune—or misfortune—to have caught the eye of Piotr Maikov, a mid-level official in the Security Ministry. Maikov had an irresistible weakness for an ancient pleasure, the ménage à trois. Headquartered in Moscow, he made regular bimonthly trips to St. Petersburg, where he never failed to visit Vera, who was ever on the lookout for a second woman. But Maikov was a man of particular tastes. He didn't want just poor students or night butterflies. Vera had to bring women with an air of respectability about them. On two occasions she even provided the wives of other government officials. (Maikov had secretly photographed these sessions.) Vera had proved to be a procuress of considerable talent, for which Maikov paid her very well.

"Right on time," Vera said, bouncing down the steps at the side entrance of the institute. She kissed Irina on the cheek and grabbed her arm, locking them together affectionately as they began walking. Vera was an irrepressibly optimistic young woman, an attribute that was almost heroic in the face of the recent sorry times.

"Nervous?" she asked with a wide grin.

"A little, yes," Irina admitted.

"No need to be. He's not very inventive."

"It's not that. It's just . . . he's a government official. That's a little scary, maybe."

Vera laughed. "Look, when he takes off his clothes, all of your nervousness will melt away. Luckily, he is a very attractive man. One of the younger bureaucrats."

"I can't complain about the money."

"Nooo, neither of us can. And if he likes you—and he can't help but like you—he'll want you several more times. He loves real blondes like you. Too many blondes really aren't when they take off their pants." She laughed.

They continued along the sidewalk for several blocks, until they reached Bolshoy Prospekt at a juncture where art nouveau architecture intermixed with the ornate buildings of the eighteenth and nineteenth centuries. Turning left, they walked on the south side of the avenue, passing strollers who lingered here and there under the maples and poplars, enjoying the evening. Still hugging Irina's arm, Vera talked animatedly about a new CD player she was going to buy through Maikov's special connections. She said he was now bringing her Lancôme cosmetics every time he came to St. Petersburg and that he had promised to get her some Italian shoes next month.

At the corner of 6-7 liniya, they started across the avenue toward a three-story art nouveau building, originally a private home that long since had been broken up into small apartments. It was here that Vera Vikulova lived, in a flat that she could afford only by the graces of Maikov's licentious taste.

Sitting at curbside, underneath the brooding trees in front of the building, was a dark-windowed American Lincoln, Maikov's pride and joy.

Irina's stomach tightened, and she furtively scanned the boulevard for Krupatin's faces. There were two. A man carrying a sack of groceries followed a little way behind them, and ahead of them across Bolshoy another man was approaching on a bicycle, coming along the side of the pink-and-white St. Andrew's Cathedral.

The two women crossed Bolshoy to the corner and stepped onto the sidewalk. As they approached the front door of the building, Irina counted four men sitting inside the Lincoln. Like many corrupt officials, Piotr Maikov had connections to Russia's *mafiya,* which were only too evident in his choice of bodyguards. Most of these thugs were avid fans of American gangster movies and freely copied the characters' posturing and clothes. But their viciousness was something they had learned on their own, and often it beggared anything they saw in the movies.

"What is your name?" someone inside the car demanded.

"Ignore them," Vera said. "The one we have to worry about is upstairs."

As they started up the stone steps to the entry, Irina noticed larkspurs blooming in tidy flowerbeds on either side of the landing. At the top they pushed open the leaded-glass door and stepped inside the building.

"We're going to be searched by a bodyguard," Vera warned in a hushed voice as they started up the stairs. "A really rude bastard. I've complained to Piotr, but it's no use. They are idiots about security. Just let him do what he wants. What does it matter, anyway? It's only touching, after all—little enough to put up with for the money."

As they rounded the second-floor landing they were met by a beefy young man with closely cropped hair. Despite the warm weather he was wearing an Italian wool sport coat, and a pair of tiny headphones were clamped to his head like padded calipers. Seeing the two women, he yanked off the headphones, leaving them hanging around his neck as he planted himself in front of Vera and Irina. Flapping the fingers of his opened hands, he beckoned them to draw closer.

"Let's have a little looky, sisters." He was somber, frowning.

Taking Irina's purse first, he opened it, felt around inside, his eyes fixed on her. She could hear the driving throb of a heavy metal band buzzing from the little pads of the earphones around his thick neck.

"Okay . . . okay . . . okay . . ." he said slowly under his breath and then dropped the purse on the floor. "Now . . ."

"Be careful," Vera warned him. "You wouldn't want me to tell Piotr you got in ahead of him."

The bodyguard pulled down the corners of his mouth in a show of indifference.

"Turn around," he said to Irina.

She did, and he started at her ankles and went up her legs under her dress, his big hands massaging her thighs all the way up. At her crotch his hand paused momentarily, and then his thick fingers dug under the tight elastic of the legs of her panties and quickly he was inside her. Irina flinched and froze. But it was not a surprise. This was routine with *mafiya* bodyguards now. Two months earlier a crime boss in Kiev had been decapitated by a woman who had hidden a small roll of piano wire there.

Withdrawing his fingers, he squeezed her buttocks quickly as he brought his hands from under her dress. Still behind her—he smelled of sour perspiration and sweet cologne—he reached around her and unbuttoned the top of her dress. Putting his hands into her bra, one side at a time, he checked the underwiring. After this he plumped his fingers around in her hair, and then pushed her away from him with a thrust of his pelvis.

She stumbled, but didn't turn around as she put her breasts in place and buttoned her dress. As she bent down to pick up her purse and the few things that had spilled out on the floor, she could hear him searching Vera behind her. He hissed once, and Vera snapped, "Stupid bastard."

As Irina stood and turned, Vera was squatting to pull up her panties and the guard was flapping his hand loosely at the wrist as if to dry his fingers. Vera's face was flushed with anger.

Vera quickly straightened her dress, and the two women walked away, their heels echoing on the wooden floor of the old building, sounding melancholy in the dimly lighted hall.

"Stupid bastard," Vera spat again, but even her practiced bravado could not hide her humiliation.

The door to the apartment was in a long, bleak corridor with wallpaper blotched with the stains of long, damp winters. At the end of the corridor a window was open to the street below, allowing the bruised glow of the White Night to fall upon the wooden floor. The sight of it suddenly brought Irina near tears, an impulse she struggled to suppress. She swallowed hard and, for a moment at least, fought off an unshakable sadness.

Vera stopped in front of her door and took a key out of her purse. She gave a little squeeze of encouragement to Irina's hand, smiled, and then turned and unlocked the door.

In the past two months Irina had come to know Vera's apartment very well, having cultivated the girl's friendship to the point that she was often invited over to listen to music and talk about their common interest in art. They entered a comfortable living room, to the left of which was a galley kitchen and a small table. In front of them was the bedroom door. To the right was a door to the bathroom, which had a second door that opened into the bedroom.

"Come on," Vera said again, taking Irina by the hand and pulling her into the bedroom. Maikov was sitting on the edge of the bed, naked, pouring himself a drink from a half-empty bottle of American whiskey. As he looked around at them, Vera said proudly, "This is Irina."

Irina managed a smile as her stomach began to crawl uneasily.

Maikov studied her in silence as Irina tried to read his eyes. But his mind was clouded by drink, and she saw nothing there, only a vacuum.

"How old are you?" Maikov asked unexpectedly, the glass of dark whiskey halfway to his mouth. "I don't mean it cruelly. You are very beautiful. I just want to know."

"Thirty-two."

He swallowed the whiskey and eyed her. He was indeed a good-looking man, well built, almost muscular. She guessed he was in his early forties.

"I *told* you, I met her in art class," Vera said, already undressing, dropping her clothes on the floor with routine familiarity. She got on the bed and went over to him on her knees, then bent over him and trawled a small breast across his back. "I didn't say she was young."

"Thirty-two *is* young," Maikov said, looking over his shoulder at Vera. "You little cow." She giggled. He turned back to Irina. "You want to get your clothes off, then?"

"I bought something . . . special," she said, holding up her purse. "Let me slip it on."

"Be my guest." Maikov shrugged, pleasantly surprised that maybe there was to be a little game in this.

Irina stepped into the bathroom and closed the door behind her, then quietly closed the door that opened into the living room. Quickly pulling a wicker clothes hamper away from the wall near the foot of an old cast-iron bathtub, she crouched down on the floor and pried at one end of a loose baseboard. It had taken her many visits to Vera's apartment to find just the right place and then to make it accommodate her needs. When the baseboard came loose, she was relieved to see the butt of the CZ 75, a Czech-made 9mm automatic handgun. Though she had put it there only two days before, she had worried about it ever since, fearful that some unforeseen misfortune would cause its discovery. But it was exactly as she had left it, the barrel pointing down between the wall studs, the silencer screwed into the barrel to keep the gun from falling out of sight. It was already loaded—and cocked.

Irina retrieved the pistol, not bothering to push back the baseboard or the hamper. She had calculated that she would need at least ten seconds after she opened the bathroom door. During those ten seconds Maikov must suspect nothing. She knew he would look at the door the moment he heard it open, so she laid the CZ on top of the hamper and unbuttoned the top of her dress, slipped her arms out of the sleeves, and removed her bra, letting the top of the dress fall around her waist as though she were about to step out of the skirt.

She picked up the CZ and took two deep, steady breaths. On the other side of the door Vera laughed a giddy, silly laugh and Maikov's deep voice mumbled a few indistinguishable words. Gripping the pistol in her right hand, Irina clicked off the safety with her thumb and let her hand hang naturally at her side, hiding the gun in the drape of her dress.

Then she opened the door and stepped into the room.

Maikov and Vera were on the bed facing each other, embracing, and at the sound of the bathroom door Maikov took his face away from Vera's breast and the two of them looked at her. Their heads were close together like those of two lovers in a photograph, cheek to cheek.

Without speaking, Irina swiftly raised both arms, brought them together to grip the CZ, and fired quickly four times. Each of the four bullets found its mark within the eighteen-inch square that contained the two faces.

She didn't know precisely where the bullets hit—an eye, a mouth, a forehead—only that the imaginary square had exploded in successive scarlet plumes punctuated by discrete gassy bursts from the silencer. It was done.

She promptly stepped to the foot of the bed, the gun hanging at the end of her limp arm, and looked at the man and the woman. They continued to die, soft liquid sounds sighing from their flesh as the two lives slipped loose of their tenuous moorings: a subtle drawing of an extended muscle, a shallow movement in the sternum. The volume of blood and the way it continued to surge from the bodies always surprised her. She stood rapt, holding her breath.

On her way out she shot the young bodyguard in the throat, then bent over and put the silencer in his mouth and shot him again. When she got to the front door and started down the steps, she saw that Krupatin's faces had disappeared, leaving death behind in the dark Lincoln at the curb.

Outside in the rosy, timeless twilight, she hurried around the corner, past the Cathedral of St. Andrew, past the white Church of the Three Holy Men, through the tunnel of locust trees, to the metro station on Sredny Prospekt.

She rode the escalators down, down into the immaculate and brightly lighted subterrane, deep below the Russian spring, and within fourteen minutes she had boarded the line to the Finland Station. There she caught the last army-green train for Helsinki. It was a six-and-a-half-hour trip, and it would take the remainder of the night.

She leaned her head against the window, and as the lights of St. Petersburg receded in the everlasting dusk, she wept, wept without ceasing, until she slept.

Two

Houston, Texas

CATE SAT across the table from an old friend in a softly lighted corner of an Italian restaurant and watched him sink deeper and deeper into gin-induced regret. Complaining was a given in his business. It came as a birthright, born of the responsibilities they accepted, of the risks they took, and of the disillusion that eventually ate away the core of far too many of them.

She hadn't seen him in nearly eighteen months, since before Tavio's death. He had been out of the country, and as soon as he was back he called her, wanting to get together. She was wary, but there was nothing she could do about it. It was inevitable that he would get emotional, and she would have preferred to avoid that. Her own road back to life without Tavio had been hard, and she didn't want to see Griffin's version of it too. She had heard that he was drinking too much again and that he had been shunted from Rome to Trieste and then eventually back to Washington and now Houston. That had taken most of a year, but Naples was still in his head as if it were yesterday.

They had finished eating an hour ago and had caught up on all the news, had covered everyone and everything except Tavio, whose absence stood between them like a pillar they kept talking around. And Griffin had settled into the point of his evening anyway, which was drinking.

"You know," he said, gesturing toward her with a fresh drink, clear gin in a clear glass with clear ice, "I never told you how knocked out I was when I first saw you. Tavio, he didn't tell me anything, the sly bastard. He knew what I was thinking when he told me he had this girl he wanted me to meet. He knew I was thinking—which I was—that she was a Mexican. He loved messing with what he called 'white-guy assumptions.' He said we were prejudiced, every last one of us, and we didn't even know it. Never let up on that. Just kind of slipped it in there. And he was right—I mean, about what I was thinking. You walked into that club . . . Remember that place? What was it?"

"Carioca."

"That's right!" He gestured quickly with the glass again, sloshing the gin. "Cari-oca! What a place . . . Anyway, you walked in, all pink and Scottish-looking, all that reddish hair, for Christ's sake." His grin was reminiscent and stupid.

Griffin was pure small-town Texas, and despite his degrees and his experience and his years of global traveling, he always would be small-town Texas deep down in the well that was his real nature. Tall and lean and nearly as dark as Tavio had been, he was almost at the end of his undercover career, at least in the front line of the DEA's foreign operations. He had strung himself out to the breaking point, playing roles inside his head for so long that the distinctions between who he was and who he pretended to be were bleeding together. It was taking him longer and longer to crawl out of the skins he crawled into in Palermo or Naples or Trieste or Salonika, and the rumor was that he was beginning to make mistakes and that he had been sent to Houston until they could decide what to do with him. He was looking more and more like damaged goods, and one of the black marks on this business was that nobody really knew how to handle damaged goods. Often the men in the offices, the men who maintained distance on everything, didn't handle this part of the business very well. In fact, it could be argued that more often than not, damaged goods were simply thrown away.

Cate looked at him and wondered how close Tavio himself had

been to this. Who knew what these men really thought? She had been married to Octavio Cuevas for five years, and though she had loved him—still loved him—and believed she knew him well, she also knew that when she married him she got only part of him. He kept a percentage—a small percentage, she hoped—to himself. But she had known that going in, and she had accepted it, though she had to admit that toward the end it had begun to have an effect on the marriage. It was nothing insurmountable. It was just that the small part he kept to himself sometimes defined more of what happened between them than she would have liked.

Griffin's smile faded, and he stared into space with an unsteady tilt of his head.

"Working together . . . so long . . ." He cut his eyes at her, almost glared at her, and then looked away again, his eyes returning to the space where nothing was. The sweat from the ice was puddling around his glass. She didn't say anything, but she wondered what it was about men that made them so damned romantic about their relationships with each other while at the same time they bravely proclaimed their independence from such dreamy attachments.

"I could *trust* him!" he snapped.

Cate frowned at the unexpected note of anger.

"That whole Naples thing was squirrelly," he said. "And I knew that—but I trusted him on it. When you start doubting your own people . . . Well, shit, you just can't do that." He shook his head slowly. "Can*not* . . . do that."

Cate looked at him. "Salerno."

"What?"

"You mean Salerno. You said Naples."

He hesitated a second too long.

"Salerno, Naples—whatever."

Now he had her attention. She had never known the details of the events surrounding Tavio's death, and she had accepted that lack of closure as a grim downside of the business they were in. Because of her own career in the FBI, and because she too had worked undercover operations, she was expected to understand the realities of the job. Both Tavio's colleagues in the DEA and her own fellow agents expected her not to pry into the particularities of operational issues. Once again, it came with the turf; you accepted the fact that there were secrets that always would remain secrets.

But something was eating at Griffin, something more than burnout.

"When I talked with Steve Lund, he told me they didn't know what went wrong in Salerno, that they still don't know," she said.

"Oh, Christ! Steve Lund. Guy's more useless than . . ."

"Then they do know."

"They know more than they told you, honey, but they don't know *anything.*"

"I don't understand that, Griffin."

"Look. You know the big story." Pause. "They know the small story." Pause. "I know the tiny story." Pause. "And Tavio, well, he knows the tiny, tiny story." With his elbow resting on the table, he raised his hand in front of his face and showed her his forefinger and thumb squeezed tightly together. "The least little scrap of it," he said, and his blue-green eyes squinted at her over the tops of his fingers.

In the simplicity of his inebriation, Griffin Younger had just summed up every undercover operation that used deeply embedded agents. At some point only the man deepest in understood everything, and it wasn't a rare thing for him to keep some part of it stored forever in that small percentage of himself that he never shared with anyone.

"So tell me the tiny story you know," Cate said flatly.

The big story—the one she knew—was that Griffin and Tavio had been working undercover on a single drug-trafficking case for almost two years. It had started small in Houston, grew larger in Colombia, and became enormous, drawing in other agencies, when it moved to Italy, where it merged into a drugs-and-arms operation utilizing the infamous "Balkan route" along which two thirds of the burgeoning worldwide heroin trade reached its Western European destinations. The case, of course, had been convoluted. While Tavio had burrowed deeper and deeper, Griffin's role had played out. He was disengaged and installed in Rome to become Tavio's case agent.

For nearly seven months the only communications Cate had from Tavio were through DEA back channels, and they had been rare. A call from an agent who was "out" and had seen Tavio in Brindisi. *He sends his love.* A cup of coffee with an agent who had just returned from Milan, where he had shared a meal with Tavio in the Galleria. *Tavio sends his love.* A voice she had never heard before, a DEA cryptographer at three o'clock in the morning. *Tavio sends his love.* The DEA was a small family. Everybody knew and everybody cared. *Tavio sends his love.*

And then one day when she arrived at the office she found her squad supervisor and the DEA's Steve Lund waiting for her. Lund was visibly shaken but managed to get through the sketchy account of Tavio's death with as little bureaucratic fuss as possible. Cate remembered the sudden pungent taste that had burst into her mouth from somewhere back behind her sinuses, and she remembered that her first thought had been a mental image of Tavio's body in the Salerno morgue, an image that had proved to be eerily accurate when she actually saw him there, with her own eyes, twenty-two hours later. She had insisted on bringing back his body herself.

It happened—not that often, yet often enough for her to know that she had to accept it without outrage, without suspicions that there had been an egregious miscarriage of responsibilities that had cost Tavio his life. She had accepted Lund's explanation, and she had accepted the account she had read in the inquiry files months later, when Lund was kind enough to let her see them when she asked. Because she was an FBI agent, she had been allowed access to more information than normally would have been given to a civilian wife. Aside from blind misfortune, she saw nothing in the account of Tavio's death that prompted incredulity. But then, she wasn't looking for anything, either. Her only interest in the details had been a desire to share Tavio's last hours in an effort to alleviate her own pain because she hadn't been able to be with him.

"The son of a bitch," Griffin said, shaking his head slowly. He was looking at her, and his eyes reddened and turned oily. "He got, you know, mixed up . . ." His voice thickened; he stopped.

"Mixed up?"

Griffin couldn't talk, just shook his head and tightened his lips, trying to gain control.

She didn't want to see this. Something about his year-old grief angered her.

"What?" she said. "He was confused about something? You

mean about the business in Salerno? I didn't see anything in the file about a mix-up."

"*Mixed* up . . ." Griffin took a deep breath and finished off the rest of his gin. "With a woman, honey. He just the fuck couldn't leave them alone . . . Got himself killed because of it."

His words knocked the wind out of her. She flushed hot, then grew faint with a chilling nausea that caused her forehead and the tops of her breasts to grow clammy. She fought the nausea as she watched Griffin's face react to her expression. When he reached out to touch her hands, which lay on the table, she jerked them back.

"Them." She heard her voice from somewhere else.

"Cate . . ."

She was confused by his anguished expression. Was it for her? For himself—or Tavio?

"That's how it happened?" Her voice was a strained, disbelieving rasp. "He was set up—a woman set him up?"

Griffin looked at her, sensing through his vaporous haze that he had unleashed something, that he had made a huge mistake. But he was too drunk, too deep into the gin, to make any kind of recovery. His nod was sloppy and mournful.

Her eyes bored into him. "And there were others?"

He looked at her. "Cate . . ."

"There were *others!*" she screamed, causing the slumping Griffin to flinch and creating an instant silence in the restaurant, making the two of them the epicenter of attention. She could see Griffin trying to calculate through the fog. Did he dare try to placate her? He continued to gape at her, his calculations glacial and offensively obvious.

He nodded again.

"How many?"

"What?" He was honestly confused.

"How . . . many?" Her voice was even, seething.

"Oh, Christ, Cate."

She could hardly control her breathing now, aware of an inward, swelling agitation.

"Always? The whole time . . . ?"

"Oh, Christ, Cate."

He seemed unable to say anything else. He made her sick. Without looking down, she let her left arm drop to her side and picked up her purse. Griffin was hardly conscious now, feeling the full effects of the gin, which had been creeping up on him with every fresh drink for an hour. She held her purse in her lap, making sure she had a firm grip on it. She stood slowly, and her voice started low.

"You . . . son . . . of . . . a . . . BITCH!" she shrieked, and without thinking she grabbed the edge of the tablecloth and jerked it with all her might, sending everything on the table flying across the dining room, crashing, splattering, and rattling behind her as she stalked out of the restaurant and into the sultry, mean heat of the June night.

Three

South Kensington, London

WERE YOU SLEEPING?"

"I was, yes," she said, looking at the clock beside the bed. She didn't know the voice and didn't wonder about it. It was two o'clock in the afternoon.

"Sorry." There was a pause. "I've got your things for you."

"Oh. Well, then, I guess you should bring them around."

"Now?"

"No. Give me some time . . . quarter to three. Can you make that?"

"Of course."

"Thank you. Goodbye."

She lay on the sheets in her underwear, the afternoon light shattered on the foot of the bed, broken by the trees in the garden outside the window. This was a very nice place, she remembered. Large. Clean. Well furnished. He had all kinds of places, shitholes and country homes. She never knew where he would put her, and she lived in all of them with equanimity. She had been here only once before, passing through. She had arrived in darkness, slept, and departed in darkness.

The sunlight on her legs was faintly warm, and she moved them on the sheets to enjoy the crisp cleanliness of British cotton.

Through the leaded windows she could hear London, the city sounds dampened by the lush vegetation of the park across the road. She hoped her layover here was for several days; she needed the rest, though he didn't care anything about that. But there might be a chance of it. The documents were supposed to arrive in the afternoon. She had business in the evening, and then tomorrow—maybe—there would be the briefing. The tight schedule was unusual, but she had done it before. It was inescapable, and like any horrendous effort, you did it and then wondered later how you ever got through it.

Actually, she had no complaints about this part of the work, being whisked from country to country without knowing where she was going until just before she got her briefing, and he let her go again. At least she was able to spend most of her time alone.

Feeling a slight cramp tug at her lower abdomen, she rolled over on her side and looked out at the sunny street. She reached up to her throat with her left hand and felt the locket around her neck. She never took it off. She couldn't. To remove it, even in those terrible moments that threatened to taint it, would cut her loose entirely. She wanted in the worst way to open it now and look inside, but she wouldn't yet. Too little time had passed since Bolshoy. She was still too near the darkness and could not risk having this special bit of weak, hopeful light extinguished.

Wearily she tried to calculate how much time had passed. The train from St. Petersburg had arrived in Helsinki in the gray Baltic dawn, and she had gone straight to a musty little hotel near the harbor. She had removed her clothes and showered, then washed her underwear and dress in the sink and hung them to dry in the window. Then she spent the whole day on the bed in the puggy, cramped room, waiting for her clothes to dry. Late in the afternoon a man knocked on her door. Without introducing himself, he gave her a ferry ticket to Stockholm, a passport, an identity card, a KLM ticket to London, and a key. He told her the key was to the rooms in South Kensington. Again she spent the night traveling and spent the next day staring out the windows, this time in a sparsely furnished flat in a bleak modern apartment building in

Stockholm. In the evening she took the last KLM flight to London, arriving at Heathrow very late and taking a taxi to the South Kensington address.

The monotonous, calliope-like notes of a siren swelled and receded, probably on Cromwell Road. She rolled over on her stomach, stretched out her arms to either side of the bed, and spread her legs, stretching as far as they would go, her face pressed into the fresh sheets. She imagined her limbs stretching, stretching, slowly separating at the sockets, wrist, elbow, and shoulder, then ankle, knee, and groin, her limbs floating, slightly away from her, slightly separated, her torso limbless on the English cotton sheets, the rest of her suspended in the air around her, all in order like the exploded drawings in medical book diagrams, her blond hair flaring out around the top of her limbless trunk as though it were electrically charged.

In this disjointed state she began to think of an icon she had seen in a monastery in St. Petersburg when she was a child. It was an image of an angel dressed in flowing robes of cinnabar trimmed in gold. The angel's great, unfurled wings were black.

The man who brought her things was not Russian but German, and though he did not say, she knew he was from Berlin, where a Russian émigré community of more than 300,000 provided the staging ground for the Russian Mafia's operations all over Europe.

"Passport," he said, pulling the documents from his satchel one at a time and laying them on the dining table between them. " 'Olya Serova.' " He was big and husky, with a leisurely demeanor and a soft voice. He wore rimless eyeglasses.

Irina gathered her dressing gown and cinched it tighter. Again she had washed her dress and was letting it dry in the bathroom. She picked up the document and looked at her photograph on the first page. Olya lived in St. Petersburg. From the stamps on the following pages it seemed that she had traveled extensively throughout Europe.

"Why have I traveled so much?"

He shrugged. "They just tell me what they want." He laid a second passport on the table. " 'Vera Mendel.' Czech Republic. Prague." He looked at her. "You speak Czech, huh?"

She didn't answer him. Vera had traveled in Europe as well. But also in England and the United States.

The quiet German laid a visa on the table. "Everything is in order here. Olya leaves St. Petersburg for London. From London to Paris. From Paris to the U.S."

"From Paris?"

He nodded.

Picking up the visa, she saw that her occupation was trade representative promoting manufacturing opportunities in the Russian Republic. She was always a trade representative.

There were backup papers for each woman, whatever was required to prove her legal attachment to each country. If Olya Serova was going to Paris, it was a safe bet that Vera Mendel eventually would be returning to Prague. She checked all the documents. All of the particulars were correct—age, height, coloring, everything.

"These are personal items," the German said, placing two photographs on the table. "Olya has a husband and a daughter, it seems."

Irina shuddered. A daughter. She picked up the photograph. A complete stranger, a child. The husband, of course, was a nobody too, and was even shown with a little girl, though it was a candid snapshot and the girl could not be identified as the girl in the first picture.

"Vera has an elderly mother and an aunt," the German said, placing two more pictures on the table with the precise movements of a man assembling the pieces of a puzzle.

"Letters to leave lying around. One from Olya's husband," he muttered, placing them beside the photographs, "one from Vera's mother, who is ill and needs the aunt to do the writing." He sat back a little. "The contents are very detailed," he added with low-key satisfaction.

She flipped through the pages and put them aside.

"I think they will want you to know the details."

She looked at him. He was a man who enjoyed being exact. Neat. At this time of the afternoon his white shirt was still crisp, his tie tightly knotted. She had noticed that his hands were as clean as a freshly scrubbed surgeon's and that the nails of his surprisingly slim fingers were manicured. She could not remember when she last had seen a man with manicured nails. He did not exactly smile, but his expression was pleasant.

"One more thing," he said after a pause. He leaned forward to his satchel again and took out a small book. "An address book." He handed it to her rather than putting it on the table as he had done with the other documents.

It was of a good quality, leather-covered, roughly thirteen by eighteen centimeters, well worn. It belonged to Olya Serova. She roamed through its pages, which were filled; names and numbers were often crossed out and new ones written above or below. Some pages were more used than others, having a patina of much handling. There were doodles at the corners of some of the pages, numbers jotted beside initials, none of them identified. Since her passport reflected that she had traveled widely in both Eastern and Western Europe, so did her address book. She could tell that some considerable time had been spent on this bogus document. They had never gone to this much trouble before, and this realization gave her a sense of uneasiness.

"This is a very important item," he said with an odd sort of kindness in his voice. "More important than the others. Until you are briefed, I should be very careful with it." He paused. "It's quite important."

She looked up from the address book. "Did you prepare these documents yourself?" she asked.

He hesitated. "I simply follow instructions," he said with circumspection.

"And these"—she tilted her head at the variety of documents on the table between them—"were your instructions?"

He considered the packets of papers as though he were regarding the sale of antiques that he had some regret over letting go. "Yes."

Neither of them spoke for a moment.

"Did he instruct you about me?"

He looked up, frowning, but only slightly. "What do you mean?" And before she could answer he added, "I received no instructions whatsoever about you. No."

She knew, of course, that that was true. She carefully laid the address book on the table and studied him. He was older than she, but by only a few years. Perhaps he was thirty-five, she guessed. He wore a thick ring with carving on it. She would like to talk with him, visit really, ask him about his work, his family, learn a little bit about his life, but she knew that was impossible. She only wanted a normal conversation, but she hadn't had a normal conversation in years, and she seriously doubted whether she ever would again.

"Would you like a drink?" she asked.

For the first time he showed hesitancy, a mild uncertainty.

She stood and walked a few steps into the adjacent parlor to a liquor cabinet. Opening it, she surveyed the contents.

"There is a bottle of scotch here, that's all," she said, turning to him. He was standing, but hadn't moved. "Scotch?"

He tilted his head tentatively, shrugging one shoulder. She took glasses out of the cabinet, poured a dollop of scotch into each of them, and turned around to find that he had taken his satchel and joined her just inside the parlor. She stepped over to him and handed him one of the glasses. Lifting hers to him, she said, "Pro-sit."

They drank, standing facing each other. He was taller than she by a few inches, even though she was tall for a woman. They looked at each other. He held the satchel in one hand and his drink in the other. She crossed her left arm beneath her breasts and rested her hand in the crook of the arm holding the glass. She knew that the top of her dressing gown had worked loose as they had sat at the table and that he was able to see a good part of her breasts. In fact, he had looked at them as he had taken his drink away from his mouth.

"Do you have a happy life?" she asked. She did not adjust the loose drape of her gown.

"Compared to what?" he asked. The response surprised her.

"I'm not asking you to compare it to anything," she said. "Simply, are you happy?"

"I could use more money."

She sipped her drink and saw his eyes fall to her breasts again as he lifted his own glass.

"How long have you done this kind of work?" she asked.

"Since university. A long time."

"For these people?"

"People like these people."

"Do you travel a great deal?"

"Not more than I want. I don't mind it."

"Are you away for long periods of time?"

He shook his head. "Well, perhaps occasionally."

With this response she sensed a modest concern in his voice. She had gone too far. What had been intended to be an effort at common human communication had become, in his mind, an inquiry. Another question would drive him out the door. It was a fact that simultaneously angered and pained her. And made her feel foolish. In this dark charade that she had played for the past three years there was no room for anything but suspicion and fear and depravity. She had learned to assume that everything she saw and heard and felt was deception, trickeries fabricated by unknown others, delusions that were intended to destroy her and that she had to ferret out if she wanted to survive.

On rare occasions, and always with strangers, she might experience a moment or two of guileless kindness that she could trust. But she never accepted it, even momentarily, without walking away feeling as though she had just escaped a snare by the skin of her teeth.

She had no idea what had made her think she could talk to this man in a normal way. She had long ago forgotten what normal meant or what it would feel like if she experienced it.

"Thank you for coming," she said abruptly, reaching for his unfinished drink. Taken aback, he frowned in puzzlement, but he gave her the glass.

She put the glasses on the cabinet and opened the front door for him.

"Goodbye," she said.

He nodded to her. "Thank you for the drink," he said. She detected no note of irony.

She closed the door behind him, relieved, thinking she had narrowly escaped a disaster.

Four

Houston

SHE WAS ON the Southwest Freeway when she began to cry, suddenly and without warning, a hemorrhage of tears that threatened to extinguish the anger that she had carried like a torch in her stomach as she fled the restaurant.

What appalled her the most as she pressed her car onto the freeway was that she immediately had believed what Griffin Younger had said about Tavio. She hadn't even questioned his revelation, because it had carried the conviction of its context. Griffin drunkenly had blurted it out as an unthinking mistake. He had not meant to give away Tavio's infidelities, but his own sorrowing fury at Tavio's foolishness had brought the truth out in a curse, a verbal fist-shaking at Tavio's licentious ghost.

Instantly she knew that all of them had lied to her—Griffin, Tavio's partner; Lund, Tavio's and Griffin's superior; and Ennis Strey, her own squad supervisor, who surely must have known all along. God, maybe he had even known about Tavio for years. Standing shoulder to shoulder, they had lied to her in the name of that age-old masculine fidelity that superseded everything and that Tavio himself apparently had found more binding than his fidelity to her.

Goddamn them all, she thought, and that was when she began to cry, the tears springing out of a livid, stuttering rage that encompassed all of them at once, tears of frustration and shock and pain like none she had never known. In that one brief moment of Griffin's gin-beclouded confession, Tavio, her most intimate other self, suddenly had become a stranger.

After Tavio's death Cate had taken a leave of absence, and her sister had come from Charleston and stayed with her for nearly two weeks, during which Cate had completely isolated her anguish in a desert of dry-eyed silence. She hadn't cried, not a tear. She simply had sat mute, staring out the window at nothing at all for days on end. Her appetite vanished. She lost weight. She got a sore throat that wouldn't go away. Every normal emotion dried up in her, shriveling to extinction. It had been a bleak two weeks, a period that seemed, in retrospect, hallucinatory.

Then one morning she woke early, just as the day was lightening the sky outside the windows, crawled out of bed, and put on a pot of coffee. She drank it alone, her ravaged digestive tract rumbling at the sudden assault of the black brew that she believed signaled her resurrection. When her sister woke up, Cate told her to pack her bags because she had booked her on an eleven-thirty flight back to Charleston.

That very day she began a diet regimen that was intended to rehabilitate a physical system completely disordered by two weeks of fasting and gut-wrenching inner turmoil. She began an exercise program. She called a real estate agent and listed the house that she and Tavio had managed to acquire by pooling their salaries. By the end of the week she had moved into a condominium on a secluded street in north Tanglewood, her adrenaline-driven recovery owing more to a denial of her emotions than a healing of them. The following Monday she was back at work.

The determined euphoria of her miraculous recovery had lasted five weeks, then it proved to be fool's gold and she had hit bottom again. Unexpectedly. After that she began a slower, more sobering and genuine climb back, a thoughtful struggle with her grief that had involved psychological counseling. The process had been incremental and less dramatic than her own version of "putting it all behind her," but it had enabled her to rebuild her life, and it had lasted.

But nothing was ever the same again. She had been in her late twenties when Tavio had stepped into her life, and she was almost in her mid-thirties when he stepped out of it. Not only was nothing ever the same, it never had been. If the psychological counseling had done anything for her, at least it had taught her to take Tavio off the pedestal on which she had placed him the instant he was gone. It was a natural overcompensation, believing that no one could ever be as wonderful as the person who had been lost, especially when that loss was a sudden blind stroke of fate, a single, unjust sweep of Death's scythe. Counseling had helped to put that in perspective.

But she had not been toughened to the point that she could deal with what Griffin Younger had coughed up from his inebriation.

So she cried, plunged suddenly into an eye-stinging blur of humiliation and anger that forced her off the expressway at the first exit and into a business plaza, a deserted boulevard, its grassy median awash in a downpour of isolated, cloudless rain from a sprinkler system. She hurriedly pulled to the side of the boulevard, ignoring the scrape of her wheels against the curb as the car lurched to a stop. Wrapping her arms around the steering wheel, she dropped her head on her arms and wept as the water drifted over the car in sheets of soft, stippling whispers that almost killed her.

Startled by her pager vibrating at her waist, she raised her head and stared at the wet windshield. She had no idea how long she had been sitting there. She looked at the pager. The number was Strey's, and there was no way she could put it off. She picked up the telephone from the seat beside her and dialed. As it rang she wiped her cheeks with her hand, wiped the tears on her dress.

"Strey."

"This is Cate."

"Hey, kid. Where are you?"

"I'm, uh, on my way home, Southwest Freeway."

"Okay. Listen, I've got to talk to you. Something's come up, and it can't wait until tomorrow."

She hesitated. "You talked to Younger."

This time Strey paused. "Goddamn. Yeah, I did. When did he get in touch with you?"

"Today. Called me at work."

"I see. Well, damn." He paused. "I'm sorry, Cate. I don't know. Griffin's a mess." He paused again. "But Cate, that's not what this is about. Can I meet you at your place?"

"Yeah," she said, holding her forehead in her hand as she looked at the water on the windshield. "I'll be there in fifteen minutes."

When Strey buzzed her from the front gate, she pushed the button to open it, and a few minutes later he was ringing the doorbell. When she opened her door he was standing there on the patio amid the palms, wearing an old polo shirt with part of the collar turned up, part down, the tail out over a pair of blue jeans. He wore deck shoes without socks, and his fifty-five-year-old face was a little pinched around the eyes from too little sleep, lately interrupted.

"Come in," she said, turning away from the door. She had had time to wash her face and run a brush through her thick, unruly henna hair. But she knew she looked frumpy, that her dress looked like it had been wadded up at the bottom of a musty clothes hamper for a week. She imagined that she looked pretty much the way she felt, which was shitty. The room was dark except for a small lamp near the sofa that she had turned on when she walked through the room as she came in. She sat down at the opposite end of the sofa and folded one of her bare feet up under her.

"What'd he think I was going to do, kill myself?"

Strey walked over to an armchair and sat down. "He was worried about you. He was so drunk it took him a while to get the story out. He said you made a pretty good scene in the restaurant."

"Did he tell you why?"

Strey nodded.

She looked at him. "You knew about this?"

"I knew how Tavio got killed, yeah." Strey was just under six feet, compact, athletic. The short-sleeved polo shirt revealed the muscles in his arms, and he carried himself like a man ten years younger. He had straight dark hair that was thinning a little in the front and graying at the temples. For the past five years he had been Cate's squad supervisor, and he was one of those rare men who had no pretensions. What you saw was what you got, which meant that you always knew where you stood with him and didn't have to play games. He didn't much like games. While he wasn't a stickler for rules, he didn't flout them and seemed to operate in large part on simple, sound common sense. And he expected the same from his agents. He liked agents who worked hard—slackers were transferred out in a snap, even after the word came down from Washington that that old trick was going to have to stop. He just flat out wouldn't put up with them, and he had enough pull with old buddies above him to see to it that he didn't have to.

"Why the hell was I given that goddamn false report, Ennis? What really happened?"

He looked at her a moment, his head tilted a little, thinking. Then he nodded and looked her straight in the eye.

"The report was correct exactly as you read it, Cate. Except for how Tavio died. He wasn't killed in an ambush, he was in bed with a woman. Lund changed that and that's all. He thought he was doing you a kindness. He didn't see why you needed to know that."

Cate stared at him, her red and puffy eyes unblinking as she swore to herself that she would not allow another tear. Certainly not now.

"The minute Tavio had suspicions that he'd been compromised," Strey went on, "he got a message to Griffin and told him that he thought he'd been made and that he was coming in to talk. They agreed to meet in Rome—"

"I read all that, Ennis," she said.

"Yeah, okay. Well, all of this happened very quickly, within eight to twelve hours, from top to bottom. He was in Salerno when he called Griffin. He also told Griffin that he was going to stop in Naples . . ."

"To see this woman."

Strey nodded. "Griffin begged him not to. Griffin had never liked . . . that woman. Didn't trust her." He paused, shook his head. "The next thing Griffin knows, the Naples *carabinieri* were calling him in the middle of the night, ten hours before he was supposed to meet Tavio in Rome."

Silence.

"And the woman?"

Strey shrugged. "Gone."

"Who was she?"

"Nobody knows. Nobody ever met her. Griffin's dislike was based on the little bit Tavio had told him and on the obvious security risk. Even so, he covered for Tavio. He just let it slide, holding his breath. Naturally, they now think she was connected. Maybe she was even the one who turned him over."

"Jesus Christ." Cate had turned her head away; she couldn't speak. The little lamp cast a feeble light; darkness was very close by.

"Ennis." She cleared her throat. "Did he have a reputation for this?" She couldn't bring herself to look at him.

"There were rumors," he said. "But Christ, Cate, you ought to know better than anybody how people talk about the undercover guys."

"Don't . . ." She stopped, got a grip on her temper, dropped her voice. "Don't patronize me. *Did* he have a reputation?"

There was a moment when she thought he wasn't going to answer at all, and then he said, "Yeah, Cate. He had a reputation for liking women."

She felt as if he had reached into her gut and grabbed a handful of her intestines. Nausea crawled at her throat again, along with the horrible knowledge that she wasn't going to wake up from this.

"While we're being honest here," Strey said, "I think you'd be making a terrible mistake if you let this wipe out everything else about the man's life. This is only a part of what he was all about. In fact, a small part. I don't expect you to understand this, not at first anyway, but those women, they didn't—"

"Oh, God, Ennis, don't say it—not any of that condescending crap."

"No, listen to me." Strey sat forward in his chair, leaning toward her. "What you thought you had with Tavio, you *did* have with Tavio. Those women, they didn't enter into the picture. I'm not making excuses for him. I'm just telling you the way it was. If we're talking truth here, then let's look at all of it, let's look it right in the face. Tavio had learned to divide himself into parts— that's why he lived as long as he did, that's the terrible reality of how those guys survive—and the part that he gave to you, that he saved for you and shared with you, was the best he had. He didn't have that with anybody else, and what he got from you, and needed from you, he couldn't get from anybody else." He stopped and looked at her. "That's the way it was. I'm not saying it's easy to deal with, I'm not saying it's right, but nothing can change it, either. Not cursing him or hating him, not even all the grief in the world."

Cate looked at him, at the shallow light of the small lamp softening his face.

"I don't know how—honest to God, I just don't know . . ." She sighed heavily. "It . . . Damn him anyway, Ennis. I can't help it."

They talked a little longer, and after a while she thanked him for coming, assured him she was going to be all right, and told him to go on home.

But Strey didn't move; he just stared at her.

"What's the matter?" she asked.

"I told you, Cate, this really wasn't the reason I needed to see you. It's something else."

She forced herself to listen to him, to bring her mind back from the shadowy hollows it had wandered into.

"Listen," he said, sitting back now, studying her. "I'll be honest with you. I wanted to talk to you about another undercover assignment."

"Undercover."

"Yeah, but it's something that, you know, you've got to hit the ground running, and . . . I don't know how you're feeling right now, if you think you can do that. Even if you wanted to."

"What is it?" She didn't like the way he had said that, as if he were afraid she might have been emotionally unhinged by Griffin's drunken revelations and imagined that she was going to have to be pampered for a while.

"You still have any interest in FCI?"

Foreign counter-intelligence had been her first assignment request when she had been transferred to Houston nearly six years earlier. But she had been assigned to organized crime instead. She volunteered for undercover operations, went back to Quantico for the training course, and then over the next few years worked three cases undercover. They weren't FCI, but they were exciting enough and challenging. That was the main thing. But she hadn't gone undercover in almost two years now. As far as she was concerned, it was way past time.

She looked at him. "Yeah, I'm interested," she said.

He nodded. "This is a Group I special, a task force originating out of the New York office. They've got a target coming to Houston, and they want a woman who knows the city. I know the squad supervisor, Curtis Hain, he's an old friend, and he'll have the ticket on this. I'll be checking in, but he's running the operation. You'll be working with a small group of people from an off-site."

"Here in Houston."

"That's right."

Cate focused on this information. A special was a case that took precedence over all others. There wouldn't have been anything else to say if he had said this at the beginning. This was an extraordinary opportunity. But she couldn't entirely suppress her skepticism.

"Why me?"

"They wanted a woman, and they wanted one with some organized crime background and some undercover experience."

"They don't have women agents like that in Washington?"

"They don't know Houston. Look, Cate, if you don't feel a hundred percent about this, then it's not for you. You know that."

"I just take the assignment or I don't? It's like that?"

"No, they want to talk to you first."

"When did you learn about this?"

"About a week ago. They contacted me and let me know they were pretty sure they were going to have a target here and they wanted to coordinate a joint operation. They said they'd need a female for undercover work. But they said it would be a few weeks away. Then a few hours ago they called and said they needed someone now. Look," he said, "I knew how you used to feel about FCI. This came up. I thought you could handle it, and I recommended you. That's all."

They were staring at each other, and she sensed his next words coming at her before he spoke them. "But under the circumstances," he said, "I don't know if it's the right thing . . ."

"No," she heard herself say. "No, it's not a problem." Instantly her hesitation vanished. She wanted this, whatever the hell it was.

The last four hours had brought about an enormous alteration in the way she viewed her life. Suddenly there were certain things she didn't want to repeat. She didn't want to go back to a tomorrow that was only a tepid variation of yesterday. She needed a dramatic change, and this was it.

"Look, I'm pissed off more than anything else," she said, fully aware of her dishonesty and hoping she could hide it. "What do you expect? It leaves a damned bad taste in my mouth, but it's not a nervous breakdown kind of thing, for Christ's sake." She paused, her eyes fixed on him, trying to read him. "I really want a shot at this, Ennis. Very much."

Strey nodded, still studying her. For a cold, brief moment she thought he was going to pull it out from under her. Then he said, "Instead of coming into the office tomorrow, just wait here. Somebody will give you a call and tell you what's next."

"Fine," she said quickly, swallowing.

Five

South Kensington, London

IRINA LAY NAKED on her side on the bed, staring at her own pearl-gray profile against the wall. She examined its contours closely and repeatedly—the reclining oval of her head, the sudden height of her shoulder falling in a gradual slope to her hip, the silhouette rising suddenly again and falling in another long slope to become her diminishing leg. This second, one-dimensional self alternately grew more pronounced and disappeared as the afternoon sun hid behind and then emerged from clouds, and then it steadily lengthened and distorted and became absorbed into the beige wall as the oblique light of late afternoon lost the ability to create any contrast at all.

The telephone was on the bed behind her, and when it rang she reached back with her arm and picked up the receiver without turning over.

"Hello," she said.

"I guess you'd better go ahead and pick up a tin of tea," the voice said.

"What kind?"

"Black tea."

"Fine. I'll do it," she said. She reached back without looking and fumbled the receiver onto the cradle.

As always, she had committed the details to memory long beforehand and hardly had to think about what to do next. For the moment, she did nothing. She stared at the wall, wondering where in it she had disappeared to, wondering what course her life would take if she simply lay there, just as she was now, until her shadow returned. She would remain there through the long evening and into the night. She would not move. She would not get up to eat. She would not get up to drink. Sometime during the night, probably in the long, interminable hours just before dawn, she would have to go to the bathroom. But she wouldn't get up. She would lie there and urinate in bed, feeling the warm liquid come out from between her legs and run down the side of her groin and thigh onto the sheets. She would stay in that wet slough through the night and grow chilled in the discomfort of her own urine. She might sleep, but she would not dream. At dawn the black walls would begin to lighten, and they would grow lighter and lighter until the actual sun would rise at her back, throwing its fire across the bed and onto the wall.

Her shadow would be red.

She sat up on the edge of the bed, her back still to the window where the weak light that refused to throw her shadow languished on the sill. Walking around the end of the bed, she went to a clothes chest near the closet and opened the bottom drawer. It was empty. Taking the drawer out of the chest, she searched for and found a small canvas tab tucked into the corner of the bottom where the wood was joined to the front. She dug at the tab with her fingernail until she could grasp it. Tugging firmly on the tab, she lifted the false bottom out of the drawer.

Taped to the real bottom were two keys, a thick manila envelope, two packets of white powder, and a pair of surgical gloves. She pulled everything loose and laid it out on the bed, then returned the drawer to the chest. Sitting on the foot of the bed, she opened the envelope and dumped out the money. She counted it. Twenty thousand pounds. And then fifty pounds in small bills. She picked up the packets of powder and examined them. One had a pressure-sensitive seal that was red; the other's seal was green. The colors were hardly noticeable unless you were looking for them.

She put all of the items on the bed into her purse, the one the bodyguards had gone through, it seemed, far in the past. The event was as vivid as if it had happened a moment before, but the circumstances surrounding it had merged with the circumstances of the other events, all of which seemed remote and long ago. This was a recent phenomenon, this psychological separation of the circumstances and the events themselves.

She went into the bathroom and dressed, taking from the wire hangers the same underwear and light cotton dress that she had worn so long ago to the Bolshoy deaths. It took her a long time to finish with the small buttons. She ran a brush through her hair and noticed in the mirror that perspiration had discolored the underarms of the cheap summer dress. Russian fabric. Everything, dresses and lives and souls, stained easily in Russia.

Back in the bedroom, she picked up her purse from the bed and walked down the hallway to the front room, where she picked up a third key from the table by the front door. She stepped outside and locked the door behind her, then began walking along the quiet wooded street in the dusk, looking for all the world like hired help, a East European girl in her plain small-patterned dress carrying a shiny black patent leather purse. Within five minutes she had reached the nearest corner and a bus stop. The bus ride to the South Kensington Underground station took less than ten minutes.

Getting off the bus, she walked a little way to a pub and waited on the sidewalk, watching the early evening traffic. She hailed the first cab that drove by.

"Yes, ma'am, where're you goin'?" the driver asked as she opened the back door and got inside.

"Wapping," she said.

He looked at her over the back of the seat, taking in her simple dress, her lack of makeup, her uncoiffed hair.

"That's a good ways," he said. "It'd be cheaper by the Underground, just over there." He jerked his head toward the South Kensington station. "Goes right to Wapping."

"Thank you, but I'd rather take a cab," she said.

He nodded, still eyeing her. This time he had picked up her accent. Immigrant. Household help or a hotel maid.

"I'm sorry, but for that distance—"

"In advance," she said, opening her purse. "How much?"

He told her, and she handed him two large bills.

"Oh," he said, surprised. He started to dig in his jacket pocket for the change.

"If you can drive me there without talking, you can keep the change," she said.

He jerked up his head and looked at her over the seat again. But his hesitation was brief. He stuffed the money into his jacket pocket, nodded slowly, turned around, put the car in gear, and pulled away into traffic.

She didn't care how long it took. Slumped in the corner opposite the driver, she watched the lights go by, watched the people in the street as the cab plowed through the early London evening. At the traffic lights she picked out individual faces to watch, but while the cab was in motion she let the lights and colors blur into streamers of confettied brilliance.

She fell asleep.

"Wapping," the cab driver said, and she started awake. "Where you want to go?"

She sat up and looked around. Wapping was part of the massive Docklands development, an eight-and-a-half-square-mile redevelopment project begun in the early eighties with the intention of revitalizing the environs of the famous Thames ship yards, which had fallen into dereliction. Responding to government enticements, real estate speculators and foreign investors had weighed in to initiate the largest urban renewal project in Europe, an effort to change the face of a landscape well acquainted with hard times, from the Tower Bridge east to the East Royal Docks. It was an eighteen-billion-dollar project. Whole blocks were razed and a new world was created, or at least conceived, with condominiums and office towers springing up in a newly designed community of commercial and residential enterprises which threw together Cockney East Enders and chic yuppies in an untested futureworld.

Of all the Docklands neighborhoods, Wapping embraced the most evident extremes of wealth and poverty. It contained one of the East End's most diverse collection of immigrants—Jews and Hindus and Muslims, Bengalis and Pakistanis, Vietnamese and

Chinese, Nigerians and Indians; an endless moil of foreign hope and determination. Through the window of the cab Irina saw the spattered blue-glowing sequins of modern office windows at night and smelled the musty water of the Thames and the pungent odors of the cooking dinners of many nations.

"The Camberwell Building," she said.

"Yeah, I know it," he said.

In a few moments he stopped in front of a block of glass structures.

"It's that one," he said, pointing to a triad of glass towers, "the one on the right." He looked at her. "It's closed at night, ya know."

"This is my first night with a custodial service," she said. "I thought I was going to be late."

She opened the door and got out of the cab.

"Good luck to ya," the driver said and pulled away.

She walked across a small tidy plaza and went between the Camberwell Building and its neighbor, heading for a third building only slightly visible from the street where the cab had let her out. Entering another plaza, she crossed to the Margate Tower condominiums. The bottom of the building was filled with darkened shops and fast-food eateries and restaurants that closed in the evenings, when the thousands of employees in the surrounding commercial zone went home to the suburbs and the city.

She used the first key to activate the elevator and punched the button for the eighth floor. When the elevator stopped, she turned to her left and walked down two corridors to number 817. She rang the buzzer. Nothing. She rang it again. And again. She was just about to get the second key out of her purse when she heard someone fumbling at the door. It opened slightly.

"Yes?"

"You ordered black tea?"

"Bloody hell," the man said. "You're right on time, aren't you?"

The door closed, the safety chain was undone, and the door opened wider. The man was in his late twenties. She didn't know how Krupatin's people found such men. He was hawk-nosed and broad-shouldered, with straight, long dark hair. He just looked at her. It appeared he had not long been out of the shower; his damp hair was roughly combed and his charcoal shirt was hanging out of his dark gray trousers, the baggy sleeves unbuttoned at the cuffs. His black loafers were alligator. He was freshly shaven.

"You ordered the black tea?" she asked again, this time with a slight smile.

"Oh, yeeeah." He was looking right through the summer cotton.

"I'm not coming in until I know you ordered the black tea," she said smoothly, almost coyly, but making the point.

"I ordered the damn tea, yeah." He looked exasperated, but she waited. "Okay, let me see." He rolled his eyes upward, remembering the exact words. "Yes-I-ordered-it-from-Clarks-on-Cromwell-Road," he said in a mocking singsong, rocking his head from side to side.

"Verrry good." She smiled brightly, her voice rewarding him for following the rules. "I have it."

He stepped back to open the door wider.

"You are supposed to be alone." She raised her eyebrows questioningly.

"Indeed I am." Now he was grinning too.

He stepped back farther, and she entered the apartment. The place was furnished unimaginatively with contemporary furnishings, a lot of glass and chrome and straight lines. The lighting was low and moody, and a massive black sound system took up most of a wall, its dials and monitors of beady colored lights blinking and winking a silent composition. The volume had been turned down. It was a corner room, and the glass walls on two sides revealed the heart of London. Whatever he had paid for the place, two thirds of the price must surely have been for the view.

"You Russian?" he asked, following her into the living room.

"When did you get in?" she asked, looking around, giving the place an appraisal.

"Flew into City Airport two hours ago." He was smiling at her, his expression flirtatious. "You're a damned fine-looking Russkie." He was very sure of himself, feeling cocky after a successful job.

"I'm German," she offered with a small laugh.

He shrugged, continuing to stand between her and the entrance, grinning. His clothes were silk, slinky and modern.

"How about a drink?" he asked. "You look like you could use

a drink. I'm having one." He gestured toward a drink on a glass coffee table in front of a crescent-shaped sofa between them.

"Sure," she said. "What you are having is fine."

"In a jiff," he said, and turned to the kitchen. She looked around.

"This is a beautiful view," she called to him.

"Ya got to love it, don't ya," he called back.

She walked to the glass wall and looked out.

He came back into the living room carrying a glass like the one on the coffee table, his manner jaunty and anticipatory. He handed the glass to her.

"Sit down," he offered.

She sat on the crescent-shaped sofa near the middle, holding her cold glass. She could smell the rum. God, who would have guessed it would be rum.

"You're a hell of a messenger," he said, sitting down and leaning back on the sofa, with one arm thrown across the back of it. He was looking at her with a silly grin, the kind of giddy expression that revolted her, the universal expression of lechery.

She raised her glass. He picked up his.

"Congratulations," she said, "on your successful job."

They drank from their glasses.

"You do this all alone?" he asked after swallowing the rum.

"They always know where I am," she said. "I feel safe enough."

"I bet you do."

She smiled. "I have something for you." She put down the glass, reached for her purse, and took out the manila envelope and handed it to him. "I have to watch you count it."

"Oooh, well, it'll be my pleasure, won't it," he said. He counted out the twenty thousand pounds and put it in two piles on the glass table.

"They want to know if you can help them another time," she said.

"My pleasure again." He picked up his glass once more and took a mouthful of rum. "When?"

She laughed. "Well, they don't want you to rush into anything. You should relax a little first." She turned slightly on the sofa and her dress fell open, revealing a good length of her thigh.

"Relax?" he asked. "I could do some relaxing . . . How about you?"

"Oh, yes. I could relax." It was incredible how little body language was required to set an imagination like his going.

He reached over and put a hand on her bare leg. She let it stay there.

"I have something that could help us relax," she said. She reached into her purse again and tossed the two packets of cocaine casually onto the table. She smiled. "One for you, and one for me." She shifted her legs and let him have a glimpse of what he wanted.

"I'm all for this," he said. "I'm bloody well all for this."

In her briefing she had been told that he was reckless and that he would not turn it down. There was a fifty-fifty chance he would pick up the right packet. She had to do it this way so he wouldn't be suspicious; she had to let him pick his own packet. If he got the red one, she would have to devise an opportunity to switch. He picked up the green.

Within moments they were on their knees laying lines on the glass top of the coffee table. She went first, taking one of the British notes from the pile on the table, rolling it deftly into a cylinder. But first she tested one of her lines, licking her finger, putting it in the powder, and rubbing it on her gums with a relishing smile. Just to make sure. Then she leaned over and sucked up a line of baking powder, throwing back her head and sniffing. Then a second line. He was rolling his own bill from the pile. Quickly inhaling and snorting like a bull, he sucked up one, two, three lines in rapid succession.

She had no idea what they had mixed for him or if the drug was simply uncut, but it didn't happen immediately. He sat up straight, smiling. He wiped his nose, he closed his eyes. His smile turned to a grin, a big broad grin that grew wider and wider, grotesquely wider, until she realized it had become a grimace. His eyes squeezed shut as his body began to tense, stiffen, and then jitter. Saliva began seeping through his gritted teeth, drooling down his expensive silk shirt. Then it began flowing, his locked teeth slowly becoming obscured as the saliva turned to froth. His eyes opened slightly; the irises had rolled upward, exposing slivers of white. He began convulsing as the saliva gushing from his mouth commingled with something lumpy and fatty yellow. She watched as he slowly slid over onto the floor, choking, groaning, shuddering.

It would take a few minutes.

Ignoring his mewling and worming at her feet, she opened her purse and pulled on the surgical gloves. Picking up her glass, she took it into the kitchen and washed it and returned it to the cabinet. She dampened a paper towel and went into the living room and wiped up the baking powder and dried the place where her glass had been sitting. She picked up the money, leaving the one bill he had used still loosely rolled next to his remaining lines of cocaine—or whatever the hell it was—and put it back into her purse.

One of his feet was rhythmically kicking a chrome leg of the coffee table, but she didn't look at him. She didn't want to look again until she had to feel his pulse.

She took the damp paper towel and went into the bathroom and flushed it down the toilet along with the red-lined bag. Coming out of the bathroom, she looked down the hallway. Three more doors, one closed. One . . . closed?

Her heart fluttered in her throat. It was the last door on the right, at the very end of the hallway. She had no weapon, but she had been lucky. She hadn't been seen. Taking several steps toward the closed door, she paused and held her breath. Now, faintly, she could hear a television. He probably had told whoever was in there to stay until he was finished with his meeting. Which made his apparent interest in a sexual encounter right there in the living room a surprising bit of audacity. That is, if there really was someone in there. Perhaps there wasn't. He might have been watching the television by himself.

She backed away from the door, turned sideways, and went back down the hallway. After stepping into the kitchen to get her purse, she headed to the living room to make sure he was dead.

She couldn't see him in the dimly lighted room where the bank of high-tech sound equipment iridesced in silence, its beady coruscation throwing nervous reflections against the darkness. When she got to him, he had coiled into a fetal ball, leaving life much as he had entered it. The room was heavy with the reek of vomit and feces. He was dead. She looked out the windows again, admiring London, and then she turned and walked out of the apartment, making sure the door was locked behind her.

Six

Houston

CATE LAY AWAKE in bed, her mind darting back and forth between the two new events, one a great weight that angered and grieved her as only betrayal can, the other an enticing question mark that she realized was as attractive to her as a means of escape, a counterbalance to the other weight, as it was a unique opportunity. All of it together put her in a state of heightened emotion that was not easily defined. There was a haunting giddiness about her situation, a feeling of unreality she could not bring under control.

But it was Tavio's infidelities that dominated the night, penetrating her sleep with unbidden images of his trysts with other women, women whose faces she could never see but whose naked bodies were all too clearly visible in her mind's eye, olive-skinned women whose limbs and loins were dusky rather than pale like hers, whose breasts were lusty shades of cinnamon and almond rather than the dusty rose of her own. She dreamed of his familiar tenderness and how he used those same ways of touching to undress the dark women of her imagination. She woke crying, drifted back into exhaustion only to awake again, her eyes matted with tears.

When the alarm woke her in the morning, she found herself lying crosswise at the foot of her bed, her spine resting against a pillow that probably had kept her from actually rolling off. For a moment she was completely disoriented, the window across the room unrecognizable and even ominous in its lack of association.

With her heart pounding, she wrenched herself off the sheets and stood, unsteady, her wiry hair disheveled, and tried to clear her head and put herself into a familiar context. Finally she fixed her eyes on her overturned shoes at the foot of the bed, and after a moment everything shifted slightly and fell into place. The same old place.

She showered and brushed her teeth standing naked in front of the mirror, left hand on her hip, studying her turbaned reflection. She looked like hell. She rinsed out her mouth and put away the toothbrush. Turning from the sink, she bent over, unwrapped the towel, and began drying her hair, her head down, staring at her own naked thighs . . . her own naked thighs. Suddenly she sobbed unexpectedly, once, then twice. She held her breath and closed her eyes, the third sob lodged deep in her throat, waiting there for her to make up her mind.

She straightened up quickly, slinging her wet hair back with a fierce snap of her head, and turned back to the sink, putting the towel aside on a stand. She opened the door of the medicine cabinet and took out Tavio's razor, which she kept on the glass shelf beside his last bottle of cologne. Without thinking, she suddenly began banging it against the edge of the sink, furiously banging it and banging it and banging it, until the handle snapped and the head went flying and skittering across the tile floor, and without looking or thinking she flung the handle too, bouncing it off the wall.

She braced herself, putting her hands on the edge of the sink, arms locked straight out, head down, fighting back the feeling that she was just a few heartbeats away from hyperventilation. She took a deep breath and then another, and then another. After a moment she reached for the towel, turned away from the sink, and bent over again and finished drying her hair. With her eyes closed.

□   □   □   □

She dressed and ate breakfast and waited. She drank too much coffee and read the paper through twice. This was the very thing she wanted to avoid—time on her hands, time that tempted her mind to fall back on itself. She loaded the dishwasher and turned it on, and while it steamed and clacked she cleaned out the refrigerator. That got her past mid-morning.

She checked the telephone to make sure she hadn't left the receiver crooked in its cradle, but it was all right. Twice she rejected the temptation to call Strey. That would be a mistake.

At noon she decided to make a sandwich, but she had been overzealous in cleaning out the refrigerator, and there wasn't much there. She made a cheese sandwich: whole wheat, mayonnaise, hastily cut chunks of cheddar and lettuce. It wasn't much good, but she washed it down with gulps of ginger ale that she had forgotten she had. It was a lousy meal, and she had no appetite, which made it worse. She felt as if she were recovering from a hangover.

At twelve fifty-five the front gate buzzer sounded, and she scrambled to the intercom button.

"Hello?"

"Catherine Cuevas?" It was a woman's voice.

"Yeah."

"Special Agent Loder."

In a few minutes Cate opened the door to a leggy, dark-haired woman a few years older than herself, smiling a crooked smile and holding up her FBI badge with her left hand to verify her identity. She stuck out her right hand. "Ann," she said.

"It's good to meet you," Cate said, shaking hands. "Just let me grab my purse."

"Uh . . ." Loder stepped forward hesitantly. "I think it'd be best if you packed some things. You know, for a few days—a week, maybe a week."

Cate looked at her.

"Sorry, there was really no way to let you know this ahead of time."

Cate caught herself. "Oh, no, it's okay. Just regular . . . clothes?"

"Yeah, sure." Loder shrugged. "Whatever you'd wear to the office." She smiled her crooked smile, and this time Cate saw her beautiful straight teeth.

"Okay," Cate said. She was determined not to show her surprise, determined to be resilient. "Give me a few minutes," and she turned and headed for her bedroom.

Loder followed her. "Catherine. They call you Catherine?"

"Cate."

"This is the way it is, Cate, with these undercover deals," Loder said, as if they were talking about shopping. She was looking around. "And with the special ops stuff, too. Most of the time they don't tell you anything until the last minute. You just gotta say 'whoa' and hang on to your socks. And then some of these guys are need-to-know freaks. They like to keep you in the dark as much as possible, as long as possible. It's a power thing."

Cate dragged a suitcase out of her closet and began pulling clothes off the hangers. Her mind was only half on the task, but she managed to remember to match colors.

"But this guy we're working with is a great guy," Loder continued. "You'll like him. I've met him once before. He doesn't play those kinds of games, which takes a load off your mind. You don't always have to be wondering and worrying about hidden agendas."

"Can you tell me what this is all about?" Cate asked, grabbing shoes from the bottom of the closet.

"Not my place, Cate," Loder said, shaking her head matter-of-factly, watching Cate pack. "We'll be doing all that in just a little while. Look, get some casual things, some pants maybe. We'll be sitting around a lot."

Cate grabbed a couple of casual dresses and a few hangers with slacks. She snatched another pair of shoes from the closet floor, then headed to the bathroom. Loder wandered after her and watched a moment.

"You know, you'd better throw in a hair dryer," Loder suggested. "This is not a hotel or anything. I forgot mine and had to buy one at a drugstore, which was too bad. I'd just *bought* a new one back at home."

Home, Cate could tell, had to be somewhere in New York. Despite her name, Loder was obviously Italian. She had high cheekbones, big black eyes, and the crooked smile that she used a lot and that somehow made you want to smile back. Ann Loder was infectiously likable.

The Loder came from an ex-husband, she explained as they

pulled out of the condominium's driveway and headed toward the West Loop. She had kept his name because it didn't give her away before she arrived. Ann Loder didn't tell you anything. Anna Mazzini, her maiden name, told you too much. She was thirty-four, had grown up in Secaucus, New Jersey, had finished the academy eight years ago, and her first assignment had sent her right across the Hudson to the city where she had remained ever since. Lately of Brooklyn.

She had a dry, world-weary sense of humor, which she didn't mind using on herself in a self-deprecating manner that conveyed the fact that she was an Italian girl with a very level head and a healthy skepticism about nearly everything.

By the time Loder had turned off the freeway and headed downtown, she had succeeded in putting Cate at ease, or at least close to it. They quickly entered a neighborhood thickly forested with pines and oaks, a quiet street in a surprisingly tony part of the city near the center. Loder pulled into the driveway, or, more accurately, the courtyard, of a one-story Mediterranean-style house that appeared to have been built in a shallow U shape, with the drive and courtyard in the open end. She parked behind the second of the two cars already there, the three vehicles forming a half-circle around a cluster of three palms in the center of the brick courtyard. The house was surrounded with thick, brambly woods that completely obscured neighboring homes, which seemed to be a considerable distance away.

"How's this for off-site?" Loder grinned, turning off the ignition and motioning toward the front of the house. "Can you beat it? God, I love asset forfeiture." She shook her head. "These butthead drug dealers. I couldn't believe this. You should see the kind of places we operate out of in Brooklyn. Jesus."

They got out of the car, and Cate pulled her suitcase from the back seat and followed Loder into the front entry, where she put her bag down beside six or eight others that were already there.

Though the house was beautiful and spacious, her immediate impression was of vacancy. The place was bare. The entry opened directly into a generous living room a step or two below the level of the entry itself, and Cate now saw that the house was actually H-shaped, the living room being in the horizontal bar between the two parallel sides. The far wall was glass and opened out onto a lush tropical courtyard, which created a jungle backdrop for the sprawling room. The dearth of furnishings in the living room made it seem even larger, and the three people waiting for them seemed dwarfed by their surroundings.

"Okay, people," Loder said cheerfully, tossing her shoulder bag into a chair. "Special Agent Cate Cuevas."

The two men and one woman were already standing, holding notebooks and manila folders that they obviously had been consulting. Other documents were scattered around on a folding card table and in half a dozen metal folding chairs sitting in the middle of the room. The nearest of the two men stepped up to Cate and introduced himself.

"I'm Curtis Hain," he said, extending his hand. "I'm the case agent on this. It's good to meet you."

Hain was in his early fifties, tall, maybe six-three, with a barrel chest that made him an imposing figure. His thick light brown hair was heavily flecked with gray and a little unruly. He wore a blue dress shirt with the cuffs turned back and no tie, dark blue dress pants that were incredibly wrinkled, and oxblood loafers. He seemed entirely comfortable with his sparse and temporary surroundings, and for some reason that Cate couldn't quite pin down, he had the air of a man who had spent a lot of hours offsite in sensitive operations. With a perfunctory gesture he tossed his arm in the direction of the person nearest him.

"Leo Ometov." Ometov's age was difficult to guess. He was a dark blond and had the kind of untroubled skin that didn't show its age. The suit he was wearing was off-the-rack European, and his shoes, which were noticeably clunky, had not seen polish in a good while. He wore no tie; his shirt was open at the collar. With a handsome long face, a precise mouth, and a nose slightly askew, he had the polite manner of a guest in a foreign country. He inclined his head as they shook hands, and his smile could only be described as one of amusement. Cate liked him instantly.

Hain swung his arm again.

"And Erika Jaeger." Jaeger was a trim young woman with an athletic manner, short yellow hair, and a healthy suntan. She was dressed in tailored chocolate slacks and a tight-fitting sleeveless blouse that hugged her small breasts in a neat, tidy package. There wasn't an ounce of anything extra anywhere on the woman, and Cate knew by looking at her that she would prove to be efficient, focused, and serious. Her handshake was firmer than Ometov's.

"Here," Hain said, motioning to one of the metal chairs. "Make yourself comfortable." He grinned at the obvious impossibility of following that suggestion. "Our accommodations are courtesy of a recently incarcerated drug dealer who had pretty good taste in Houston real estate but no luck with Miami women—didn't know an FBI agent when he saw one." Everyone sat down again. "Unfortunately, whoever's in charge of asset forfeiture sold every damn stick of furniture in the place." He motioned to the chairs and the card table. "This stuff's from the storage room in your field office here." He extended his legs in front of him, moving stiffly, and crossed his feet at the ankle, his chair creaking. "But we've got rental authorization finally. We'll be getting some stuff in here later in the day."

He looked at Cate. Out of the corner of her eye she saw Jaeger flipping through papers in her folder. Ometov, with a kindly smile, kept his eyes on her.

"Okay," Hain said. "I know you're wondering what in the hell's going on here. If it makes you feel any better, we've all just met, literally this morning. Well, Ann and I met in New York a year ago." He scratched between his eyebrows with his thumb. "Erika's an agent with the BKA, the Bundeskriminalamt—Germany's equivalent of the FBI. Leo's sort of on loan to us from Moscow's Interior Ministry, directorate for organized crime."

Cate raised her eyebrows.

"You thought this was FCI." Hain nodded. "Well, it is and it isn't. I'm from FCI, Washington office. Ann's with the Bureau's New York field office, organized crime. She's worked closely with NYPD's organized crime/Russian squad."

He paused. "Would you like something to drink? We've got soft drinks in the kitchen in there, iced tea—"

"No, I'm fine," Cate said.

"You come highly recommended."

"I appreciate that," she said. "But I'm not sure I understand why."

"Did Ennis tell you that he and I are old friends?" Hain asked, ignoring her last remark.

"He mentioned it."

"Yeah, from college."

Cate studied him during this little exchange. He had a square face with blue eyes and full cheeks. He was good-looking, but not in a handsome, rugged way. Rather, he was a clean-cut, all-American kid who somehow hadn't entirely lost that self-assured collegiate look on his way to fifty.

"What we have in common here," he said, motioning to Jaeger and Ometov and himself, "is an interest in a Russian *mafiya* figure named Sergei Krupatin. This man has been a big player in Russia for nearly two decades, for nearly a decade in Germany. Obviously, his influence in the world of international crime is enormous, or we wouldn't be here. We've received some intelligence that we think provides us with an unusual opportunity to get a closer look at the way Krupatin operates. This task force was assembled to take advantage of that opportunity. And with your help, that's what we intend to do."

Seven

South Kensington, London

SERGEI KRUPATIN was a handsome man in his early forties. He had thick hair which was prematurely gray and which he wore full and carefully barbered. He had a neatly trimmed mustache which, like his eyebrows, was much darker than his gray hair and showed the brindled color his hair had been before it had turned. He was a sad-eyed man, his eyes sloping gently at the outside, which gave him a poignant, soulful appearance. His nose was strong and straight, his face oval.

Delicate cups of English china sat between them on the table. They drank rich, strong tea, to which Krupatin was addicted. For the fourth time he put a sugar cube in his mouth and sipped the dark cream-cut tea, sucking it through the dissolving cube.

Also on the table beside Krupatin, who sat in precisely the same chair as the German forger had used the day before, were two thick notebooks. Sometimes he would reach over and idly line up the corners of the notebooks as he spoke. He was a very tidy man, even unconsciously.

"And finally, I made the deposit in the Crédit Suisse in Bern this morning."

She nodded. "And?"

Krupatin smiled sweetly in a deferential manner, opening and closing his sad eyes. "And another in the Banca Svizzera Italiana in Zurich."

"In her name?"

"Of course. Yes, yes."

Irina said nothing but put out a hand, palm up, on the table. Krupatin smirked, reached into the breast pocket of his suit, and produced two wire receipts, which he put into her hand. She read them. Later, when he was gone, she would call and verify the receipts.

This was a stupid game of Krupatin's. He always made her ask for the money, toyed with her. She never really understood why he did that, what he got out of it, but she never asked.

She picked up her own cup of tea, which she drank without cream or sugar.

Krupatin was dressed in a custom-made English suit of dark summer worsted wool, double-breasted, chalk stripe. Being a vain and intelligent man, he did not want to look like the dull-witted Russian mafiosi who had become known for their brutality, for their use of violence when guile would have served as well, if not better. He wanted to be thought of as shrewd, so he tried to look shrewd and paid close attention to his dress, which was meticulously and classically stylish. But the truth was, he really did understand violence better than anything else. It had got him where he was, and it was taking him where he was going.

"Now, to the next thing," he said, washing down the last bit of the sugar cube with more tea. "I want you to read these files." He rested a well-tailored forearm on the two thick binders, his hand hanging limply at the wrist. "These are the files on the next two targets. These you will have to know intimately before we can move to the next step. This time, Irina, we are not dealing with our lamebrain comrades."

He raised his dark eyebrows and widened his eyes at her, the visual equivalent of a trumpet fanfare. He did not smile, but he wanted to.

There was no logical reason, no actual knowledge that caused her to experience the emotion she felt at that moment. It came unexpectedly and inexplicably, a disturbing and at first subtle anxiety.

Krupatin looked at his china cup and pushed the handle back and forth a bit. This was his townhouse, furnished impeccably with British antiques, a foreigner's idea of what an English gentleman's city home should be. There was a small garden in the rear with paths of bricks in a herringbone pattern and rosebushes, all carefully tended by an old couple whom Krupatin retained on salary. Like all men whose criminal enterprises have yielded them fortunes, he was preoccupied with putting a great deal of distance between himself and the negative images of his past, hoping to push them all the way into oblivion.

"Just read the files," he said. "We have some time."

"How much?"

"A few days, a week. Something like that." He looked at her dowdy summer dress. "And please, buy some damn clothes."

"What kind?"

"Get some things for the next few days here, something nice. As for the trip . . . I'm not sure yet."

She sat with her legs crossed at the knee under the table, her thick, buttery hair pulled back and fastened with a clasp at the nape of her neck. These meetings, when she received the information about her targets, were never witnessed by anyone. From the beginning it had been that way, and she knew it would remain that way. There were often files, but never anything like this. Usually he briefed her himself.

"Why don't you tell me about these men yourself, like always?"

"Because I spent a fortune to get these damn things," he said, patting the binders. "Information like this on men like these is like platinum. We'll talk, 'like always,' but first I want you to read every damn word of this. The fact is, Irina," Krupatin said, softening his voice, a self-satisfied look settling over his handsome face, "this . . . situation has been in the planning for many months already. We are now entering the final stages. Many people have been carefully constructing this building for a long time, stopping to measure every individual brick to see that it is perfect, checking the consistency of the mortar to make sure it is strong and will not crumble"—he held up a flattened hand, turned it edgewise to her, fingers pointed up, and canted it slightly this way and that—"checking the plumb line every few moments to make sure we do not make a mistake, not even by a millimeter." He carefully lowered his hand and let it rest on the table again. "With these people, a miscalculation even by a few hairs would be fatal."

" 'Men like these,' " she said. "And we have to take special care."

He nodded.

"Because they are important men."

He nodded.

"And you believe this is necessary."

"It is imperative."

It sounded to her like Krupatin was getting ready to make big trouble for himself and maybe for many others as well. The vague anxiety she had experienced a few minutes earlier now became a distinct, well-defined fear. It suddenly seemed that all the risks she had escaped during the last four years were gathering together and turning on her, forming a phalanx of old debts wanting their due at last.

"Listen, Sergei," she said, slowly dropping her eyes, wrinkling her brow as she began to shake her head. "This doesn't sound like something that I would be good for. If it is this delicate, I don't think I am up to it, to the tension. The truth is, you've used me too much already. I should tell you . . . I don't . . . the last few times . . . Sometimes I feel like I'm losing my mind." She swallowed. She should tell him; she should let him see her state of mind. "Sergei . . . I don't believe . . ."

Krupatin shook his own head slowly, looking at her with a serious expression that said he would not listen to this.

"Irina, the fact is you are *perfect* for this. *The* perfect one. You have the best English. You have your fancy university degrees— and in *art,* for God's sake! You will see how perfect this is when you read the files." He sat back in his chair and stretched out his arms, opening his hands to her. "And you're beautiful!"

There was silence.

"Sergei . . ."

"What are you talking about, dammit!" he blurted fiercely, slapping the Regency table so hard his spoon leapt off the saucer and hit her hand. His face was tumid with anger.

It was futile for her to say anything else. She stared at her teacup, her finger lightly touching the thin gold rim, the intricate cobalt pattern.

Krupatin was silent. The house was silent, and then a wall creaked, the way a house will do when one is alone, and Irina clung to that sound as though it were an actual piece of wood, a plank of drifting wreckage to keep her afloat in the deep, ominous sea of her disconsolation.

"Irina, what are you talking about?" The tension had vanished from his voice, which now conveyed only a cajoling irritation.

"Nothing," she said. They both knew she would not bring it up again, and she would not talk about it even if begged to do so.

"You're tired," he said, his voice lilting to sympathetic tones, "and you should be. Of course. I should have waited a few days to bring these to you. But I was so eager—I just didn't think. Look, why don't you just sleep tomorrow, then, in another day or so, look at the files. I'm asking too much of you. I'm sorry."

He reached across the table and took her hand from the teacup and gently held it in his own.

God, how she hated his condescension, his door-to-door salesmanship that was so insultingly transparent. She didn't know whether he was mocking her or he really believed that this pots-and-pans psychology was effective.

She had known Krupatin a long time, had seen him emerge from the human debris of the Russian criminal world by sheer will and unrelenting cunning, and she had benefited from and suffered with him as his fortunes rose and he had dragged her along by his cruelty. He could buy all the expensive suits that the British tailors could make, he could become more handsome than a film star and accumulate even more wealth to separate him further from his former poverty, but she always would see Satan in those sad eyes. And always she would fear that he would carry out the only threat he had ever made against her, which had served to bind her more closely to him than the acts of sexual intercourse of the past, and which reached further into her being than she ever could have imagined, even into her own death and beyond.

She thought of this now as he looked at her, and she thought she could see a glimmering of his old desires. She had learned that they were complicated desires, fueled by ambition and power and the erotic aura of what she had come to represent to him. She was afraid that in his mind she had come full circle: the Red Angel of Desire and the Black Angel of Death were beating their great wings in the back of Krupatin's soul. There they were engaged in a tumultuous struggle, like two celestial cocks who in the frenzy of their carnage had become indistinguishable.

Eight

Houston

"ALMOST TWO WEEKS AGO," Hain began, speaking directly to Cate, "I got a teletype lead in my office in Washington from legat Moscow. He had received pretty good source information that Krupatin's going to be making a trip to the U.S. and that he's probably headed here, to Houston. Now, this isn't the first time he's been to the States. There's a sizable Russian émigré community in Brighton Beach, Brooklyn, and Russian organized crime is well established there. Krupatin's been to Brighton Beach three times in the last two years—that we know about. We think he's also been in under false documents on a number of occasions."

"The Russian *mafiya* gangs operating there now are not actually organized," Loder picked up. She was sitting with her purse in her lap as she brushed her hair, pulling it back in a ponytail. "They're a bunch of bad guys, street-wise, smart, and getting smarter. Even though the *mafiya*'s been around in one form or another since the beginning of communism, it's never been organized in the sense we're used to thinking of. In fact, it's been notoriously *dis*organized—and fractious. That's why Krupatin's appearance on the scene is a big deal. He's the type of operator we're going to be seeing more of, the future face of Russian crime. And the future face of international crime. Even though his games are the traditional stuff—fraud, including gasoline taxes, Medicare payments, counterfeit credit cards; narcotics; counterfeiting; extortion—the difference is that Krupatin *is* organized. A lot of his people are educated. They're making alliances with certain Sicilian groups and with some of the Asians, just like they did a few years ago in Europe. The important thing is, these different ethnic groups are not warring. They're cooperating."

She paused, took a rubber band out of her lap, and wrapped it a couple of times around a handful of jet hair.

"And they kill at the drop of a hat," she went on, leaning over and crossing her arms on her knees. "On each of his three visits to Brighton Beach, Krupatin held a number of meetings with men who had been running the most lucrative rackets there. Krupatin left and within a few weeks these guys turned up dead. New faces took over, things started being done a little differently. All the operations are slicker now, and we've found it more difficult to tell what's going on. In each situation we think the organization is branching out. The details are in the files there," she concluded, nodding at the paper-cluttered card table.

"The Russians' willingness to use violence is pretty damn impressive," Hain continued. "The Italians and the Asians go through periods of violence when they fight over turf, but they also know the value of keeping peace when it's to their advantage. Russians see violence as *being* the advantage. We know that they've assembled hit teams of ex-KGB agents they've hired out to the Sicilians in Europe. Contract killing is a staple service wherever the Russian *mafiya* establishes itself, or wants to establish itself. Probably our best file on these people has come out of Germany, where these hit teams have been operating for a long time."

Hain lowered his head toward the BKA agent sitting across from him.

"Erika, give us a quick picture of the situation in Germany."

Jaeger nodded and sat forward on her chair. Though she seemed to be wound up tight, her face showed the strain of jet lag.

"Well, of course, you must know that after the Berlin Wall fell in 1989, we were overrun with East Europeans," she said. Her accent was heavy, but she had no trouble expressing herself in English. "Everybody—Romanians, Czechs, Bulgarians, Hungarians, Yugoslavs, Poles—they all came. We were overwhelmed; it became a nightmare. Already we had a large Russian émigré population that had drifted into Germany over the years. Criminals quickly established protection rackets among their own people. When the new, younger criminals arrived after the wall came down, they moved in on the older gangs, selling their own protection to the émigrés, 'protecting' them from the people they were already paying protection money to in the first place.

"Car thefts exploded." Jaeger shook her head. "You can drive to Moscow in twenty hours from Berlin. That first year, twenty-four thousand Audis, Mercedes Benzes, and BMWs made the trip out of Germany, going north. Within a few years the car thefts were up to a hundred and thirty thousand annually. It was absurd."

Jaeger leaned her forearms on her knees, her feet apart on the floor—a distinctly masculine posture—and clasped her hands. She did not try to hide the fact that the situation she described agitated her. She took it personally.

"In Germany we have had the Sicilians since the 1960s, with the yakuza and the Colombians following close behind. But they established themselves gradually, a little here, a little there, and before we knew it we were infected with another parasite. But not the Russians. No. These people unleashed a blitzkrieg. Within *three years* they illegally transferred into German banks and businesses more than $7 billion that they had pillaged from their disintegrating homeland. And in that same period of time they became directly involved in one third of the organized crime in our country. There are many Russian gangs, and like here, they are not organized, they do not always cooperate. Very quickly there were . . . what, ground wars?"

"Turf wars," Loder said.

"Yes, these turf wars between the Georgians and the Chechens. Very bloody. Suddenly we had dead Russians turning up everywhere, not just in Germany but all over Europe. By 1993 Krupatin and his Chechens had become the leading crime group, and they had allied with the Cali cartel and with Israeli traffickers. Through these connections, tons of cocaine poured into Europe. Krupatin had import-export companies headquartered in Berlin, with daughter companies in Holland, Belgium, Luxembourg, Hungary, South Korea, New York, Los Angeles. What traveled between these companies were diamonds and cocaine and heroin, cash of every kind of currency to clean—to launder—stolen antiques, radioactive materials, chemicals for processing drugs, stolen arms. A blizzard of forged documents supported these companies and moved goods all around the world.

"In short," Jaeger concluded, sitting up straight again and offering her open hands in a gesture of frustration, "we woke up one morning and discovered we were at war once again, this time with criminals. In the world of organized crime, Krupatin's operation stands out. His financial empire is awesome. He is now involved with legitimate business, and his illegal systems are so complex and powerful that it scares us." She paused and looked around. "When the Americans came to us with ideas of cooperation against the Russian *mafiya,* we were ready to talk."

Hain didn't even allow a pause.

"Okay, good," he said. "Now, a few days after this first teletype from legat Moscow, we got another one: Krupatin had left St. Petersburg. A few days after that we got a teletype from legat London: Scotland Yard's computers flagged Krupatin coming through Gatwick. We were looking for that. The guy loves London, but for him it's neutral territory. Aside from Berlin"—he glanced at Jaeger—"it's his most frequently visited city outside Russia. A lot of his money is there, and he uses it as a home away from home. Only thing is, Scotland Yard never knows where the hell he is. They suspect he owns as many as half a dozen houses in the city—all deeds in somebody else's name—that he and his people use when they're in London."

Hain shifted in his chair; his big frame seemed to require periodic adjustments in position. Cate guessed he had been an athlete in college and it was about time for his muscles and bones to begin paying him back for former abuses.

"Two days ago," Hain said, holding his thigh just above the knee as he extended and bent his leg to work the stiff joint, "a Russian male showed up at a travel agency on Cromwell Road in London and bought two British Airways first-class tickets to

Houston in the names of Nikolai Yelyutin and Vasily Matveyenko. Probably false names, forged passports. The departure date is tomorrow morning, nine fifty-five London time. That'll put them into Houston at two-thirty tomorrow afternoon. In addition, these two guys applied for business visas. London legat sent us their passport photos, but we don't recognize them from any of Krupatin's known associates. So we don't know exactly who they are or what their specialties are within Krupatin's organization."

"We know your OC people have opened preliminary inquiry files on three Russian groups here within the past year," Loder said, nodding at Cate. "But these guys, they're insignificant. It doesn't seem logical that Krupatin would be coming here to bother with them—unless they represent something we don't know anything about yet. But we're not convinced of that. We think he's up to something else."

"So here we are," Hain said. "We don't know what the hell for, but we're here because he's here—or will be. He may be on an extended visit, or he may touch down for a few days and *poom,* he's gone. Whatever he does, the five of us"—he swung his arm around the room at the others—"are gonna be his closest friends as long as he's here."

"And what about surveillance?" Cate asked.

"Your people. I'll be working on that with Ennis. Everyone's scrambling to get all that straight now."

"What about wires? Isn't this kind of short notice?"

"Covered. FCI guidelines apply here. We can put up a wire on anything the guy thinks about while he's in the States."

Hain paused, furrowed his brow, and leaned forward in his chair. He seemed to want to choose his words carefully.

"We know you haven't had this kind of undercover experience," he said. "But we know you're no stranger to the stresses of the job." He studied his big loafers.

"If Krupatin should decide to stay here for a while," he said, "we want to become a part of his scenery." He looked up. "I want to be able to get closer to him than just sitting in a car with a camera or in a tech van listening to them ordering takeout food. We know from the Germans' experience that Krupatin has first-rate counterintelligence of his own, but we also know he doesn't always bring that with him when he comes here. He did once. The other two times he didn't. So we may have an edge on him. Surveillance against him will be expensive and hard to sustain over the long haul. So if he does settle in, we want people who can become part of his environment."

Hain tilted his head in the general direction of the others without taking his eyes off Cate.

"You, Ann, and Erika are going to be a part of Krupatin's background," he said. "But we don't know exactly how yet. We'll have to work that out as soon as we see what kind of situation we're going to have."

There was a pause. Ometov hadn't said a word, and it appeared that he wasn't going to—yet. This breathing space, it seemed, was for her benefit. How was she feeling about this? She wasn't sure, but she did have one question, which had lodged at the back of her mind the moment she walked into the barren living room.

"Three women," Cate observed. "That's no coincidence."

"That's right," Hain said. "My preference. The fact is, for these kinds of guys this is still a man's world. That goes for whatever ethnic group you're dealing with—Italians, Asians, Russians, whatever. Criminal organizations are not a hotbed of equal opportunity employment. It's man's work. Men do all the important doing and women have their place, usually flat on their backs or in other interesting positions. Otherwise they're pretty much disregarded. Clerks, maids, cashiers, waitresses, housewives, secretaries—as long as they're not so good-looking as to attract attention, they're invisible."

"Curtis's dream team is five postmenopausal women with gray hair, bifocals, no makeup, no tits, and lots of undercover experience," Loder explained, laughing.

"Damn right," Hain said. "I'd love that. Those guys wouldn't have any secrets. Anyway, when Krupatin's men are scanning for surveillance, they're going to be looking for other men. They know all about camouflage surveillance, men posing as telephone repairmen or plumbers or maintenance workers, service station attendants, delivery people, all that kind of thing. The only time they'll be especially leery of women is when it comes down to sex. The honey trap. They do a pretty good job of using it themselves."

Cate felt her face burn. If Hain knew about the circumstances of Tavio's death, or of the events of the previous evening, he certainly wasn't showing it.

"If the opportunity even remotely presents itself," he said, "we're going to put you three right under Krupatin's nose."

Nine

London

SHE BOUGHT CLOTHES but took no pleasure in it. Rather, she shopped like someone buying equipment required for a particular job. She knew instinctively what Krupatin wanted, at least until he told her otherwise. Krupatin liked drama. But elegant drama, always in the best of taste, which he knew she had and which he expected her to use. He liked her to wear smart dress suits that complemented her hair and complexion. Strong colors like scarlet and black and emerald. He liked sometimes a slight military touch, an ivory suit with brocade on the sleeves and bodice, or scrolled soutache. A fiery red bouclé suit with black cord trim. A black coat-dress with a white shawl collar and white cuffs. Double-breasted suits of dark peacock or claret. For casual wear he liked trapeze dresses and sheaths, with the hemlines well above the knees to play up her long legs, or fine knit cottons with darts to emphasize her waist and bust. He favored liquid silk that draped over her body like a thin skim of water.

For two full days she did nothing but shop, trying on clothes, dictating precise alterations, and ordering things made up from fabrics that she preferred to the ones in stock. Then she had everything delivered to the townhouse in South Kensington. She unpacked it, put it all away, and settled in with the files Krupatin had left for her to absorb.

He called on the fourth day.

"Have you shopped?"

"Yes."

"Have you read the notebooks?"

"Yes."

"Fine. We'll go to dinner this evening and talk. You've got something to wear for dinner?"

"Yes."

He hesitated. "You sound surly."

"I'm sorry. Maybe I'm a little tired."

"Take a nap. I'll be there at eight o'clock."

She wore a black silk evening dress with a jewel neck and an upper bodice and long sleeves of skin-tight chiffon, mere smoke next to her golden skin. A single pendent black pearl dangled from each ear.

Krupatin had reserved an alcove table for them at a French restaurant called Geneviève in Belgravia. He was at his charming best, and she saw him looking about with relish as heads turned to follow them through the crowded, intimate room to their table.

"You've lost nothing—*nothing,* Irina," he said as they were seated. He saw no indelicacy in this remark. Did he think that what he had put her through in the past year would have affected her appearance? Did he think she might begin to rot like garbage?

He sat facing the mirrors so he could watch the men behind him stealing glances at her.

"God, I don't know why you won't dress like this all the time," he said. "Why you don't live a better life . . . You know, your kind of beauty, it's perishable. You ought to enjoy it while you still have it." He took his napkin, flapped it open, and picked up the wine list. "Good God, you have this martyr complex or something . . ." His voice trailed off as his attention turned to vintages.

After the wine steward took his order, Krupatin crossed his forearms on the table and leaned toward her with a smile of anticipation.

"Okay," he said. "Wei Tsing."

He was attractive, his rich gray hair particularly striking in the soft lights of the restaurant. And he was repulsive. He did not consider her a human being. If God was a Jew, she thought, Satan had to be a Russian.

"Fifty-two years old," she began slowly. "Born and reared in a wealthy Hong Kong family. His father was a taipan for an Australian construction conglomerate. Educated in Britain—he received a master's in economics from Oxford University. After returning to Hong Kong, he took most of the trust money from his father and invested it in establishing a new trafficking organization to bring heroin out of the Golden Triangle. This was during the Vietnam War, when drug consumption was exploding in the United States. By the age of thirty he was a multimillionaire. But Tsing was intelligent—"

"Wei," Krupatin interrupted. "With Chinese it's backward. If you call him Tsing, you're using his first name. You can't do that. It's Mr. Wei. It's pronounced *way* in English."

"He smuggled arms to the North Vietnamese and black-market goods to the South Vietnamese. With his profits he bought real estate in London, Paris, Los Angeles, and New York."

"And Sydney," Krupatin reminded her.

"Yes, and Sydney."

The wine steward arrived, and she stopped while he served them, arranged the ice bucket, and left.

"With these large real estate acquisitions, he began to see the advantages of distancing himself from the operations of the drug trade. He hired shrewd subordinates and won their loyalty with lavish salaries. He established legitimate corporations in Hong Kong as fronts and created shell companies to launder his own money. Then, in a big leap, he began laundering for the yakuza and triads."

"At . . ."

"Twenty percent."

Krupatin nodded and grinned. "That son of a bitch was getting that kind of money even back then."

"He's still doing it for them."

"Yeah, but at twenty-*seven* percent now. He says it's getting harder to do, with all the new international laws, with countries trying to cooperate. He told me that himself. Bullshit."

"Anyway," Irina continued, "his legitimate business ventures in

Hong Kong grew enormously. Now, for the past two years, he has been busy trying to get them out before the Chinese take over in 1997. He has moved them primarily to Canada and the United States . . . one in France."

She stopped and watched Krupatin refill her wineglass and then his own. He looked at her breasts through the smoky chiffon, the way he had done when she first met him and he had enjoyed the seduction game. She felt nothing. He might as well have been staring at her purse. He had fallen to his death long ago, and in doing so he had grasped at her heart in an effort to save himself. The plunge had killed them both.

"In the United States," she said, "he has outgrown his Cosa Nostra ties and is expanding outside the Asian community. He is laundering drug money there, too. Counterfeiting. Prostitution. Gambling. And, of course, smuggling Asian aliens into the country—he made almost one billion from that in 1995. And heroin, as always. Also, for a percentage, he is facilitating Hong Kong capital flight to the U.S. The total flight money in 1994, the last year for which you have solid figures, was nearly six billion dollars."

"Very good, Irina." Krupatin sipped his wine, a happy glint in his eyes. "Now what about his personal life?"

She drank from her glass. The wine was very expensive, very smooth and clean.

"He married a Hong Kong Chinese," she said, "a woman from a family well established in the colony's social elite. From the time he was a young man he has had mistresses. His wife knows this. He has never had an Asian mistress. They are always American or British or European. Well, there was an Israeli girl once, and an Argentine. With these women he often enjoys a ménage à trois—in fact, more often than not."

Krupatin shook his head in amusement.

"The grass is always greener, huh?" He laughed. "You can be the richest shit in Asia, but all the money in the world can't buy you even one tiny blond Asian pussy. They just don't make them that way." He laughed again, enjoying very much this observation of Asian genetics.

"He is a long-time collector of ancient Asian art but in the last few years has turned his attention to East European religious icons and relics."

"*That's* absolutely providential," Krupatin said, smacking his lips. "I thought you would like that, huh? The fact is, some months ago I acquired a pair of very high-quality Macedonian icons for him. He has requested more, which we are going to get."

"Three of his mistresses came to bad ends," she went on, "after having been dismissed by him. One died of a heroin overdose in Paris. Another died in a boating accident on Lake Como. A third died in a helicopter crash on Corsica."

"And there were rumors . . ." Krupatin coaxed.

"Yes, rumors that they had been indiscreet about his sexual proclivities."

"Which are . . ."

"Various things," she said, refusing to indulge him. "He has an exotic imagination."

Krupatin leaned back in his chair and laughed, softly, deeply, as much at her refusal to give him details—which he already knew anyway—as at Wei's weaknesses. Krupatin always thought other people's weaknesses were humorous.

The majordomo brought their menus; the headwaiter took their order. Krupatin scanned the mirror for signs that they were still being admired. He seemed satisfied and preened.

They talked more about Wei. Krupatin quizzed her through the cold hors d'oeuvres to make sure she had retained the details. He quizzed her through the soups. By the time their entrées arrived, they had finished with the Chinese.

"Now, Carlo Bontate," Krupatin said.

"A third-generation Sicilian Mafia son from Palermo," she began, reciting Krupatin's expensively acquired information as if it were the Underground timetable. "Responsible for introducing his family to the new realities of modern drug commerce. Very helpful to the Colombians as a distributor of their cocaine in Europe, where the Sicilians already had the connections that the Colombians found hard to establish. Bontate's family launders for the Colombians also, and that's when you got involved with them, helping them by providing rubles. They also hit for the Colombians. From us they have established an arms connection, which they market to Western Europe and to the Colombians. Of course, they are involved in the traditional Mafia business in southern Italy.

"Now, apparently, Bontate has visions of establishing more serious operations in the United States, like those of some of the other Sicilian families who are already there. His influence there is growing, and la Cosa Nostra has been severely weakened by recent law enforcement successes. Now the Sicilian presence is probably bigger in the United States than that of la Cosa Nostra itself. Bontate has ambitions."

"Personal life."

"He has few interests besides the Mafia and his family. He married the daughter of a capo in an affiliate family and has three children. He also has mistresses, but they are Italian, regional women whose backgrounds are familiar to him. He is not a socially sophisticated man, but he is clever. Of the younger generation of Sicilians, he is the acknowledged man of influence that everyone else has to contend with."

Krupatin had been eating all this time, nodding approval as he listened. He wiped his mouth as he finished chewing and picked up his glass.

"His American ambitions are the most important thing to him right now," he said. "As a matter of fact, they are the most important thing to all three of us right now." He drank his wine, looking at her as he washed his mouth with it and swallowed. "Wei, Bontate, and I have worked together, have been useful to each other in Europe. We all have a foothold in the United States, but in different areas of influence. We all want more than a foothold, and none of us wants to wait too long to get it. We think we can be mutually helpful. We're going to talk about it."

Irina had taken advantage of his remarks to eat a few bites of her venison fillet. A few bites was all she cared for; her appetite had vanished. As Krupatin continued, she turned back to her wine and stole glances around the softly glowing dining room. Krupatin could not be ignored easily, but she caught the attention—for an instant—of a few men, of a woman, people who had no idea what they were seeing when their glance met hers in the thin margins of this London evening.

Krupatin undressed her slowly, peeling away the tight sleeves and bodice of black smoke until she was naked in front of him like an essence of his imagination, something pure though entirely barren of purity. She had never completely understood why he felt such a need to humiliate her. Perhaps it was shame, an emotion of which she did not believe him capable, though she could think of no other explanation. Shame over the way he used her—not sexually, that was the least of it, but as though she were soulless, an android from a future that had not yet arrived. So the way he treated her, in the context of the present time, was not yet allowed; it was blasphemy, and it haunted him, and he hated her for it.

There was only one thing of integrity between them, and that one thing lived in the locket that hung around Irina's neck and swung on the chain in the air between them. He dealt with her body however he wanted; that was her stoic concession, her part of their unspoken collusion. But he never touched the locket, and Irina never took her eyes away from it, glittering, spinning between them. Set in motion by malevolence, it was the only thing of light between their two darknesses, a kind of *sacramentum* in the abyss, a promise that the darkness was not forever.

Ten

Houston

LEO OMETOV had remained silent throughout the first part of Cate's briefing. He slumped uncomfortably in his metal chair, crossing and uncrossing his legs in a languorous manner that would have appeared restless if it had not been done with such sluggish indifference. He seemed preoccupied, only half attentive to Erika Jaeger's account of the rising influence of Russian organized crime in Germany. Much of the time he was turned sideways in his chair, staring out the glass wall at the tropical courtyard, his elbow on the back of the chair, his chin in his cupped hand.

But when Curtis Hain began talking about Krupatin, Ometov regained interest in what was being said. He was especially attentive when Hain began talking about using female surveillants and penetrating Krupatin's circle.

"Yes," he interrupted, "yes, yes. This is extremely important." He looked at Hain. "I am sorry, please, but it is so important for her to understand Sergei's personality. This is so essential. In fact, it is the most important element in what we want to do."

He had straightened up in his chair and was leaning forward as Jaeger had done. Cate noted that Ometov had apparently learned his English in Britain. The resulting accent was crisp but peculiarly nuanced.

"Mrs. Cuevas," he said, putting stress on the last syllable of her name. "Cate. Sergei Krupatin is a complex man." He glanced at Hain, not so much to seek permission to speak as to let him know he was going to say what he wanted to say. "It is important for you to know," he went on, "that he is a Chechen. You know all about Chechnya from your news, I'm sure. All about the war. What you may not know is that for centuries the Chechens, being in a remote region, have created a kind of closed society. They are a law unto themselves, both psychologically and as a matter of practicality. They are an isolated and secretive people. Chechnya has been the spawning ground for Russia's most vicious criminals for generations, much in the same way Sicily has been for the Italian Mafia. In the post-Communist era the Chechens have become the worst of the worst.

"Today they are the most violent of all of Russia's gangsters, killing readily and indiscriminately. It is their first response to any challenge, their first solution to any problem. Chechen criminal organizations are especially strong in Moscow, but for a number of years now they have been a ruthless presence in all the major cities of Western Europe. They like to travel—they are not provincial peasants."

Ometov seemed to be a man given more to thinking his way through to solutions than to acting, but he had an air of savvy about him that made Cate suspect he once had been an agent himself, though he had long ago gravitated to the cerebral end of operations.

"Sergei grew up in a smuggling family," he went on, clearly immersed in Krupatin history, "and by the time he was a teenager he was in charge of his own gang, bringing cigarettes and whiskey across the Black Sea from northern Turkey into Georgia. He quickly graduated to gun-running and heroin. When he was eighteen, he was with his father and three of his brothers and some cousins when they were cornered by a Soviet coastal patrol on the Russian coast of the Black Sea. They were smuggling Turkish arms to rebels in southern Russia through ports in the Crimea. But they were betrayed by some of their own people. The father and oldest brother were captured, and while Sergei and the others watched from their hiding places in the rocky cliffs above the beach, those two were tortured by the militia. They were dragged naked up and down the beach behind a jeep while the soldiers used them for bayonet practice, jabbing at them until they were in shreds, falling to pieces. Then they were left there on the sand. Sergei and his other two brothers could not fire on the patrol for fear of giving away their positions. They watched in silence.

"Afterward Sergei made it his personal business to discover who had betrayed them. It was a cousin. Sergei made the man watch as his house was burned down and then while his wife and two daughters were gang-raped until they were dead. Then Sergei himself disemboweled the man with a shovel.

"A few years after this, Sergei moved to Moscow, where numerous Chechen gangs were already well established. But he did not go to work for one of these many gangs. Instead he did something that was to become a trademark of his operational style. Rather than start his own black-market scheme or set up his own protection racket, he took time to study the world in which these gangs operated. What was the hierarchy? Some gangs were more influential than others. Why? What rackets yielded the most income? Which were the best controlled? Which ones had the best connections with city politicians or influential party members? When he had satisfied himself regarding these questions, he and his men picked a 'business' they liked and simply took it over. It was a black-market food operation. Five men died quickly within eighteen hours, and Krupatin was established, literally overnight, as a major black marketeer.

"Within the next three years he did the same thing with a car theft ring, a prostitution ring, and a major protection racket. He used violence ambitiously, precisely, and without hesitation. Once he focused on a business, there was no denying him."

Ometov paused, seemingly to decide how best to proceed. His pale gray eyes, which had been so much a part of his quick smile earlier, had grown calm and thoughtful. He seemed more tired than the others.

"By the early 1980s," he continued, "Sergei had become a very rich man. But he was still a thief among thieves, and he wanted that to change. He decided to pay huge bribes to several officials in the central ministry in order to obtain import licenses, which were very difficult to acquire. This he did. At this time the Soviet Union was flush with profits from its oil exports. The embargo had driven world oil prices to thirty-five dollars a barrel, and the Soviet Union, because we had vast oil reserves, was collecting windfall profits. But the rest of the country's infrastructure was in shambles—our factories were outdated and falling apart, our agricultural programs were unproductive, nothing worked. Virtually every kind of consumer item imaginable had to be imported. So Krupatin became a major importer with a government license, liberally bribing officials to back up his counterfeit bills of lading. He bought at low world-market prices, everything from shiploads of wheat to railcars full of porcelain toilets, and sold to the central government at inflated prices, always paying off party officials whenever he had to. He could afford it. From 1982 to 1985 he made staggering profits and began opening bank accounts all over Europe.

"Because of his established government connections, he was standing in the doorway of opportunity when perestroika walked through, the beginning of the golden age of organized crime in Russia." Ometov sat back and crossed his arms thoughtfully, shaking his head.

"Free market economy. Well, Gorbachev, he was desperate. Everything was collapsing around him, poor bastard. The only people who had money to invest in these 'free enterprises' were the party barons, who had spent their careers siphoning money from the government, and the gangsters, whose black-market economy was in fact the real economy that kept Soviet society from imploding. So who do you suppose put their money into this new 'private commerce'?" He nodded wearily. "Black and gray money flooded into joint ventures with Western entrepreneurs, it flooded into the stock exchanges, into cooperatives and banks and joint stock companies. During the six years of perestroika, Krupatin became a criminal giant. And he was not the only one."

Ometov sighed hugely and stood up. He put his hands into his pockets and walked over to the glass wall. He stared out a moment, his sloping shoulders the very caricature of weariness. He turned around.

"In August 1991, the Soviet Union fell apart. Fifteen new nations emerged, and the criminals really went to work. Russia was like a helpless woman being gang-raped by her own children.

There was an immediate hemorrhage of Russia's natural resources, tons and tons every day, day in and day out—aluminum, petroleum, cobalt, nickel, steel, timber, cesium, uranium, titanium, silver, tin, and on and on and on. The independent republics—the former Soviet Union—plundered the country with the help of the *mafiya,* which had the money and the connections to obtain the material.

"And armaments. My God. Every crooked general who had any control over a military installation of any kind used its armory as his personal property—and sold it to the *mafiya.* Tanks, missiles, planes, automatic weapons, mortars . . . you can imagine. And who did the *mafiya* sell these weapons to? Everyone! Criminals, terrorists, drug traffickers, military establishments. Warring Third World armies.

"Our little Sergei was right in the middle of this. Money poured into his pockets. With these profits he entered the international drug trade on a scale that dwarfed his former efforts. Now that Russia's borders were porous, he used them as transshipment avenues. He made contact with the Sicilians; he knew they were trafficking cocaine for the Colombians, who had no distribution network of their own in Europe. He offered his import companies as venues. It began to snow the year round in Europe. European consumption of cocaine jumped to two hundred tons annually—ten billion dollars' worth on the streets. Krupatin's drug profits quickly quadrupled."

Ometov paused, pursed his mouth, and thought a moment. "Sergei traveled. He followed his money like a rat follows garbage, and he followed his businesses, which were now thoroughly established in Holland, Luxembourg, Belgium, Sweden, Germany, Britain, and the United States. His Chechen thugs were raising the crime rate in every country, laundering money, dealing drugs and weapons and stolen antiques and stolen cars, extorting, blackmailing, running protection rackets. It was a Russian holiday.

"Krupatin himself was long out of the day-to-day operations of all this, however. Today he simply travels from one major city to another, touching base with his lieutenants to make sure everything is running smoothly. If it isn't, people die."

"Okay, I have a question," Erika broke in. She had followed Ometov closely, and now she sat with her legs crossed, ankle on knee, leaning back, her hand open and cocked to stop Ometov. "How much do you know about Krupatin's assassins?"

Ometov gave her a wry grin. "How much do I know?"

"Yes. The biggest problem for law enforcement in the European Community is—"

"Sharing intelligence. No one wants to share intelligence," Ometov said with a weary nod.

"Exactly." Erika closed her hand into a fist. "In the EC we have twelve different governments with twelve different political philosophies and twelve different legal systems. But police agencies are the same everywhere—they don't trust anyone else with their intelligence. So these people, Krupatin's people, can kill in one country, drive a hundred miles and kill in another country, catch an hour's flight and kill in yet another country, and as far as the law enforcement agencies know, it is as if three different guys did three different hits. There's no way to build a file on these people. Krupatin's enforcers essentially have a free hand, because nobody's keeping a running record from country to country."

Ometov, who was leaning on the sliding glass doors and looking out at the courtyard beyond, had turned sideways to listen to her. He said, "You have a lot of palms here. I like palms. Very tropical."

"The question is," Erika said, throwing a look of exasperation at Hain, "who are Krupatin's hitters? We know he has used his close Chechen friends. We killed two of them in Berlin six months ago, after they hit three Dutch traffickers. But does he use only Chechens? How does he set them up? How do they operate?"

Ometov looked down, seemed to study his feet, and then turned to the others again.

"Initially, of course, they were his Chechen associates. Thugs." He shook his head. "Just thugs. There was very little need for finesse."

"Initially," Erika said.

"Yes. As time passed, as his organization became more sophisticated and his targets were men of greater importance, it was essential that the killings be conducted more . . . surgically. He began using active KGB agents who took assignments from him off the record. Of course, after the fall of communism there was no shortage of these men. There was no trouble moving across borders. Sergei has always had superb forgers. Documents are no problem."

"The KGB agents are not so hard for us," Erika said. "Our foreign intelligence from the cold war years is good there. But they are not the only hitters."

"No, you're right," Ometov confirmed. "Often in other countries he uses 'disposables,' people who are hired to do the actual work and who are killed themselves when they return home— wherever that might be." He paused. "And then there are a few 'surgeons'—Krupatin's specialty. These are the top assassins. They are usually highly educated people, professionals who are not from Krupatin's world but who have had the bad luck somehow to cross his path. These people usually have access to someone special, someone who would otherwise be nearly impossible to get to without attracting sensational attention. But the surgeon has no problem, because he is one of them. He is a banker. An executive. A bureaucrat. A lawyer. Krupatin's theory is, if you want to kill a politician, get a politician to do it. If you want to kill a stockbroker, get another stockbroker to do it. Because they are on the inside, they know how to do it without disturbance. And because they have no motive, they are never suspects."

"What are you talking about?" Erika frowned.

"In very simple terms, these people are approached by Krupatin's lieutenants and are given a choice. Either they do a job or a wife is brutally raped and murdered by thugs. Either they do a job or a child disappears. Either they do a job or an elderly parent dies in a house fire. They are told they have to do it only once, only one job—a piece of knowledge that helps them rationalize the choice they have to make. They say to themselves, this is a war without uniforms; this is a struggle for survival. It is either this one man or my daughter. Either one executive or my wife, one banker or my parents. And if they ever doubt the seriousness of Krupatin's threat, he gives them a taste. A cousin dies, a next-door neighbor, a good friend. After the taste, they all believe. And they all decide to do the job."

Eleven

South Kensington, London

IRINA LAY beside the Devil in the dark. There were roses on trellises across the front of the windows, and the streetlamps cast their shadows against the wall like a tracery of black rosettes, the long, climbing stems reduced to vague spiderwebs of gray.

She lay on her side, and behind her the Devil stirred in his sleep. Desolate in her depression, she felt like a long-reformed whore who after years of abstinence had returned again to loveless sheets, preferring even one moment of counterfeit affection to endless nights of genuine loneliness. Nothing compared to moral failure in its resulting isolation. For momentary comfort you were left with only the sour aftertaste of everlasting regret.

She looked at the clock: it was one-thirty. Carefully she laid back the sheet and got out of bed, hoping he would not awaken. It would be too cruel to have to look at him now, to have to talk to him immediately after.

She walked into the bathroom, squatted on the bidet, and washed herself, washed with soap, dry-eyed and dolorous, feeling ugly in her nakedness, the chill tile as unforgiving as glass underneath her bare feet. When she was through she dried and then washed her face, again using soap, rinsing over and over until her skin felt oilless and clean, perhaps the only clean thing about her. She took a new dressing gown off the hook behind the bathroom door and slipped it on, turned off the light, and walked through the darkness of the bedroom and out into the hallway, closing the door behind her.

In the kitchen she turned on a small lamp on the cabinet counter and began heating water to make a cup of tea. She leaned against the counter and waited in the dim light for the water to get hot, and when it was ready she poured it into a blue porcelain pot. Within moments the smoky aroma of lapsang souchong was penetrating the smudgy corners of the large square room, and its fragrance carried her to places, so many places, where she had gathered memories, sweet and ugly, a library of emotions that she never had managed to put in order, never managed to organize. Everything was there, but it was bedlam; she never knew what she would find when she went looking.

She poured the tea into a cup and took it outside to the garden. The bricks were damp on her bare feet, and there was a layer of damp air around her legs as she walked to a table and chairs and sat down. The city sounds were distant at this hour, muffled by the dense vegetation of other gardens all along the street. Pulling her feet up into the big comfortable chair, she wrapped her gown around her feet and hugged her legs. The smell of plants and damp soil hung in the dark, occasionally punctuated by a waft of the strong tea, its aroma prowling the air around her in invisible tendrils.

Suddenly the kitchen door opened and Krupatin stood there, his silhouette backlit by the frail light of the kitchen. He peered out. He was dressed.

"Irina?"

She could hardly bring herself to speak. "Yes." Her voice was weak and died out in the cushion of the vegetation and the night.

Krupatin lighted a cigarette, and for a moment his face flickered like a carnival mask, then went black. "Just a minute," he said, and he turned back into the kitchen.

Her heart sank, and tears of exhaustion and frustration welled in her eyes.

Krupatin appeared in the doorway again, carrying a cup of tea.

The cigarette glowed in his mouth as he approached her along the brick walk.

"It's almost too dark," he said, the unintended double entendre losing all meaning for her except its metaphorical sense, which seemed an omen.

He made his way to her and sat down in a garden chair across the table from her.

"We might as well talk now," he said, taking the cigarette out of his mouth and blowing a luminous plume into the still air. "I was going to come back tomorrow, but, well, now we're here. Now is the best time."

He lifted his cup and blew over the top of the tea. The nearly exhausted light from the kitchen door highlighted his silhouette, creating a gold seam that outlined the shoulders of his suit, his head, the edges of his arm when he lifted it to smoke or sip tea. She could see lumps of sugar lining the edge of his saucer. When he turned his head slightly, the side of his face was gilded.

"This meeting—in Houston, Texas, did I tell you that?"

"No."

"It was very difficult to arrange. Wei's people and Bontate's people and mine have been talking forever. Talking, talking. They're cautious bastards, both of them. But they smell a lot of money. Mmmmmm . . ." He pulled on his cigarette. "And you know how that is. As the potential profit rises, so does the temptation to take risks. Still, they're not your average men, these two. Cautious—to a fault, I hope."

He gave a humorous snort at this, put a sugar cube in his mouth, and lifted the teacup. She heard him sucking the liquid through the porous cube. Though he was wearing his suit, he had not put on his tie, and she noticed that his hair was neatly combed. He was very handsome, rakish in the casual way he wore his tailored suit. She found his every move hateful.

"We have established an elaborate system of rules for this meeting," he continued. "Bontate insists on certain things; Wei responds with requirements of his own. I accommodate. Then I insist on some things too, of course, and they accommodate, or counterpropose. We go back and forth, back and forth, gradually arriving at something with which everyone is equally uneasy."

"Whose idea was this meeting?" Irina asked.

He paused. "Wei's. He has these big ideas about cooperation. A consortium."

Irina sipped her tea. Krupatin continued.

"As time went on and I saw how much Wei wanted this thing," he said, putting out his cigarette, "I outcautioned their caution. I said, look, I've made some serious moves in the U.S. recently, and as far as the law enforcement officials there are concerned, I am somebody to watch. Wei knows this, of course. Our moves there have given us a big bite of a lot of things—that's why Wei wants us involved in this consortium idea of his."

Krupatin's silhouette was immobile, one forearm resting on the table, his fingers on the teacup.

"I insisted on a low profile. I said I couldn't be driving all over Houston to meetings."

"Why did they choose Houston?"

Krupatin paused again. She couldn't see his face, but she knew her questions were making him impatient.

"That was Wei's idea too. Houston has a huge Asian population. He thinks his people will be less obvious there."

"Less obvious than New York, than Los Angeles?"

"What? What the hell does it matter? Why are you asking these questions?"

"I wanted to know, Sergei, that's all."

There was a longer silence this time. His face, lost in the shadows, could tell her nothing.

"I told them," he went on. "I said, when we are down to the last conversation, to the final agreement where everything is spelled out, then I will show up and do my part. Until then, I said, I want all of the negotiations from my side to be handled by my most trusted emissary. This emissary, I said, will do all the legwork, all the preliminary negotiating."

He stopped, his silhouette motionless. Then he raised an arm and pointed at her, gold rippling down the length of his dark suit.

She looked at him. Not being able to see his face was beginning to bother her. His arm was still extended toward her.

"What is it?" she said.

"You are my emissary. Olya Serova."

She couldn't believe it; it was an absurd idea. "You're crazy."

"No, this is perfect," he said, dropping his arm.

"This is your big plan? This is how I'm supposed to get close to them?"

"Absolutely. I will send you back and forth, back and forth. They'll get used to you. Your coming and going will become routine to their subordinates. You will become familiar to all of them. Familiarity. That's the key to this, Irina. 'Oh, it's Krupatin's woman. Yes, yes. Go through.' That's the idea."

"That's insane, Sergei. They're not going to get that used to me in the short time it will take to do this—what, a week, two weeks?"

Krupatin's silhouette shrugged. "Whatever it takes. But listen, Irina, I'm not going to wait until the last minute to introduce you."

"What does that mean?"

"Wei is in Paris. He wants to meet you."

"Oh, my God. No, this is just too stupid."

"It's already been decided," Krupatin said flatly.

"And Bontate?"

"The day after. You will fly from Paris to Palermo."

"To Palermo?"

"It's all been arranged."

She stared across at him. "And what did you tell them about me? You have known these men for a year now. You have done business with them. How in the hell did you explain me to them when they have never seen me or heard of me all this time? And I'm supposed to be your most trusted emissary? They can't possibly believe such a thing."

"They believe," Krupatin said. "I told them, I said, this woman is the only one I trust to do this. I want her to meet you before we all get together in Houston. I want her to see for herself the two men she will be dealing with in the U.S."

"But what am I supposed to say to them, for God's sake? They're going to ask me business questions. They're going to try to trip me up, catch me in some mistake."

"No," Krupatin said. "Because you come from me, you already have authority. You don't need to prove yourself to them. If they try to do that, don't fall for it. The point is, I am sending you to look *them* over, not the other way around. The way I see it, you just go to visit. You have a couple of meals with them, pretend you are just trying to get a feel for them. Make them like you, feel comfortable with you."

"That's it? You don't have any specific directions for me, no objective?"

"Not for these trips, Irina. Whatever you fabricate, do it to suit yourself. Say whatever you must to make yourself comfortable, whatever will put you at ease when you meet them in Houston. When you come back from Paris, from Palermo, we will meet, and you can brief me. Then we will put our heads together and work out the details for the rest of it."

And what if I refuse? The question hardly formed in her mind, much less on her lips. This was madness. Her heart was beating irregularly, and she felt moisture beading at her hairline. This could be the end of her. It was highly unlikely that she would come away alive from such a bold plan. And Krupatin, of course, was well aware of this.

She looked at him. "Sergei . . ."

"Irina." His voice stopped her, and he paused to take another cigarette out of his pocket and light it. The carnival mask again. And again the immediate darkness. "Irina," he said, the smoke thickening his voice and rolling from his mouth into the damp London night, "I am prepared to make this your last one."

She was stunned again. Did she believe this? She didn't. Even if she could believe it, it was in fact a worthless promise, because the odds of her surviving this kind of operation were, surely, nonexistent. And what if he did mean it? What was she going to do, get him to sign such a promise and have it notarized? What was a promise from a man like this? He was prepared to make this the last one? He was *prepared?* What did that mean? What did it mean when Satan spoke to you and told you he was prepared to strike a bargain? How much more absurd could life become? And what did this mean? It meant that she was lost, that's what it meant.

Irina felt the chill moving about beneath her chair, prowling along the bricks. South Kensington slept while Irina sat in a garden chair with her bare feet tucked up under her dressing gown, talking to the Devil.

"You will receive your tickets to Paris tomorrow," Krupatin said, making the ember of his cigarette glow like a small red eye in the center of the black place where his face should have been. This time when he blew the smoke into the air, the side of his face caught the gilt light in an uneven contour for just a brief moment and then was gone. "For the trip to Palermo, you will be informed when the time comes."

Krupatin was silent a moment, and then he leaned forward and put his elbow on the table between them. The raised hand held the cigarette.

"Listen to me, Irina. Listen to me." The ember on the cigarette danced in the dark between them as he motioned with his hand. "This is the most important thing you have ever done. Do this right, and it's over for you. All of it. You won't have to worry about it anymore." He hesitated. "Don't throw this away. You can do it. You're probably the only one who can. If you've ever done anything right in your life, it should be this. Believe me."

She was so dumbstruck, so numb, she hardly comprehended his words, which surely must have been distorted both in meaning and in tone, because to her his promise sounded like a death knell. There was nothing she could do.

She sat in the garden in the dark long after he was gone.

Twelve

Houston

LATE IN THE AFTERNOON a van pulled up to the off-site house and began unloading the rental furniture Hain had ordered. It was the bare minimum: a sofa and an assortment of chairs, two long folding metal tables, and a filing cabinet for the empty living room; a dining table and chairs; and a bed and a chair for each of the five bedrooms. The real luxury was that each of them did get a private bedroom and bath.

Since the deliveries already had interrupted the briefing, Ann and Cate took one of the cars and picked up sheets and blankets and pillows for the beds and towels and washcloths for the bathrooms. They stopped by a discount store and bought cheap dishes, plastic utensils, and an electric coffeepot. Then they went to a grocery store for all the necessities they could think of on short notice.

By the time they returned to the house, the tables had been set up in the living room and the files that had been scattered all over the place were being organized by Erika and put away in the filing cabinets. The tech people from the Houston field office had been over and set up computer terminals that tied them in with all the necessary Bureau communications. Two more telephones had been installed as well and were sitting on the folding tables, which had been arranged back to back, making one large rectangular workspace facing the courtyard.

Then Neil Jernigan arrived. As squad supervisor of the Special Operations Group that would be responsible for surveillance on the arriving Russians, Jernigan wanted to know what Hain was expecting in the way of countersurveillance from Krupatin. Cate was reassured by Jernigan's presence. She had worked with him before and knew him to be unflappable and uncommonly observant. He considered surveillance an intricate dance, a tango with feints and slides and innuendos of chase. He was an olive-skinned man with thick, straight hair and features that suggested Bombay or Delhi, though he was clearly not Indian.

Jernigan's queries resulted in another long session in which Ometov, Jaeger, and Loder related their experiences with Krupatin's techies. They were sophisticated. He used ex-KGB officers, which meant they used methods and technologies that weren't altogether unfamiliar to FBI counterintelligence. But a lot had changed in Russia and it had changed fast, and people like Krupatin were no longer behind the times. He could afford the best technology, and he would have it. He could afford the best people, and he would have them.

By the time Jernigan left, the long day was beginning to wear on everyone. They all agreed to retire to their rooms to unpack and take a few minutes alone.

One of the corridors of the house had three bedrooms opening into it, and the three women moved into these. Cate's room was at the end of the hallway on the inside corner, so that two of her windows looked out onto the house's interior courtyard—which contained the palms Ometov had admired—while two others looked out into the dense woods at the rear of the house. One of the city's bayous was not far away.

She unpacked her clothes, double-checked to see whether she had indeed brought anything that matched, and was relieved to find that she had packed better than she remembered. In a few minutes everything was hanging in a closet, the several dresses looking bereft and temporary and somehow a little depressing. Without any clothes chests, she had to keep her underwear in her suitcase, which she put beneath her clothes in the closet. She took the sheets out of their plastic wrappings and made up the bed, putting the pillow at the head and the blanket across the foot. Then she went into the bathroom and spent some time scrubbing, making the place her place. As she worked, she thought about the people she had been listening to for the past several hours, and she thought about Krupatin. Once she even thought about Tavio, but she quickly shoved him back into oblivion. That was where she needed to keep him until she had enough balance, enough time, to turn around and deal with him.

When she was through cleaning, she washed her face and forearms and wiped the back of her neck with a fresh damp washcloth. She brushed her hair and tried to make herself look like she wasn't as tired or as tense or as confused as she really was.

She walked back into the bedroom and stopped. Her single bed reminded her of a prison cot in the center of the bare room. She sat down on the edge of the bed and looked around. The house must have been vacant for some time, because it had that slightly chalky smell common to empty houses. She saw nails still in the walls where God knows what kind of pictures had hung, and there were scrapes against the walls at about waist height, where the back of a chair or a table had rubbed away the paint. She wanted to lie down but decided against it. The hectic loss of sleep of the previous night was taking its toll. She was weary, but her mind wouldn't shut down for a long time now, and she found herself impatient to hear more about Krupatin.

Getting up, she smoothed her dress and walked out into the hall and back down to the main part of the house, where she found Jaeger, Ometov, and Hain opening bottles of beer that Hain was pulling out of a plastic ice chest.

"Hey," Hain said, seeing her come in, "how about a beer? Ice cold. Your only other option is water."

"Well, then I'll take the beer," she said. She was glad to see they were bottles of beer rather than cans, and when Hain popped off the top for her, the cold, sweaty bottle felt good in her hand.

Ometov was sitting in one of the newly arrived chairs looking out at the courtyard, where the sun was still burning through the trees in shafts and splinters of light. He finally had shed his suit coat and rolled his long sleeves to his elbow.

"This is June," he said. "So it will be this hot for two more months?"

Cate grinned. "I've seen it stay like this into November," she said, sitting down near the tables.

Ometov looked at her, astonished. "November? You're joking."

"No, the heat's only going to get worse during the next two or three months."

"Into September?" Ometov couldn't believe it.

"Krupatin picked a great time to visit," Hain said. He was standing near the tables, looking at the computer setup.

"I just hope the bastard actually shows up," Erika said. She was sipping unenthusiastically from a bottle of beer, and Cate guessed she was not much of a drinker of any kind of alcohol.

"I think the intelligence is good," Ometov said. "I think the odds are good."

"Damn right," Hain said. "I can tell you, our budget masters wouldn't have let us go this far if they thought the intelligence was iffy."

"He must know he is very important here now," Erika said. "He will be more careful. His people here—his own intelligence— must be telling him to watch his step."

"No doubt," Hain agreed, "and he will. But that won't stop him from coming."

Erika rolled her head to the side and gave a skeptical lift of her eyebrows, but she let it go. Cate wondered how Erika had gotten this assignment. She assumed the BKA had given their decision a lot of consideration. Erika Jaeger, Cate guessed, was an interesting story.

"What do you think about our little boy?" Ometov asked, looking at Cate with his amused smile, his shambling manner more apparent as he slumped in a shirt so wrinkled it looked as if he had washed it in an airplane lavatory and put it in his bag to dry.

"Before I answer that, I have a question," Cate said.

Ometov nodded.

"What kind of man would I see if I were to meet Krupatin now, if I had no idea what he did other than that he was a businessman?"

"Ah, a good question, a very good one." Ometov beamed.

"What kind of man." He swigged from his bottle, staring at the bare floor. "Well, if you were to meet Sergei Krupatin today, if a friend introduced you, you would see a handsome man," he said, looking at her. "Prematurely gray hair, a clean-cut dark mustache, a good straight nose. One scar, horizontal, here." He drew a finger under his right eye. "He would talk to you intelligently, using passable English, and he would be very sophisticated in his manners, obviously intelligent. If you asked him his occupation, he would say something vague like 'international commodities' or 'international investments.' He would be dressed immaculately in a British tailor-made suit. If you talked to him for several hours, you would be impressed. If you talked to him all day, you would see things that would make you begin to wonder. If you talked to him for several days, you might well decide that he was not the kind of man you wanted to know, and you would avoid him in the future."

He gestured vaguely with his beer bottle. "But of course he can be irresistibly charming, and that, along with his good looks and wealth, makes him honey to butterflies. Women do not quickly see the real Sergei, which is never far below his superficial refinement. If you were inclined to succumb to his advances, you would discover that he has a proclivity for brutal sexual involvements. Two women—that we know about—have died from his 'affections.' What is it your prostitutes call men like that?"

"Rough trade," Cate said.

"Exactly. Rough trade. But that was years ago. Now his women are more respectable—a little higher up on the predatory evolutionary chain, one might say."

"He's never been married?" Cate asked.

Ometov smiled, and seemed delighted once again by her question.

"No," he said softly, and then his smile faded as though he were about to discuss a great sadness. "Sergei has never been married. In fact, with one possible exception long ago, the man is incapable of forming any kind of real attachment to a woman. He just doesn't need them, except for sex, and that is easily taken care of by anyone."

"One possible exception," Cate said.

"Yes." Ometov nodded, knowing she would ask. He sighed with a melancholy tilt of his head and tried some more beer, pursing his lips at the taste of it. "Sergei was already a big man when he met her. This was maybe ten years ago. Anyway, he was wealthy and had a lot of living behind him, a lot of bad history. He was already traveling very much out of Russia. In the autumn he was in St. Petersburg and saw a girl on the sidewalk. It was that simple. She was a student at the Repin Institute, a very prestigious academy for artists, difficult to get into. She was from a respected family of academicians—her father was a professor of literature at the University of St. Petersburg, her mother an art restoration specialist in the Hermitage Museum. A very fine family, not well off financially, but brilliant people. Good people. She was an only child.

"Krupatin courted her with all seriousness. He knew immediately, of course, that these people were at the opposite end of the cultural scale from himself. Not only was he truly in love, I think, but he knew very well that to have her on his arm, so to speak, would enhance his image, give him a patina of sophistication that he did not otherwise have.

"For a good while the ruse worked. He charmed her; he charmed her family. He lied most flamboyantly about his past and his present and created a new persona, one that he knew they wanted to believe in, one perhaps that he wished he had. These people, they didn't see through him for a while. Remember, by this time Sergei had already discovered his London tailor. He had come a long way from Chechnya, this importer and international businessman."

Ometov finished his beer and looked at the bottle thoughtfully. "She fell in love with him; I think it's fair to say that. Shortly after they met she finished her six years at the Repin Institute, specializing in restoration art, like her mother. She also received a scholarship to study in a special program here in the United States. It was arranged by the Hermitage. Krupatin could not talk her out of going. She left and was gone a year.

"When she returned, he was there to meet her at the airport in St. Petersburg. He covered her with gifts, with attention. He paid for a wonderful apartment, far nicer than where she had been living with her parents. He dressed her like a society lady, treated her in a way that would have spoiled a woman twice her age. But she was an extraordinarily level-headed girl and went on with her work. She had received a coveted position at the Hermitage—

naturally, since she was groomed for it almost from the time she was a child."

Ann Loder came into the room and got a bottle of beer from the ice chest. Ometov took the opportunity to get another. His stories seemed to create a time frame of their own. Cate noticed that now, as earlier in the afternoon, there was a reluctance on everyone's part to interrupt his train of thought. He went back to his chair and looked out into the courtyard again.

"The next two years began in triumph and ended in tragedy," he went on. "She was now highly trained in a specialized field. Other museums all over Europe paid to have her travel there and hold seminars on painting restoration, to give lectures, to advise. And of course she was the darling of the Hermitage, and the fact that she was in such demand was good for the prestige of the museum, and for Russia. She traveled a great deal, to the Deutsches Museum in Munich, to the National Gallery in London, to the Schweizerisches Institut für Kunstwissenschaft in Zurich, to Venice, to Rome. To the Prado in Madrid. She was wonderfully gifted.

"The tragedy began when Krupatin decided he couldn't live without her and followed her everywhere she went, all over Europe. She loved him, but she loved her career as well, and Krupatin could not tolerate her divided attention. Sometime in 1989 he must have made a conscious decision to change that. She was a passionate woman, very romantic, and he played up to this. Somehow—God knows how, I can't imagine it was voluntary, but it was never clear—he introduced her to cocaine . . . and heroin."

Ometov sighed hugely again and stared at the palms, which were turning black against the dying light.

"Everything she and her parents had worked for since she was fifteen unraveled slowly and painfully. The drugs, you know, finally took over her life. As Krupatin followed her from one assignment to the next, always feeding her drugs, demanding more and more of her time, enticing her with a corrupt and luxurious life, she became unreliable. Her work suffered. Sometimes she wouldn't show up at the museum workshops at all, and sometimes when she did she was unable to work. The word got around that she was in trouble. Finally the Hermitage called her back, but she didn't go. By then she was just something Krupatin owned. He had used the drugs to make her useless to anyone but himself.

"Eventually she even lost touch with her parents, who were anguished to the point of insanity. For a long time no one heard from her. She traveled with Krupatin, trailing along after him like a creature, living increasingly in his world, which was alien to her, and separated from her own by a drug-induced nightmare. There were rumors about her, but her old friends saw her only rarely, and the stories they had to tell were frightening. She had become a ghost.

"In late 1991 I discovered that the girl was no longer with Krupatin. Not only that, he was frantically looking for her. Somehow she had escaped. I don't know if it was with the help of friends or . . . I don't know, but she was gone. I eventually found where she had been, but she had already left there as well. It was a private clinic in Zurich. According to their records, she had arrived there alone, using fake identification papers. She was seeking a cure from the drugs—rehabilitation. She was also pregnant. As far as I could discover, she had never been visited by anyone even remotely resembling Krupatin.

"After nearly five months, she left. Alone. The baby was due within a month. The director of the clinic said she had been a remarkably determined patient, that she was strong-willed, and he had every reason to believe that she might be one of the few people who could conquer her addiction.

"Following that, I made an extraordinary effort to keep in regular touch with her old friends, the ones from her art-school days. Eventually I began to hear rumors again. These old friends were fiercely protective. She had had the child, a little girl. She was living in Paris. She was living in Zurich. She was working in an art gallery in Berlin. She was working in an art gallery in Brussels. Again she was in Zurich. Then, late in 1992, the rumors stopped. Every time I talked to one of her friends, they would begin their response by saying, 'The last time I saw Irina . . .' She simply vanished."

Ometov had finished his story. The room was silent. He appeared weary and drained, and though Cate knew it had been a long day for him, she knew also that this girl's story, and his role in it, had required a price of him.

"I'm sorry," Cate said. "You . . . It seems personal for you."

"They were old friends," Ometov said with a dismissive shrug that was not entirely convincing. "Her parents, I mean. Krupatin has been my preoccupation for many years. It's been my job. But when the girl got involved, it became personal. You know, Krupatin destroyed their lives. They were already in middle age when the girl was born, and she meant everything to them. When Krupatin came into the picture and began to dominate the girl's life, he made them count for nothing in their own minds, made life unsavory to them. He created a vacuum where once there had been a family full of love and intelligence. They both died, the parents. They never saw their daughter again. That's a terrible thing to do to people. And what he did to the girl—how do you account for something like that? And they are just three people. There are hundreds of other stories like theirs. Sergei Krupatin has a lot to answer for."

Thirteen

South Kensington, London

SHE SAT IN THE GARDEN long after he was gone, the dew gathering about her on the roses along the paths, the damp distilling on the garden chair in which she sat, her feet still pulled up under her and covered by her gown.

Krupatin's plan was complex, too complex. It was not that the other assignments had not required careful planning. They had. But she had been on her own. Krupatin had briefed her privately about the target and had provided her with the nameless faces for backup if she needed them. But the plan and its timing had been hers alone. Now Krupatin had interjected her into the middle of a complex operation, one that seemed to exceed a reasonable expectation of success. It seemed to go out of its way to invite risk, to flirt with failure. How could she, a new figure in an equation that had worked perfectly well without her for a year, be totally accepted by these two shrewd men? And even if she was, could she be accepted to the point that she would have both the opportunity and the privacy with them to do what she had to do . . . and escape? They would have to be killed within half an hour—or less—of each other. Even then, the timing would have to be calculated by moments. She would have to rely heavily on Krupatin's faces. And all of this in an American city with which no one was familiar.

Staring across the small garden, her preoccupied gaze catching whatever was visible in the pale thread of light from the kitchen door, she wondered if she had indeed reached her limit. Was her suspicion a result of paranoia or legitimate caution? How much of this could she endure, even for the sake of the only thing dear to her?

At three-thirty she started awake, surprised that somehow she had slipped seamlessly from lucid thinking into abstraction. Moving stiffly, she unfolded her legs, cringing as her warm feet touched the cold, wet bricks. She took the cups and saucers and went inside, where she left them on the kitchen table. In the bedroom she stripped the sheets off the bed, and after throwing them on the floor in another bedroom she went to sleep on the bare mattress, covering herself with a blanket she found in the closet.

She woke shortly before noon, threw off the blanket, and went straight to the front room, where she found the airline ticket inside the front door; it had been pushed through the mail slot. Quickly opening the packet, she looked at the departure time: Gatwick, British Airways, five-forty in the afternoon. There was a handwritten note on a piece of paper stapled to the ticket that said Wei had arranged for her to be met at the airport. She would be taken to his home in the city.

She packed first, everything except her cosmetics and the dress she was going to wear on the flight. Then she made coffee and sat down at the dining table to go over the files of the two men again. But it was difficult to concentrate. Her mind kept gravitating to the thought that without a doubt, both Wei and Bontate had similar files of their own. Their intelligence sources were at least as good as Krupatin's, and she was suddenly gripped with the fear that "Olya Serova" would be identified as an imposter almost from the beginning. She could not shake the idea that she was walking into a trap.

When she walked through the gate at Charles de Gaulle Airport, she was surprised to be met not by the usual escort of suited men but by an Asian woman, who introduced herself as Mr. Wei's assistant. She was accompanied by an Asian man who was clearly a bodyguard and who stood back deferentially and without introduction.

The woman had impeccable manners, and during the drive into the city in Wei's ash-gray Bentley she managed to carry on an intelligent dialogue without touching on anything of substance regarding Irina's visit. Irina guessed that she was connected to Wei's legitimate world and probably had no idea of her employer's darker involvements. She felt sure that the same was not true of the bodyguard, who was also the chauffeur. He wore small headphones and a tiny microphone bent round in front of his mouth, into which he spoke from time to time. Irina caught his glance only once in the rearview mirror as they glided silently deeper into the city, at an hour when the lights were just coming on in the failing light.

Wei Tsing lived in the heart of the sixth arrondissement, an exorbitantly expensive piece of real estate on a narrow cobblestone street that was like a private passageway between the Place St.-Sulpice and the Luxembourg Gardens. The houses that lined the street were of the *ancien régime,* shaded by chestnut trees that seemed nearly as old as the houses. He lived in a seventeenth-century *hôtel particulier,* its cut stone walls softened by vines that climbed its full three stories. It was the blue time of the evening, and as the Bentley pulled smoothly through the iron gates and into the drive, Irina noted the warm glow of soft lights in the tall ground-floor windows. As they stopped under the arched portico of the front door, she was surprised to see Wei himself coming down the steps to greet her. He was alone. He opened the door of the Bentley and helped her out.

"Welcome to my home, Madame Serova," he said in English. "I hope you had a pleasant trip?"

He closed the door of the Bentley, which purred away, taking the prim assistant with it. A maid in black uniform appeared and whisked away Irina's bag as they ascended the few steps to the entry.

"Would you like to go upstairs to your suite for a while?" he asked as they entered a cavernous hall punctuated with marble columns that led to what appeared to be a ballroom at its far end.

"No, not at all," she said, "as you know, it is a short flight."

Wei was exactly Irina's height, with thick black hair that he combed straight back and that was so precisely barbered as to draw attention. He was wearing a white dinner jacket and black tie, a formality seldom seen in a private home, and blue velvet opera slippers. His facial features, like his hair, were sculpted and precise, his skin flawless. There was no sign whatsoever of a beard beneath the smooth flesh of his face.

"I thought we might have a little wine before dinner," he said. "It's in the library."

The floors were quadrate white marble with black diamond insets. Interspersed between the columns was a series of stone pedestals, each holding a small sculpted female figure, every one carved of red stone, none more than a foot in height. Lighting from an obscure source washed the figures in a soft illumination that heightened their translucence, causing them to stand out almost as if they were scarlet holograms burning in the dusk of the great hallway. The effect was so unusual, so stunning, that Irina could not help but pause before one of the pedestals.

"Do you like my seraphim?" Wei asked, obviously pleased that she had stopped.

"They are exquisite, but I doubt they are seraphim," she said, seeing now the autoerotic postures of the naked women. These could not be ancient. She was not aware of a single example of female masturbation in Greek or Roman visual art.

Wei laughed. "They are carved of what the ancients called carnelian—red chalcedony. The detail is remarkable, isn't it?"

Irina could feel his eyes on her as she moved along, examining each of the sensuous images.

"I bought them from a dealer in Bern who claims to have acquired them from a well-known collector in Istanbul. No one has been willing to assign a provenance to them, but I hardly care at this point. I have never seen women more candid about such pleasures, have you?"

"Not in stone," she said dryly. The figures were incredible pieces, their lubricious self-absorption as fascinating in the detail of its portrayal as in the inventiveness of their acts. She had never seen anything quite like them, inspired arrangements of execution, subject, and color.

"Please," he said, touching her arm gently, "I have other things I want you to see," and he led her farther along, past two more of his ember-red ecstatics. "You see, I knew two things about you in advance, Olya. Is that all right, may I call you by your first name?"

"Of course."

"I knew that you were beautiful—Sergei was specific about that—and I knew that sometime in your past you were an expert in pigments, the restoration of paintings. That's all he told me." Wei smiled. "It was a shameless enticement. I would like to hear more about it."

Irina's skin prickled with a warm flush of adrenaline, and she suddenly found it difficult to breathe. She needed to take a few deep breaths, but to do so would be unthinkable. Sergei was insane to have mentioned her background to this man. It was only blind luck that Wei had mentioned it in the very first moments of their meeting. Her mind was scrambling to discard the ideas she had put together during the flight, the fabrications she had assembled about herself that she was prepared to give to Wei and Bontate. Now she would have to improvise on this bit of truth Krupatin had passed along without her knowing. Now she would have to demonstrate her knowledge—and it had been so long ago—and keep in mind all the while that she could not afford to dip too deeply into her own reality. Anything she said would give him clues for a background search. And yet she could not afford to stumble now, not at the very beginning.

Now they were at the doors of the library and Wei led her inside, where rich rosewood bookcases lined the rectangular room. The cases were no higher than five feet, and above them, reaching to the fifteen-foot ceiling, the walls were crowded with paintings and drawings. The books on the shelves were all dedicated to one subject, art: art histories, biographies of artists and collectors, scholarly monographs, catalogues of special collections.

"This is my passion," he said. "At least, one of them."

A silver urn of chilling white wine and two long-stemmed glasses sat on a baroque gueridon just inside the doors of the library. Wei poured each of them a portion of wine.

"Would you like to take a little tour?" he asked, gesturing with his glass toward his collection. "I would be delighted to have your opinions."

"It's been a long time," she said vaguely. "I'm no authority on taste. As I'm sure you know, Sergei knows so little about such things that anyone who knows a modest amount becomes an expert in his eyes."

Wei looked at her with an expression of amused surprise. He had not expected to find this kind of irreverence in Krupatin's most trusted emissary.

"I am sure," he said with a hint of admiration in his voice, "that yours is an opinion I would value regardless of your credentials."

He placed his hand gently at the small of her back and guided her toward the long row of pictures on the right side of the generous room. There were the requisite French Impressionists, which Wei admitted he had bought early on in his collecting career, along with a few exquisite Italian quattrocento panels. Even better was a small collection of fifteenth-century Venetian and Florentine drawings that any major museum would have coveted. Surprisingly, there was a significant representation of *fin de siècle*—Klimt, Schiele, Czeschka, Khnopff, von Stuck, and a smattering of the French Symbolists as well.

Irina's slow and isolated footsteps marked their progress on the marble floor as Wei moved silently on slippered feet beside her, talking softly about his collection, stopping here and there to examine an artwork or to relate an anecdote connected to the acquisition of another. They rounded the far end of the library and started up the other side, eventually coming to his growing collection of icons. Apparently Krupatin was not the only dealer in stolen art who had been supplying Wei's appetite for contraband sanctity. There were scores of invaluable icons that were most surely undocumented, ivory diptychs from Turkey, chased silver and gold from Georgia, mosaics from Greece, frescoes from the Balkans, tempera on wood from Russia—a collection of smuggled art that could have put him in prison for the rest of his life.

And then they came to Wei's most recent enthusiasm, for Irina a life-saving stroke of luck: Asian painting on paper and wood and silk. Some of Irina's research on pigments had been done with these very artists when she had worked with the Freer Gallery in Washington. She knew the materials intimately.

When they came to the doors of the library again, Wei paused and turned back to face the length of the room.

"I have reached the point in my life when these works mean

more to me than just about anything else," he said. "I don't know why, and I don't even bother to analyze it anymore."

He took the wine from the urn and offered her another glass, which she accepted, waiting as he poured more for himself as well. Not once had he asked her anything specific regarding the works in his collection, anything that would have allowed her to demonstrate her reputed knowledge. She knew that it was up to her to provide the confirmation he was looking for.

As he shoved the wine bottle down into the ice again, she walked a little way toward the center of the library and stood in front of one of the Asian pieces.

"I was a color restorationist," she said without introduction, looking at the painting. "My training was academic, and during the time I was studying I worked with some of the very best scholars in my field. I studied internationally. If I hadn't, I would never have seen the work of this man." She gestured toward the picture she had been admiring, on which her eyes were still fixed. "Chao Yung, fourteenth century." She turned to Wei and was delighted to see him looking at her with an expression of stunned surprise. "Am I right? This is a Chao Yung?"

"Yes, incredibly, it is," he said, clearly amazed.

Irina laughed casually and turned again to the painting. "The key to restoration, of course, is knowing the chemistry of the pigments you are working with," she went on. "You could destroy a painting in seconds if you were ignorant of the composition and properties of its original pigments." She stared a moment at the painting in front of her. "The red in that horseman's robe, for instance, is vermillion, which in its natural mineral form is called cinnabar, the crystalline form of mercuric sulfide. But the Chinese had discovered a dry-process vermillion—synthetic cinnabar—by combining mercury, which is derived from cinnabar, and sulfur, which creates a black product, and subliming it to form the red modification called vermillion. It is a relatively stable pigment, but capricious. Sometimes it holds its color for centuries . . . but sometimes not."

Wei was looking at her as if he couldn't believe his ears. Irina moved to the next work.

"This is of the Nanga school. I'm guessing the artist is Watanabe Kazan, Japanese, nineteenth century."

"Good God . . . you are absolutely right."

"The color of that kimono is made with malachite, a moderately permanent pigment. Under certain conditions it tends to blacken, but the malachite areas on frescoes from medieval Italy are still quite brilliant."

She moved to the next painting. "I have no doubt about the identity of this artist. Ishikawa Toyonubu, Japanese, eighteenth century."

Wei nodded, beaming.

"Look at the white in the fleshtones on this courtesan. That is achieved by the use of a pigment made of pulverized oyster shells called *gofun*. This makes a more subdued white than the heavy metal whites and enables the creation of these subtle but almost luminous fleshtones. This is a superb example, too. You should be proud of this one especially."

If Irina had had any doubts about winning Wei's acceptance, they faded rapidly with each disquisition as she moved from picture to picture. Several times she did not know, or pretended not to know, an artist or a date, which gave Wei an opportunity to reciprocate with his own expertise. Though she had been terrified that she would never be able to recall enough of her long-out-of-use scholarship to impress him, she was delighted to find that the more she talked, the more she remembered. And in truth, if she got some technical bit of information wrong about this pigment or that one, she had no real fear that Wei could possibly detect the bobble.

They had dinner together in a small dining room not far from the library, served by silent French maids who wore only their stockings, no shoes. The food arrived silently and the used tableware disappeared silently, and never during the evening did she observe Wei giving even the subtlest signal to tell them when to come and go.

Wei was indeed a beguiling man, and it was clear to her that he was finding the evening much to his liking. Krupatin, Irina now realized, had not done this with any lack of cunning. Keeping her in the dark about Wei's knowledge of her art training was a stroke of genius. This last-minute discovery, while disconcerting for her initially, provided a spontaneity that might not have been present if she had been allowed to plan everything down to the last detail. Not only did she recover beautifully, but the concentration she had to summon to do that allowed Wei to see her at her least calculating, and she found the instant reimmersion in her old profession stimulating in a way that was surprisingly refreshing. And she had to admit, Wei was unabashedly charmed by her. Again Krupatin had been shrewd. He had given Wei an evening to remember, combining his two passions: art and Western women.

But in his typical disregard for Irina, Krupatin had not foreseen everything. Irina herself was finding the evening stimulating. It was only with the greatest difficulty that she reminded herself to do her job. Wei was a supremely self-confident man and had the casual self-assurance of those who have been wealthy from childhood and have never known anything else. He had that immaculate sexuality that was peculiar to Asian men, appearing meticulous in his dress and manner, his dinner jacket crisply cut to his compact physique. He had only the first creases of crow's feet at the corners of his eyes to hint that he was not as young as he seemed.

Irina watched him carefully. For some reason he never ate all of any course put in front of him. Once she even saw him start to eat a last bite of something, then stop himself and lay down his fork. He was left-handed and wore a carved gold ring with a Ceylon-cut ruby on the finger where a wedding band should have been. Sometimes he tended to listen to her talk by turning his head slightly to his right, as though he had better hearing in his left ear.

Twice during the evening a telephone was brought to him at the table, with someone already on the line. Irina never heard a telephone ring, and neither time did he indicate any surprise or impatience at being interrupted. Both times he apologized to her, put the telephone to his ear—his left ear—and began talking without verifying who was on the line. He spoke in Chinese and seemed to give information and receive none. His tone of voice was the same as he was using with her: gentle, polite, relaxed.

Irina found herself actually intrigued by him, or by the evening in general, and had to remind herself of the fate of his three mistresses. She also found herself wondering if perhaps the demise of these women was not a bit of disinformation Krupatin had added to Wei's dossier as a hedge against the possibility that Irina might not be sufficiently repulsed by the man she was being positioned to kill.

Fourteen

Paris

"DID YOU SLEEP WELL?" he asked.

The terrace was shady, but the late morning sun was falling obliquely through the towering chestnut trees that predominated in the wooded grounds onto the lawn below. The perimeter of the lawn and the grounds was made up of thick shrubbery that formed a barrier inside the wrought-iron fence that faced the Rue Férou.

"Very well," she said, approaching the table. "Thank you."

She had been awakened by an Asian maid with coffee on a silver tray. The maid had informed her that Monsieur Wei wished her to join him on the terrace in forty-five minutes. Did Madame want her to run her bath? No. Did Madame want her to run the shower? No. Did she need any assistance in the bath? No. Did she need assistance dressing? No. Very well. If Madame required anything, please ring number six on the telephone.

"Sometimes a strange city, a strange bed, can be disconcerting," he said, standing to hold her chair as she sat at the marble-topped table.

"It never bothers me," she said. "Besides, Paris is no strange city to me."

Wei raised his eyebrows inquisitively.

"I lived here for over a year, not that long ago," she explained. "Ever since then it's been a friendly city to me."

"But you live in St. Petersburg now," Wei said. "Coffee?"

"Please. Yes, St. Petersburg is my home. Most of the time, anyway."

"You travel a great deal, then?"

"A good bit," she said.

They chatted a few minutes over coffee while she ate a few samplings from the tray of pastries on the table. She noticed *Le Monde* and the London *Times* at his elbow, each folded several times after having been read. Crows called from the tallest trees on the grounds, and faintly in the background, barely audible, the noises of Paris seeped through the woods.

After she had toyed with her food for a sufficient length of time, Wei turned his chair sideways to the table and faced her, crossing his legs, his thin hand on a fresh cup of coffee.

"This is very unusual, what Sergei wants to do," he said without preamble.

"What's that?" she asked, to give herself a second.

Wei smiled as though he knew she was being disingenuous. "Wanting to employ a 'trusted emissary.' "

"If you didn't insist on meeting in the U.S., it wouldn't be necessary," she said.

"Perhaps I will change my mind."

She shrugged and nodded as if to say, yes, that would do it.

"Have you done this sort of thing for him before?"

"Yes, this sort of thing."

"I think he is being paranoid."

"Do you?"

"What do you think?"

"I have found that more often than not, Sergei Krupatin knows exactly what he is doing."

He smiled. "Well said. Then you don't think he is being paranoid."

"You must know, Monsieur Wei, how I must answer that."

Wei stared at her. She had no idea how to read his expression, which hinted, perhaps, at admiration.

"Sergei did not tell me how he knows you."

She looked at him and sipped her coffee, keeping her eyes on him over the rim of her cup. He was smiling faintly.

"Really?"

"No."

She put down her cup and sat back in her chair. "He must have thought it wasn't important."

"Perhaps. But still, I would like to know."

She regarded him a moment, and then she felt that it was her turn to smile. "Why?"

But Wei was not so easily drawn out either.

"How long have you known him?"

She didn't want to answer this. Her sense of self-preservation warned her that she should not give him any more information than she could possibly afford.

"I hardly think that's relevant," she said.

"But if I think it is, that's what is important, isn't it?"

She looked at him, paused, then slowly pushed her coffee cup away from her. "Monsieur Wei, I am a very private person. I feel sure that is something you can appreciate. With all respect, I do not want myself investigated any more than you surely must have done already." He did not react to this. "I am agreeing to do this for Sergei Krupatin because I owe him a favor, not because I have to. But my need to repay that favor is not greater than my own desire for privacy. If you are not satisfied with me as you find me, you should tell Sergei Krupatin, and he will find someone else for this role. And I will not be offended, I assure you."

As if by theatrical cue, bells began tolling from St.-Sulpice at the end of Rue Férou, and others, more faintly, from St.-Germain-des-Prés, nearer the Seine.

Wei's expression had grown more serious as she spoke, but when she finished and the bells lilted in the clear morning air, he let a placid smile return to his smooth Asian features.

"I can see why Sergei has chosen you," he said with a slight nod of acquiescence. "But please excuse me. I did not want to make this sound like an inquisition. Perhaps the circumstances here have made this more awkward than necessary. My interest, Olya, is more personal than professional. I am not interrogating you. I am . . . well, simply curious, as a man is curious about a woman because she is a woman, not an emissary."

She was taken aback. It was not a staged reaction, but it was in fact the proper response. She could see this in his face.

"I simply would like to know if your relationship with Sergei Krupatin involves more than business," Wei said. "Or do I have the liberty to get to know you better?"

She looked at him, privately astonished that Sergei's bet had paid off so quickly. He was Satan's psychologist; he had known exactly how his man was going to respond to her.

"Our relationship is strictly business," she said, and then added quickly, "but I am not at all sure that what you are suggesting is . . ." She didn't want to insult him. ". . . a good idea under the circumstances."

"I am only suggesting less formality between us," he said unconvincingly. "We have so much in common, as we discovered last night."

"I suppose the question is which of us knows him better," she said. "I know him well enough to think he would see that as . . . a curious development."

"You think so?" Wei allowed himself another amused smile.

"I do."

"Then you feel obligated to tell him everything that passes between us?"

"Not obligated, no. But I do have a responsibility not to compromise the position I am supposed to represent here," she said.

She had to be careful to strike the right balance. The Chinese was no fool. Perhaps he was playing with her. She had to remain independent, possessing some authority of her own, but at the same time she could not put herself in a position that Wei himself would find disloyal if she were working for him instead of Krupatin. And yet she could not afford to give up the seduction factor. It could be the key to everything she needed.

She was given another lucky break when one of Wei's shoeless and silent maids glided across the terrace with his telephone.

"Excuse me," he said.

As he spoke on the telephone she turned her face away from him, presenting her profile. She knew he would be watching her, and she wanted to portray just the amount of uncertainty that she guessed he would want to see. He would want to think that his charm was working on her, that she was tempted. She imagined that he believed any woman would want a taste of this life—his obvious wealth, his refined manners, and yes, even his considerable sexuality. A fling at least, surely. She knew that scores of women had had similar propositions from him, and she thought she could guess with some certainty what the results had been.

She lifted her chin and stared out across the lawn, absently stroking the side of her long throat with the back of her fingers. She knew he was watching. She straightened her back, lost in thought, and felt his eyes on her breasts as surely as if he had laid his hand there. Wei murmured in Chinese, and the crows of Paris called their ageless calls across the stone churches and ancient narrow streets of the Rive Gauche.

When he finished talking on the telephone, she continued staring, seemingly lost in thought about the conversation they had just had, perhaps uncertain as to what she was going to do about it.

"Olya."

She started, her thoughts interrupted, and turned to him. The maid was gliding away across the terrace.

"What were you thinking?" he asked.

"Nothing." Dialogue older than the churches.

"You never answered my question."

"I was supposed to come here to put your mind at ease about my role in the negotiations. Have I done that?"

"Of course. I couldn't possibly have any objections."

"Very well," she said. "Then I think we should leave it at that."

"No, I don't think so," he said.

She stiffened inside and regarded him closely.

"What do you mean?" She was terse. She had seen these kinds of men turn vicious with the tenderest words on their lips. If that was the case here, she was well prepared to meet the situation with bravado, if nothing else.

He looked at his watch. "I have just made arrangements to have you taken to Sicily on one of my planes. You are supposed to be there by one o'clock this afternoon, which means you will have to leave within the hour. You are not actually going to Palermo but to Carlo Bontate's estate, which is inland, in the hills south of Palermo. My pilot has been to Marineo before and knows it well."

"This was the original arrangement?"

"Sergei has agreed to this. And Bontate," he said, not directly answering her question. He hesitated a moment. "You have not met Carlo?"

"No."

"We are quite different people," he said.

She wondered why he felt it necessary to tell her that.

"When you have finished in Palermo, my pilot will bring you back to Paris."

"To Paris?"

"Sergei did not object to your spending one more night here on your way back," Wei said. "To talk about art again . . ." He smiled. "If you have no objections. I would consider it an honor to have you."

Fifteen

Houston

IT HAD BEEN A LONG DAY, beginning in Washington for Ometov and Hain and in New York for Loder and Jaeger.

When Cate and Ann returned to the off-site with pizzas and salads and several more six-packs of beer, they all gathered around the rented dining room table and ate, their conversation falling into a general discussion about the differences in law enforcement procedures in Russia and Germany and the United States.

This casual exchange only highlighted Ometov's weary sense of humor and Erika Jaeger's natural inclination to sobriety regarding just about everything. They were both exceptionally inquisitive, sometimes asking questions about the validity of impressions they had gotten about the United States from American films. The dinner conversation ranged over a wide variety of issues, none of which had anything to do with their reason for being there. There seemed to be an unspoken agreement to set it aside for a while, if only for the length of time it took to eat a pizza. Which was only as long as it lasted.

Putting a last bite of pizza in his mouth, Curtis Hain sat back in his chair, one hand resting on his bottle of beer as he crunched the crust. He was thoughtful for a moment and then looked at Cate.

"Cate, we've been holding out on you a little bit," he said. "Well, not holding out. Maybe holding back is a better phrase."

Cate felt her face flush and simultaneously realized she had no reason to be having this reaction. Still, in her own personal spectrum of emotions, his remark had the effect of the other shoe falling. But it didn't frighten her. It simply verified the vague feeling she had had all day that for some reason she was not getting the full picture here, despite the fact that much of the briefing had been directed to her specifically. Everyone else was already up to speed.

She took her eyes off Hain, looked at the olive on the slice of pizza she was holding, and then put the slice down on her plate. She was a slow eater; she wasn't through, but her appetite suddenly had deserted her. Giving a little shove to her plate, she wiped her mouth with her napkin.

"Okay," she said. "What is it?"

"I'm going to get right to the heart of this," Hain said. "You've been buttonholed for a special job here. I mean special even among this special group of us. And you've been selected for a number of specific reasons. One, to be blunt, Ennis Strey said you had the balls for it. Two, you've got the right looks for it. Three, Ennis Strey said you had the brains for it."

"In that order of importance?" she asked.

"Actually, yeah, it's pretty damn close," Hain said. He took a swig from his bottle of beer. "We want to try to put someone personally close to Krupatin, especially if it looks like he's going to set up here for a while. We don't have a lot of time to try to do that, but we have a card up our sleeve that we hope will give us an edge." He stared across at her. "A couple of years ago Krupatin set up one of his most trusted lieutenants in New York. Brighton Beach. His name is Valentin Stepanov. He seems to be the cornerstone of Krupatin's infrastructure here in the States. Stepanov has been summoned to Houston by Krupatin. That's the real reason why we're so sure he's coming here. Stepanov is ours."

"Christ." Cate was stunned. She looked at Ann Loder and then back at Hain. "How did that happen?"

"It's complicated," Hain said.

"You should tell her," Ometov put in. "If we are going to ask her to do this, she ought to know everything, all the details."

If Hain was irritated by this intrusion, he didn't show it.

"Stepanov came up through the ranks with Krupatin," he said, "ever since the early Moscow days when they were blasting their way into criminal stardom. Stepanov and Krupatin were equals, best friends, but as their careers progressed, Stepanov's position gradually emerged as subordinate to Krupatin's. He became Krupatin's most trusted lieutenant rather than his equal. As Krupatin's fortunes rose, so did Stepanov's, though not as extravagantly as Krupatin's. There's never room for more than one at the top. When Krupatin made his move to the U.S., he put Stepanov in charge of holding the ground here."

"A while back Stepanov made a mistake," Ann said, nibbling on a slice of cucumber. She looked weary; her eyelids were sagging, gravity having its way at the end of an exhausting day. "We got him on tape setting up, in detail, an extortion arrangement. Big bucks. Corporate-level stuff. He was looking at a big chunk of time without parole. We talked to him, and he rolled over."

"When was this?"

"Nine months ago."

"Then he's opened up on Krupatin?" Cate asked.

"Oh no, he's tougher than that," Hain said, shaking his head. He picked up a piece of pepperoni and put it in his mouth. "But for starters he gave us some stuff on one of Krupatin's big German operations. The BKA handled it very well and broke up a deep, multiheaded organization there. Losing that organization cut seriously into Krupatin's German interests. That's where Erika came in, working undercover in that operation."

"Stepanov could do that because he knew the cell there," Ann said. "He used to run it. Being all the way across the Atlantic and not having been directly involved in it for nearly two years, he was well protected from suspicion. But he was stubborn about the U.S. operation. He said if he gave it up, Krupatin would kill him, whether Krupatin could prove he had had anything to do with it or not. The boss heading the German operation was blown up, along with his three guards, as he was being transferred from one prison to another in Mainz. That's the way it works. Krupatin never lets anything slide. You screw up, you pay."

"Then we got the intelligence from legat Moscow." Hain was

leaning his chair back, rocking on its back legs. "We immediately contacted Stepanov. He admitted he'd received communication from Krupatin to meet him in Houston. Swore to God Almighty he knew nothing more than that. Wouldn't, or couldn't, help us out, threats or no threats. But he did agree to help us put someone inside."

There was a pause.

"Why me?" Cate asked.

"The reasons I gave," Hain said.

"What did you mean when you said I had the right looks for it?"

"There were four women in the running for this," Ann Loder said. "One in the San Francisco field office, one in the Chicago field office, and one in our Brussels office. And you."

"And?"

"We showed Stepanov all the photographs," Loder said.

"You understand," Ometov interrupted, speaking softly, politely, "Valentin has known Sergei all of their lives. He knows him . . . intimately." He shook his head, and a soft smile of inevitability accompanied a slight shrug. "His finger"—Ometov tapped the table beside his plate—"selected your picture. 'This is the one,' he said."

It was the most curious procurement procedure that Cate had ever witnessed, especially since it was directed at herself. There was no need for an explicit elaboration of the ramifications of accepting such an assignment. She knew them. Once she was inside—if she got inside—no one was going to ask her how she got her information. If it was indeed information they wanted. They were not going to be asking for a breath-by-breath account of how she got what she got. She would be on her own in matters of intimacy. You went however far you had to go. The realities of the business were that the information was so important that no one was going to blame you for anything you had to do to get it.

All of them were looking at her, but her eyes were still fixed on Ometov.

"You're wanting information, I assume."

"To be precise," Ometov said, "anything—everything."

She looked at Hain. "You're not going to ask me to wear a wire, are you? That's impossible."

For a millisecond Hain looked as if he didn't know how to

frame a response, but before he could put something together Ann Loder leaned forward with her forearms on the table.

"Cate, have you ever used Norplant?"

"No."

"But you know how it works."

"Sure."

"The techs at Quantico have come up with two devices. Same size as Norplant. Same application. One is a very sensitive, incredibly sensitive microphone, uses human tissue as a kind of antenna or something. Shit, I don't know. It doesn't matter. The other is a burst transmitter. Left arm, right arm. We know where you are at all times."

"And you hear everything . . . all the time."

Loder nodded. "It never turns off."

"I'd be a walking microphone."

"It *never* turns off," Loder repeated significantly.

There was silence for a moment.

"Jesus Christ," Cate said. "And what is it you expect me to do?"

"Stepanov has agreed to take you with him. He's married. You'd be his mistress."

"I thought I was supposed to be . . . available to Krupatin."

"Krupatin . . . well, he has a reputation for taking what he wants. The fact that you're Stepanov's mistress is irrelevant."

"Oh, shit."

"No, no no no," Erika said quickly, eager to correct a possible misunderstanding. She looked all around the table before her eyes settled on Cate. "Look, it's not so . . . *ungehobelt*—what, crude. He is not a beast, not in that way. No. He will not hesitate to take you away from Stepanov, but he will do it with guile and romance, with some civility. Insulting to Stepanov, no doubt, but not insulting to you. He is not going to jump on you, have sex with you right there in front of everyone."

"Then how does it work?" Cate asked. "What could I expect?" She couldn't believe she was having this conversation. In her own mind she really wasn't committed to this. But she was curious, very curious.

"As I said." Erika frowned and furrowed her clear, unwrinkled brow. "He will flirt with you. This is common with him. He just does it if he wants. He would flirt with the Virgin Mary in front of

Jesus Christ. You know, no rules in this. What belongs to his lieutenants belongs to him—if he wants it."

"What you're saying," Cate said, trying to read between the lines, "is that to some extent I could control the situation. I don't have to be afraid of rape."

"God, no." Erika shook her head. "The smarter you are, the longer you can drag it out. He likes—what, the game of it. But," she said, holding up a hand, index finger extended in caution, "if you have to have sex with him, you had better be prepared for a crazy situation. When I was undercover in Berlin, I talked to women who had slept with him. He is cruel. It's that simple. Watch out."

Erika's blunt references to the sexual possibilities in this assignment were like a splash of water in the face. Her European frankness was far out in front of what either Loder or Hain would have ventured, but Cate noticed that neither of them was rushing in to qualify her remarks. Clearly everyone felt that the stakes here justified a considerable ethical leniency.

It was quiet as Cate looked at her plate: scattered crumbs, a bit of lettuce or green onion, a charred corner of pepperoni, an oily drool of salad dressing. She thought how odd it was that these trivial scraps would even catch her attention. The proposition put before her was entirely out of proportion to anything she had ever done.

"What about backup?" she asked. "Just how far out there am I expected to operate?"

"I don't think we need to go into operational details at this point," Hain said quickly, dismissively. "What we need to do is to give you some breathing space here. We're all exhausted. It's been a hell of a day. Let's clean up this mess and get to bed. Cate, think about it. Sleep on it, if you can." He smiled weakly. "Tomorrow morning we'll talk. But we've got to know then. This is tough, I know, and I'm sorry we're having to do it this way, but we haven't been given a lot of time. If you decide to pass on this—and you're perfectly welcome to do that, it doesn't affect your career one way or the other . . . this is an off-the-record proposition. But if you pass on this, we've got to know soon so we can get agent number two down here pronto. Understand? This is pressuring you, I know, but this is the way it's got to be."

▫ ▫ ▫ ▫

It seemed she had lain awake for almost an hour without having made any measurable progress toward a decision. The pros and cons were so integrated as to make her choice nearly impossible. She played them all out, strung them in scenarios that resulted in everything from laudatory success to grim disaster. She had never imagined having to make such a choice. And yes, she thought about Tavio. She made all the comparisons, made all the rationalizations about how this was different, but she was inwardly embarrassed at how easily she paled at what he had done routinely for years. Too many years.

She was just about to slip into an exhausted sleep when she thought she heard voices in the hallway. But when she lifted her head from the pillow the aural perspective changed, and she realized the voices were coming from the courtyard. Throwing back her sheet, she got out of bed, went to the window, and parted the blinds slightly. The only light in the courtyard was the glow from the city reflected off the gulf clouds that had drifted in with the cooling temperatures of the night. A stone barbecue pit was built against the rear wall of the courtyard, and Curtis Hain was sitting on the side of it with his arms folded across his chest, head down as he listened to Ann Loder, who seemed to be delivering a heated monologue, leaning toward him and occasionally gesturing with one arm, flinging it toward the sky to make her point.

Cate watched the two of them for a moment, and then as she started to close the curtains, she happened to see a third figure a few steps away. Sitting in a lawn chair in the shadow of one of the palms, Leo Ometov was calmly listening to Loder's diatribe, his chin resting on one hand as he smoked.

Sixteen

Marineo, Sicily

LIKE MOST COUNTRY HOMES in the *campagna,* Carlo Bontate's villa was not actually in the little village of Marineo but well off in a valley to the northwest of the hamlet, which consisted primarily of two ancient chapels around which a small community had encrusted itself on the top of a hill. Irina could see the little whitewashed town with its terra-cotta roofs shimmering in the distance from the porthole of Wei's jet as it touched down on the tarmac strip in the middle of a dusty plain.

The airstrip itself was a sign of the new generation that Bontate represented. Such a sign of wealth, even in the isolation of the Marineo valley, would have been forbidden a decade earlier. These sorts of extravagances were left to Mafia holdings outside Sicily. At home, humble appearances were the rule. The Sicilians differed in this from the Colombians, who flaunted their wealth under the dirty noses of their own impoverished peasants.

But youth and expediency often brought about changes soundly decried by tradition. Such was the way of the world, even for the families of the Sicilian Mafia.

When the plane made a slow turn at the end of the runway, Irina saw two Mercedes sedans sitting side by side along the edge of the tarmac. The familiar sight of bodyguards leaning against the sides of the cars was not particularly comforting to Irina as the Falcon 2000 whined to a stop fifty yards from them.

Bontate's young men were clearly not the local country boys who were so famously loyal to the older mafiosi. These sun-shaded and surly loyalists wore silk shirts and fashionably baggy suits and seemed to consider accompanying their boss during re-treats to the country house a hardship duty. Their black city shoes were caked with dust, and the expressions on their faces revealed an impatience with this country business and a desire to be back on the streets of Palermo, where a man's shoes would stay shiny and he could get a *caffè corretto* at the snap of his fingers from a trattoria always close at hand.

Two handsome *palermitani* met Irina as she stepped out of the jet and ushered her into the back seat of their sedan. The pilot got into the second sedan with two other men, while two more re-mained behind with the plane and with Wei's security guard, who always traveled with the pilot but never let the aircraft out of his sight. The two cars sped along the dirt roads of the valley toward the rising land and the foothills opposite Marineo itself.

Bontate's country house was an old two-story villa of stone and faded ocher stucco. It sat atop a hill, like Marineo, and faced northeast across the valley to the bright little village eight miles away. On either side of the road that wound up to the villa were alternating fields of grain and olive groves and vineyards, and everything near the road was glazed in a chalky dust that baked under the summer sun. The villa was enclosed by a high wall, which was thickly planted on its outside perimeter with lemon and lime trees, punctuated here and there by tall palms whose fronds hung over the inside of the dun-colored wall.

The two Mercedes cruised through the gate in the wall and turned to a sudden stop on the gravel drive. Immediately the bodyguards were out, opening Irina's door just in time for her to be engulfed by their own dust, which had followed them into the courtyard on the heavy summer air.

One of the young men, beckoning her with manicured fingers and a flashing diamond ring, led her across the gravel and into the shade of a portico. She sensed someone to her right and turned to see several people sitting in a garden under the dappled shade of trees. They were all women, three or four of them in wooden lounge chairs, fanning themselves in the heat. Books and magazines were lying about, and on a small round table nearby were glasses and a bowl of fruit and a pitcher of some kind of iced drink. All of the women turned to look at her as well, as did a little girl in a baggy white dress, who was pushing her black hair out of her face with one hand while her other hand gripped a string attached to the neck of a speckled chicken.

Irina froze, her eyes fixed on the child. Then, almost instantly, she realized she was staring and quickly turned to follow the bodyguard into the villa's gloomy entry hall.

The stone walls were thick here, as were the shadows that kept the inside of the old villa cool. The yeasty odors of a wine cellar lingered on this bottom floor, but the bodyguard immediately started up the stone stairs that ascended on either side of the hall. Irina followed him up along the curving balustrade to the second-floor landing, where an open mezzanine wrapped around both sides. Immediately at the head of the landing double doors led into a large square reception room with parquet floors and heavy dark furniture. Tall windows along the walls let in muted afternoon light as they crossed to a second set of double doors, which opened onto a deep shady loggia. The view from here was stunning, a sweeping perspective of the valley and the mountains beyond, the rolling landscape brilliant in the summer light. Huge meringue-white clouds drifted in from the coast to the north, dragging behind them smears of stucco-colored shadows that moved over the groves and fields below.

"Signorina Serova."

Irina turned to her left and saw a heavyset man in rumpled trousers and a short-sleeved plaid shirt getting up from a chair and coming toward her. She recognized Bontate from the photographs in Krupatin's file.

"Welcome to the country," he said, extending a hand without a smile.

"Thank you," she said, glancing over his shoulder behind him. No one else was there.

"Let's sit down over here," he said, turning his back on her and walking to the small table with a chipped and discolored marble top where he had been sitting. There were several chairs and on the table a bottle of wine without a label and two glasses. There was also a pack of American cigarettes and the tin lid from a widemouth jar, which he had been using as an ashtray.

"I was just out looking at my vines," he said, motioning for her to sit down, "when I saw your plane. This isn't the very best land for wine, here around Marineo, but I am experimenting with some *moscatos.*" He shrugged. "I don't know."

An old brown fedora, its band stained with sweat and dust, was hanging on the back of his chair. The underarms of his shirt were dark with perspiration, and the upper part of his forehead was pale where the fedora had shielded it from the Sicilian sun.

He poured a small bistro glass of wine and set it in front of her without asking her if she wanted it. He did not ask if she wanted to freshen up or if she cared to have something cool to drink. He looked and acted like the caretaker of this property rather than its owner.

"This is a little unusual," he said, getting right to the point as he poured wine into the other glass for himself. Like Wei, he spoke English, but Bontate's English was heavily accented. In his early forties, just shorter than Irina, he had tousled dark hair with flecks of sandy brown. His face was round and sunburned and stubbled with a day's growth of beard. But his most striking feature was his eyes. They were bright amber and shielded by long, soft lashes. The rich honey of their color seemed almost to glow in contrast to his deep Sicilian tan.

"Perhaps," she said, setting her shoulder bag on the floor beside her chair. "But Krupatin was hoping that having me meet you would put your mind at ease."

"My mind is not uneasy," he said, sitting back in his chair. "All the same, this is a little unusual."

"What strikes you as unusual?"

"Well, we have never done this before. Doesn't that make it unusual?"

"Yes," she said, "it does. I will be happy to answer any questions you might have." She reached for the small glass of wine and took a sip. She was surprised to find that it was very smooth.

Bontate picked up the pack of cigarettes lying on the table and lighted one, blowing the smoke out his nostrils as he crossed his legs, grunting a little. He put his hand on his bistro glass, hesitated, then picked it up and sipped the rich red liquid. He held the cigarette deep in the fork of his fingers.

"If he is so afraid of the American police, why doesn't he just tell the Chinese we have to meet somewhere else?"

"Would you do that, Signor Bontate?"

He looked at her. "I would ask the Chinese to have the meeting somewhere else."

"Maybe he did."

"You don't know?"

"No, I don't. Signor Bontate, I should tell you that I do not work for Sergei Krupatin. I agreed to act as his emissary on this one occasion, for these negotiations only, in return for a favor I owe him. After this we are even, and I don't want to have anything more to do with him."

Bontate pulled on his cigarette, looking at her. "It must have been a pretty big favor."

"It was."

He turned his face to the valley, where the clouds and shadows were traveling south over his vineyards and groves, and squinted into the bright light.

"How do you know Sergei Krupatin?"

"I met him when I was a university student in St. Petersburg, years ago. We got to know each other. A few years passed, and I decided I didn't want to know him anymore."

Bontate was still staring out into the light. "That happens."

"He didn't like it, but he had a certain regard for the way I saw things. He still does."

"What is he paying you?"

"Nothing. I told you, I owe him this."

"You don't like this man, but you still think you owe him something? If you don't like him, why do you respect an old debt?"

"For some people, an old debt has little to do with the person it's owed to. It has more to do with something inside the person who owes it."

Bontate turned to look at her, his amber eyes glinting out of his dark face. He picked up his glass and lifted it in salute to her and took a drink. He smoked, continuing to look at her.

"I have a picture of you, did you know that?"

"No."

He shook his head. "Krupatin. Shrewd bastard." He sighed. "Did you see those women down there?"

"Yes."

"My wife. Her sister. My mother-in-law. I married three women."

Irina couldn't help herself. "And the little girl?"

Bontate looked sharply at her. "My daughter. A better woman than all three of them put together. Did you see her chicken?"

"Yes."

A slow smile grew on Bontate's face, the first expression besides a scowl since Irina had arrived. He laughed silently, his stomach moving under the plaid shirt.

"The hooli-booli man gave it to her."

"Who?"

"Oh, a street magician in Palermo. He put a black seed behind her ear, and when he brought it out, it was that damned speckled hen. For some reason she thought it came out of her head, and so she says they are sisters. This chicken . . . She has taught this hen to peck out the Father, Son, and Holy Ghost in the same order you cross yourself. You know." He made the sign of the cross. "Damnedest thing I ever saw."

Irina watched this Italian don laugh at his beloved daughter's religious chicken and tried not to think about what she was supposed to do to him, or what he would do to her if he ever discovered Krupatin's traitorous intentions. There was so little distance between one and the other that she could hardly believe what she had gotten herself in the midst of.

As if Carlo Bontate had read her thoughts, the smile on his face faded, and he once again soberly pondered the light on the slopes of the land below his house. He smoked his cigarette. Pigeons fluttered and burbled along the eaves of the loggia, and as if the little girl knew she was in her father's thoughts, she laughed somewhere near the mimosa where her mother and aunt and grandmother were lazing in the lacy shade.

"No," Bontate said, as if interrupting himself in the middle of a conversation, "it's logical that the Chinese wants to meet in Houston. Once the arrangements have been settled, we are going to want to talk to our people. Being the kind of men we are, we are not going to want the others to get ahead of us. The Chinese is impatient. And Krupatin, he has already proved that he can move very fast."

He took one last pull on his cigarette and mashed it out in the tin lid. Letting the smoke roil from his nostrils, he picked up his glass and drank, swallowing a mouthful of wine and smoke. He looked at her quickly.

"What do you think about the Chinese?"

"In what way?"

"In any way you wish."

"I'm not supposed to think about him. It's not part of what I have to do."

"What do you have to do?"

"Deliver messages from one party to the other and keep my mouth shut."

"Oh." Bontate nodded. "Very strict instructions from Sergei."

"Yes."

"Well, as a woman, then. Forget your job. What do you think of the Chinese?"

Irina looked at Bontate. What was he trying to do? Surely with all that was at stake here, he wasn't going to play a macho game with her. But why did she think that he wouldn't? Wei had only played a smoother version of the same thing.

"He's an interesting man."

Bontate laughed softly and turned to her. "Signorina Serova, I do not believe that Sergei Krupatin does anything—*anything*—without first counting the benefit to himself. Is he ignorant of the penchant Signor Wei has for European women? I don't think so. You are a nice marzipan heart for the Chinese. This is good for Krupatin, for negotiations." He paused, shaking his head thoughtfully. Then he resumed. "Now, I can only expect that Sergei has something special in mind for me too. Something to appeal to my special tastes as well. But what can that be?" He raised his eyebrows and dropped his face in mock consternation. "What can that be? The same woman? I don't think so. But what can it be?"

Irina stared at him. Just when she thought Bontate was easing back on his tension, he revealed it once again, in so subtle a way that it caught her by surprise. His suspicion was far from allayed. He was not satisfied. The worm, it seemed, never rested in Carlo Bontate.

"Do you understand my confusion?" he asked. "I think even those clouds out there are guided by a purpose," he said, lifting his chin to the plain below. "My job is to find out if that purpose has anything to do with me. And if it does, then I have to know if it means to harm me or to help me. That is as natural to me as breathing and having sex. I have thought like that since I was ten years old, so you can't expect me to think any other way now. When my good friend Sergei Krupatin sends me a beautiful woman such as yourself and tells me that I should trust her in everything she says and everything she does, what am I to think?"

He paused, tilted his head at her, and shifted his eyebrows in a sympathetic appeal.

"And then—such a surprise—my good friend Signor Wei volunteers to fly you here to see me in his own private jet. Well, this is even something more to think about. What do I imagine from this? I squint my eyes and think to myself, this is something. This is something I need to think about very hard."

Irina looked into Carlo Bontate's face. The bright amber eyes were narrowed slits, glowing at her like a cat's. Nothing but a conspiracy would satisfy this clever, thick-jowled Sicilian. Nothing but a new angle would sound sensible. If Irina wanted to survive this intrigue of Krupatin's, she was going to have to be as inventive as a poet. She was going to have to pull angels out of the sky and send them to this Sicilian with a secret that would compel even the Great Deceiver to believe.

Seventeen

THEY TALKED ON into the late afternoon. From the second-floor loggia of Bontate's villa, they watched the lengthening silhouettes in the olive groves as the gnarled trunks of the trees melted into their own shadows as if in a Surrealist painting, spilling across the hard Sicilian soil in uniform ranks away from the falling sun.

The shade grew deeper on the loggia as they emptied two of the don's unlabeled bottles of wine. They were now nearing the dregs of the third. Irina excused herself to use the bathroom, and one of Bontate's young men emerged from the somber reception room and escorted her down the corridor, where he waited a discreet distance from the doorway. After finishing, she washed her face with cold water. Though Bontate's vines had produced a surprisingly smooth wine, she should not have taken so much of it on an empty stomach. Bontate himself seemed deliberately to be seeking a numbing level of consumption, a considerable task in view of his healthy girth.

Returning to the loggia, she was relieved to see that a meal had been set up on a second table beside the one where they were sitting. The table was laden with grilled meats, a platter of bread, and bowls with a variety of olives. There were serving dishes of baked squash, potatoes roasted with peppers and onions, and platters of cheeses, fresh tomatoes, and sliced fruits. There was also another bottle of wine.

Bontate was finishing a cigarette, which he ground out in the tin jar lid.

"I was hungry," he explained. "Anyway, it's time to eat."

Without ceremony, he handed her a crockery plate with a knife and fork lying on a white linen napkin in the middle of it and took a second plate for himself. Then, still without speaking, he began serving up the food.

They ate as the setting sun turned the white village of Marineo to pinkish gold on the foothills across the valley. Nighthawks came out, darting in the dusk for insects, and down in the *moscato* vineyard a bird with a languorous, quivering trill sang among the rows of vines.

Bontate ate like a laborer, in silence, preoccupied, often gazing out to the darkening valley that fell away from the villa. Irina could only wonder what kind of progress she had made with this man of simple habits and violent reputation.

As dusk passed into evening, dim lights came on along the loggia, and Irina could hear the domestic sounds of women's voices and the opening and closing of doors echoing through the tile hallways and cavernous rooms. Once or twice she heard the small voice of the child, Bontate's daughter, the keeper of the speckled hen, gift of the hooli-booli man.

Bontate ignored all this until the last light in the sky was gone and the voices in the house had receded into the quiet places of privacy that were peculiar to the rhythms of every household. It was a strange, silent meal, a moody repast that had the effect of stealing away the appetite that Irina had brought to the table. She ate mostly vegetables and bread and olives—and drank more wine.

Suddenly Bontate laid down his fork loudly and wiped his mouth with his napkin. He looked at his watch and then at Irina, his amber eyes aglow in the soft light of the loggia.

"Signorina Serova," he said, pushing away his plate and picking up the cigarettes again. He lighted one and exhaled thick blue streamers of smoke through his nostrils, and picked up his bistro glass. He drank the wine as if it were water.

"I still believe it is an odd thing that Sergei Krupatin wants you to do," he said, "but life is full of odd things, and they are not all necessarily bad. That's true."

He smoked.

"And I think I understand what kind of woman you are, doing this thing to repay a debt . . . which is an honorable intention that I respect."

He drank his wine.

"Now, I want you to understand what kind of man *I* am." His stomach lurched with a suppressed belch. "I want you to go into Palermo with me. I want you to see something."

He smoked.

"Have you had enough? I don't want to rush you." His voice was not solicitous.

"No, I'm through," she said, shaking her head and wiping her mouth. At this moment she was grateful that she had drunk enough wine to sedate her nerves. An abrupt invitation to go to Palermo at night with Don Carlo Bontate was not a thing to be desired. But Irina had no choice. She was already deep into her game.

Bontate stood and leaned over the stone parapet of the loggia.

"Nino," he called down into the courtyard, "let's go."

There were shouts below as young men relayed the message to each other. Hurried footsteps crunched across the gravel, and the motors of the two Mercedes started up in preparation for the trip.

"Have you ever been to Palermo?" Bontate asked, motioning for Irina to precede him. "It's not too far—about forty kilometers to the neighborhood where we are going."

When they got to the bottom of the stairs and stepped out into the graveled courtyard, the car doors were open and waiting for them. Young men with serious expressions stood by each of the opened doors, waiting for a word from Bontate.

As Irina got into the back seat of the second car, Bontate stepped to the first and spoke with several of the young men, who nodded and nodded, listening to him. Then he came and got into the back seat with Irina, and the two cars pulled out of the courtyard and started down the dirt road from the villa, passing once again through the vineyards and olive groves. The Villa Bontate slowly receded behind them, its windows glowing yellow in the blue evening.

They sped across the valley, throwing up dust that hung like a dun mist in the still darkness of the *campagna*. They climbed up into Marineo, where they encountered pavement and the big Mercedes roared through the cramped streets. Soon they were on a tortuous, narrow highway that the young drivers maneuvered with relaxed abandon, careening around curves and hurtling into the straightaways. Shortly they reached the main highway and turned north toward Palermo.

"This is an interesting story," Bontate said to Irina as he settled into his corner of the back seat, oblivious to the reckless driving of his youthful chauffeur. "It has to do with a woman named Emilia." Bontate had grown listless, finally showing the effects of the huge volume of wine he had consumed. "Emilia was the wife of a Palermo magistrate, a pompous old rooster who was twice her age and only half as clever. She was—and still is—a beautiful woman with a full and generous body. She was a good wife and, as the old rooster wished, entertained all the right social and political people in their *palazzo* near the Quattro Canti. There was always a lot of talk there. Gossip.

"But Emilia was too spirited for that old man. She had yearnings. Desires. It happened that I got to know her," Bontate said vaguely, looking out the window indifferently, "and we were seeing each other quite often—and secretly—during 1992, when all of Italy exploded in a fit of wailing after the assassinations of Judge Giovanni Falcone and Judge Paolo Borsellino. Palermo was already a boiling pot because of Falcone's self-righteous 'Mafia investigations,' and since the magistrates were often at Emilia's house for social dinners, she was hearing all the talk from the government side of the situation. With the help of her information, I was able to keep my family out of the turmoil altogether and even to make lucrative arrangements with the Colombians and the Turks while some of the other families were preoccupied. Also, because of some things she told me, I was able to blackmail an industrialist in Milan and a banker in Rome. So the relationship was a very good one."

"And why was she doing all of this for you, Signor Bontate?" Irina asked. "Did she love you?"

Bontate shrugged. "Maybe. But probably it was because I was putting a lot of money in a Swiss account for her."

The cars were now flying toward the outskirts of Palermo, the city's lights throwing a pale glow in the distance.

"The old rooster died," Bontate went on, "a stroke of good fortune for Emilia and bad luck for me. She was no longer any good to me. But that was okay. She had made a lot of money *for* me, and she had made a lot of money *from* me, so it had been a good bargain for both of us. Well, she inherited the *palazzo* near the Quattro Canti, but as soon as she got everything straightened out legally, she bought a place in Rome and began spending most of her time there. The truth is, Palermo was always too small for her anyway. Sometimes I would go to see her when I was in Rome, but after a while we lost touch."

Bontate stopped, leaned forward, and tapped the shoulder of the young man sitting beside the driver. He made a drinking gesture, and the man handed a flask over the seat. Bontate unscrewed the lid and took several deep swallows. Irina could smell the liquor, and she wondered how he could handle it on top of the heavy wine.

"A year ago Emilia contacted me," he went on, resting the flask on his thigh. "When I met her in Palermo, where she had come for the weekend, she told me that she had made some acquaintances who might interest me. It turned out that she was seeing an Israeli businessman who wanted to buy a great quantity of heroin. She gave me a lot of information about him, and I had my people check it out. He was ex-Mossad. He was connected with some very big names in Eastern Europe. Sergei had done business with him. And Wei, too. We talked to the Colombians. We did all the right things. This took several months, but in the end he seemed to be someone we could work with. Finally, over a period of five months, we sold this man a total of three tons of heroin, moving it through Europe for him, pushing it through our channels. We got our money. He ordered more."

Bontate took another long drink from the flask, capped it, and tossed it into the front seat with a gesture of disgust.

"Then four days ago we learned he was an American DEA agent." He looked out the window again. "Last night he was killed in Brindisi."

They were entering the outskirts of Palermo. For the last four or five kilometers they had been on the major motorway, but now they turned off and were making their way into the belly of the old city. Palermo was a city of romantic decay. The streets were narrow and cobblestoned and lined with crumbling shops and dilapidated *palazzi*. At night dim lights and darkened doorways led to mazes of courtyards and secluded piazzas. History was a potent force here, where the dense architecture evoked the past and every stone held memories of Saracens and Normans and Spaniards.

Familiar with the serpentine streets, Bontate's young men wheeled their cars swiftly through ancient passageways and pulled into the walled courtyard of an old *palazzo* where a sallow light glowed within the barrel-vaulted portico of the front door. Car doors flew open, and the young men spread out in the courtyard. Bontate sighed hugely and crawled out of the back seat with a stoic groan. A single light burned in one of the tall ground-floor windows.

Irina walked with Bontate into the portico, where one of his men was already waiting by the front door. They stepped inside and entered an enormous and gloomy *sala grande* furnished with elaborate antiques in the formal manner of a bygone era and revived only in the homes of the wealthy in love with the past. To one side of this room, sitting at a small, ornate game table, was a woman as dark as a Gypsy, who looked at them with sultry eyes that bore an expression of philosophical melancholy. She wore an evening dress which bared her lovely shoulders and displayed a generous décolletage that was the perfection of seduction. She held a deck of cards, and beside her elbow was a liquor bottle and a glass.

She stared at them as they crossed the room.

"Who is this, Carlo?" she asked, her voice sad and gently scolding.

"It doesn't matter, 'Ilia," Bontate said. "A friend."

Emilia drank from her glass, her eyes on Bontate. She was drunk, but it was the steady inebriation of a woman used to the condition. Putting the glass on the green baize of the table, she lay down a few cards and looked at them. Irina saw they were Tarot.

The woman studied the cards a moment and then looked up at Bontate.

"I thought, perhaps, one last seduction," she said, turning her heavy eyes on Irina. "But . . ." She tilted her head to one side in resignation and looked at Bontate. "Go ahead, Carlito, sit down."

Bontate sat across the card table from her, his manner respectful and polite, all the coarse country mannerisms he had displayed at his villa subordinated in deference to this compelling woman. They looked at each other in silence.

"What got into you?" he asked. The question carried a tone of regretful disappointment. The only light in the cavernous room came from a lamp near the entry and a rustic wrought-iron floor lamp beside the card table. The deep gold light pooled around the two of them, but the shadows in the upper reaches of the high ceiling loomed above them like brooding clouds.

She looked at him, almost in tears, and her mouth quivered into a smile.

"Passione, mio caro. The same as always. It was so crazy."

"You couldn't find passion somewhere else? It had to be with this man?"

Shrugging her beautiful shoulders hopelessly, she said, "I'm foolish."

Bontate was not finding it easy to talk. "I loved that about you."

"That and my lovely breasts," she reminded him.

He nodded. "And your lovely breasts."

One of the young men stirred slowly through the eddies of shadows at the edges of the room, moving like a trick of the eyes around behind Emilia, who chose to be oblivious to him.

Bontate lifted his pudgy chin at the cards on the game table. "So what have you learned from these?"

Emilia pulled her eyes away from him and looked down.

"Tonight, nothing. They are lying to me."

"How do you know this?"

"They keep coming up with signs of good fortune."

Without taking her eyes off the cards, she reached for her glass and sipped delicately from her drink. Bontate watched her.

Finally he said, "I cannot understand why you did this, Emilia. Surely you had to know it could only come to a bad end. Did you think it would last forever?"

She looked up at him with eyes swimming in glycerin.

"I often think some passionate thing will last forever, Carlo. You know that. That's what the *passione* is all about. Believing in forever." She paused. "It is a kind of wishful magic." She paused again. "Tell me, *mio caro,* all those nights between my thighs . . . at these breasts"—she tried to smile—"didn't you ever think, even once, for a little moment, that it would last forever?"

The silence that followed was painful, and Irina's heart ached as she earnestly wished that Bontate would tell a compassionate lie to this woman, who, even in their shared mercenary passions, clearly had meant something to him.

"There's a difference in believing and wishing, 'Ilia," Bontate said. "And in those days, more often than you would think, I wished that it would last forever."

It was a cruel man's honest distinction, as close as he could come to showing compassion. Emilia seemed to recognize this, and her brave smile faltered to sadness.

Bontate reached across the game table and took both her hands in both of his, a suitor's gesture of endearment as he looked at her fingers, her bare arms, and her generous breasts, which she had so generously given to him to enjoy.

"No regrets?" he asked.

"Oh, Carlito, there are always regrets," she said.

The cord passed over Emilia's head so quickly and gently she never saw it.

"Addio," Bontate said.

She lurched up in her chair, her back arched, her bosoms thrust forward and heaving—the same motions that in another context would have made Carlo Bontate's loins ache. But these were only postures of reflex.

Bontate braced his feet against the floor as he gripped her hands and kept her arms pinned to the green baize surface. The table legs stuttered on the tile floor. As her back arched almost to the breaking point, Emilia's eyes remained fixed on Bontate. But there was no scorn or blame in them, only acceptance and a natural fear of the coming darkness. Involuntarily she began grunting rhythmically as the garrote squeezed a deep and fatal furrow into her neck.

Bontate remained seated, his hands locked on hers, watching her face as her eyes received him, their last earthly image, before they ceased to see forever. With her arms quivering awkwardly, she finally achieved in death what a sybaritic life had denied her, a moment that lasted forever.

Eighteen

Paris

IT WAS NEARLY ELEVEN-THIRTY at night as Wei's Falcon
lifted off in the Sicilian darkness and made a wide turn over
the Marineo valley. Irina had been in the company of Carlo
Bontate for more than eleven hours. Emotionally drained to exhaustion, she kicked off her shoes and sank back into her seat,
resting her head against the rich brandy leather as she watched the
occasional lights fall away through the porthole beside her.
Within moments they were drifting over the dazzling lights of
Palermo and then out over the dark Tyrrhenian Sea. Her mind
was weak from concentration, and only moments seemed to have
passed when the lights of Sardinia crept into view and then
quickly gave way to the black western Mediterranean.

She closed her eyes and waited for the coast of southern France.
It wouldn't be long. She wanted to see more lights, wanted to
watch them drift below her window, occupy her thoughts, dis-
tract her from the web of complicity she was weaving, which
would grow increasingly complicated before she was able to rid
herself of this last of Krupatin's horrors.

She had not had any preconceptions about what she would encounter with Carlo Bontate, so she was not really taken aback by the contrast between him and Wei. There had been only Wei's remark that the two men were vastly different, and that could have meant so many things it was hardly of any help at all.

Nor had she had any illusions about Bontate's ruthlessness. Krupatin's file had prepared her for that. But the strangling of an old girlfriend whose carelessness had jeopardized one of his drug routes was an object lesson she could have done without. She did not have to be told that taking her along to witness the event was a none too subtle cautionary warning.

In practically every way, Don Carlo was more straightforward and less cryptic than Wei. He had little patience or use for veiled language, which made Irina's task more complicated. Wei found vague language useful. It provided options, never closing doors, never committing, never cutting off possibilities. But Irina had had to be straightforward to gain Bontate's trust, something that was very hard to do when the whole essence of her job was deception. It was the sort of thing Krupatin said she did better than anyone, a bit of perverse praise that baffled her, since she invariably suffered an overwhelming lack of confidence whenever she was required to call on these resources.

So she had spoken sincerely to the Sicilian don. She had taken yet another risk and in doing so had played yet another card in a hand that she increasingly feared was allowing her fewer and fewer options. How many cards were left in the deck? All the spent ones lay before her—she could remember in sickening detail how she had played them—and the small stack that remained to draw from was there too. But there was no time to count, no way to calculate what her chances were with the few cards that remained.

When the earthly stars finally glittered into view again, she realized she never had taken her eyes off the porthole. What were these stars? Marseilles? Nice? Monaco? They moved in glacial time past her frame of view. Paris was not that far away. Another drama, another act, another role. It would not be so bad if anything ever lasted from these theatricals, but the whole point of them was termination. She had to step over the corpses to get off the stage, and she always exited alone. There was no one to talk to. The isolation was a torture, as was the absence of continuity.

She had no one to share a memory with, but even worse, few things she wanted to remember.

There was darkness again: the French countryside. The lights had been turned down to a low glow in this luxurious cabin, which she occupied alone. She hardly had moved since she sat down, and her weariness was so all-encompassing it was the sole thing that defined her. Reaching up to her chest, she felt the small, lozenge-shaped locket hanging safely between her breasts beneath her blouse. When she moved her head slightly against the leather seat, she felt moisture beside her face. She hadn't even realized she was crying. Was that possible, to cry without being aware of it? Apparently it was. But it was also a sign that she was fragmenting. Soma and psyche were moving apart. And she felt there was little she could do to withstand it.

She woke when the Falcon made its first steep turn on its approach to Orly. Outside her window Paris lived up to its name as the city of lights, its dazzle scattered across the night in an extravagance seldom appreciated by the earthbound.

The Bentley came to the Falcon, and Irina had to walk only a few steps on the tarmac before she was surrounded by leather once again, speeding into Paris rather than over it. The bodyguard was her chauffeur, as before, but the pretty Asian girl was nowhere in sight.

Arriving at Rue Férou, she found the street shrouded in the silence of the small hours. She was met at the front portico not by Wei but by one of the shoeless Asian maids, who accompanied her through the huge stillness of the silent house, along the marble hallways, past the ember-red and self-absorbed courtesans and up the flight of marble stairs to her room. Nothing stirred in the house but them; no sound could be heard but the sound of their own presence.

When she dismissed the maid at the door, the woman smiled and bobbed her head submissively. "Please," she said softly and opened the door, indicating that Irina should precede her. Following Irina in, the maid closed the door behind them and went straight into the bathroom and started the water in the shower. Returning to the bedroom, she insisted on helping the weary Irina undress. Too tired to protest, Irina closed her eyes and allowed herself to be waited on.

When she was naked, she turned and walked into the bathroom and got into the shower, immediately putting her head under the falling water. She would have liked to stay there for hours, but exhaustion lay upon her like a cape of lead. Opening her eyes to push back her hair, she was startled to see the maid in the bathroom again, also undressing. Through the spattered glass Irina watched the woman slip out of her uniform, fold it neatly, and put it on a marble bench. After taking off her underclothes, she unpinned her hair, which fell, indigo-black, against her olive skin.

Irina did not move as the maid reached for the shower door and stepped in, joining her under the spray. She did nothing as the maid took the scented soap and began lathering her from head to toe. Though it was a delicious relief from the day's unrelenting tension and a wonderful way to shed the dust of Sicily, the shower was nonetheless a utilitarian operation. The maid did everything, as though her hands and fingers were Irina's own, tending to the business of bathing with a thorough, practical intimacy.

Succumbing to an emotional twilight, Irina was only minimally aware of being led back to the bedroom wrapped in a large towel, which disappeared as she lay down on clean white sheets. She felt strings of oil trail across her body, filling her mind with strange scents as the small hands of the Asian began to transport her, muscle by muscle, to another plane of reality. It took only moments for the hands to lose their identity as hands and become a breath wandering over her, and then a current within her, moving through the layered muscles, coursing through the veins and arteries, until Irina arrived at the only place where she could find any peace at all—oblivion.

She woke once during the night, sobbing, fearful and aware of an approaching horror. Then she felt herself embraced, her body pulled next to another's, a realization she grasped with a grateful yearning to be comforted. Pressing her face against the Asian's breasts, she grasped her tiny waist. Small hands caressed her hair and neck, and a small mouth moved softly against her ear, whispering words that were unintelligible to her except for their unmistakable compassion.

Nineteen

Houston

CATE'S DECISION to go ahead with the assignment was met with businesslike sobriety, no congratulations, no pep talk, no expressions of appreciation. It was a job, and all of them were feeling the pressure of being behind the curve. They wanted to move on.

Valentin Stepanov, who had arrived in Houston during the night, was reached at his hotel, and arrangements were made to meet him at another hotel later in the afternoon. Hain got in touch with his contacts at the Bureau's reclusive Engineering Research Facility at Quantico and told them he was ready for their help. He was told they would send down one of their technicians with the devices as soon as possible.

After everyone had a breakfast of coffee and packaged doughnuts warmed up in the microwave, Cate was given Valentin Stepanov's considerably thick file, and she retreated to her room to concentrate on it. Ann Loder had been responsible for putting it together, and she had done a first-rate job. The thing read like a novel. For the next two hours Cate pored over the file, taking notes and making a list of questions. Twice she got up to refill her coffee cup, and each time she looked into the living room and noted that the computers and at least one of the telephones were constantly in use.

She had no trouble concentrating on Stepanov's dossier, and found herself almost calm with a keen anticipation. Actually, all the butterflies had vanished when she had made her decision to go ahead with the assignment. She was, in fact, eager to get on with it.

"The thing to keep in mind about Stepanov," Ann said, sitting at one end of the folding tables and talking over a notepad lying open in front of her, "is that he is always looking out for Stepanov. No matter what happens, that one concern never changes. He's committed to his role as traitor—to save his skin—but he hasn't gotten used to it yet. Since he was eighteen his life's been tied to Krupatin's, but he's only been a traitor for nine months. And most of the effects of that have been long-distance, in Germany. Now he's going to meet Krupatin face to face for the first time since we turned him."

They were all sitting in the living room again, and Cate had Stepanov's file in her lap, along with her questions. Hain was sitting at the far end of the folding tables, his shoulders turned away from them, a telephone pressed to his ear, his head bent, intent on the conversation. Cate had never seen anyone work telephones the way Hain did.

Erika and Leo Ometov were sitting in two swivel armchairs the rental agency had delivered, facing Cate. Everyone was drinking coffee.

"Always in his mind," Ometov interjected, tapping his forehead with his middle finger, "is the question of whether he has been found out."

"How do you think Krupatin would deal with it?"

"Their relationship is such that if that were the case, it is highly likely Krupatin would take care of Stepanov himself." Ometov sipped from his mug. "But that would happen later, on Krupatin's way out of town."

"How does Stepanov feel about having to work with me?" Cate asked.

"He doesn't give a damn," Erika said in her heavily accented

English, "one way or the other. Besides, it doesn't matter whether he likes it or not."

She was the only one who actually had worked with him in an undercover situation. During the German operation, Stepanov had flown into Munich once, on a U.S. military flight, to meet secretly with the BKA. His job was to identify a Krupatin cell leader whose identity was known only to him. The BKA had never been able to get a photograph. Stepanov met the man at a little tavern, where the BKA was to arrest him. Something went wrong, and in the altercation Stepanov killed the man, later claiming he had had to defend himself. Erika was in the tavern at the time and wrote in her report that in her view the killing had not been necessary. She suspected that Stepanov had not wanted the man taken alive.

"Is he going to be able to do this?"

Erika grinned. "This definitely will be the most important acting job of his life. The man is like most of the con men I have known, a natural actor. He is a . . . what, a bullshit-ter. He talks a lot. He is very shrewd. Even though he is talking, he is watching you, watching how you react to what he is saying. Is he going to be good at this? Of course. This is his natural environment, like a beetle in a shit pile." Erika lowered her gaze at Cate. "But that is the question he is asking himself about you right now. Is *she* going to be any good at this? He is going to be very skeptical of you, so be ready for him to, you know, challenge you, to see how you respond."

"Then you think he'll be able to fool Krupatin?"

Erika shrugged. "That's what all of this is about. But if anybody can, he can." Her eyes slid away, and she fanned the pages of her briefing book. "They know each other like old married people. You will be the one out of touch. Things will pass between them that you will never see. If Stepanov doesn't fool Krupatin, you will never know it. And in my mind, that is the most dangerous situation you will face here. You will not be aware of the explosive nature of the chemicals they will be mixing with each other. The slightest little thing . . ." She snapped her fingers.

Cate looked down at her notes and thought a moment. Then she looked up at Ann.

"Do you really think I'm going to be able to get in close enough to be privy to anything significant? We have so little time." She glanced at Ometov. "It just seems like such a long shot. These are big people."

"Yes," Ometov said immediately, nodding vigorously, "you can. Several reasons." He held up a thumb. "One, and most important, you belong to Stepanov. All these guys have women, and when you are at Stepanov's level, no one questions you. It is his responsibility to make sure you are clean. If you are not, there is the usual penalty—he goes to hell."

He raised his index finger. "Two, it is true that Krupatin is obsessive about security and that this obsession is applied with savage discipline to his underlings. But at the top, as far as we can tell, they are guilty of making assumptions. Just like people at the top everywhere, they assume all the basics have already been taken care of by the time they step in to do their part. Krupatin has a number of managers at Stepanov's level, people all over the world who he contacts routinely when he travels. He doesn't deal with the underlings anymore. These are essentially business meetings. There is an assumption of obedience at this level, that all the way down the line everything has been taken care of beforehand. It is an incredible opportunity we have here. The first time ever."

Hain hung up his telephone and turned around in his chair. Sipping from his mug of coffee, he listened.

"Besides," Erika said, "girlfriends who talk have their tongues pulled out and their throats cut. In that order. That is one of the first things impressed on you when you become a girlfriend."

"But if you can keep your mouth shut, it's a good life to be a girlfriend," Ometov said.

"They can't possibly say *everything* in front of these women," Cate protested.

"No, maybe not." Erika shrugged. "But we know from experience they say enough. When they get comfortable with their women, they get loose tongues. You know," she said, not afraid to display her disdain for male frailties, "it is a kind of male swaggering. Big talk. They are peacocks."

"In this profile," Cate said, tapping her notebook with her pencil, "Stepanov comes across as pretty smooth. What makes him sweat? Have you ever seen him strung out?"

Hain shook his head. "He's pretty slick. When we first approached him, after we had the tapes, had him dead on, he squirmed. In fact, he was pretty rattled throughout the negotiations, up to the time he agreed to work with us. After that, after some assurances that we weren't going to use him and then hang him out to dry, he began to level out." He looked down thoughtfully. "As to what makes him sweat? I don't know."

"Krupatin," Erika said. "I really believe that Krupatin is the only thing that scares him. Krupatin is the last great ghost before death."

"Yeah, maybe that's right," Ann said. "He sure as hell didn't flinch at any of the things we asked him to do in Brighton Beach. I mean, as far as operations went. He'd do anything."

"Except give up the American organization," Cate said.

Ann shrugged.

"But he *is* willing to give up Krupatin," Erika emphasized.

"No, he's willing to help us put someone inside," Hain clarified. "There's a lot of difference. He's not really giving up much, if you think about it. He's just providing access, positioning."

"It doesn't really matter," Erika said, "how little or how much he is doing for us. He is under a death sentence all the same. In his eyes, by refusing to give us the organization here, he is only delaying the inevitable end. I sometimes think he is a little fatalistic about that. It's the big gamble for him. It's either prison now—and for the rest of his life—or a roll of the dice with Krupatin. Not much of a choice, really. But he is human, after all. He will gamble with the future. The present is too soon for him. Premature. You know, he clings to the hope that something could happen later to save the day for him. There's always that possibility."

"You don't seem to think much of his odds," Cate replied.

"No, I think he is a dead man," Erika said, shrugging again. "You have to look at the history of stories like this. They never end well—rarely, anyway. Stepanov is a soldier, a lieutenant. We've used that term ourselves. Krupatin is a general. Generals survive wars, not soldiers. Behind all his bluster, Stepanov knows this."

"These two guys coming in from London—you've shown their passport photos to Stepanov?" Cate asked.

"Sure."

"Nothing?"

"No, he doesn't recognize them. Krupatin has told him someone's coming to advance him, but he hasn't told him who it will be."

"Isn't that a little worrisome? If Stepanov's been around so long, you'd think he'd know these two guys coming to this important meeting."

"Yeah," Hain agreed, nodding, "that's worrisome. It's worrisome to all of us, but it's got to really bug Stepanov. It *is* unusual that he doesn't recognize them. No doubt about it."

There was an awkward pause after this remark.

"Okay," Cate said, "all these people are coming to Houston. Where are they staying?"

"We don't know," Ann said. "The way it works is that at prescribed times Stepanov calls his answering machine in New York. There's a message there, too brief to trace, telling him what to do next. That's been the routine. We have no way of knowing if these two guys know where they're going or not."

"What about backup?" This was the question Hain had avoided answering the evening before. Erika looked at Ann Loder, but it was Hain who responded. The buck for this operation stopped on his desk. He leveled his eyes at Cate.

"There is no backup," he said.

No one spoke up to fill the silence. It was clear this was a bombshell they had been carefully waiting to reveal to her, and with those four words it became instantly clear for the first time how well they had played her. The hard part, the deal-breaker, had not been revealed until they had given themselves the opportunity to employ every available inducement, to present every enticement to make her want this assignment in spite of this crucial difficulty. These people knew quite well what personality types volunteered for undercover assignments. And they also knew that given the right agent, the right timing, and the right circumstance, the greatest obstacle could also become the greatest seduction.

"Go on," Cate said. She felt as if she had just taken the first step into the damp, slippery slope of a labyrinth. She could feel all of them looking at her, but her attention was fixed on Hain.

"A number of reasons for this," he said. "First of all, we don't see this as a potentially volatile situation you're stepping into. I mean, you're not going to be buying or selling drugs or guns or laundered money. The opportunity for violence is not built into it—it's not an integral part of the mix."

Cate didn't quite see it that way, but that wasn't a surprise. It was like the issue of unequal pay for doing the same work, like arguing about the color red with a person who saw only gradations of gray.

"Second, if you're able to get inside, we don't want to run the risk of discovery. It'll be a rare thing to do and we don't want to risk blowing it with a conventional backup structure that could interfere with your mobility. If you constantly have to try to stay in touch with a backup, there might be things you wouldn't want to do, places you wouldn't want to go because it would weaken or break your link with your backup. Trying to avoid these conditions could attract attention and suspicion. If there's no backup, you're entirely independent."

And vulnerable, Cate thought.

"Third, the Russians' countersurveillance is damned significant—they have a lot of cold war expertise and the finances to make it work. If Krupatin chose to bring all this into play—we don't know if he will, but if he chose to do so—we'd have to spend a mint to put together a backup system that they wouldn't pick up. A lot of agents, a lot of technology."

Hain nodded at her arms. "The implants will eliminate the possibility of your wire being discovered, and they will eliminate the constant threat that goes with discovery. Essentially, you're our fly on the wall, Cate, and flies don't get backup."

Cate looked at the notepad in her lap. She rolled the pencil in her fingers, feeling the long ridges thrumming against her flesh.

"Strey knew about this from the beginning?" she asked.

"Yeah, he did. In detail."

That was interesting, she thought. Very interesting.

"What about Stepanov? Does he know about the implants?"

Hain shook his head. "Absolutely not."

Twenty

THERE WAS NO USE in having a lengthy discussion about the absence of a backup. That was the job assignment. She didn't appreciate that they had handled it the way they had, but she understood why they felt it was necessary to do so. The operation was the important thing here, not her feelings. If she were the sort of person to take such things personally, she wouldn't be doing undercover work. They had, in fact, judged her correctly. This was clearly an important operation. The players were about as big as they got, and it was being run by an elite group of agents, domestic and foreign. She definitely wanted to be a part of it. The down side would have to be a hell of a lot steeper than it was now to cause her to walk away from it.

And it mattered significantly that Strey had been fully informed about the details and still had recommended her. That was immensely gratifying and did wonders for her confidence. If anything, the thoughts that ran through her mind in the few moments following Hain's revelation only solidified her conviction to stay with the operation. She had been carefully chosen for a one-of-a-kind job. She wasn't about to let it get away from her.

They arranged to meet Valentin Stepanov in one of the business hotels on the Katy Freeway, a twenty-mile stretch of traffic and commerce, soaring cloverleafs, corporate centers and commercial parks, glass and steel crowding right up against the hurling transportation of product and persons in a ceaseless bidirectional stream of mercantilism reaching west from downtown into the flat coastal plains on the way to San Antonio. Stepanov was waiting for them. He stood up anxiously as they filed into the room: Ometov, Erika, Ann, and Cate. His physique was not unlike Curtis Hain's, large-boned, stocky, but he was a decade or more younger. Cate was surprised that he was good-looking, with rough, unrefined features, dark brown hair graying at the temples, his hairline low on his forehead. He wore a good suit, white shirt, and tie and was clean-shaven. His dress was completely Western, and nothing in his appearance would have led her to believe he was anything but a fifth-generation American.

Smiling easily, he shook hands with Ometov. It was clear that they had worked together before and that Stepanov was pleased to see him. They exchanged several phrases in Russian before Stepanov turned to Erika and again exchanged a few phrases, this time in German. He was equally warm with Ann, even a little more familiar, nearly flirtatious. Since she was the one who had turned him, he had known her longer than any of them, and his attitude toward her seemed to contain an honorable respect for the victor. When Ann introduced him to Cate, Stepanov's gaze fluttered all over her, confirming his first impressions from the pictures he had been shown.

"Please, everybody sit down," he said, sweeping out his arms, "but Cate, please, sit here." He indicated the corner at the foot of the bed. He sat down immediately in front of her in an armchair, looked at her a moment, and then turned abruptly to Ometov.

"Leo, I called my machine. I will be staying at a hotel called the Chateau Touraine."

Ann looked at Cate. "Know it?"

"Sure. It's big, expensive. Private grounds. Very exclusive."

"Okay," Ann said, getting up and going to the telephone. "I'm going to let Hain know there's a good chance our boys in the air may be headed there when they get on the ground." She looked at her watch. "Which won't be any too long now."

Stepanov turned back to Cate, instantly ignoring everyone else in the room.

"I'm not going to ask you how you feel about this because you are here, obviously agreeing," he said. His accent was soft; he had done a good job of picking up American pronunciations and jargon. "But I must tell you, for me this is a life-and-death situation, and so I am going to be very strict and tell you that you have to do everything I tell you to do if you and I are going to stay alive." He looked at her. "Do you understand that?"

But he didn't give her time to answer.

"I know American women," he said, nodding with assurance. "Feminists' rights. Independence." He shook his head. "Let me tell you, you have to screw feminists' rights if you want to get out of this. No Russian man would have anything to do with a feminist. You are 'our women.' " He opened his hands in a gesture of finality. "That's it. Okay? If this is impossible for you, decide right now."

There was silence for two or three beats while he and Cate stared at each other.

"I don't have any problem with doing what I have to do to stay alive," Cate said.

"Sometimes I will have to treat you in a way that will insult you if you have feminist views," Stepanov went on, as if he hadn't heard her answer. "You have to put that out of your mind. Do you understand what I am saying? I say this to you right up front because I am guessing this is going to be hard for you. I say this to you because I don't want to die, and if you cannot deal with this, then don't waste my time. The only thing I care about is getting out of this alive."

He stopped and glanced around the room at the others, then turned his attention back to Cate.

"Look, I don't care about you, okay? I'm going to be too fucking scared to want to play with you. But I may have to deal with you in such a way that you will feel like you are taking a lot of shit." He jerked his head at Erika without taking his eyes off Cate. "Ask her."

The room was silent for a moment as Stepanov stared at Cate.

"I understand," Cate said. "And I agree to it. But if you go any further with me than I think you have to, I'm going to eat your balls when this is over."

Dead silence. Stepanov's face was an absolute blank, but only for a second.

"Let us say I have seen you naked in every way you can imagine," he said, his expression unchanged. "What have I seen?"

This question seemed so abrupt and provocative that Cate suddenly realized what was happening. Stepanov was being deliberately offensive to see how far he could go with her. He was making it plain to her that he wasn't going to worry much about her feelings, and he wanted her to know that from the start.

For an instant she imagined herself naked, imagined herself trying to explain the shape of her body to him.

"I have a birthmark on my right hip," she said, "halfway down." She hesitated, but only instantaneously, nothing noticeable, she hoped. "I have a small tattoo of a red flower, a poppy, just above my genital hair . . . right of center."

"Anything else about the tattoo? Somebody's initials?"

"No. Well, a small green leaf below the poppy." She suddenly felt stupid. Hell, she didn't know. It infuriated her to have to tell this man something so intimate, the secret results of a crazy weekend with Tavio before they were married.

"That's it?"

"I can't think of anything else out of the ordinary," she said. "Anything you'd need to know," she added pointedly.

"I want you to shave between your legs," he said.

"What?"

"My women do that. Sergei knows it."

"Oh, for Christ's sake—" Ann began, but Cate stopped her.

"No," she said, her eyes fixed on Stepanov. "I'll shave between my legs."

"Good," he said quickly. "Now, that's all of that."

Still ignoring everyone else there, he continued to study Cate as he thoughtfully took an ashtray from a dresser beside his chair, put the ashtray in his lap, crossed his legs, and lighted a cigarette. He exhaled the smoke, not bothering to turn his head away, his eyes fixed on her.

"I should explain something to you," Stepanov said. "Under normal circumstances this would be impossible to do. If Sergei had wanted to come to New York, no. We could not do this. In

New York I need bodyguards, because . . . well, I have a history there. These people would know you are not my mistress. But on this trip Sergei told me to come alone, leave the bodyguards in New York."

"Come alone?"

"Well, a woman." He shrugged dismissively. "It goes without saying."

"What about him?" Cate asked. "He'll bring bodyguards, won't he?"

"Maybe. I don't know." Stepanov frowned. "When he has high-level, very secret meetings, he will actually travel without bodyguards. A big change from the old days, I can tell you. He doesn't like showing up with an entourage, like the Italians. He thinks of himself as a businessman now. When businessmen come to do business, they don't have all these men hanging around. They only attract attention, opening doors, kowtowing. There's no need to make a show of strength here. There's no danger here. Moscow, St. Petersburg, Berlin, New York, that's different. But here, he wants to slip in, have a few business meetings, slip out. That's the new way. It's not like the movies."

They were all aware of the movies.

"You don't have any idea why he's coming, then," Ann said.

Stepanov turned to her. "Business. That goes without saying."

It seemed that a lot went without saying for Stepanov.

"He didn't tell you what business."

"No."

"Is that unusual?"

"Yes. Well, it's happened before, but it's not usual."

"How do you feel about that? Does that make you uneasy?" Cate asked.

"No, it just tells me that this is probably a high-level, very important meeting."

There was a pause in the conversation as Stepanov mashed out the end of his cigarette in the ashtray. He reached up and put the ashtray back on the dresser. The hotel room was spare, depressing. Outside, commerce raced to and fro on the expressway.

"So how is it going to work?" Cate asked. "What do we do from here?"

"We will have to arrive at the hotel together. You need luggage, clothes. A week of clothes." He looked at Ometov and then Ann.

"I really don't expect this to be a trip in which Sergei is intending to play a lot of games. He did not have me prepare that way. He is sending two people ahead of him, which is normal. If he feels something odd about her"—he jerked his head at Cate—"he might have them go through our room. You have a history for her already?"

"We're working on it," Ann said.

"Okay," Stepanov said, "good. I need to have that as soon as possible." He turned back to Cate. "We don't have time to create a long story about us. I think it should be this way: I have been to Houston a number of times. Sergei is interested in a couple of Russian operations here. Anyway, I think you should be my mistress for these trips. I see you when I come to Houston. There is something good and something not so good about this. Good, he will not expect us to be so familiar with each other. He will not expect you to know the people I know. So there is less of a chance of tripping up on your story. You stay with whatever background they are making for you, and you will be all right."

"And the not so good?" Cate asked.

"Well, not so good is that Sergei is going to be less inclined to discuss business in front of you. But maybe there will be opportunities. I will try to make opportunities. If he is a little concerned, but not too concerned, he will probably speak Russian. I'll just have to tell you what he said later."

"Will you be carrying a gun?" Erika asked.

"Yes." He looked at Cate. "Smith & Wesson forty-five, model 645. Do you know this gun?"

"I've shot it."

"You had better know it well. It will be the closest gun to you if you have to use one."

"When do you think Sergei will arrive?" Ometov asked.

"Tonight, I think."

"These two guys from London are supposed to be in this afternoon," Ann said. "That's not much time for them to do advance work."

"I'm guessing."

"But he doesn't know where you are staying?"

"Of course not. Not where I am staying now."

"How is he going to contact you?"

"I am supposed to check in at Chateau Touraine. There will be a message there for me with the names of the two men who will be my contacts. That's all I know. It would be best if we arrived today. Tonight is all right. Can she be ready tonight?"

"We think so."

"When will I know?"

Ann looked at her watch. "Let's set a time when she can join you."

"Nine o'clock?" Stepanov said.

"At the Four Seasons, downtown?"

"Yes. But in the parking garage. I'll check out and meet you in the parking garage. Level two. Okay?"

"Level two. Four Seasons. Nine o'clock."

Cate sat listening to them discuss her transportation as if she were a piece of luggage. It all seemed to be moving too fast. It seemed there were huge holes in the planning. She had a thousand what-if and what-about questions. Suddenly the timetable was racing, and she was feeling frighteningly unprepared for what was about to happen.

Twenty-one

Rue Ferou, Paris

WHEN IRINA WOKE in the middle of the morning, her limbs were leaden, and the heavy-headed effects of sleep were difficult to shake. Suddenly remembering the Asian woman, she reached across and felt the empty bed. She tried to remember the woman's face. It wasn't difficult. Though the episode was almost like a dream, she could remember details of color and touch and fragrance, and most of all the feeling of being comforted, of not being alone.

As she lay in bed, the bedroom door opened, and through blurry eyes she saw a woman in a maid's uniform enter cautiously, carrying a silver coffee service. She held her breath expectantly as the maid moved out of the shadows into the light nearer the bed.

"Madame?" It was the maid of the morning before.

"Yes," she said with disappointment, "I'm awake."

The maid placed the coffee on the small table near the bed and proceeded through the same series of questions as on the previous morning. Did Madame want her to run her bath? No. Did Madame want her to run the shower? No. Did she need any assistance in the bath? No. Did she need . . . No, thank you, she needed nothing. Very well. Monsieur Wei wished her to join him on the terrace in forty-five minutes. If Madame required anything, please ring number six on the telephone.

Irina showered again, washing off the oneiric fragrances, all that remained of a nocturnal experience that had been all too rare in her life. She chose a dress that would be comfortable on the flight back to London and went downstairs to the terrace.

Wei, dressed in a summer suit of off-white silk, stood as she came out onto the terrace. He took her hand and held her chair for her to be seated.

"I apologize for not being available when you arrived last night—or rather, this morning," he said, sitting down and pouring coffee for her from the silver service on the table.

The morning was a precise duplicate of the day before—the rosy late morning sun, the faint sound of Paris muffled by the surrounding woods, and the crows cawing in the tops of the towering chestnuts and pines.

"I wouldn't have expected you to be awake," she said, looking at him as he handed her coffee to her.

"Did you get enough sleep?"

"Yes, thank you." She saw nothing in his face that indicated he knew about her episode with the maid. But then again, perhaps this was not something unique for Wei's guests. He lived in a manner that might seem exotic to most of them. She decided he knew everything about last night. She also decided she didn't care.

Wei sat back in his chair with a fresh cup of coffee for himself and smiled at her.

"So how did you find Signor Carlo Bontate?"

"It was an enlightening visit," she said, buttering a croissant from the tray on the table.

"A long visit."

Irina assumed the pilot had been debriefed before he was allowed to go to sleep in the small hours of the morning.

"A long visit," she said.

"Did you like him?"

"I did," she said. "He is very direct."

Wei laughed. "Yes, he has that in common with Sergei. They are not all that different in many respects."

"Really? What else?" Irina thought it was time Wei himself was quizzed a little.

"Ambitious. Direct." He paused to choose his words carefully. "Aggressive. Not given to . . . finesse. Not for very long, anyway." He looked at her, and his smile faded briefly. "Both men have a utilitarian view of women."

"You object to that?"

"Perhaps I view it differently."

"It?"

"The issue."

Irina nodded and took another bite of the pastry. She was starving. Stress was upsetting her metabolism, and she seemed to be constantly hungry.

"Eleven hours is a long time," Wei said, finally getting to the point of his conversation.

Irina swallowed the bite of croissant and sipped her coffee. Wei was very curious, but she was under no obligation to tell him anything.

"Yes, it was," she said, looking at him.

"You were hardly here eleven hours. Much less did we talk that long."

"And we talked about considerably different things," she said. "I did not discuss art with Bontate."

"What did you discuss?"

"He was less comfortable with me than you were. He had to be . . . reassured."

"And how did you do that?"

She looked at him a moment before answering. She did not want to appear to be readily submitting to his interrogation.

"I answered his questions," she said.

"You told him what he wanted to hear."

"I don't know how you feel about Carlo Bontate," she said. "I mean, how you personally feel about him. But I did not find him to be a man who would be satisfied with that kind of response. He did not strike me as someone who would tolerate being patronized."

"Well, I think you are right on that point, Madame Serova."

"I did not try to deceive him any more than I tried to deceive you, monsieur. But to be candid, you are suspicious men, and I'm not sure how well I succeeded."

"Meaning?"

"I doubt that either of you is entirely comfortable with me. You are more polite about it, but you keep your feelings more in check. But I doubt if you are accepting me without serious concern."

"You seem to want to defy what is apparent. Have I not told you I trust you?"

"Yes."

"Then I don't understand."

"Of course you do. Sergei trusts me too, but I am not so naive as to believe he is not watching my every move, checking with each of you after my departure to see that I have acquitted myself as I was supposed to."

"That is only good management."

"Call it what you will. I am sure that all three of you have talked since I left Marineo last night. I know you have already worked together. You wouldn't be working together again if you didn't trust each other at some level. I am only an element, a temporary element, made necessary by the special logistics of your new venture. I am no more than that. I do not want to be any more than that. I have nothing invested in this and want nothing more than to see it done and over."

Wei had crossed his legs and was regarding her with his favorite wan smile of amusement. He nodded, studying her.

"You are a very direct woman," he said, pushing his cup away from him and folding his napkin carefully on the edge of the table. "Which is good. I would not have expected any less from Sergei."

He looked away momentarily toward the light angling across the lawn, a gesture that caused Irina to hear the crows again, their mindless cawing drifting away from them, away toward the Seine. When he turned back to her, there was no smile of amusement on his fine features. She had no doubt that what he was about to say was going to be business at its most intense. At some point, even the polite Asian had to drop all pretense and get to the essence of what he considered important.

"You know, Olya, that men like us have enormous resources for information. You know, I am sure—you have said as much— that you have been the subject of intense investigation by information brokers. This is necessary. I know you have loyalties to

Sergei Krupatin, which I accept. All three of us surround ourselves with people we trust, people we believe will be loyal to us under the most extreme circumstances.

"This entire . . . operation is my idea and has come about through my careful planning. You are a new element in it and therefore come under considerable scrutiny." His left hand was lying on the table, resting on the napkin he had just folded. At this point he raised and lowered it from his wrist, a gesture of finality. "I trust you. We will go on with this as planned. But you must know that I will not stop watching you. If I suspect you are deceiving me or in any way working against me, I will have you killed. Without warning."

They stared at each other.

"I told Sergei this," he added. "And I told him I was going to tell you. Carlo did not have to be told. He feels the same way I do."

Irina said nothing. Wei did not ask her to respond.

"I know you understand this," he said. "Now, having said that, I want to say something else. Your debt to Krupatin is something I cannot evaluate. I only know what you tell me about it. But I would like to make a bid for your fidelity as well."

He let these last words hang in the air, where they took on a prismatic dimension, a dimension of potential and possibility but also of malevolence, a dimension of finitude as well as infinitude.

Wei's voice grew soft, and he spoke more slowly. "If at any point in these negotiations you should find yourself in possession of information that would be crucial to me, or if you should discover yourself in a position to be helpful to me, you would find me as generous in that instance as you would find me uncompromising in the other. I am not asking you to betray anyone—you must be clear about that. But if *I* am betrayed—if something is about to occur that works to my disadvantage and that I do not expect—I would look upon a warning as an act of loyalty worthy of generous reward. I am not seeking an advantage by making you this proposition. Rather, I am wanting to forestall a *disad*vantage."

By making Irina this offer, Wei had immensely complicated an already sophisticated game. She was gathering secrets from each of them; each of them was binding her to the negotiations with something that none of the others knew about. In a very real—

and dangerous—sense, she was being woven into the fabric of this triad to a degree that wrapped her in a complex pattern of lies. Truth became a single small thread smothered and hidden deep within the warp and woof of a dense cloak of deception.

"Why have you said this to me?" she asked, trying to be as clinically frank as Wei. "I am obligated to take this to Krupatin. Surely you know, and understand, that."

"I know what you've told me," Wei said. "But I have to protect myself. I have to believe that you belong to me in this negotiation as much as you do to Sergei. That has to be the way of it. I would be surprised if Carlo has not done something similar. Don't you see, there is no such thing as your loyalty to only one of us. That simply is not possible. You have to belong equally to all three of us. Sergei knows this. That is why he sent you around. It may be that each of us will bind you to himself in a different way, to be sure. But I can assure you, once you are bound, the only real way to gain a separation is through surgery . . . a necessary loss of blood."

Irina regarded the Asian's smooth face with as much calm as she could summon. He had to know that she was just as audacious as he was; he had to know that she would not flinch, nor would she be bought into a betrayal.

"Monsieur Wei, I appreciate your position, but you must appreciate mine as well. How can you trust me if you know that Krupatin cannot trust me? You are asking me to arbitrate, to decide on my own when you are being taken at a disadvantage. I am not qualified to do that. I wouldn't know how."

"No. I am not asking you to betray Sergei. I am asking you *not* to betray me by your silence if you should become aware of anything kept from me that works to my disadvantage."

They were playing word games now. The syntax had to be massaged to the point where each of them could live with an acceptable ambiguity. That was the apparent game. The darker game, the game of the subtext, was one that made Irina's face and chest burn as though she had a fever. She was the point at which all of the vested interests came together, and all of them wanted *her* to insure that those interests were secure. How in God's name did Sergei Krupatin think she would be able to accomplish what he wanted? The road from here to there was choked with snares. Whatever Krupatin's plans, she thought he had made a mistake in making her a pawn in their negotiations. At first she had thought that he intended this arrangement to give her access to her targets. Now she was not so sure. Now she wondered if Krupatin did not have more targets in mind than just the Sicilian and the Asian.

"I can only tell you this," she said finally. "I will not be a part of any betrayal, yours or his. I don't want to spend the rest of my life afraid of what is waiting for me around the corner. I want to be able to sleep."

Wei studied her in silence, nothing showing in his face except concern.

"I believe you," he said.

Twenty-two

Paris

WEI EXCUSED HIMSELF only moments after this exchange and left Irina sitting alone at the table on the shady terrace, her heart still pounding from his statement that she had been the subject of an intense investigation. Surely Wei and Bontate had access to the same information brokers as Sergei. These sellers of intelligence were more mercenary than arms dealers and would sell to the highest bidder, good or bad or indifferent. They made no judgments. They gathered information; they sold it. If it resulted in thousands of deaths or one, or none, that was nothing to them.

It always had worked to Krupatin's advantage that he came from a closed society. In the world of international crime, the Russians had benefited greatly from the fact that they had no past. In the former Soviet Union, secrecy was a way of life, and the information brokers were confronted with perpetual darkness when they sought to buy information within that great gulag archipelago. But with the disintegration of the Soviet empire, with the collapse of the economy—even if it was a false economy—

came a new rapacity for survival. Now the files of the secret police, the files from the prison camps and transit centers and espio-
nage organizations, the files of the KGB and State Security, were
as valuable in the world marketplace as the FSU's nuclear weapons components, which caused so much concern.

What had Wei really learned about her? How good were his
sources in Russia?

Suspecting she was being watched, she poured another cup of
coffee and sat back to "enjoy" it. It was important that she appear, if not calm, at least not unnerved. Taking another bite of her
croissant, she gazed across the lawn toward the splinters of sunlight slicing through the trees. The pastry almost stuck in her
throat, as her mouth was too dry to help her swallow. She forced
herself to think logically over the sound of her heart pounding in
her ears. If she could believe Wei's threat—and she didn't doubt it
for an instant—she must still have the advantage, since she was
still alive. It was small comfort, since the margin of advantage,
whether it was one or one hundred, was an unknown factor.

"Madame."

Irina flinched. She turned and managed an unperturbed expression. "Yes?"

"Monsieur Wei informs you that he had to leave and would
you please forgive him."

Irina nodded.

"Monsieur informs you that a car will be waiting for you in
half an hour in the portico."

Irina looked at her watch. "Thank you."

She supposed there also would be an airline ticket in the car
and directions as to what to do next. This triumvirate of Satans
worked very quickly and enigmatically. As best as she could tell,
she had passed muster and would be seeing a good deal of Wei
and Bontate. Krupatin would be most pleased.

She quietly finished her coffee and croissant, her mind flying in
a dozen different directions at once. She hadn't felt so unsure of
herself since the first one. And yet she had passed through a world
of hells since then, and she was no longer the same woman. Even
her doubts now had more assurance in them than her former
confidence had contained. The deep well of her doubts had been
filled with the stones of experience and a fatalistic belief that isolation was her only safe refuge.

Suddenly she remembered the time and checked her watch. It was time to go. Putting down her napkin, she got up from the table and left the terrace to go upstairs to pack her small bag. Inside the house she walked alone through the marble hallways and up the marble staircase to more marble halls. She glanced around to see if she might glimpse the maid of the night before, but the woman was nowhere in sight.

When she got to her room, she found her bag already packed and sitting in the middle of the floor. She went into the bathroom to see if they had missed anything, but they hadn't. The suite of rooms was as immaculate as if she had never occupied it. There was just her overnight bag sitting in the center, a symbol of her expulsion from this Asian Eden in the heart of Paris.

No one came to carry her bag, which was unnecessary anyway, and she saw no one in the hallways as she descended to the main entrance hall and headed for the portico. She saw no one as she followed the white light of day that glowed from the entrance. Just as she got to the door a car pulled up in front of the steps, so she never even broke her stride as a doorman appeared and opened the outside door for her. A man got out of the front passenger seat of the car—it was not the Bentley this time but a glistening black Mercedes—took her bag, and opened the back door for her. As she stepped into the back seat, she was startled to find someone already there.

"Well done, Irina," Krupatin said.

She sat down beside him. The car smelled faintly of leather and the French lime cologne he favored.

"What are you doing here?" She tried to act unconcerned, as though his unexpected appearance did not shake her. The Mercedes pulled out of the drive at Rue Férou and glided down the narrow lane toward Rue de Vaugirard.

"I came to get you," he said, adjusting the white cuff of his shirt at the sleeve of his dark suit. He was neat, precise, not a single gray hair out of place. His mustache was perfectly trimmed, his face as smooth as a polished stone.

"I see that. I could have flown to London without your help."

"I'm sure. But we are not going to London."

She looked at him.

"We are on our way to the airport, Charles de Gaulle."

"We?"

He nodded affably.

"I hope you know what you are doing," she said. Her heart was pounding again. They had never once traveled together since she had started working for him. When she was on an assignment, she always traveled alone. He was very deliberately thousands of miles away from what she did.

"I know what I'm doing," he said.

"I suppose it doesn't matter that I have no clothes." It was a stupid thing to say, but it was all she could think of. She did not like what was happening. This departure from the usual had a terrible air of finality about it.

"No," Krupatin said. "Listen, I've talked to both that fat Sicilian and the Chinese. They love you. Wei wants to have sex with you."

Krupatin laughed and shook his head and laughed some more. Irina turned away and stared out the window. Paris. It would be a good place to die. If there was nothing after that, then at least your last thoughts would be thoughts amid the sounds and sights and smells of a beautiful city. In the end, what more could you want than beauty? It was free. Anybody could appreciate it—the wealthy, the poor, the healthy, the dying. Paris would be a good place to die.

"What in the hell did you tell them, anyway?" Krupatin asked with a lewd smile. "What kind of promises did you make? Huh? Irina?" he said, nudging her as she continued to stare out the window. They had turned onto Boulevard St.-Michel and were approaching the Seine. "Hey, tell me, huh?" He was grinning, in a good mood.

"Did Wei tell you he would kill me if he suspected me of deceiving him?" she asked, still looking out the window.

"What? Oh, of course. He says things like that."

"He told me he did a background check on me."

"So?"

"What could he find out?"

"Not very damn much, huh? You would already be dead, wouldn't you? No, Wei is satisfied. Believe me. I swear to God, he was absolutely charmed. That business about the painting—pigments. I knew that would work. Good God. You would have thought he had met a queen."

"You might have told me some of that," she said. "If you are going to create background for me, you'd better let me in on it."

"I didn't have to. That *is* your background."

She turned on him angrily. "What's the matter with you, Sergei? This is no game, damn you. If you want me to do this, then let me do it. You're going to get us both killed if you insist on *dabbling* in this. I can't even believe this is happening. What do you expect me to do?" She glared at him. "How in God's name do you think we can do this?"

Krupatin let this frantic burst hang in the air between them a moment. They looked at each other.

"This one has to be different," he said calmly. "Dramatically different. Just the opposite of the others, in fact. Irina," he said with sarcastic composure, "you are not on your own this time. I am going to be directing you, and you have to do as I say. I know these two men. I know how they think, what they want, and what they will do to get it. I have studied these men, and I know what they are thinking right now. I know what they will be thinking in two days. I know how they are going to react when you meet them again in Houston."

"When will they both be in Houston?"

"Two days."

Her eyes held his unblinkingly. "What happens if you make a mistake?"

He stared at her. "You would be surprised how little thought I give to that possibility."

"Then you are a fool, Sergei."

Silence.

"Five years ago you may have been able to say that with some authority," he said, "but not anymore. I know you too, Irina, just like I know them. I know that inside that beautiful body you carry around on your skeleton is an emotional disaster. I can see it in your eyes. I even felt it in your sex." He shook his head, an expression of bored pity on his face. "You don't have long to go, I can tell you that. So do you think it makes sense that you should be giving me advice? Every time I see you I have to put you back together, and every time it gets harder and harder to do. So I'm relieving you of all the responsibility of planning this time. All you have to do is follow instructions—go here, go there, say this, say that, do this, do that. I have it planned down to every . . . last

. . . breath." He smiled at his double-entendre. "Listen, you do *one* thing exceedingly well. Do it two more times, and then you can go to hell."

She turned away and looked out the window of the car again. The beautiful city was passing by outside her window—the Boulevard de Sébastopol.

"Of course, you always have a choice," he said. "In that respect, this time is no different from the others."

It was like reminding a leper of her disease or a saint of her salvation; the choice was never out of her mind for a moment. She could neither ignore it nor forget it. It was both her bondage and her deliverance; it drove her toward madness and rescued her sanity; it was, in fact, the one thing that defined her.

The beautiful city was passing by outside her window.

She had no idea how much time streamed away, how many people saw her face in the window of the car, how much architecture she saw without comprehending it. The car moved on, and she moved with it, she and smirking Satan, riding to hell together in his black Mercedes.

Twenty-three

Houston

"Our two boys from London arrived while you were out," Hain said as soon as they walked in the door. He was standing at the tables in the living room, the telephone to his ear, holding.

"When?" Ometov was suddenly animated. "Where are they now, right now?"

"They came in a little over an hour ago, spent some time clearing customs, renting a car . . . They're halfway into town from the airport." He cocked his eyes at the telephone cradled at his neck. "This is Quantico." He nodded at the table. "Those are photographs faxed to us from our people at Intercontinental. Good pictures of these guys coming through customs."

Ometov shambled quickly to the tables and sat down, picking up the photographs. Erika was immediately at his side. Together they began poring over the pictures. In the background the radio system the SOGs had set up to enable the off-site to monitor the surveillance team's progress was turned on low, and calm, sporadic voices punctuated the silence with irregular, sometimes monosyllabic communication.

"How'd it go?" Hain asked, looking at Cate.

"Good. Fine, I think," she said, tossing her purse into a chair. She saw Hain glance at Ann, who went straight to the kitchen to get a soft drink.

Ometov studied each individual photograph, passing them to Erika.

"These are extremely clear photographs. A lot of them. This is very good." Even as he spoke he was taking the photographs back and laying them all out on the table side by side. Erika hadn't said a word.

"Leo, what about it?" Hain asked, still holding the telephone.

Ometov shook his head. "I don't know these guys."

Hain frowned.

"Erika?"

"No. I don't know them either."

"Leo, you know all of Krupatin's regulars."

"Yes, yes, yes, I know them," Ometov said a little testily, frowning, peering at the faxes. He shook his head again, then looked at Erika. "You know what I think? I think these men are disguised."

"What?" Hain was still holding the telephone to his ear, but the word "disguised" almost made him forget about it. "What do you mean? Both of them? Disguised—you think they're both disguised?"

Erika raised her eyebrows and picked up a fax in each hand, looking back and forth between them. After a moment of studying them, she slowly began to nod.

"Yes, I see . . . Okay, a very good possibility," she said.

"They're disguised?" Hain was incredulous.

Ometov ignored him and sat down at the table, reaching for his notebook file of photographs of Krupatin's bodyguards and associates. He began flipping through the notebook, and after a moment he settled on two photographs. Cate was now looking at the faxes too. Ann had walked in just as Ometov had spoken.

Frustrated at being on hold to both Quantico and Ometov, Hain almost seemed on the verge of hanging up the telephone when he suddenly got someone on the line. "Yeah, yeah, I'm here," he said. He listened. "Great—no, that's great. Thanks," he said, looking at his watch and tossing down the receiver. He leaned toward Ometov. "They're disguised?"

"Yes." Ometov was nodding. He looked up at Cate, who was standing over his shoulder. "Look at this man. Forget his face. See his build, the way he stands, the way he holds his shoulders, this one a little higher. Even the way he carries his head. Now look at our new arrivals. You see the similarities?" He tapped a photograph from the airport customs line, which had been labeled "Nikolai Yelyutin." "Grigori Izvarin," he said.

Cate was struck by the cosmopolitan clothes of the two men who had checked through customs a little over an hour earlier. They could have been well-heeled businessmen from anywhere in the States. Unlike Ometov, there was nothing Russian about them. The man Ometov was referring to was tall and well built, and the way he held himself conveyed a clear athleticism.

"What the hell kind of disguises?" Hain persisted.

For the next few minutes Ometov went over the details of the appearances of the two men and pointed out what he believed were alterations in their features. In the case of Izvarin's companion, he swore the man was even wearing false nose putty to broaden the bridge of his nose. The discussion bounced back and forth until Hain asked the question everyone was thinking.

"You don't think this guy's Krupatin, do you?"

Ometov pondered the faxes laid out in front of him.

"You know," he said, "he could be."

"That's hard to believe," Ann said. She was looking at the faxes too, all of them, bending over the table.

"The size is right," Ometov said. "The weight. Take into consideration the altered nose, the hair . . ." He shrugged. "Maybe."

"Jesus, don't you know him well enough to be able to tell?" Hain asked impatiently. "These two guys match their passport photographs. What're they gonna do, dress up again to leave the country?"

"Why not?" Ometov asked.

"Hell, a better question is why," Ann said. "I mean, why do this? It's not like they're going to fool us with stage makeup."

"Apparently that's exactly what they're doing," Hain said pointedly.

"We don't know that," Ann said. "Leo's already spotted this Izvarin guy."

"This isn't Krupatin," Erika said, shaking her head with the finality of a personal conviction. "I don't think so. No."

Ometov looked at her. She sat down in her chair and scooted it away from the table.

"Even if the disguises are professional—and we really don't know if this is Izvarin, Leo—but all that aside, Sergei Krupatin would never do this. This is undignified. Sneaking into the United States."

"He's been in here before under false passports," Ann reminded her.

"Certainly," Erika said, "but not *disguised,* for God's sake. There's some dignity in walking through customs with magnificently forged documents, having all the confidence in the world that your brains are better than the brains you are working against. That takes . . ." She grasped her crotch and looked at Ann.

"Balls," Ann said.

"Yes, the balls. But putting on a false nose . . ." She shook her head once, with finality. "No."

"Maybe she's right," Ometov said. "That is good psychology."

"Or maybe that's just the kind of thinking he expects from us," Hain said. "Jesus."

"Well, where are they now, Curt?" Ann asked. "What does surveillance have on them?"

"About ten minutes ago they were on the Northwest Freeway, on their way into town." He nodded at the radio on the table, its monitors a flickering trill of green lights visually mimicking the spoken voices. "Sounds like they're poking along. Probably reading all the highway signs, trying to figure out where the hell they are." He shook his head, looking down, pondering.

"Okay," he said, wheeling around and going to the telephones. "I'm going to have Jernigan get a photographer over to the Chateau. If these guys take off their disguises in the car and check in under new names and IDs, I want to see it on film."

Everyone waited while Hain worked the telephones again. When he was finished, Ann didn't give him time to catch his breath.

"What's the situation with the implants?"

"They've got a guy in the air," Hain said. "He's on a charter flight, so . . ." He checked his watch. "He ought to be arriving at Houston Intercontinental about eight-thirty."

"Shit," Ann said, looking around. "Erika, you'd better get in touch with Stepanov and tell him it'll have to be tomorrow."

"He said he wanted to check in tonight," Erika said tersely. "And if these two men get there ahead of him . . ."

"Then what?" Ann snapped. "Nothing, that's what. They just get there ahead of him. I didn't hear him say anything about who was supposed to be there first, for Christ's sake. I'm not going to rush this implant thing. I want to make sure it's working right, and I want to make sure Cate's comfortable with it. Work out something for tomorrow. And tell him about our new arrivals. See what he has to say about that."

"We could have him look at these faxes," Erika said. "Maybe he could see something."

"Yeah, good idea," Hain said.

"He'll be meeting them sooner or later anyway," Ann said. "There's plenty of time for him to see those if it turns out this isn't developing like we think it will."

Erika turned with a petulant jerk of her shoulder and walked around the table and picked up one of the telephones.

"Cate," Hain said, reaching for a manila envelope, "these came in from Washington a little while ago. It's your legend."

Cate took the envelope and retreated to a chair in a far corner of the room, next to the glass wall that looked out onto the courtyard. The afternoon sun was beating down on the palms and bougainvillea, sharp light and deep shadows. Erika was going through the telephone machinations necessary to reach Stepanov while Ometov continued laboring over the photographs of the two Russians. Hain and Loder had put their heads together in a private conversation.

The envelope contained six pages of single-spaced information and a Texas driver's license in the name of Catherine Miles, the name she had used the two times she had worked undercover for the organized crime section. Her residential address was a duplex in northwest Houston where the other side of the duplex was owned by a special support group member—one of a number of freelancers known as Gs, who provided minimal support for Bureau operations for a fraction of the cost of a full-time agent—

who knew to cover for her if anyone showed up at the door trying to verify Cate's residence. Her legend was an amalgam of the legends she had used before as well. She was an assistant manager in the personnel office of a large architectural firm. Her telephone number would be answered by an agent in the Houston field office who was Hain's liaison in the event he needed local support. If anyone actually went to the company to inquire about her, the real personnel director was a long-time support group member and would field the inquiry.

Everything had been covered. Cate was reading through the legend a second time, double-checking the details, when Ann Loder came over and pulled up a chair.

"You have trouble with any of this?" she asked, nodding at the legend.

"Nope, seems like they took most things into consideration."

"You can change anything you want. We just need to talk about it."

"I don't want to change anything."

"Okay, good. Another matter, we need to come up with a word you can use if you want to bring everything to a halt, if you feel threatened or whatever—if you've simply had enough. A common word, but not too common. You don't want to use it by accident, because it's going to bring everything to a standstill. A phrase, maybe."

"A personal reference," Cate said. "I guess that would be best. Something about how I feel. Uh, what about 'I feel hot,' or 'I'm burning up'? I do that sometimes just before my period starts."

"Whatever."

"Okay, that'll be it."

"Fine, I'll put it in the operations notes, make sure everyone who needs to know is aware of it. Now, what did you think about our man Stepanov?"

"The bastard has a lot of gall," Cate said, laying down the papers in her lap. "It's going to be quite a ride."

"Yeah, I think it will be. It's hard to comprehend the magnitude of what's at stake for him. He's putting a lifetime on the table here."

"What about his wife and son back in Russia? He's just going to walk away from them?"

Ann nodded. "According to him, it's been a bad marriage for a long time anyway. He's got a girlfriend in Brooklyn. Of course, the family in Moscow was supposed to be the sword Krupatin was holding over his head in case he screwed up."

"Even for longtime buddies?"

"Oh, yeah. It's business. Everybody understands these things."

"So what will happen to them?"

"It depends on how this plays out. If Krupatin is really pissed, they'll die. Sergei is big on revenge."

"Then in essence, Stepanov is giving them up."

"We can't be sure of that."

Cate shook her head. "Jesus."

Ann turned her head slightly and glanced in Hain's direction, then turned back to Cate. "Look, about the living arrangements with Stepanov," she said, her voice low. "He knows better than to pull something stupid, but if he tries, you don't have to take anything off him. That's not in the game."

She looked at Cate. It seemed as if her gut wanted her to say something else, but her brains and her training kept her from coming out with it.

"You're not going to tell me this is a war?" Cate asked. "That we're soldiers, and soldiers sometimes have to do things that are ugly?"

"I don't think I have to tell you that," Ann said without irony. "The question you have to ask yourself going into this is just how ugly you're willing to get." She glanced at Erika on the telephone and then back at Cate. "She made some mistakes. Not operational ones, not legal ones. Well, legal—sometimes legal goes out the window in these operations. Sometimes it just stops being a relevant framework for consideration. Anyway, her mistakes were personal, soul-shaking. When you're undercover, those are the real dangers, the lasting ones. The operation will be over sooner or later. They always are. People move on to a new assignment, a new operation. But the stuff that happens inside you is never over. That's where you've got to protect yourself. That's where you have to have a good inner understanding of where the lines are drawn." She paused, her eyes motionless and deep. "Just don't forget who you really are. And don't do anything you won't be able to live with when this thing is over."

"Ann." Hain was leaning forward on his forearms on the table, his head thrust toward the radio monitoring the surveillance team. "Looks like these guys are going to that hotel."

"Chateau Touraine?" She got up and walked to the table, carrying her soft-drink can.

"Yeah," Hain said, touching a dial, fine-tuning the radio. "Yeah, they are. This ought to be interesting."

Twenty-four

CATE SPENT THE REST of the afternoon with Ann, Erika, and Ometov once again taking her through her paces as Catherine Miles. Erika told anecdotes about Stepanov that revealed more about his character and that unintentionally told Cate a little about Erika herself. Neither of them, it seemed, had any shortage of audacity, and Stepanov apparently resorted to bluster to buy time, or any other advantage he might gain, whenever he found himself in a questionable situation. This explained some of his overbearing manner when they had met earlier in the day.

Late in the afternoon the two Russians who had flown in from London checked into a suite in the Chateau Touraine wearing new faces and using new names. Jernigan's photographer was able positively to identify Grigori Izvarin, who now presented himself as Anton Nakhimov. His companion registered as Rudolf Bykov, and his photograph was quickly faxed back to the off-site for identification.

In another surprise move, when Nakhimov and Bykov registered, they also reserved another suite—for one—in Nakhimov's name. Since Stepanov already had made his own reservations, this was important information.

Everyone realized that the Touraine was going to be a gathering place of considerable significance. Jernigan's team quickly swung into action to establish a serious communication station in the hotel. They made contact with the hotel management and arranged for someone to be on registration desk duty at all times. They tapped the telephone lines to the suites occupied by the Russians and set up a system whereby the bedroom in Stepanov's suite would be swept regularly for bugs and thus would remain a "safe room" if Cate and Stepanov needed to talk. They would have to watch what they said in the other rooms. The team also immediately surveyed the hotel's two dining rooms, locating positions where directional microphones could be installed. The installations were designed to be adjustable so the agents could target whichever table the Russians occupied after entering the dining room. It would take an agent only a few minutes to redirect the microphones to wherever they were needed. One microphone was placed in an air conditioning vent that was accessible through one of the kitchen storerooms; the other was installed on a rolling dessert cart, hidden behind a white lace screen attached to a decorative sconce on top.

The tech team stopped short of installing wall mikes in the Russians' rooms. There was some concern from the look of Nahkimov's and Bykov's luggage that they might have arrived with sophisticated debugging equipment. The SOGs were trying to come up with a plan to check this out so they would know what kind of devices to use.

"So the extra room's for Krupatin?" Cate said to no one in particular. Again they were gathered around the table in the dining room, eating takeout dinners. They all had agreed on seafood. Even Ometov, who had proved to have an insatiable appetite for hamburgers, had been persuaded to forgo them this one time. The radio had fallen silent, since surveillance activity was at a standstill at the hotel. The Russians had not left their room since checking in and had ordered room service for dinner.

"Anybody," Ann said, eating little pieces of scallop with a toothpick. "Could be anybody."

"I wouldn't rule out Krupatin," Hain mused. He was peeling

boiled shrimp, dumping the shells into one of the takeout sacks and piling the pink striped shrimp on a paper plate. A bottle of Heineken was sweating beside his plate.

Erika stabbed a fried oyster with her fork. "Shit, I wouldn't rule out any*thing* or any*body*."

"When do the techs think they can have something in the room?" Ann asked.

Hain shook his head. "They're still talking it over, still a little spooked about the equipment."

"This Bykov bothers me," Ometov said, looking at the fax of the photograph taken when Bykov registered. "I don't know what a completely unknown player is doing in this mixture of old hands. This doesn't seem right." As he ate, he studied the picture with the kind of concentration usually seen in jigsaw puzzle enthusiasts, as if he were just on the brink of assembling all of the blue sections of the enigma.

"Nothing from London about Krupatin leaving there?" Cate asked.

"Nothing."

"You know what's going to happen, don't you?" Ann said. "He's just going to show up at the hotel. Just like he shows up in Brighton Beach, out of nowhere."

"That's fine with me," Hain said.

"Yeah." Erika nodded. "I just want the bastard to show up."

The doorbell rang.

"That's Jernigan and John Parmley from the tech squad," Ann said, wiping her mouth and looking at her watch as she stood up. "You've worked with Parmley before, right?" she said to Cate.

Cate nodded.

"They picked up the guy from Quantico at Intercontinental about an hour ago," Ann said, heading for the door.

Cate tried to ignore a momentary stirring in her stomach and continue eating her fried shrimp. She had to do a better job of keeping herself on an even keel, not allowing her adrenal glands to squirt all over her every time something came at her unexpectedly.

The agent who came into the dining room with Ann and the other two men was in his mid-forties—sparse hair, bespectacled, and thin as linguini. He wore a wash-and-wear plaid shirt with short sleeves. His suit coat was draped over his right arm, and in his left hand he was carrying a thick aluminum suitcase.

"Alan Geller," Ann said.

Geller sat down with a Diet Coke while they finished their dinner. Since this operation was a special, he said, the Bureau had flown him down in a charter that was on a twenty-four-hour lease. As soon as he took care of things here he was going right back to the airport and right back to Virginia. No thanks, no shrimp, he said. He had eaten one of those wonderful airport hot dogs in the car on the way into town. He took off his glasses and wiped his face with a paper towel. "So what's the deal here?" he asked. "Is there a heat wave in Houston, or what?"

"They told you, I guess," Geller said a few minutes later, opening the suitcase on the tables in the living room, "that it's basically like Norplant. You ever use Norplant?"

"No," Cate said, glancing at Ann, "but I know how it works." She and Geller were sitting facing each other at the end of the tables.

"Okay, fine."

The suitcase had a foam filler with more than a dozen cut-out spaces filled with rather specific-looking equipment. Geller took out a pair of surgical gloves and began pulling them on.

"Believe it or not, I had to take a three-day kind of nursing course for this," he said with an expression of pained impatience at the bureaucratic overkill. "Just for the hygienic aspect of this procedure. I need your sleeves up. On both arms."

He took out a bottle of alcohol and some cotton swabs. "I'm going to sterilize the areas of implant. Same identical procedure as Norplant, even the same device used for it. These implants are identical in size to Norplant."

"Why don't you explain to me how it works?" Cate said.

"Sure." Geller continued to work, getting all the components ready. "I'll explain to you the *principle* of how it works, because the actual how is highly technical and of course classified, blah, blah, blah. But I went into it in detail with them on the way in from the airport," he admitted, jacking his head in the direction of Jernigan and Parmley.

"This is the burst transmitter," he said as he began the procedure of inserting the implant in her right arm. "It's a pretty straightforward device, same as always, but improved in many ways for clearer signal and durability of transmission. It's not nearly as sensitive to disruption as the older devices."

Everyone watched as Geller deftly placed a single rod into the inside of Cate's upper arm.

"Under any conceivable circumstances this thing's going to transmit a receivable signal."

"What are the inconceivable circumstances?" Cate asked.

Geller grinned. "Okay. You're in a lead-lined room. You're in a radiation-bombarded room. You're under more than seventy feet of water. Stuff like that. I wouldn't worry about it. I'm going to insert five mike rods here," he continued as he turned to Cate's left arm. "The biggest drawback with wiring somebody with the conventional method, of course, is the size of the device—getting caught with the thing, discovery. Naturally, with chip technology we've overcome that.

"Let's see," he said, pausing between insertions. "Let's just say this is like one of the old integrated systems. Each one of these rods is battery-driven, and the power the battery produces is much stronger than the body's ability to absorb it. But the batteries wear out quicker because this superior ability draws more energy. So what we have here is five rotating battery systems. When one goes out, another kicks in. Like time-release medication."

"How long do we have in these five rods?" Hain asked quickly.

"Ten days," Geller said, pushing the last rod through the syringelike applicator into Cate's arm. "Two days each. Easy to remember. That's it," he said, looking at Cate.

"What about detection?" Cate asked. "What about debugging equipment?"

Geller was already shaking his head. "Got you covered. These things are undetectable with such equipment. They're not going to find these things by any conventional method."

Cate rubbed the slightly raised ribs that splayed out in a rising-sun pattern on the soft flesh of the inside of her upper arm. She felt the strange but familiar stirrings of excitement—a mixture of fervor and foreboding—that eventually rose to the surface at the beginning of every undercover operation she had worked. Every undercover agent experienced something similar. It was unlike any other emotional experience, at once elemental and sophisticated. It was as simple as the challenge of survival and as complex as aberrant sexuality. It was an open-ended invitation to risk the unknown.

"One more thing," Geller said, taking a small package from his suitcase. He handed it to Cate. "These are a dozen adhesive plastic strips that look exactly like Band-Aids. And they work exactly like Band-Aids. But the absorbent pad is actually a thin sheet of lead." He turned away from her and began putting his utensils back into the suitcase.

Cate looked at him. "What do I do with them?"

Geller didn't look up. "Just put one over the rods if you want to prevent transmission," he said.

Privacy. Discretion. A way to close the bedroom door. Cate looked at Hain. "So who's going to be listening, then?"

"Me, Leo, Ann, and Erika here at the off-site," Hain said. "It's going to the tech room in your regional office. Ennis will determine who can listen there. And Jernigan and Parmley. Remember, even if you put the patch over the wires, do *not* cover the burst transmitter. We've got to know where you are at all times, even if we can't hear you."

"But Jernigan isn't going to be here," Cate said.

"No, Neil's running surveillance on the Russians. They'll be expecting that, so even if Neil's people are spotted it won't be a big deal. But we're not tailing Stepanov. Just the two guys who flew in tonight. When you and Valentin leave the hotel, you will not be tailed either. If Krupatin has countersurveillance in place, they won't see anything. Nothing."

Cate nodded. Hain decided to address what she might be wondering.

"If you need help," he said, "it'll probably come immediately from Neil's people. They'll be on the street, and Neil's going to keep someone in the right part of the city, though they won't know where you are until he tells them. But they'll know there's an undercover agent out there and that they're on standby for an emergency. It'll be quick."

They spent the next hour making sure that Jernigan and Parmley knew how to operate the unusual receiver for Cate's transmissions. The receiver—which turned out to be something like an electrical relay that enabled the transmission to be picked up by a designated number of conventional receivers—was under the foam pad in Geller's briefcase. It was a strange-looking computer, having a panel of digital readouts, a peculiar keyboard, and a high-resolution screen.

"Now," Geller said with undisguised relish, "this little device is the *future*. We've put a Houston street map chip in here. It'll tell us *exactly* where the burst transmitter is located." He punched a key. "The street address." Another key. "Tells us if the address is residential—house, condo, apartment—or if it's commercial—retail, strip mall, high-rise, hotel, shopping mall, convenience store, parking." Another key. "Gives us the location of the nearest fire department, EMS station, police, hospital, all that. Shows greenbelts, vacant lots, bridges, alleys, on and on and on." He paused and looked around.

"Only thing it can't do—but we're working on it—is read elevations." He looked at Cate. "If you're in a seventy-story office building or a two-story duplex, this can't tell them how high up you are. It cannot show vertical locations, so they're never going to know what floor you're on. If that's going to be important, you've got to provide a verbal cue. Just keep it in mind."

They traveled around the city in cars as they tested the devices. Cate transmitted while walking in a crowd at a shopping mall, while sitting next to the noisy kitchen in a diner, and even while watching computer play in a video arcade. Hain, almost giddy with satisfaction, pronounced the equipment superior to anything he had ever seen.

After an additional half-hour of questions by Cate and Hain, Alan Geller left his direct-line number with them and flew back to Virginia.

Cate covered the rods with a patch and went outside into the courtyard to think. It was late, but she had to have some down time before she could ever hope to close her eyes and sleep.

Twenty-five

THE NIGHT HOURS finally swallowed enough of the day's heat to make the evening merely unpleasant rather than miserable. The temperature and humidity were just below the point where people would perspire when simply sitting still.

Cate sat in one of the wrought-iron chairs looking toward the house, where the others were still talking. When she left, the conversation turned to speculation about what Sergei Krupatin would do next and how he would do it. As she watched them leaning toward one another over the tables, nursing cups of coffee, Leo Ometov's shambling figure stood up in the dim light of the living room. He stretched to his full height for a moment to relieve his weary back and then stepped to the courtyard door and pushed it open. He came outside, closing the door behind him. After pausing for a moment to let his eyes adjust to the darkness, he reached into his coat pocket and took out a pack of cigarettes. As he dug into the pack, he started toward Cate.

"If you would prefer to think alone . . ." He gestured tentatively with a cigarette as he approached her.

"No, of course not," she replied, though she really didn't know how she felt about it one way or the other. "I wasn't aware that you smoked," she lied, remembering seeing him smoke the night before when she had looked out her window and seen him here in the courtyard with Hain and Ann Loder.

"Not inside," he said with one of his most genuine smiles. "I am in self-imposed exile."

He lighted the cigarette, sat down in a wrought-iron chair near her, and turned obliquely to the house.

"How are you feeling?" he asked, blowing smoke into the still, heavy air.

"Eager," she said. "Which, I confess, rather surprises me."

Ometov lifted his head in a half-nod. "I understand that. This kind of work is exhilarating. It is challenging to match your intelligence and cunning against a formidable adversary. But losing has such . . . threatening consequences." He smoked for a moment. "The old axiom is true, after all, that some people are never more alive than when they are most at risk of dying."

"Jesus," she said.

Ometov laughed softly. She could see his face in the reflected light from the house, and for some reason it was comforting to see him laugh.

"You didn't have much to contribute to the brainstorming going on in there," she said. "I'm guessing you didn't want to say what you were thinking."

"Oh? No, nothing so mysterious. I don't really know what I think Sergei is going to do. I'll simply have to wait—wait until Sergei gives me some more information."

"And you're sure he'll do that?"

"Oh, most definitely. It is unavoidable."

"Unavoidable."

"Of course. If you live, you produce information about yourself. Information is a byproduct of living."

"Like making a choice."

"Pardon?"

"It's impossible not to make choices. Even refusing to make them is choosing. Life is making choices. Little ones. Momentous ones."

"Precisely like that, yes." He smoked. "And Sergei will make a

choice soon, and then he will produce some information for me."
He laughed softly again.

"May I ask you a personal question?"

"Please do." He smiled. "I may not answer it, but you may certainly ask."

"I sense that for you, pursuing Krupatin is more than a job." She paused. "That it's personal."

"Ahh." Ometov raised his head and tilted it back slightly toward the sky. "Okay, an observation."

Cate waited, but Ometov did not say anything else. He simply stared across the courtyard, his cigarette lifted beside his face as his elbow rested on the arm of the chair. She sensed that he was not pondering whether to address her question but rather how to address it.

"Of course it is personal," he said. "I told you of my friends and their daughter. That can cut very close to the soul, you know."

"I was thinking . . . more personal than that, perhaps."

"Really?" He looked at her. There was no smile this time as he regarded her across the distance of a few feet in the anemic light. "That's good. You are very observant, Catherine." He looked at her. "Cate. Diminutive. Russians are very enthusiastic users of the diminutive as well, like Americans. But it has lost its intent, I think, over the years, the diminutive. It was originally meant, you know, to be an endearment, but over time . . . Well, to me it often now seems more utilitarian than endearing. As though we do not have the time to pronounce an entire name. Which is too bad. The entire name is often very beautiful."

Cate said nothing. Ometov's aside was simply a setup for his response. She had come to appreciate his reflective manner of speaking. He was sitting with his legs crossed, and once he seemed as if he were going to swing his leg and then caught himself.

"I told you the story about Sergei's smuggling exploits off the coast of the Crimea, when his father was killed."

Cate nodded.

"I was a young lieutenant then, in the Soviet army. I was the one who recruited the cousin who betrayed them. I say recruited . . . I bribed him, offered him certain concessions. It was my patrol that cornered Sergei and his father and brothers late that day. Only by a minute chance misfortune did we miss getting them all. A mistake in signals, a misbegotten chain of events. Bad luck. All the things that are too familiar to military men everywhere, the little things that cause the great disasters.

"I was a new officer, with responsibility for this patrol for only four months, but my first sergeant had been on the Black Sea coast for six years. He was intimate with the Krupatins, in the way that enemies are intimate. Sometimes they can be closer than lovers." He paused to smoke and think about this last remark.

"Anyway, there was a lengthy exchange of gunfire before we captured Krupatin's father and brother. We lost two men. One of these men just happened to be a good friend of my first sergeant. The sergeant was livid that the trap had not succeeded in catching all of them. And he was overwrought about the deaths. He and the Krupatins had harassed each other up and down the coast for six years, and for this sergeant, this was the last straw. He knew Sergei and his brothers were hiding in the cliffs, and he decided to torture our captives to draw them out.

"When he proposed this to me, I refused him. And then something happened that all young lieutenants fear when they are put in charge of an older, more experienced group of men. Without anyone's saying so, they refused to obey my order. They were going to do what they wanted to do regardless of my directive. All the men stood there beside the sea and glared at me, daring me to try to enforce my command of refusal. Two of their own were lying there dead on the beach beside us, caked with sand and blood. If I tried to stop them, I would lose my life. I knew it. They knew it."

"Then you didn't even try to stop them."

He shook his head. "No. Of course, that is what I should have done. I mean, it would have been the honorable thing, from a military discipline standpoint. But when it came right down to that moment of my death, I was a coward. It was either my life or the lives of those two men kneeling on the sand." He stopped, then shook his head slowly.

"No, actually that wasn't even the choice. My men were going to kill those two smugglers regardless of whether I died or not. So as the sun fell slowly into the cold waters of the Black Sea, I watched them do it. I watched them drag the father and son up and down the beach between a gauntlet, each soldier jabbing his bayonet into them as they passed by, like jackals snapping at a wounded, dying prey. The sergeant was screaming up at the rocks, ranting, foaming at the mouth, shrieking with each jab of the bayonets, taunting Sergei, who was hiding in the cliffs as his father and brother were sliced and jabbed to shreds, until they were no longer recognizable as human beings, just meat, some rags of flesh dragged behind the truck and caked in bloody sand. It was the longest dusk of my life."

Ometov dropped the end of his cigarette on the tiles of the courtyard and put his foot on it. He didn't grind out the burning cigarette, just put his foot on it. He sighed heavily, as though the story had drained him of oxygen.

"After that," he said, pulling another cigarette out of the pack, "I was no longer any good as a lieutenant. Of course we all lied about what happened. That coast patrol was a kind of outpost. Whatever we said was what went into the reports. No one had any sympathy with the smugglers anyway. They were considered vermin. The headquarters in Moscow didn't ask many questions about how we conducted ourselves in that remote region." He lighted the other cigarette.

"I put in for an immediate transfer, naturally. But I was there for another miserable year before I was sent back to civilization in Moscow, my obligatory tour in the outposts completed." He blew smoke into the dark and watched it lift up into the palms.

"These palms are wonderful," he said. "They remind me of Istanbul. Istanbul when I was a young man."

"Was that all there was to the incident?"

He shook his head. "No. The man I recruited, remember, was Sergei's cousin. I told you what happened to him. And the outraged sergeant—he had been in the outposts far too long. Eventually he made it back to civilization too. He was a career enlisted man, a brutal man with a brute's intellect. Sergei knew him well, since they had been adversaries so long. So when Krupatin eventually made it to Moscow too, after he became important in the criminal world there, he looked up his old friend the sergeant. It was only dumb accident that I ever knew what happened to him.

"After the army I joined the Moscow militia—our police. Because I was educated, I rose quickly. I became a director in intelligence. It was there that I came across the sergeant's name after he died. He was murdered, either by Krupatin or at Krupatin's directive. I suspect Sergei was there. The sergeant's body was found in a section of Moscow that 'belonged' to Sergei, in a warehouse. He was hanging from a winch on meathooks. They had lowered him upright into a vat of some kind of acid, I don't remember what kind. He was alive when they did it. They submerged him up to just above his navel in the vat. He had thrashed about there while it melted his flesh away from his bones. It took a while—they made sure of that. Then, when he was mostly a skeleton below the waist, they raised him up, and the rest of his viscera just fell out the bottom of his rib cage."

Ometov smoked.

Cate could not avoid asking the obvious question. She doubted whether Ometov expected her to.

"Has he tried to kill you too?"

"He killed three other men who were there on the beach that late afternoon. Again, they were enemies a long time before I came to the outpost." He sighed. "As for me, I don't know. He has never made any attempt to kill me." He shrugged. "He probably never even knew who I was. Or maybe he saw everything that happened. Maybe he knew I was against it, tried to stop it, but didn't try hard enough. He couldn't blame me for that. After all, he did the same thing. I wouldn't give up my life to save his father and brother, and he wouldn't either. He hid in the rocks and watched. And I watched from the sand."

Twenty-six

Mexico

WHEN THEY BOARDED Krupatin's Gulfstream V, which was hangared at the Aéroport Charles de Gaulle, Irina went straight to her cabin, took a couple of sleeping pills, removed her clothes, and went to bed. For more than three quarters of the trip she was lost in a fitful oblivion, a dark angel in flight from the demons within and the Satan traveling with her.

Nine hours later she surfaced from a restless unconsciousness and lay drowsily among the sheets, passing in and out of the present until the leaden edges of the pills' effects wore off, leaving her more numb than rested. After a while she got out of bed and went into the bathroom. As she sat on the toilet to urinate, she bent forward and held her head in her hands, trying to steady the floating sensation in her brain. After finishing, she straightened up and let her arms hang limp at her side as she leaned her head back against the bulkhead, her eyes closed. She didn't know why she hadn't taken the whole bottle of tablets so that she could have slipped mercifully from sleep into eternity.

Opening her eyes, she summoned her strength, stood up, and

went about the business of washing and cleaning up. When she was finished, she pulled on a silk robe she found hanging on the back of the bathroom door and stepped into the main cabin, where Krupatin was smoking a cigarette and watching a soccer game on television.

He glanced at her with lingering disinterest as she groggily collapsed into one of the plush leather seats and pulled her feet up under her. She stared out the porthole beside her. After a moment Krupatin flipped off the television and pressed a button that summoned a steward. He ordered a fresh pot of hot tea and stared at Irina. His left arm rested on a desk built into the cabin wall, papers scattered over its surface.

"You look like hell," he said, puffing on the cigarette. He was still wearing his suit trousers, and his deep blue shirt with its white collar was wrinkled and undone at the sleeves and neck.

Irina ran her fingers through her hair and continued looking out the window. Blue sky and clouds down near the sea.

"Where are we?"

"Approaching the Caicos Islands. Cuba dead ahead."

"How much longer?"

"An hour, an hour and a half." She felt him studying her. "You'd better pull yourself together," he said. "If that's possible anymore."

She ignored him. The sky below was Caribbean blue, the clouds Viennese white.

He turned and picked up a passport from his desk and tossed it at her. She flinched when it hit her lap. The little green booklet slid off the silk covering her thighs and fell on the floor. Unfolding her legs, she reached down and picked it up. When she opened it, she saw her photograph and the name Helen C. Kurner, Mexico City, DF.

"Kurner?"

"A lot of Germans live in Mexico City," Krupatin explained.

"And you are Mr. Kurner?" she asked wearily.

"Until we cross the border."

"Then what?"

"Then I'll let you know."

She looked away, out the porthole again. The huge Gulfstream slipped through the sky like a world unto itself, a small, beautiful hell, luxurious and barren.

"You don't have to do anything," he said. "Just look pretty and be pleasant. You don't have to think at all until we cross the border."

"I don't have any clothes," she said. "I had only the one other dress in Paris."

"You can get some more in Houston."

It didn't really matter; she only wanted to complain. By now she was used to buying clothes and then suddenly walking away from them. She had left complete wardrobes all over the European continent.

The steward arrived with the tea and served Krupatin first—English china cups and saucers, silver sugar tongs, fresh cream, and chocolate-covered strawberries on two little silver trays. Krupatin popped a strawberry into his mouth and began preparing his tea in silence.

Irina watched him, holding her cup and saucer in her lap, her feet once again folded up in the seat. The desolation she felt was indescribable. Being alone with him in the cabin of this airplane was like being buried with him in a coffin. She desperately yearned for the presence of others, anyone who might absorb or deflect some of the malignancy he exuded. She wished that the steward, however groveling he might be, would return, move about the cabin, do anything rather than leave her alone with this creature.

"When do Wei and Bontate arrive in Houston?" she asked.

Krupatin shook his head. "I don't know. We have an appointment in two days. What they do until then is no concern of mine. I don't give a damn, so long as they show up when they are supposed to."

Even though he had just eaten three of the chocolate-covered strawberries, he popped a sugar cube into his mouth and sucked his tea through it, as was his habit. Irina watched him. Though he was tending to gain weight, he was still handsome, still self-absorbed. But the thing that caught her attention now was his self-contained silence. Usually when they met between assignments he was loquacious, either because he was ebullient about what she had done—having rid him of some real or imagined thorn—or because he was slightly giddy with anticipation at what she was about to do. Either way, death animated him, even at a distance. She knew from experience that his familiarity with death, his intimacy with it, was closely aligned with his sexuality. Long ago she had realized that the emotions he experienced from each were actually indistinguishable to him. It was a volatile confusion of passions.

But now he was brooding, and his insistence that it was not necessary for her to be privy to events until just before they happened alerted her to a new development, one that she instinctively read as a threat.

As he sipped his tea he pretended to study some papers on his desk, ignoring her. This would have satisfied her perfectly if it weren't for the nagging suspicion that if she neglected to address this behavior, it would be at her own peril.

"Sergei," she said, surprised at the weakness of her voice, "do you have no doubts about what we are about to do?"

He looked around at her. "We?" His face was expressionless. "I am doing this. You are only an extension of me. I am doing this."

"Okay, fine."

"Not even a second's doubt." He looked at her for a long moment. "Tell me," he said, swiveling his chair around to face her, holding his cup of tea in one hand. "Which one of our partners troubles you the most?"

"Troubles me?"

"Who do you think will be the most difficult to hit?"

She made a quick, radical calculation. "Wei."

"Really?"

He seemed surprised, a reaction that made Irina's heart lurch.

"Why?" he asked. "He's attracted to you."

"That's why," she said. "No matter what his attraction, he is not going to lose his head. He will always be suspicious that what he wants might very well have a lethal consequence."

He looked at her a moment. "Then that should make you all the more desirable."

The remark said more about Krupatin than Wei.

"Maybe." She shrugged. "All I know is, it makes my job more dangerous."

Krupatin nodded and sipped his tea, his eyes never leaving her. It was as if now that he had deigned to acknowledge her, she was the only thing he wanted to see. And her own stupidity hadn't helped any. In her drug-lagged state she hadn't paid attention to her gown, and Krupatin had picked up on her carelessness. Instinctively she wanted to cover herself where the slippery silk had fallen away from her thigh, but she knew that such a reflex would bring his attention to her reluctance to have him look at her. So she sat there, afraid to protest in even the smallest way with a modest gesture, while his eyes sucked at her as if she were one of his sugar cubes.

"We will talk about the details later," he said. "But you ought to think about this: we cannot afford to let either of them get away. At the faintest hint of something fishy, they both have to go. Getting only one of them is not good enough." He sipped from his cup. "So you see, it's not a consideration."

"Did you think I thought it was a consideration?"

"I don't waste time wondering what you think," he said. "I'm just telling you."

The jet hissed over the tiny Caicos Islands, a silver fleck against the sun over Cuba. It turned a few degrees north and slipped into the clear bright sky over the warm waters of the Gulf of Mexico.

Irina was not a fatalist. She would not be in the position she found herself in now if she were. But she did recognize the foul breath of dread, and she smelled it now, like the staleness of dead flowers in a vase of cloudy, stagnant water. It was the odor of the end of her life, and it came from the mouth of Satan, staring at her naked thigh.

They landed under a low, hot Mexican sun a few miles inland from the coast, on an isolated airstrip flanked by sugarcane fields. A new but dusty Land Rover waited at the end of the strip for them, along with a glistening clean pearl-gray Mercedes.

When Krupatin stepped out of the Gulfstream, he was met by a thin, silver-haired Mexican in a rumpled white linen suit and a white shirt open at the neck. The Mexican was flanked by two gun-toting guards. Krupatin spoke to him, and then the two men moved a few steps nearer the tall stalks of sugarcane and held a brief discussion. After a subdued conversation, the Mexican tossed his head in the direction of the Mercedes, reached into his pocket, and took out a set of keys, which he gave to Krupatin.

They unloaded what they needed from the plane and put it into the Mercedes. Krupatin visited with his pilot, and then he and Irina got into the Mercedes and the Land Rover pulled out in front of them. They followed it along a dirt road away from the sugarcane fields and the airstrip to a paved highway.

Within fifteen minutes they were negotiating the tight, narrow streets of the port of Tampico. Eventually they made their way out again to the coastal highway, which followed the beaches north past shaggy palms and dunes clustered with woody sea grapes. After a while the Land Rover slowed and Krupatin passed it. But it stayed behind them in the distance, making sure they did not fall victim to the occasional criminal opportunists who were becoming increasingly evident on Mexico's isolated highways. The guards would stay with them all the way to the border.

The afternoon was turning hazy and pale. Irina knew that on the other side of Mexico the sun was just now balanced on the horizon. But here the light already had softened to mauve above the gray-green surf, and a bruised evening was approaching, dragging the night along with it.

Twenty-seven

KRUPATIN DIDN'T WASTE any time. He pushed the Mercedes hard toward Texas under a clear half-moon. It was a little over three hundred miles to the border, and luckily the coastal highway was not particularly crooked or heavily populated. Slumped behind the wheel, he drove somberly, as if he were on the Autobahn, flat out, the Mercedes sucking at the black asphalt that ran north in straight stretches—with occasional slight adjustments in direction—between the Gulf of Mexico and the Sierra Madre Oriental. In silence they hurtled through the star-sparkling night toward another country.

It was Irina's job to navigate, using a road map that had been provided with the car. Every time an intersection appeared out of the darkness, she gave Krupatin the highway number he was to take and the name of the next town or village. Her directions were the only words spoken for several hours as the headlights of the Mercedes flashed over the roadside terrain, giving a fast-forward, tunnel-vision glimpse of Mexico's isolated coastal spaces. There were miles and miles of nothing, vague notions of desert, glimmerings in the distance, a collection of shacks, a stalled truck and the faces of two bewildered men caught for an instant in the Mercedes's lights. More vague notions of desert. The moon followed them, racing over the Gulf of Mexico outside Irina's window.

When the dim lights of Reynosa finally appeared in the distance, the Land Rover escort pulled to the side of the paved road and wheeled around. The red taillights signaled that Sergei and Irina were alone.

The border station was not difficult to find, but Krupatin turned into a street a block away and pulled to the curb. The streets were poorly lighted and had more potholes than pavement. Mexico did not put its best foot forward in its border towns, and Reynosa was no exception. Krupatin had parked on a street filled with bars, but it seemed to be a sluggish night and there was a scarcity of clientele. Only a few cars were parked along the high curbs, and a haze of dust hung suspended in the night, casting a romantic veil over the neon lights that quivered above the sidewalks.

"We had better check with the border guard," Krupatin said, lighting a cigarette. "Go in there," he said, nodding at an open bar and pulling a piece of paper from his coat pocket, "and call this number. Ask for this name." He looked at her. "He's on the U.S. side. When he identifies himself, hang up."

She did as she was told, a blond, fair-skinned woman in a dark cantina, dark faces turning her way, white eyes flashing. Jerky music, accordion and guitar and horns, obscured her conversation. The man she wanted eventually gave his name, in a twangy accent like those of Texans in the movies.

Before she was even inside the Mercedes, two men appeared at the door of the club to see where she had gone. They watched as she closed the door of the car behind her.

On the Mexican side of the bridge they were waved on. It was too late at night even to engage in a little game for a *mordida*. They drove slowly across the darkness, and only once did Irina see a brief glint of moonlight on the little bit of water. She thought fleetingly of the Neva.

On the U.S. side she pretended to be asleep. It was brightly lighted and only one agent came out of the building. He was a

Mexican and did not look like his name would be the name written on the piece of paper. When he spoke, she knew he wasn't. She kept her head against the back of the seat. He asked Krupatin for their papers and read them. Why are you coming to the United States, Mr. Kurner? Tourists. How long are you planning on staying? Two weeks. Where are you going? San Antonio for a few days, then to Dallas.

Irina turned restlessly in her seat and through squinted eyes looked inside the station. Another agent was studying a computer screen in the bright fluorescent light. He glanced up once, but continued working on the computer without taking notice of the routine procedure outside. The two agents did not communicate. Then the agent questioning Krupatin handed their passports back, told him to enjoy his stay in the States, and backed away from the car.

Krupatin never showed the slightest concern. He had been crossing borders all his life.

They drove seven miles in from the border to a town called McAllen, where Krupatin stopped at a service station and made another telephone call. Irina watched him as he made a few notes on a piece of paper, looking down the street and nodding, asking a question, looking down the street and nodding again. Finally he hung up, and they drove down a palm-lined boulevard until he pulled off at an all-night café. He parked in a corner of the parking lot, away from the streetlamps, and they went inside, where he chose a booth next to a window. They quickly ordered something to eat, neither of them having had anything since they left Tampico.

As he always did, Krupatin looked around at the people in the café to see whose company he was keeping. It was well after midnight now, nearly two o'clock, and the few other diners scattered around in the booths and at the tables were a sober-looking lot, people who were familiar with the small hours of the morning and who tended to keep their own counsel. When the waitress brought them coffee, Krupatin lighted a cigarette.

They had been there twenty minutes, Krupatin had finished his cigarette, and they were already eating when another Mercedes pulled into the parking lot, made its way over to their car, turned in beside it, and parked. Krupatin watched it with unconcern, with no more particular interest than that with which he had been watching the occasional car passing on the boulevard.

A man got out of the Mercedes, which was dark blue and larger than the one they were driving, and opened the trunk. Then he went around to the passenger side of their car and opened it. Krupatin had left the keys in the ignition. The man took the keys and opened the trunk of their car and transferred the luggage that was there to the dark blue Mercedes. When he had done that, he closed the trunks of both cars, got into their Mercedes, and drove away.

If anyone in the café had noticed this little transaction, Irina could not tell. It had taken no more than three or four minutes, during which Krupatin's expression had never changed. He had continued eating, not even bothering to watch the exchange of luggage.

It was two-thirty when they pulled into a large motel a few miles down the road. It was a new establishment built like a Spanish hacienda, with balconies and arched walkways. There were palm trees and magenta bougainvillea and potted plants all around the swimming pool, which was bright and clean.

As soon as they checked into their room, Krupatin opened a briefcase on the table near the windows. The briefcase was full of neatly organized identification documents: travel visas, passports of various colors, credit cards, and papers identifying them as a variety of married couples as well as unrelated individuals. Helen and Gunther Kurner had disappeared with the pearl-gray Mercedes. None of the data they had presented at the border would ever be seen again.

Now they would be whoever Krupatin wished them to be. Irina knew that he would play these documents skillfully, so that their drive to Houston would leave no trace whatsoever. How he would use these identities in the city was another matter. It all depended on how invisible he wished to remain.

Once he finished with these documents, satisfying himself that he had received what he had ordered, he returned everything to the case and closed it. Then he opened a second briefcase. This one contained cash in American dollars. He counted it—this man who had billions in foreign accounts all over the world—counted this cash as if he were a traveling salesman, carefully, meticulously tallying up the day's receipts to make sure every penny was accounted for so his commission would not be shorted.

Irina was exhausted. She hung up her two dresses, hoping most of the wrinkles would hang out of them during the night. She took off her underclothes and took a shower. Then, with a towel wrapped around her, she washed out her underclothes and draped them from hangers to dry during what remained of the night. When she finished Krupatin was still at the table, almost through counting. She lay down on the bed farthest from the windows, farthest from him, and turned out the bedside lamp. Stoop-shouldered, he continued to count, his profile to her, the room lighted now only by the lamp beside his table. A hank of hair fell over his brow. He was tired and looked tired, but would not stop.

She went to sleep holding the locket that hung around her neck, as the Devil counted his money a few feet away. The dollars might just as well have been souls, his tally for the day, another score sent to hell. The Devil was insatiable, gathering to himself every tiny soul, never enough, never enough, greedily raking the lost into his abyss like so much loose change, a shekel, a kopek, a penny, a life. It was all the same. Profit and loss.

Twenty-eight

Houston

AT SEVEN O'CLOCK the next morning, Cate and Ann Loder left the off-site and drove to Cate's apartment, where she picked up more clothes, this time nicer dresses that would be more appropriate for her relationship with Valentin Stepanov. Then they drove to a restaurant just off the West Loop and had breakfast.

Cate was hungry, but her stomach was uneasy and her breakfast did not settle well. She guessed it didn't have anything to do with the lousy meals they had been having for the past forty-eight hours. Lousy meals were part of her routine. But she suspected it had everything to do with what she was about to throw herself into.

"Butterflies?" Ann asked, holding a cup of coffee in both hands, looking at Cate.

"It shows that much?"

"Actually, not at all. I just knew you'd have them."

Cate nodded. "I feel a little weird." She turned her wrist up on the tabletop, exposing the inside of her arm. "These things are going to take some getting used to."

"You'd do best just to forget about them."

"Oh, sure," Cate said. "That's best. I'll do that." She ate another bite of her egg and spread a bit of orange marmalade on a piece of toast. She put down her knife.

"Last night, when we tried them out—how sensitive are they?"

"Pretty good," Ann said. "Pretty damn good."

Cate took a ballpoint out of her purse, pulled a clean paper napkin from the dispenser on their table, and wrote, "Can they hear me peeing?"

Ann grinned. "Well, I don't know if I'd worry about that . . ."

"Goddamn." Cate rolled her head and wadded up the napkin.

"Come on. Look, it's not that sensitive, really."

"Yeah, well, I believe you, Ann . . . really."

"That ought to be the least of your worries."

Cate looked away, out the window to the expressway. "No, I don't have any shortage of worries."

"You remember the code word?"

" 'I'm burning up' or 'I'm hot'—some reference to that."

"Okay. Just make sure you're not vague about it."

"You can bet on that."

Ann studied her for a moment. "I shouldn't say this, but you can back out anytime you want to."

Cate looked at her across the table and said evenly, "I wouldn't back out of this if my life depended on it."

The phrasing was unfortunate; both of them realized it but chose to ignore it.

"That sounds determined," Ann said. "It also sounds like you think you've got something to live up to—or live down."

"Maybe. Both, maybe."

Ann shrugged. "Well, that's a lot of baggage to carry into this. But people go into this work for all kinds of reasons. Any way you cut it, this is a pretty strange business, when you just back up and look at it." She set down her coffee cup and picked at a crumb beside her plate. "People have all kinds of reasons."

"Why do you do it?"

Ann looked up. "No, I *don't* do it. I'm always sitting back at the home fire. *You* do it. People like you. Erika does it. People like her. I'll run you, but that's it. That's enough pressure for me. I won't go out. I won't do it myself."

Cate studied her. She wanted to ask why she wouldn't do it, but she was afraid to. She had no idea what Ann's answer might be, but now was not the time for her to hear it, no matter what it was.

By the time they got back to the off-site at nine-thirty, Valentin Stepanov had called and left instructions for them to meet him in an hour at a particular location in the parking lot of the Town and Country Village, a shopping mall in the northwestern part of the city, at the intersection of Interstate 10 and the Sam Houston Tollway. Just as Cate and Ann were getting their things together to leave, one of the telephones rang on the table. Hain's bank of equipment seemed to be growing. Still another telephone and computer monitor had been added, and the tangled drapery of wires and cables that provided intravenous power to these systems was threatening absurdity.

Erika raised the telephone. "Cate."

She took the telephone.

"Are you bucked up for this?" It was Ennis Strey. She was relieved to hear his voice.

"I'm ready," she said, trying to sound game and to ease any anxieties he might be feeling on her behalf.

"You'll do fine." There was a slight pause. "I'm in the tech room. We've got someone on you round the clock, too. You've got lots of company."

"Thanks, Ennis. I appreciate it."

"Take off," he said.

Cate hung up and grabbed her purse. Hain was instantly beside her. His aging schoolboy face was concentrated as he walked beside her through the living room toward the front door.

"Careful not to slip and let Stepanov know about the mikes," he said, stooping a little toward her as he spoke.

"Fly on the wall," she said, not slowing down.

"Yeah," he said, "that's about it." One, two, three, four steps. "Any last-minute double-checks? Anything you want to reconfirm? Clear up?"

"Not a thing."

They were at the door. She turned and glanced back at Ometov. He was waiting for that, with his hands in his pockets, his face smiling. He nodded and gave a small tilt forward from the waist, a baggy bow of deference to her temerity and a quiet sign of his respect for what she was about to do.

Outside, Neil Jernigan's car was waiting behind Ann's. John Parmley was sitting in the front seat wearing tiny headphones and looking down at his lap, undoubtedly already tuned to her body's receptions.

Jernigan opened her door for her, a means of having one last word with her.

"Cate, I know I don't have to caution you, but be careful with any verbal communication you might want to make directly to us. Even if you're alone. When you're in their territory, you've got to assume you're in bugged territory. They'd pick it up. If you want to talk to us, do it rarely and carefully."

She nodded. "Okay, Neil, thanks."

"Good luck," he said, and closed the door.

Within ten minutes of leaving the house, Jernigan's car dropped out of sight. For the next few minutes the only words spoken were Cate's occasional directions to Ann. When the telephone rang, Cate picked it up.

"Cate, it's Erika. I wanted a few private words before you join Stepanov." She paused. "I am thinking maybe you should not be too defensive with him. Believe a few of his lies. It will make him a little comfortable. We need his ego on our side." She paused again, cleared her throat. "It's just a thought I had."

"No, I can see that. That's good thinking."

"Good luck," Erika said curtly. She was off the line before Cate could thank her.

Cate put the telephone on the seat beside her. They were all crossing their fingers, tossing salt over their shoulders, rubbing their rabbit's feet. Ann Loder said nothing.

It was well after ten o'clock and the parking lot of the mall was moderately full. They found Stepanov's rental car where he said it would be, outside the main entrance to one of the mall's anchor stores, near an oak tree and a park bench. But Stepanov was not in it. Ann Loder cruised past it, slowed, and went on. They circled on the far side of the lot until they found a vantage point from which they could clearly see the rental car and parked. But no sooner had Ann turned off the ignition than Stepanov came into view, walking across from a fast-food restaurant and sipping a cup of coffee. When he got to the car, he leaned against the driver's side door and crossed his feet, prepared to wait.

Ann said nothing, watched him a minute, then started the car.

They pulled up behind Stepanov's car and stopped. He made no display of greetings at seeing them but simply stood upright, pulled his keys out of his pocket, and opened the trunk of the car.

Ann looked at Cate. "We'll let you know how you can get in touch with us. Circumstances will dictate."

"Okay," Cate said.

"Don't screw up." Ann grinned at her.

"I'll hold that thought," Cate said and opened the door.

They transferred Cate's bag to Stepanov's trunk, and Stepanov slammed it shut.

Ann looked at him. "Be careful, Valentin." It was more a warning than a cautionary remark.

"Oh, I'm sure you will keep a good eye on us," the Russian said without humor. "I'll take good care of her, don't worry."

Ann nodded and looked at Cate. "Keep in touch. Good luck."

That was it.

Ann got into her car and Stepanov watched her drive away. "Come on," he said. "Get in."

They got inside his car, which was in the shade of the oak, and Stepanov put his keys in the ignition, but he didn't start the engine. He simply sat there, looking out the windshield at the traffic coming into the mall lot, watching people get out of their cars and walk through the aisles of vehicles to the mall. Then he rolled down his window. He sipped his coffee, looking as though he were pondering just how to say what he was going to say.

Cate thought he was bigger than she remembered from the day before. He filled up the car seat and loomed over the steering wheel, which seemed proportionally too small for him. She studied his profile and in those few moments recognized the strain in his face. Though he was presenting a picture of equanimity, the stress on the inside was manifested in a weariness in his eyes that he could not disguise.

"Well," he said finally, continuing to stare straight ahead. "Are you wired?" He was almost pensive. The question seemed routine, lacking any real curiosity.

"No," she said.

"They'll find it if you are, and that will be the end of it. I hope your people weren't that stupid."

"You can check me if you want to," she said.

He looked at her and smiled. "No," he said, and then turned his gaze back out the front of the car. "You know, whoever Sergei sends, at some point they will go through everything in our hotel room."

"I'm okay. There's nothing to find."

"They have debugging technology," he observed. He looked out into the sunlight. "He is going to be surprised at how hot it is here." He smiled to himself, a gallows smile.

"Your two friends checked into the Chateau Touraine late yesterday afternoon," Cate said.

Stepanov turned his head to her. "Really?" His face showed no surprise.

"When they came through customs they were disguised."

"Disguised? You're kidding." He shook his head.

"By the time they arrived at the hotel they had removed their disguises, and Ometov has identified one of them as Grigori Izvarin."

"Izvarin." He nodded. "Of course," he said with a weary jerk of his head. "Who else but him? And the other one?"

"Leo doesn't know him."

Stepanov raised his eyebrows in mild surprise. "Leo knows Sergei's people pretty well." He sipped his coffee. "That's interesting. So they've checked into the hotel." He thought about this a moment. Then he shrugged and tossed his coffee cup out the window into the parking lot. "Let's drive and get some things straightened out." He turned on the ignition and started the car, then looked at her. "You look nice," he said.

Twenty-nine

VALENTIN STEPANOV maneuvered the rented Cadillac out of the parking lot of the Town and Country Mall and worked his way to the entry of the Sam Houston Parkway, where the driving was not complicated, he said, and they could talk. They headed south.

"So, I need to know about your legend," he said.

She nodded. "Catherine Miles . . ."

"Miles? M-i-l-e-s?"

"Yes."

"Okay."

"I'm an assistant manager in the personnel office of an international architectural firm," she said, and told him how she had used this before and how it was covered by backup.

Stepanov listened to her elaboration and seemed satisfied, nodding and mumbling his assent.

"Okay, good," he said. "So how did we meet? At a hotel bar. I have told you I am with a firm that promotes international business cooperatives, and I am here doing that, blah, blah. This is the fifth time we are together. You are staying with me at the Touraine rather than at your home because it is fun. When I am in town, I take you to fancy restaurants, buy you things, pay for everything. You get to stay in luxury hotels instead of your dreary duplex or whatever it is. It's like a working girl's vacation when I come to town. We party. We have good sex. You just pack up a bag and move in with me for a week or so. This time we were lucky, because you had some time off—what, it's . . . when you have worked extra time and you can take off?"

"Comp time."

"Exactly. So you see, it is basically a good time. Nothing more. I don't tell you all that much. You are not asking a lot of questions. Both of us are in it just for the good time."

"Is Krupatin going to question this at all? It's a little hard to believe he's not going to be suspicious of me."

"Oh, he will be suspicious. Sergei would be suspicious if I did not have a woman with me. He would think, what is the matter, Valentin always has a woman. What does this mean, no woman? What is going on here?"

He shook his head, checked the rearview mirror, and changed lanes.

"What can you tell me about Grigori Izvarin?" Cate asked. "What's his background?"

"Grigori is the son of an old friend who is now dead, someone who helped us out in the early Moscow days. He is thirty-two years old, one of the next generation of KGB agents—the generation that never happened. But he had all the training and was active for five or six years—not a long time by those standards—before the so-called empire blew to shit. Of course, all the time he was on Sergei's payroll. Sergei always kept four or five KGB on his payroll.

"You will have to watch Gori. He thinks Krupatin is God, and he wants to be Jesus Christ. But he is a watchful Jesus, and he sees a Judas in every face. I have had my share of run-ins with him. The bastard is viciously amibitious. And you know, no matter how smart a man is, that kind of slavish devotion is flattering. Gori is making headway with Sergei, he's coming up in the ranks."

"So he's here to make sure Krupatin's not walking into something."

"Yes, I think so. But even if that is not his specific job here, that is always on his mind."

"They're going to have guns."

"Of course."

"How are they going to get them?"

"Those people I come down here to see, they have explosives and firearms connections. That will be their job. They have already been contacted."

Stepanov changed lanes again. Cate guessed they would be driving for a while because he was curious about being tailed. He obviously wasn't trying to dry-clean himself. He was just curious. It was the kind of thing he did without even thinking.

After a few minutes he looked at her. "How are you going to communicate with your people?"

"Telephone."

"Oh, that's ingenious," he said with mock admiration.

"It's safe," she said.

"I guess there's not much to say anyway."

"What do you mean?"

"There are probably small little FBI agents hiding inside your pants." He laughed, but it wasn't altogether comfortable.

"I'm covered well enough," she said.

"That's good. When you get killed, I want them to know it was not my fault."

"I understand you picked me from a photograph."

"That's right, the same way I pick out a piece of meat at the butcher's. Something nice and pink. Something I can really get into."

"In your dreams," she said, and forced herself to smile at him. An easy, inviting smile, something he would like. And he did.

He laughed again, looking at her, this time a genuine laugh that showed surprise at her jest, and then smoothly and quickly he exited off the parkway. Without explanation he pulled into a service station, parked to one side of the drive, and got out of the car. She waited and watched him walk to a telephone booth, step in, close the door, and put a quarter in the slot.

"He's . . ." She stopped. She was going to tell them what he was doing, and then she remembered Jernigan's advice not half an hour before. Was Stepanov giving her a chance to hang herself, or did he really have business on the telephone? He even had his back turned to her, giving her permission to go ahead and talk. He was making it too easy. She kept her mouth shut, wondering where he might have hidden a tape recorder in the car.

He remained with his back to her for nearly ten minutes. Cate waited in silence and wondered what they were thinking in the tech room in the field office, in the off-site, in Jernigan's car. It would be a long time—if ever—before she would get used to her broadcasting condition. She still couldn't get over the fact that she had let this happen to her, that she had simply walked into it with everything hanging out as if she were Mata Hari. Christ.

Finally Stepanov hung up the telephone and walked back to the car, jangling his car keys, which she had noticed he had taken with him. Old habits.

"Did you have a nice time?" she asked as he shut the door.

"I can't always explain everything I do," he said, turning the ignition, starting the car. "Get used to it." He pulled out of the service station and at the next opportunity got back on the parkway.

"Aside from your people," he said casually, "have you seen any other surveillance?"

She looked at him. Then she smiled slowly. "You haven't seen our people, Valentin."

"What do you mean?"

"It's a mystery," she said. "Get used to it."

Stepanov laughed openly. "Okay," he said, "okay."

They continued on the parkway, this time going back the way they had come, Stepanov again driving casually, switching lanes, watching his rearview mirror. She didn't exactly understand what he was doing. His maneuvers were too cursory for dry-cleaning, and yet they were more deliberate than aimless wandering.

They went on talking. He asked her about her family, and as she talked he stopped her occasionally to ask, "Is that Catherine Miles you are talking about, or Cate?" It was both and neither.

A good undercover agent, Tavio always had said, never left his real self behind. The new self was just a thinly disguised old self. This trick had two functions. First, you didn't have to memorize a whole new personality with a whole new set of personal facts from birthdate to that very moment. Essentially, you were still you, with only a few facts changed so you could assume a new identity with a reasonable amount of comfort. Catherine Miles and Cate Cuevas had the same favorite color, liked the same kind of music, saw the same movies, had the same taste in clothes, bought the same kinds of foods at the supermarket. So ninety percent of the time, when she was answering Stepanov's questions, she was answering them honestly, accurately, naturally, without having to keep a tally of lies. This created no tension, no memory problems.

The second function to this trick was that you never identified too closely with your new associates. This was one of Tavio's cardinal rules. Too many times, he said, he had seen undercover agents, men and women who had been under a long time, forget their essential selves. Sometimes in this business you came to realize that some people who did horrible things were, in all honesty, likable. It was easy to get next to them and to like being next to them.

But, Tavio said, that was the way to destruction. Cate Cuevas did not like the same people Catherine Miles liked, and it was essential to her survival that she never like the same people. Cate Cuevas never forgot who she was, never forgot what her standards were, who her friends were, where her loyalties lay. Catherine Miles might eventually get to like Valentin Stepanov, even sympathize with him, as she learned more about his personal history, the way life had been unfair to him. But Cate Cuevas would not and could not.

Ninety percent of the time, Cate and Catherine could be friends; they even could be the best of friends. But that last ten percent would alienate them forever; it was the territory of moral values. The smallest part became in fact the defining part. Like a drop of gentian violet, it was the dye that prescribed the differences that gave meaning to a life, the differences that gave meaning to believing or disbelieving. That last ten percent was, in the end, all that mattered.

"What about you, Valentin? Have you forgotten who you were?"

He did not answer quickly. They had left the parkway, having traveled again over the same territory. Then, at Cate's suggestion, they turned onto the Southwest Freeway and headed downtown. Once there, they came back out again onto the West Loop, not that far from the Chateau Touraine.

"Have I forgotten who I was?" he asked. "Who I *was*?"

As Cate looked at his profile, she realized he was not a handsome man after all. His features were coarse. A slightly too large nose, a slightly too small mouth. His lips did not have smooth lines but had too much of an upward tweak in the center, where the dimple underneath his nose formed a too-delicate juncture. He had heavy jowls. His body was bulky, conveying strength without the grace of a well-defined musculature. He was more buffalo than athlete. His eyes were forgettable—almost. Physically they were not striking, but if you looked at them closely, separated them from the rest of his features, you could see an emptiness in them that was disconcerting. It was not what she could see there that gave her a momentary shudder; it was what she didn't see. Something was missing, something that distinguished a human eye from an animal's. If his eyes conveyed anything at all, they conveyed a realization of damnation. It was a sobering thing to see. It was even frightening, as though she were allowed to speak with a man who was guaranteed to go to hell. And knew it.

"As a matter of fact . . ." he said, and he paused, and his face took on a momentary difference, as if he were delving far, far back into himself, as if the question were absolutely original to him and his thoughts were thoughts that were surprising. "As a matter of fact," he said, "I have."

Then he laughed, a dry laugh lacking joy or amusement but genuine all the same. He laughed a long time.

Thirty

McAllen, Texas

"THREE HUNDRED and forty-five miles," Krupatin said, bending over the map in the restaurant. They were having a late breakfast. "That's . . . five hundred fifty-five kilometers. Good God, nearly six hours!"

He slapped down his pen on the restaurant table and took another sip of coffee. His suit had a few sharp creases at odd angles in it, because he hadn't bothered to unpack it before collapsing on the bed early that morning. He was not wearing a tie with his white shirt, but his face was freshly shaven.

Irina didn't pay much attention to him. She was looking out the window at the palm trees, finishing the last bites of her pancakes.

"It has to take that long," Krupatin added, thinking out loud. "The state police are supposed to be strict bastards about speeding."

There was a breeze outside, and the deep green palm fronds rocked and lilted like hula dancers against the bright blue sky.

Krupatin looked at his watch. "That will put us in Houston

about six o'clock or so, seven o'clock if we stop to eat. Not night yet, this time of year."

Krupatin's trademark, Irina thought as she watched a maid in a white uniform push her cleaning cart along the loggia on the other side of the swimming pool. He knew everything he had to know to do what he had to do. Speed limits on the highways. Time changes. Daylight savings time. She knew about that too, a strange concept. She did her homework too. Krupatin was thorough, but he was thorough for Krupatin. He did not pursue his efficient planning beyond his own interests.

"You know how we are going?" he asked, looking at her, nodding at the Texas map on the table.

He knew she did. She had memorized the highways, the intersections. But the map had no marks on it. That was an old habit too.

"You don't have much to say." He glowered at her.

She took her eyes off the calm scene outside and looked at him.

"What can I say, Sergei? I don't know anything."

"It's for your own good," Krupatin said matter-of-factly, popping a last bite of bacon into his mouth. "If this doesn't go by the mark, it will fall apart. The only way I can control it is to do everything myself. As much as I can, anyway." He wiped his hands on his napkin. "You ought to understand that. That's the way you work, isn't it?"

"All alone, huh? No boys?"

He raised his head in a half-nod. "And a few boys." He leveled his eyes at her. "Incidentally, they don't know any more than you do. That's just the way this has to be."

A waitress came by their table and filled their coffee cup, then moved on.

Krupatin glared after her. "I don't believe this. This is the third time she's done that. She doesn't even ask. She just comes up behind you and . . . Christ. That's goddamned irritating." He lighted a cigarette and pushed the coffee away. "Christ."

She studied him. "What kind of time frame are we working with?"

"I think you've asked that."

"I don't remember. What kind of an answer did I get?"

"I'll let you know."

They looked at each other. She was having to swallow a matrix of emotions. Fear. Anger. Impatience. Fear was foremost, but it was complicated by a ferocious will to survive. At times, at black times, she doubted she would ever be rid of the embrace of his dark wing. At other times, when she thought of Félia, she imagined herself crawling out of an abyss, her daughter's face in the distance before her, small and pale and yearning. At those moments her resolve to be free of him was fierce and irrepressible.

But even when her resolve was at its strongest, she had to admit to herself that she was suffocating under the weight of what she was doing. In the beginning, after each of the first two killings, she had vomited immediately, on the spot, leaving the contents of her stomach behind with the bodies. After the next two she had managed to hold on to her nerves until she was well away, until she was alone, down on her knees in a public bathroom, in a train station. She still remembered the smell of the public toilets and the hollow sound of her own retching echoing off the tile walls.

Her instincts, however, sobered her. She knew if she was not able to control herself she would make a mistake, a fatal mistake. The margins for error in this business were thin and brittle. So she called on the only greater power she knew. Much to her shame, she prayed for strength. Before each of the next jobs, if she was in St. Petersburg, she went to the Alexander Nevsky Monastery, through the woods to Trinity Cathedral. The church was often crowded, foggy with incense, glimmering with candles, worshipers kneeling and praying, kissing icons, moaning their faith in mumbled prayer. So did she. She implored the Father and the Son and the Holy Spirit for the will to kill without anguish, to steal lives to save a life, to murder again and again in order to preserve again and again. She implored the icons, their gold and silver glinting in a vast hazy gloam of lifted prayers. The faces of all the madonnas and all the angels became Félia's, peering down at her through the smoke of candles and incense in gratitude for salvation through the delivering hand of Irina's executions.

The next two times the killing itself was easier, but she was entirely unprepared for what happened to her afterward.

The first time it happened was in Prague. She met her man in a coffeehouse near the Charles Bridge. They had coffee and pastries, then walked to his car, parked in one of the tight, narrow streets nearby. It was summer. Dusk. His hand was under her dress, fumbling at the elastic of her pants, his face burrowed in her breasts. She slipped the hypodermic needle into his neck. The cyanide gave him time only to recoil. He gaped at her, and the single word "Greta" escaped through the rising phlegm in his throat. The name hit her face like a strew of blood. Greta? She had studied her target thoroughly, as always. There was no wife named Greta. No daughter. No sister. No mistress named Greta. The identity of this woman whose name was the last word spoken by a man she had killed began to haunt her. She began to look for the name in newspapers, listen for it in overheard conversations on trains, in restaurants, on the street. She dreamed of faceless women. It was months before she could shake loose of it. After much prayer, incense, and candles.

Then she had to kill a woman in Bern. When the woman answered the doorbell at her house in a secluded section of the city, Irina shot her in the face. The blast sent the woman sprawling backward, her arms windmilling as she reflexively tried to maintain her balance even in the moment of her death. This odd, moribund ballet stuck in Irina's mind. Again it populated her dreams; people everywhere were windmilling their arms in death. She had one vivid, gruesome dream in which she visited a city where the head of every tenth person she met exploded, and they windmilled backward, staggering for balance. The other citizens of the city paid no attention to this and went on about their business with unconcern.

Then without warning the fixations stopped, and the killing became a cold routine. She killed with no more feeling for her victims than if they were soap bubbles that she clapped into extinction between her hands. She continued to pray for this soothing insentience. Félia continued to live, ignorant of her absent mother's sins on her behalf, ignorant of the money that piled up in the accounts in her name in the Crédit Suisse in Bern, in the Banca Svizzera Italiana in Zurich.

"For God's sake," Krupatin was hissing in a stage whisper, "what the fuck are you *doing?*"

He was looking at her hands. She looked down and saw that she had pushed one of the tines of her fork through the thin weblike skin that separated the base of her forefinger and middle finger. Blood and syrup were running down the back of her hand.

"You stupid . . ." Krupatin was looking at her the way he might look at a new Mercedes whose engine had inexplicably burned up. The failure was infuriatingly inconvenient for him. Her psychosis was enormously discommodious.

"Relax, Sergei," she said with equanimity, withdrawing the fork from her hand and laying it down. Casually she wet her napkin in her water glass and wiped her hand, daubing at the wound to stanch the blood.

Krupatin gathered up his map and picked up the ticket. "Fucking crazy cow," he muttered, and got up from the table and went to the cashier to pay.

They drove north in the midday heat, across the long stretch of coastal plains and ranchland to Kingsville, turning slightly eastward, roughly following the coastline that lay just out of sight beyond the hazy horizon to the east.

Krupatin never took his eyes off the highway. Irina followed the map closely and otherwise gazed out the window at the alien land. The large Mercedes, heavy and comfortable, lazed along the highway at the posted speed limit, a pace that seemed to make the landscape crawl by, stretching out the long afternoon interminably. Four hours later they stopped at a truck stop outside Victoria. They refueled the car, bought hamburgers to take with them, and pulled back onto the highway. They were still a hundred and thirty miles away from where they wanted to be.

The Houston skyline had been in front of them for over half an hour, sitting on the horizon like a mirage, growing imperceptibly, its size swelling without appearing to do so like the surreptitious movement of the minute hand on a clock. The highway traffic increased; suburbs rose out of the coastal plains in the distance all around them, far off at first, then creeping closer to the highway until they were moving through a solid outlying civilization, the subdivisions and businesses gradually thickening to become urban instead of suburban, and they were suddenly in the city, its architecture softening, turning slate blue in the paling light of the lowering sun.

They were on an expressway, and Irina noticed Krupatin watching for an exit, something suitable for his purposes, which he had yet to share with her. Finally he switched lanes and entered the down ramp of an exit onto an access road. The tall, unlighted neon sign of a restaurant loomed ahead of them, and Krupatin pulled off the access road and into the parking lot.

Turning off the ignition, he reached over the back of the seat and picked up one of the briefcases. He flipped it open and put it on the seat between them. The roar of the traffic above them throbbed like Irina's own heartbeat.

"Okay, now you will need to use your Olya Serova documents," Krupatin said. "They've been put in your largest suitcase, along with the address book that was brought to you. The address book is important."

He reached inside the briefcase and took out several strapped bundles of cash.

"Five thousand dollars." He handed the money to her. "Do you remember Valentin Stepanov?"

"Of course."

"He will be staying at the Chateau Touraine also, and so will Grigori Izvarin, who will be registered as Anton Nakhimov, and Valery Volkov, who will be registered as Rudolf Bykov. Nakhimov will be holding a suite for you in his name. You will get a taxi from here."

"Then they are expecting me?"

"Izvarin and Volkov know that one other person is coming. They don't know it is you. Stepanov knows that two of my people will meet him there, but he doesn't know who."

"And what about you?"

"I'll be staying somewhere else. None of you will be able to reach me, none of you will know where I am. This has to be the situation in order for Wei and Bontate to be convinced of my intentions. You have to be the actual conduit."

"And Stepanov?"

"He will have a job to do too," Krupatin said, slamming down the lid on the briefcase and snapping the latches shut. "There's really nothing for you to worry about for a while. At the proper time I will let you know our means of communication."

"Where will I be meeting Wei and Bontate?"

"I don't know. They will make their own arrangements. They know where you will be staying. That was all worked out ahead of time. They will contact you."

"After I arrive at the hotel, do I contact Grigori and Valery, or do I wait to hear from them?"

"You should contact them," he said. "You will tell them that I intend to remain out of the picture here, that I will communicate with them through you."

"Grigori is not going to like that."

"Just tell him. Tell them they may have to wait several days before I will have any instructions for them."

"Do they know about Wei and Bontate?"

"No."

"Then what do they think they are doing here?"

"I just told them to be here and that they would receive instructions when they arrived."

He reached into his suit pocket, pulled out a checkbook, and gave it to her.

"This is on a London account. It's unlimited, and the authorization can easily be checked by any store. When you buy new clothes, choose well. I want you to be very smart, very fashionable." He took the keys out of the ignition. "I'll carry your bags to the restaurant."

Thirty-one

Houston

STANDING IN THE FOYER of the restaurant, Irina looked out at this city that was foreign to her and thought of all the other times she first had set eyes on an unfamiliar city. So many years, so many miles, so many worlds. So many deaths.

But there was something different now, here. She was no longer intimidated by encountering cultural and geographic unknowns. Kruptatin had thrown her into this business with only a single, powerful motivation to sustain her: threat. The consequences if she did not accomplish what she had been assigned to do far outweighed any natural intimidation resulting from being plunged into a foreign environment. She had had to be self-sufficient in so many foreign countries, to get up to speed in so many foreign languages among unfamiliar traditions and conventions, that she had come to realize that people were essentially everywhere the same and that for the most part, only the details of their dress and manners and customs differed. Human nature was consistent. This she could depend on, and once she fully had grasped this concept, crossing borders had become less daunting.

The difference she was now sensing had nothing to do with common timidity. It had everything to do with something Krupatin had given her inadvertently as a result of his brutal despotism: a highly developed sense of survival. From the very beginning, Krupatin had thrown her into the water to sink or swim. And she understood, as surely as she understood her own fear, that he didn't care about the outcome. If she survived it, she would be useful to him. If she didn't, it saved him the trouble of looking after her.

So she received a briefing: here is the target; here is a file. Study the file. Kill the target. He didn't give a damn how. And her own survival was a matter of developing her cunning. She had to learn to kill—as she would later understand it—in a vacuum. She and the target's life left the scene, the city, and the country almost simultaneously. This was no more than common sense, a woman's and a mother's instinct for survival, and had nothing to do with sophisticated KGB training. Krupatin had never offered her that, though he could have. The fact that he had not bothered to do so said as much about how worthless he considered her as anything he had done.

But in retrospect, it may have been her unconventional training, or lack of training, rather, the gut-driven evolution of her native instincts, that had made Irina such a success at her grim profession. There was a science, a psychology of assassination that had developed over millennia in the name of governments and religious fanaticism and prejudices and greed, a manner of individual killing that had, by the end of the twentieth century, developed to a prescribed art form. Irina partook of none of this. She didn't know the rules of the game she played; she didn't know the history of traditional deceits. Which worked to her advantage, for she left no patterns, no signatures, her adversaries could recognize. She did not use the tricks of the trade. Every hit was different, and she went about it in isolation. She was simply a woman without recourse, which made her unpredictable, resourceful, and dangerous.

Therefore, it was with a finely tuned sixth sense that she waited for the taxi she had called. If there was one thing she knew she could not do, it was to trust Krupatin. And yet that was exactly what he was asking her to do. Rather, that was exactly what he was requiring her to do. She had no choice.

The taxi came, driven by a young woman in well-worn blue jeans and cowboy boots and a plaid shirt with the sleeves cut out at the shoulder seam. Her chestnut hair had a masculine cut and her freckled face was a little pinched by the sun and weather, but her gray eyes handled Irina with a tenderness not hinted at by her appearance. In a flash she summed up Irina's London fashion, and as she held open the back door of the taxi she relished what she could see of Irina's breasts and long legs as Irina bent to get inside. A country boy could not have yearned more ardently for what he saw.

Irina played tag with the taxi driver's eyes in the rearview mirror as they drove through the Houston streets, which were just now slipping into evening. The lights were coming on all around them, and the city was beginning to sparkle, the heat of the day giving a clean coolness to the evening, deepening the blue that belonged, in this particular hue, to dusk.

She was surprised at how heavily wooded the city was—pines, it looked like, and oaks, everywhere a thick canopy, dense woods, houses and offices set back in darkened greenish shadows. Landscape lighting created pale pools of jade.

The taxi swooned smoothly into a wooded lane and wound its way toward a stout stone chateau, the softly lighted facade of which Irina glimpsed through the surrounding pines. They passed through tall iron gates thrown open from massive pillars and slowed when they approached a paved compound formed by high stone walls, which reached out from the gates to embrace the two wings of the chateau that extended from either side of the main structure. Loggias fronted each wing of the hotel, and shiny, dark cars were parked in a line along the hedges, facing outward like soldiers in a dress parade: Mercedes, BMWs, Rolls Royces, Jaguars, Bentleys, black and midnight blue, sparkling chrome and dark windows.

When the taxi pulled up under the porte cochere, the doorman was instantly at Irina's side, holding open the door and extending his hand to her. She ignored him and paid the driver, who looked at her over the back of the seat and handed her a card as she accepted the overpayment. She smiled at Irina, who hesitated, nodded at her, and looked at the handwritten number on the back of the card. Irina looked into the gray eyes again, then turned and got out of the taxi, leaving the attendants to take care of her luggage.

Inside, at the marble registration desk, Irina gave her name as Olya Serova and said that a suite was being held for her under the name of Anton Nakhimov.

Yes, of course, the concierge said, her rooms were already waiting for her.

"Excuse me," Irina said. "Will you show me where they are?"

Of course. The concierge produced a floor plan and pointed at the location of Irina's suite with the gold nib of her fountain pen. She said that for Irina's convenience, the suite was right next door to that of her colleagues and had a private courtyard and garden of its own. Irina studied the plan.

"And Mr. Stepanov?" she asked. "Is he nearby also?"

The concierge presented a satisfied expression, and the gold nib of her pen moved directly across the corridor. "They are here," she said.

"They?"

The concierge hesitated, but it was subtle, and she quickly recovered. "He and his woman friend," she said.

"Oh, of course." Irina shifted her eyebrows indulgently and smiled wanly at the concierge, who returned the smile, a woman-to-woman exchange. "Okay. Well, good, then, you've thought of everything. And they have all arrived?"

Yes, indeed.

"Excellent," Irina said. "But you know, this is my first visit to the city, and though I appreciate the convenience of the ground floor, and the proximity to my friends, I would much rather be on an upper floor—with a view."

The concierge again hesitated only slightly. "But this was a special request of Mr. Nakhimov's."

"And that was kind of him, but I really would prefer a higher floor," Irina graciously insisted. "The third floor, the topmost. You have suites available there?"

The concierge, unflappable, consulted her computer, tapping a few keys. In three beats she had located another wonderful suite, with an exquisite city view. But it was slightly more expensive.

"That's fine. Where is it?"

The concierge again employed the gold nib of her pen to point to the map, describing the suite as Irina again studied the plan.

"Perfect."

The concierge was pleased, delighted that she could have been of service.

"A woman?" Hain reared back in his chair in front of the computers, holding the telephone in one hand, a cup of coffee in the other. "A good-looking woman?" He looked at Ometov on the sofa, with his shoes off, his legs stretched out as he studied a folder of documents in his lap. "Olya Serova?"

Ometov, looking back at him, shrugged. Hain glanced at Erika, who sat in an armchair with her feet folded up under her, reading a magazine. She shook her head at the name and then got up and went to one of the computer screens. She bent over, tapped in the name, and waited.

"Where is she staying?" Hain listened. "That's interesting. I'll be damned. Okay, thanks. Listen, when can you get us a picture?" He looked at his watch. "Okay, great, we'll be waiting."

As soon as he slammed down the telephone, he turned to Ometov.

"Okay, what the hell's this, Leo?"

Ometov had sat up and placed his socked feet on the floor. Looking down, he was pondering. He didn't answer.

"Krupatin's woman?" Hain suggested.

"The name is not in the files," Erika said, looking at the computer screen. "S-e-r-o-v-a. Right?"

"Right," Hain confirmed. He was looking at the Russian intelligence officer.

Ometov tilted his feet back on his heels a couple of times, a thoughtful, rhythmless gesture, his forearms on his knees as he stared at the floor.

"Not a mistress," he said finally. "Not a mistress."

"Why not?"

"Not this time. He wouldn't do that, ferry in his favorite woman. It's too cumbersome. Not for this, I think."

Hain looked at Erika.

"I don't know," she said. "I think maybe Leo is right."

"Okay, then." Hain shrugged his huge frame at them, looking back and forth between them.

Ometov rose slowly from the sofa and padded to the windows that looked out into the courtyard. Earlier he had found the switch that turned on the landscape lights, and he delighted in looking out at the palms and the sagos and the bougainvillea.

"You asked where she was staying?" he asked.

"Yeah. When she checked in, she asked where the others were staying. When they told her, she said she preferred to move higher up, because of the view. She was new to the city and wanted a view. She looked at a layout of the place and chose a suite on the top floor."

"A suite," Ometov said thoughtfully, gazing out at the court-yard. "Very expensive, I suppose."

"That's right."

Ometov said nothing for a while, his hands clasped behind him, looking out at the night palms.

"To be honest," he said at last, "I don't have any idea, Curtis." He pronounced Hain's first name as "cur-TESS." "It could be that this woman belongs to someone else." He turned around. "I don't know why I refuse to believe it is Krupatin, but it simply is not right for some reason. I'll think about it. It will come to me. I am sure I am right, but it may take me a little while to understand why."

The fax machine beeped, and Hain went over and waited, im-patiently grabbing the paper as it came out of the machine and holding on to it until the machine let go. He looked at the photo-graph.

"Jesus. Well, she's good-looking. They were right about that."

Ometov came toward him, holding out his hand, and Hain gave him the photograph. Ometov quickly turned it around and frowned at it, pushing his mind to grasp the image as quickly as possible. Then, abruptly, all the anticipation and tension fell away from his face, and he backed up two steps and sat down on the sofa.

"My God," he said. "My . . . God."

Thirty-two

THE KNOCK ON THE DOOR was unexpected. Cate and Valentin already had unpacked. They had three rooms. The door to the suite opened into the main sitting room, furnished with sofas and armchairs; it was large and spacious, with French doors opening out onto a garden. A bedroom adjoining one side of the main room also opened onto the garden. And on the opposite side the main room opened into a kind of office–sitting room, with a desk, computer, fax, and answering machine, a number of armchairs, and a television. The garden, which was enclosed by high brick walls for complete privacy, was beautifully landscaped with an abundance of flowering plants, a bistro table, and chairs. A stone statue of a nude woman bending to dry her feet was partially hidden among the vines behind a small fountain.

They ordered room service and ate. Afterward, as Cate sat looking out at the garden, sipping the last of a glass of wine, Valentin decided to take a shower. He hadn't been gone ten minutes when there was a knock at the door. Her heart lurched, but she took another sip of wine and a deep breath. In this kind of hotel the maid did not knock at the door to see if you wanted her to turn down the sheets. They had not rung room service to take away their dinner things. They had been there three hours and had not heard a word from the two Russians.

She took another sip of wine—actually a mouthful—and swallowed it as she crossed the main room to the door. She did not put on her shoes.

"Hello," the first man said. His companion was just behind him, looking away, down the corridor.

"Yes?"

"We are friends of Valentin's. Is he in?" He was smiling, agreeable. The first thing she noticed about him was that he was rather tall and had a simpering mouth, a rather prissy way of holding his lips closed as he smiled. He was blond, with fashionably cropped hair, longish on top. His face was smooth and flawless, with flushed cheeks that looked as though they had just been smartly slapped. He wore a beige tailor-made suit that draped his body elegantly, fluidly, and a black, long-sleeved cotton knit shirt buttoned at the collar.

"Well, actually he's in the shower."

"The shower." He beamed. "Valentin is always so *clean*." He beamed even more brightly. "I'm sorry," he said. "Forgive me. My name is Anton Nakhimov, and this"—he turned slightly without looking around—"is Rudolf Bykov."

Bykov looked around at the sound of his name and smiled. He was paler than Nakhimov, shorter, with a receding hairline of dark hair. He had none of his partner's charm or flair; his dark suit and white businessman's shirt would have made him anonymous in any city in the world. Whereas Nakhimov's complexion was almost Technicolor, Bykov's skin was pasty, grayish, a genetic misfortune rather than the result of a lack of sun. His lips, niggardly in their thinness, were a darker gray than his skin, with perhaps a hint of a slightly bruised darkness to them.

"Well," Nakhimov said, still beaming, "might I ask to whom I am speaking?"

"Uh . . . Catherine Miles," Cate said.

"A friend of Valentin's."

"Uh, yeah."

"You're living here with him for his stay, I suppose."

Cate nodded. "That's right."

"Well," Nakhimov said, looking down at his feet with a smirk, "would you mind if we waited for him . . . in there?" He looked up at her again. "We are the reason he has come here. Business—with us."

"Sure," Cate said, smiling a little foolishly. "I'm sorry. I just wasn't expecting you."

"Of course." Nakhimov beamed on, coming into the room almost more quickly than Cate could back away from the door. "We should have called, but we, you understand, thought it would just be Valentin."

He was inside, looking around, checking out the second room, looking out into the courtyard, sizing up the situation, while Bykov sauntered in more slowly, looking only at Cate. She closed the door. Nakhimov wheeled around, thrust his hands into the generous pockets of his trousers, and beamed.

"So, Catherine, how long have you known Valentin?"

"Oh," she said, "a year, maybe." She picked up her glass of wine. "Not longer than that."

"Not longer." Nakhimov nodded, looking her over. "And where are you from? New York?"

"No, no. I live here in Houston."

"Oh?" He raised his blond eyebrows. "A Texan, then. A cowgirl," he added brightly. He was mocking, but it was clear that he had every confidence Cate would not have the bad manners to object to it. He was too charming; she would not protest. But she would know she was dealing with a superior.

"Not hardly," she said, not offended.

"What do you do here in Houston, Catherine?"

"I work for an architectural firm. In personnel."

"Really? What firm?"

"Guillen and Boardman."

"And what do your architects build?"

"Whatever their clients are willing to pay for," she said. "They're international."

"Oh, international," he cooed, smirking primly, amused at her effort to put her employer's best foot forward and perhaps to impress him.

He walked to the cart that had carried their dinner in, where the leftovers had grown tepid amid soiled linen napkins. He examined what was left.

"And how often do you see Valentin?"

She didn't answer immediately. She was letting Stepanov's words seep into her brain, reminding her of her place. She was so tempted to take this guy down to size.

"Whenever he comes to Houston," she said, sipping her wine. "Whenever he wants. Not often."

"So it's kind of a party when our Valentin comes to town," Nakhimov said, using the tips of his fingers to lift the wine bottle by the neck and pull it partway out of the ice bucket so he could read the label.

"You might say that. He likes to have a good time."

Nakhimov let go of the bottle, and it slushed down in the bucket.

"What do you do?" Cate asked. She sat down in a plush chair, drew her legs up after her, and sipped the wine, managing a pleasant face for Nakhimov. "You're Russian too, right?"

"Emphatically," he said. "And I do what Valentin does. Has he told you what he does?"

"He doesn't talk about it much. International business or something."

"That's right, Catherine. Businessmen. We are world-traveling businessmen." He looked at his watch. "International, just the way your architectural firm is international. Perhaps we could do business."

She sipped her wine and didn't say anything. During all of this Bykov was obviously bored. For a few moments he wandered into the office part of the suite, but he wasn't there long enough to do anything more than count the chairs. He came back in, stepped out into the courtyard, looked at the wall that separated this garden from the one next door, and came back to the living room. He sat down in one of the armchairs and crossed his legs, ankle on knee. His socks were too short, and a band of white hairless ankle brightened the space between his trousers' cuff and the top of his sock. Cate guessed that Nakhimov's socks reached all the way to the tops of his calves.

"I might've known it would be you," Stepanov said, suddenly standing in the bedroom door. He was wearing one of the hotel's white monogrammed robes. His hair was still wet but slicked back with a comb. His face was also damp, and he was lighting a cigarette. He puffed on it and put the lighter in the pocket of the robe.

Nakhimov was beaming at him, his hands in his trousers again. "Valentin," he said, "we have just been visiting with Catherine."

Stepanov grunted and pulled on the cigarette.

"How long have you been here?" Nakhimov asked.

"Where's your boss?" Stepanov ignored his question.

"All in good time," Nakhimov said. "We didn't know you would be having a guest."

Stepanov looked past Nakhimov at Bykov and nodded.

The putty-faced Bykov nodded back. "Valentin." His voice was a surprisingly handsome baritone.

"Nice that we have these opposite suites," Nakhimov said. Cate could see no reason for his pointing this out.

"I noticed when I checked in, Anton, that there's another one waiting," Stepanov said.

"So did I," Nakhimov said.

Then Stepanov switched to Russian. *"The boss?"*

"I only do what I'm told to do, and I wasn't told to say anything about the other suite," Nakhimov said.

"Which means you don't know anything either."

"I know that you are in the dark, Valentin. I know that."

The telephone rang, interrupting the conversation. Cate picked it up as they all turned to look at her.

"The telephone line's clean," Ann Loder said, "but just for this one call. Don't use it again. Apologize. Act embarrassed, tell them it's personal. Turn away from them and stay right where you are—they'll probably go on talking in Russian."

Cate did as she was told. Stepanov turned back to Nakhimov and continued.

"The other guy's going to have half an ear on your conversation," Ann said, "so throw in something every so often. You need to know that a woman named Olya Serova has just checked in to Nakhimov's reservation, but she's moved upstairs to Suite 316. Her real name is Irina Ismaylova, and she is the woman Leo told us about who used to be Sergei's lover. We don't know what she's doing in the picture here. Tell Stepanov after the others have left. They don't know she's here yet."

Cate mumbled a few phrases about what one friend said about another friend.

"Leo wants you to get close to the woman if you can. His guess is that she's definitely going to be seeing Krupatin. Ask Stepanov if he knows anything about Bykov. Leo knows nothing. We'll get back to you."

Suddenly the line was dead. Cate acted out a few more exchanges and hung up just in time to hear Stepanov saying to Nakhimov in English, "I wouldn't work too hard at being a prick. It rarely pays off in the end."

"You can testify to that," Nakhimov said.

"You two sound like a couple of pussies," Bykov said, lighting a cigarette. "It's not the first time any of us has gone into something like this not knowing whether to piss or puke. Why don't you try to relax until you can find out what's to get excited about?"

"If you only came to pay your respects," Stepanov said, "consider them paid. Do you have any messages for me?"

Cate noticed that his face was still wet, and she wondered if perspiration had replaced the shower water.

"No messages," Nakhimov said with authority.

"Good," Stepanov said with unmistakable finality. He stood in the middle of the room like a glowering Cossack.

Irina had replicated this moment many times. Wrapped in a hotel robe, she sat in the dark, near the window of a hotel she had never slept in before, and looked at the lights of a city she had never visited before. Or perhaps she had been there before, but always as a stranger. When she was not in St. Petersburg, she was a stranger in all cities. Perhaps Zurich was not so lonely for her, or Paris. But those were exceptions. She never could relax in any of the others, and this one was no different.

She drank vodka and thought of the people below her. Stepanov. She had seen too much of Stepanov. Over the years she had watched him simmer under Krupatin's lordship. But there could be only one top man, and Krupatin had brutally claimed that position for himself. Not that it made any distinguishable difference. A sea of people had died at a spoken word from Stepanov as well. And before his word carried that kind of weight, he had done the work himself. She had heard talk. Ever since he had taken over the operation in the United States, he had had to restrain himself. The level of violence he wreaked elsewhere had to be reined in here. Though the profits could be enormous, the law enforcement agencies were better than their counterparts around the world. The risk was greater.

Grigori Izvarin was just another version in the shape of a new generation. Young and handsome and well trained by the KGB before it folded, he represented Krupatin's vanguard. He had the good sense to use his head once in a while, but he was impatient, and brutality was close at hand. He was bisexual and vain and ambitious. He was mercurial and absolutely untrustworthy.

Valery Volkov. Yet another variation on a theme, and by now she was beginning to understand the music very well indeed.

And of course Stepanov would have a woman. He dragged them along everywhere he went or picked them up wherever he happened to find himself. He and Krupatin had that in common too. They were like adolescent boys, always wanting to see under yet another woman's skirts, always peeping down women's blouses, wanting to touch them. The fact was, if that was as far as it went, it might be considered prurient or wanton but not necessarily destructive. But neither man ever found enough satisfaction in these pubescent curiosities. Long ago, when they were in fact pubescent, these men/boys had been awakened to the psychology of necrophagia. In one way or another death served them; it became nourishment for them and sustained them. A steady diet of death kept them alive.

The telephone rang. She didn't even flinch. She took another drink of the clear vodka. The telephone rang in the darkness, and she listened to its bleating, bleating, bleating. Lifting her wrist, she looked at her watch. By now, the overeager Izvarin would have discovered her arrival. And Stepanov would know. They would have talked by now, these two creatures. They would be discombobulated by a woman's name in the register. They would be suspicious because she had moved to the top floor.

The vodka had begun to soothe and calm her, to smooth out her nerves, to make her care less. The vodka and the darkness allowed her to retreat, to withdraw into a womb from which she could see only the lights of the city and none of its wickedness.

She carried time with her into the womb, time on her wrist.

The telephone rang and rang. Then stopped.

Thirty-three

THE BAR WAS CROWDED with people having drinks as they waited for their tables in the restaurant. It was a popular place, a place to be seen, hip and up to the minute.

"It's almost like the old days, the early eighties," the brunette said, taking the plastic toothpick and olive out of her drink and testing it with a sip and then a big gulp. She knocked the ash off her cigarette and turned around to glare at the guy on the barstool behind her, who had just jabbed her in the small of her back without even noticing.

"You've sure had a hell of a month," her friend said. The women were facing each other, opposite elbows on the bar, their long legs crossed on the high stools, hems to mid-thigh, leaning in to each other to talk.

"Can you believe it? *I* can't believe it. Incredible." She pulled on her cigarette, leaving fresh red on the filter. "Remember a couple of years ago I had this German guy who came into town and was buying property for a not-to-be-identified client, and he paid in full right there on the spot, writing checks on a Brussels bank?"

"From London—the guy was from London and bought a place in the Amberson Towers."

"Yeah, right. Paid one mil five for that. Slam-bam."

"God . . ." Her friend stretched out the word enviously.

"Well, he's back in town." The brunette held up her crossed fingers. "And I'm showing him some more toys."

"Jesus. I wish I had a big one like that—a guy who kept coming back for more."

The double-entendre was unintentional, and when they both realized what she had said, they burst out laughing.

"I'll tell you what, though," the brunette said, puffing on her cigarette and then rocking her wrist back, elbow on the bar, talking past the smoke. "That whole thing was a little strange. After this guy bought that Amberson property, he put an English guy in charge of building it out. He wouldn't use any of the remodeling people on the Amberson's recommended list, no—used his own people. Had them come in there and line *all* the exterior walls with lead sheeting. Soundproofing. I mean, they just rolled the stuff out like you're putting on wallpaper. You have any idea how expensive that is? *Way* expensive! Then they put another layer of gyp board on top of that, painted it. New molding. Real slick." She shook her head.

Her friend tugged at the hem of her skirt, which was working up past expectations, almost up to tutu level. She had the figure for it and didn't mind the guy four barstools down peeking past his date's shoulder to take in the creeping hemline. But she didn't want the damn thing up around her waist either. She smiled at the guy, a kind of oh-so-embarrassed smile, and tugged again.

"Then this client's a computer freak, too," the brunette said, picking up a pretzel dusted with cayenne pepper. "So here comes another special crew. Spent a month in there doing some kind of special installations. He's afraid of 'hacker intruders,' so he has special crypto crap put in." She bit into the pretzel and chewed. "Digital stuff, I don't know. Same way with the telephones. Everything was very special, very secure, first-rate. Lots-o'-dough is what it was."

"You ever meet the guy?"

"No way." She shook her head, sipped her drink to calm her

burning taste buds, puffed on her cigarette, and blew smoke up into the smoky air above the bar. "I don't know of anybody who's ever met him. Tell you the truth, I don't think these third-party people have ever met him. It's like he was Jack Nicholson or somebody. Has all this stuff done in somebody else's name, has everything set up the way he likes, then one day he just puts on some sunglasses, drives into the garage, takes the elevator up, and there he is. Hell, he could be living there a year and no one would know it unless somebody just happens to get a glimpse of him coming or going. And this guy, you wouldn't recognize him if you saw him. I mean, he's not famous, just rich." She took another big swig of her drink.

"Then you don't even really know his name. His lawyers and bankers did all the transactions of the sale. Just his people in London."

"You got it. That's right. Listen, there are a lot of people like that coming in here again. All kinds of Arabs. French. Mexicans. Canadians. Germans. Japanese. Things are definitely looking up."

She paused and looked around, gazing down into the restaurant, frowning. "Jesus, what about our table?"

"I was surprised," Izvarin said as he strode impatiently along the corridor to the main lobby of the Chateau Touraine. "I thought Valentin would know who was going to be taking the other suite."

"Maybe he does and just didn't say anything," Volkov offered. "That's the way you handled him."

"The prick. What did you think about his woman?"

"Very pretty. Good tits."

"Tits." Izvarin rolled his eyes.

It was relatively early in the evening, and the lobby of the Touraine was not by any means sparsely populated. But even with the milling guests, the inevitable loiterers waiting amid the splendors, people for whom time seemed at their beck and call as they drank daiquiris and manhattans against a backdrop of ornate *boiserie*, beneath chandeliers, lounging on damask sofas and armchairs—even with all of this, Izvarin had only to turn his lean, elegant frame toward the registration desk for the hotel staff to move in his direction like a school of herring.

"Yes, Mr. Nakhimov?" the young woman said, her blue eyes

centered on him, her only wish to accommodate him. He preened inwardly that she knew his name.

"I was wondering if my colleague had arrived yet."

"Oh, yes indeed. She registered half an hour ago."

She?! Nakhimov managed to control his face.

"Well, I didn't make the reservation in her name because I didn't know which representative the commission was sending," he said, leading the woman to offer assistance.

"Oh, I see." She moved to the computer, tapped a few keys, waited a millisecond. She looked up, smiling.

"Ms. Serova. Olya Serova."

"Wonderful." Nakhimov beamed.

At the lobby entrance, the ever-watchful doorman had Izvarin's car waiting for him only moments after he reached the steps of the porte cochere.

He tipped the young man who brought the car and held the door for him, and slipped in behind the wheel. Volkov got in on the passenger side, and the rented black Cadillac motored softly away from the Touraine, through the iron front gates and into the tunnel of dark pines that took them to the open city streets.

"Who the fuck is Olya Serova!" Izvarin blurted suddenly as they cleared the front gates.

"What?"

"Olya Serova! She checked in to the reserved suite."

"A woman?"

"Yes! A woman, yes. You ever heard of her?"

"No. I've never heard of Serova," Volkov said.

"And she changed suites!" Izvarin was livid. "What is Sergei doing? Did he bring *his* woman along too? Imperious bitch, changing suites. I'm going to go up there when we get back and find out what's going on."

"I'd think twice about that, Gori," Volkov said.

"What the hell does that mean?"

"We've been through this kind of thing before with Sergei—not being told anything, just being sent on a trip, knowing we'll receive our instructions when it is time to receive them. Sergei does this."

"Not to me. Not in a long time, anyway."

"Not to me either. But what are you going to do, tell him you are too important now to be treated this way?" Volkov shrugged.

"I am just telling you, if he wanted you to contact her, he would have told you to. I wouldn't do it."

"You're not going to do it," Izvarin snapped. "I am."

"Go ahead, then."

"If this is such an important trip, I don't know what he's doing letting his pussy get in the way," Izvarin went on.

"We'd better get down to business," Volkov said.

"Shit," Izvarin swore, and then shut up.

Both men had memorized the route. The first thing they did was to drive somewhat indirectly to their destination, though anyone watching them would not know this, for they did not stop but cruised slowly by without changing their speed or braking to indicate they wanted to look it over. Then they began dry-cleaning.

It took them an hour and a half, not at all an unusual length of time for such a process. First they went through a whole routine of double-backs and turnarounds, going in and out of residential driveways and into dead-end streets. Then they got on the South Loop and drove around the south side of the city to Alemeda, where they turned southwest onto a stretch of street that ran out of the city proper and into the flats—scattered houses, fields, only a few side roads. It was an excellent place to catch a tail. When they got to one of the most deserted stretches, they pulled off to the side of the road, cut their motor, and got out of the car. Both men leaned on the car and looked up at the sky. They were familiar with light plane surveillance and waited nearly twenty minutes in the quiet absence of traffic, listening to the skies, before getting back into the car and continuing. Finally back in the city, they drove to an upscale residential area not many miles from their hotel and pulled into the parking lot of a health club.

Izvarin waited in the car while Volkov took a black workout bag out of the back seat and walked across the parking lot and into the club. The place was bright, new, and luxurious. Mirrors everywhere, a health bar. Glass walls so that you could see the weight rooms, the racquetball courts, a juice bar, a track, a pool. It was so late there were only a few people scattered throughout the club, two in the weight room, a couple in the juice bar, a lone man swimming laps.

Volkov knew exactly where to go, for this too had been well rehearsed. He walked past the front desk, past the massage room, and into the men's dressing area. Without hesitating, he moved through a maze of lockered enclosures, past a solitary bather in the showers, and into an enclosure near the back of the men's section.

He rounded a corner to a dead-end aisle and approached locker 276. He was the only person in the dressing room. Reaching into his pocket, he pulled out a key. He opened the locker and took out an athletic bag just like the one he was carrying and replaced it with his own. He closed the locker and made sure it locked. Then he picked up the new bag and retraced his steps to the front of the club. The bag was heavy, and he had to strain to walk naturally, so he wouldn't look like he was lugging it.

Just as he was making his way to the front door, he stopped, turned back a few steps, and walked up to a pay telephone tucked in behind a screen of palms. He put a coin in the slot and dialed a number. He waited and hung up the receiver. Then he put in another quarter and dialed again. His party answered, and he conducted a short conversation, no longer than four minutes.

Without any further diversion, he walked out the front door and back across the parking lot to the black Cadillac.

"You got it?" Izvarin asked as Volkov slammed the door.

"Got it."

Izvarin started the car. "It took you longer than I thought it would."

"Yeah, me too, but I stopped twice."

"What happened?" Izvarin pulled back onto the city streets.

"Some guy stopped me to ask if I had seen someone. I think he was more your type."

"What was that? Thirty seconds. That's nothing."

"Then I saw two women helping each other on these weight machines. They were wearing bright, tight little exercise suits, and one of them was pushing some weights up and down, up and down. She had these great tits."

"Open the damn bag," Izvarin snapped.

Volkov grinned and unzipped the bag. "Okay," he said, looking inside, "we have two TEC-9s with thirty-six-round magazines, two Smith & Wesson 659s. Half a dozen boxes of Black Talons."

"Well, they got something right," Izvarin said.

They started back toward the Chateau Touraine, driving in silence for a while. The smell of the oiled munitions intruded in the car, the metallic odors of steel and lead.

"I think Stepanov knew about her," Izvarin said, picking up the old thread. "He knew. That's why he brought his own woman."

"Stepanov always has a woman, Gori. You know that."

"But something big is going on here, and I can't believe he would let one get in the way if he didn't already know this Serova would be here."

"Then you think she's only Sergei's sleeping partner."

"What else? I don't think he's ready to start turning operations over to women. She pissed me off, but I'm not worried about her. What worries me is that Stepanov knows what's going on here and I don't. Why didn't Sergei inform me about this? What's the situation here that he can talk to Valentin and not to me?"

Volkov shook his head. "You're sounding like a jealous old queen, Gori."

"Screw yourself."

"Look, you don't even know what business we have here. If Sergei was clear about anything, it was that we were to do only what we are told to do. Exactly what we are told to do. I don't know what is going on here either, but I don't want any part of some harebrained scheme to improvise."

"Talking to her is hardly an improvisation. My God."

"Unless he doesn't want us to talk to her."

"How can that be?" Izvarin's tone was shrill. The fact was— and Volkov knew this—Izvarin was almost beside himself precisely because he didn't know what was going on. He was an inside man, very close to Krupatin, and he was not used to being treated once again like a common hireling who simply did what he was told. Long ago he had left behind that way of life, and he was frantic to know why he seemed to be in that position once again. It was as if a general had been bumped back to the level of an enlisted man. For Izvarin it was humiliating, a bad dream.

"Wait a little while and see what happens next," Volkov cautioned. "Play Sergei's game with a little patience. Look at Stepanov. I imagine he's just as much in the dark as we are. It's clear he doesn't have a clue. Whatever's happening, it's got to happen this way or Sergei wouldn't be doing it."

"Stepanov," Izvarin said with a surly evenness.

"Look. We are here. We have our positions. We know where

we stand. All of us are lieutenants. Don't get your nose twisted out of shape just because you can't read Sergei's mind. None of us can. So relax."

If Izvarin did not exactly relax, at least he had calmed to a smoldering silence by the time they drove back through the Touraine's front gates and pulled into the aureate light of the porte cochere.

Thirty-four

STEPANOV CLOSED THE DOOR behind Nakhimov and Bykov, turned toward Cate, put a vertical forefinger up to his lips, and pointed to the bedroom.

"Listen," he said, "why don't you go ahead and shower? Then we'll get a drink or something."

He went into the bathroom and turned on the shower, then returned to the bedroom and pulled the door closed behind him. Even though he was aware that the room was to be swept regularly by Jernigan's tech team, he stood close to Cate's face and talked in a hoarse whisper.

"What the hell was that telephone call?" he rasped.

"It was Ann—"

"Are they crazy? Are they fucking crazy!"

"Look," Cate said, stepping back from him, "there's no need for this stage-whispering. That was important. She wanted you to know that a woman had checked into the extra suite."

"A woman?" Stepanov narrowed his eyes, puzzled.

"She registered as Olya Serova, but they've identified her as Irina Ismaylova."

Stepanov's eyes changed, pulled taut, then flattened, but his face did not change. "Incredible," he said, letting his eyes drift aside as he considered this. Then he cut them back at her. "You know about this woman?"

"Ometov's briefed me."

"Okay. This is very strange indeed." He turned his head aside and wiped his face with the arm of the bathrobe. "You know what? I don't think Krupatin is going to show up here at all."

"Why?"

Stepanov's eyes moved away again, as though he couldn't look at her while he was thinking. Close to him like this, she noticed tiny pockmarks in the deep creases on either side of his unattractive mouth.

"I was very surprised," he said, "that Izvarin apparently is as much in the dark as I am about Krupatin's plans here. I'm sure he didn't know about Ismaylova." He turned and walked to a dresser, picked up a pack of cigarettes, and lighted one. "This is very goosey, what is happening here. I don't know about this."

"Leo wants to know if you know Bykov. Do you know anything about him?"

Stepanov nodded and held a huge inhalation of smoke inside his chest. He let it out slowly.

"Valery Volkov." He wiped his face again. The moisture was indeed perspiration. "Another former KGB. He was a sabotage expert in Afghanistan. Years ago Sergei put him to work organizing the drug routes out of Afghanistan, Tajikistan, Kazakhstan, and Iran. He was also responsible for feeding money to the radical Islamic groups in Pakistan who raised hell in different places around the world whenever Krupatin created a bloodbath to eliminate rivals and wanted it covered by some terrorist story. These people could be manipulated, and Volkov was very good at it. So he's spent most of his time in Krupatin's eastern business. That's probably why Leo hasn't come across him."

Stepanov shook his head and began walking around the room. "Whatever Sergei is up to, he has brought together a strange crew to accomplish it."

"Do you think they're on to you?" Cate didn't know whether

this was a stupid question or not, but she wanted to know what he thought.

He shook his head some more. "I won't know that until I talk to Sergei. If he had his doubts about me, he wouldn't tell these guys."

"Leo told me that Irina Ismaylova had dropped out of sight," Cate said.

"She might have dropped out of Leo's sight, but not Sergei's," Stepanov said. "Not for long, anyway. When she disappeared to take the drug cure in Zurich, she was able to hide from him for nearly two years. But then he found her."

He paced back and forth in front of the glass doors to the courtyard, looking like a figure in a museum diorama.

"And she had a baby?"

"Yeah, a baby."

"Krupatin's?"

"I don't know. Maybe." He shrugged; the baby didn't interest him. "Then she really disappeared."

"What do you mean?"

"Sergei took the baby and sent it away to live with some people, and Irina just vanished. I don't know what happened to her. I knew she wasn't dead. People saw her, but just here and there, now and again. Nobody knew anything, and nobody was asking questions. She became another one of Sergei's mysteries." He pulled on his cigarette. "Shit, Sergei has a hell of a lot of mysteries."

Cate watched Stepanov fall silent, his cigarette burning down in his hand as he stared at the floor in front of him, his body, if not his mind, momentarily stalled.

"I take it this isn't developing as you had imagined, is it?" Cate asked.

"Oh," Stepanov said, looking up from his preoccupation, "it's not that. You never know how it's going to develop with Sergei when he decides to do one of these magic operations. It's one of his favorite techniques, and if you are around him long enough, you are not so shaken by it." He paused and smoked, one hand jammed into the huge pocket of his robe. "Unless, of course, you start to imagine that you are not part of the plan but instead you are the object of the plan."

He gave her another one of his grim smiles. The hand holding the cigarette rose up and he tapped himself on the chest. "And that is where I am, Catherine, wondering if I am going to be terribly surprised here."

Cate looked at him a moment, watched him return to a deep pondering posture, holding his cigarette next to his chest as he forgot about her. She tried to put herself in Hain's position. What would Hain want to know right now? What questions could she ask Stepanov that they hadn't already asked him? What questions might he be inclined to answer if she asked him, rather than Hain and Loder? What questions might he answer now, as a result of the developments of the last two hours, that he might not have answered before? Suddenly her responsibility to draw out information seemed daunting.

"Valentin," she said, doing her best to sound like a woman rather than an agent, trying to make use of the attributes that had caused her to be chosen in the first place, "I'm going to go ahead and shower."

He nodded, but didn't really come out of his abstraction. Cate walked to the closet where they both had hung their clothes and began to undress. She had no idea how difficult this moment was going to be. She couldn't even imagine it. But as she unbuttoned her blouse with her back to him, she found it to be the easiest thing in the world. It was nothing. Probably because she knew that nothing was going to result from it, and probably because the other events were so momentous that they overrode the timidity of taking off her clothes. It was pretty sobering to be in the same room with a man whom everyone clearly thought would be dead in the near future. It was not something that added an element of titillation to the situation.

But she knew that Stepanov was more used to close-range danger than she was, and she knew that it had never been a retardant to his sexual drive. She could only hope that seeing her with few or no clothes would put him in a different frame of mind. Maybe when she got out of the shower she could make a drink and they could talk. Erika had said she should try to relax with Stepanov, not be so defensive. She realized that she was going to have to be more accessible to him if she was going to get him to spill what he was thinking.

She took off her blouse and hung it on a hanger, unbuttoned the waistband of her skirt and let it fall to the floor, then hung up the skirt. Then she removed her slip and began peeling off her pantyhose. Standing with her back to him, in only her panties and bra, she took a robe off the hanger on her side of the closet and walked into the bathroom and closed the door—but only halfway. She removed her underclothes, dropped them on the floor, and got into the shower, which was still running from Stepanov's having turned it on fifteen minutes earlier.

As she showered, she kept an eye on the half-open door, and sure enough, as predictable as a compass needle, Stepanov appeared in the open space, not right at the door but back a little way in the room. From there he watched her, and she watched him, catching glimpses of him as he stood with one hand in his robe pocket, the other rising and falling periodically as he continued to smoke. She did not try to hide anything from him, not even the fact that she had followed his instructions and shaved between her legs.

As she finished and came out of the shower, his image disappeared, and she dried off in privacy, wondering what he was thinking in the room alone. She dried her hair but did not put on more clothes. Instead she wrapped her robe around her and went into the bedroom. Stepanov was not there. She went to the bedroom door and found him in the living room, mixing a drink.

"What are you making?" she asked.

"Gin and tonic," he said. "A lot of gin, a splash of tonic. Do you want something?"

"I'll take some of that," she said. "But—"

"Less gin, more tonic."

"That's right."

She noticed that the room service cart was gone, but there was still the faint, lingering odor of food. She sat on the sofa, but when Stepanov turned around he tilted his head toward the bedroom.

"Come on," he said and walked into the room.

Cate swallowed hard, got up from the sofa, and followed him. He closed the door behind her, handed her her drink, and then walked away and sat in one of the armchairs near the French doors that led out to the garden. She moved past him and sat in an opposite armchair. He looked at her, raised his glass in a toasting gesture. She did the same, and they both drank.

"How is that?" he asked.

"Perfect. Thanks."

Stepanov's hair, which had been slicked back with water from his shower, had dried, loosening its coifed grip so that it was falling loosely over his ears and forehead. He ran his fingers through it self-consciously. She may have been looking at it.

"This is a hell of a situation," he said. He wasn't smiling this time. It was simply a statement of his predicament.

She shrugged. "I'm not really sure what kind of a situation it is. I feel pretty much in the dark." She took a drink. "To tell you the truth, I'm feeling a little at loose ends. This . . . All of this seems, well, almost random, not very well planned. I didn't know that so much of it would have to be played by ear."

"You haven't worked too much undercover," he said. "I thought so."

She looked at him. "How does that make you feel?"

"It scares the shit out of me." Again he wasn't smiling.

"Why didn't you say something to Ann, or Ometov? There were other women."

"No. The others would have been maybes. You are a sure thing." He drank, not sipping but drinking, until he had consumed half the tall, thin glass. He looked at her, holding the last swallow in his mouth a moment before he finally let it go down.

"You're talking about me being bait," she said.

He nodded. "I just don't know how you are going to react when the shark takes a bite." He raised his head. "That's what you would understand if you were more experienced. I really like this phrase, 'to play it by ear.' That's the way it is. You know, you have this objective. In our case, to see how much of Krupatin's onion we can peel away. And then you have to make a decision to go for it. Everything else in between has to be played by ear."

He looked at her. He held his glass in one hand, and with the other hand he used his forefinger and thumb to stroke the glass downward, wiping away the sweat: a continuous gesture.

"Sometimes," he said, "the people you are playing with are tone-deaf. But you don't discover that until it's too late. That's when people die."

Cate looked at him and sipped her drink. "Where do you think I'm most likely to make a mistake with him?"

He studied her. "You may be too smart for him to believe you. You may be too interested in him."

"He's good-looking."

"You can notice him, let him notice you noticing him, but don't move in his direction. Let him come to you. You can enjoy his attention. That's a natural reaction, but I wouldn't ask him any questions, no matter how innocent they may seem to you. What you say and what he hears will be two different things."

"But you said earlier you didn't think he was coming at all."

He turned his head aside in impatience. "Look, I was thinking with my mouth open. A mistake. There's no doubt he will be here—Izvarin and Volkov assure that. And Irina. Everything points to that."

He took a mouthful of his gin and looked at her bare feet. She wasn't sure he was seeing them; he was thinking, and his eyes had focused there perhaps without his being aware of it. She felt as if she were entirely naked.

"Let's say," Stepanov said, "just for argument, that Sergei has discovered my . . . new situation, and he wants to kill me. Then what? Replace me here with one of these other two? Izvarin? Volkov?" He shook his head. "Neither of them has any experience with the U.S. I do. That's why I'm here." He took another drink. "More likely he has suspicions about me, maybe. These two men are here to take a look. Izvarin would like to see me disappear anyway, so of course he will say, yes, yes, the bastard's a traitor. As for Volkov, I don't know. He doesn't suck up like Izvarin. I don't know about Volkov."

He raised his glass and finished off the gin.

"And what about Irina?"

"That," Stepanov said, "is a puzzle." But he didn't seem too bothered by it. It didn't seem to cause him any anxiety. He looked at his empty glass.

"You want some more?" he asked, holding up his glass.

Thirty-five

WHEN THE DOORBELL CHIMED in Irina's suite, it startled her awake. She had fallen asleep on the sofa, curled up in her robe, unaware that she had gotten chilled by the air-conditioning sometime during the past hour. When she awoke she was cold, and she wasn't entirely sure what she had heard. Then the chimes sounded a second time.

Expecting Stepanov or Izvarin, she stood, snugged up her robe, and walked through her bedroom to the door. When she opened it, two dark men were standing in front of her, one of them holding a finger in front of his lips. He was young and handsome. Italian.

The two men came into the room, and Irina closed the door. One of the young men leaned close to her ear.

"Please, Don Carlo and the Chinese wish to see you," he said softly and slowly, his breath warming her ear, his cologne reminding her of his youth. "Please don't talk. Dress. You will be safe with us."

And she knew she would be.

They escorted her down the hallway to a stairwell and then followed her all the way to the basement, where they made their way to the hotel's kitchens. From there it was a short walk to the loading docks at the rear of the chateau, where the three of them stepped through the open doors of a laundry van. The van pulled away and left the grounds of the hotel, and within ten minutes they were pulling into the underground parking garage of a hotel near the Greenway Plaza. When the laundry truck stopped, they stepped out and got into a dark Mercedes. The driver started the car, and they circled up the maze of ramps and left the garage.

Knowing nothing of the city, Irina had no idea where they were going. The large car was gloomy inside. One of the young men sat in the front seat with the driver and the other sat in the back seat with her, well over into his corner. These were Bontate's Sicilians. A radio emitted short bursts of communication. No one spoke. They were taking their job very seriously.

Though they remained in the city, they drove for what seemed to be miles through thickly wooded streets, the car's headlights illuminating a green corridor ahead of them. The houses were large, even grand. High walls sprang up on either side of the lights, and they passed gated drives with entry lights set into the stones, softly lighting the driveways. The car slowed and then turned and slipped through a set of narrow gates. Irina saw guards standing in the green shadows cast by landscape lights.

They stopped at the front door of a modern home, a seemingly new two-story structure that was nestled among ancient trees. Its angular facade was oddly backlighted, so that it seemed to hide its contents behind a flat front embossed with simple interlocking geometric designs.

The young men escorted Irina up three short flights of three steps each set into a thick groundcover and entered the house from an entry positioned at a right angle to the facade. They came into a high, vaulted foyer; a stairway of seven red granite steps rose to another level. On either side of the stairs a waterfall took up the rest of the space in the enormous entry, each fall descending over scores of terraces of polished black granite that rose nearly ten feet high and easily twice that in width. Though the water slipped over the granite at a gentle velocity, its sheer volume produced a resonating, soft burbling, an aural magnet that reflexively drew her attention away from everything else.

Still following the two Sicilians, Irina made her way up the steps and down a broad, straight corridor with oblique lighting from the floor and the ceiling. The beams of pale light from above and below converged rapidly at the far end, where a huge stone circle was embedded in the wall, forcing one to turn either left or right. But before they were halfway down the corridor they turned aside, where two red doors parted, retracting into the walls, and Irina was ushered into a large sunken rectangular room where Wei Tsing and Carlo Bontate were sitting amid plush mandarin-red modern furniture.

Wei stood and came toward her, up three steps, extending a hand, which she took. He kissed her hand.

"Welcome to my home," he said, and held her hand as they stepped down into the living room.

Bontate stood as they approached. He was wearing a suit, and a well-cut suit too. He looked rather handsome, with his sun-darkened skin off-setting the dark suit and white shirt. His hair was carefully barbered, and his amber eyes settled on her as he stood and shook her hand. He did not smile, but his beautiful eyes handled her gently.

"Would you like anything?" Wei asked softly. He was once again wearing a white dinner jacket, dark trousers, and opera slippers.

"Nothing," Irina said.

"Then, please, sit down," Wei said, waiting until she did before he sat also, as did Bontate.

Irina looked at the two men in front of her. "Sergei said you would contact me. I didn't expect it would be this way. Or this late."

"Oh, we keep very late hours," Wei said comfortably. But there was no small talk. He got right to the point. "We need to decide how all of this is going to happen. The logistics of coming and going."

"Coming and going where?" Irina asked.

"Here," Wei said.

"Sergei hasn't told you anything different, has he?" Bontate asked.

"So far he's told me nothing," she said.

"You don't know where he's staying," Wei said, asking with a statement.

She shook her head. "I rather thought we might have our meetings at the chateau."

"That would require us to move about too much," Wei said. "Though we are not in the same predicament as Sergei, neither do we wish to advertise our presence. This is more discreet. We can guarantee you won't be followed here and therefore can guarantee our anonymity. Don Carlo's men will always arrange your passage from the Chateau Touraine by whatever means they deem necessary. Sometimes they will bring you directly here, sometimes they will transfer you to my people somewhere in the city. The point is, they will always provide your transit to guarantee you are not followed."

"We have people staying at the chateau also," Bontate said. "We know about Izvarin and Volkov. What are they doing here?"

"I have no idea."

"What is Stepanov doing here?"

"I don't know. Sergei said he had business with him."

"Who is the woman? Did she come from New York with him?"

She shrugged. "I have no idea. I haven't yet spoken to either of them, or to Izvarin or Volkov. Anyway, you know Stepanov better than I do, and I understand that that is his habit."

They looked at her, Wei with a vague smile on his smooth lips, Bontate as sober as a village priest.

"Wei and I have talked," Bontate said. "We want this series of meetings to end in four days. Like Sergei, we would like to be gone as soon as possible. We brought a substantial number of security people, and regardless of how careful we might be, such a number will inevitably attract attention."

"As soon as Sergei contacts you," Wei said, "we want you to tell him we want his response to the following proposals. It is understood that this is the first of numerous meetings among us with the purpose of developing broad cooperative efforts. We have already put our accountants through a rigorous examination of the financial potential in these plans, and all of us agree it can be enormously beneficial. But these are first steps. We want to develop them methodically, carefully. The days of gangsterism are history. What we are doing now is developing a more efficient way to cultivate the potential of the American market."

"You don't have to remember all of this," Bontate said. "Before you leave we will give you a laser-disk recording of this meeting, which we want you to give to Sergei. The disk has . . . certain properties designed for security. It cannot be read by common machines. Sergei has all the technological details and has access to the proper equipment."

"Number one," Wei began, "we agree, as in previous conversations, that Sergei can have the right to move in on all the East European entities already operating in the U.S.—the Albanians, Yugoslavs, Serbs, Croats, all of them. We agree that these countless free-lance groups need to be brought under an oversight organization.

"Number two, Carlo will provide RICO legal consultants. Any of us who are developing enterprises that will put us in danger of susceptibility to these statutes must meet with his legal consultants in setting up the enterprise. This has two obvious benefits. First, the consultants will be able to provide legal advice that can help us avoid stupid mistakes. Second, meeting will keep the three of us informed about what the others are doing, the directions in which they are moving, so we don't overlap enterprises and create unnecessary violence. It also means that if we are planning enterprises that could benefit from mutual cooperation, we will be able to see it early enough to make the most of such arrangements.

"Number three, all international operations—any enterprise that requires regular trips across American borders—are to be coordinated through my international unit. Once again, we can benefit from established transshipment lanes whether we are handling drugs, arms, money for laundering, any kind of product. There is no need to duplicate efforts, that is, to have the drug operations develop their own networks, the arms and munitions dealers develop yet others, and on and on. My international unit will be responsible for coordinating all border crossings. This means both Carlo and Sergei will have to give up some traditional connections to their operations with the Colombians, the Mexicans, and other Latin Americans. The Latin Americans will have to be informed of this in detail. Some of them will not want to cooperate. We will have to explain to them how this is going to benefit not only us but them as well.

"Number four, the issue of legitimate business enterprises. Our laundered funds are going to have to be invested more intelligently than in the past. We must distribute capital investments more wisely. We have received the report from the accountants regarding adjustments in our shell companies. With the new changes in the U.S. Congress, our people feel there are new opportunities for us if we re-examine our shell companies' strategies. We can explain this in more detail after we agree on the basic premise that we hire these people to oversee this for us. Remember, these are men educated at Harvard and Stanford, Americans who understand the subtle complexities better than we do. We're letting too much money get away from us because we are not placing our funds in the most efficient high-yield opportunities. We can do better.

"Number five, regarding a centralized counterintelligence section . . ."

Irina sat listening to this methodical list of planned criminal enterprises that these three powerful men had begun to put together. It was clear that international organized crime was going to be guided from boardrooms. The only place it would appear to the public to be "criminal" was at the street level, where the coarser elements of these money machines did their dirty work. She could not help thinking of the misery these men were creating for common men and women all over the world, the suffering they sowed in order to reap prosperity for themselves. They rested in luxury, their pampered bones cushioned by the sighs of anguish rising up from the millions they disregarded, the countless number to whom they laid waste to satisfy their insatiable avarice.

Wei droned on. As in Paris, occasionally a silent maid would drift in on stockinged feet and leave a drink or a platter of canapés. These young women appeared to be Hispanic, though they were dressed like the maids in Paris, their white stockings adding a strange note of another age to the modern setting. Wei would stop long enough to eat a few bites and then move on. He never referred to notes, never paused or hesitated to deliberate over a word or phrase, never uttered a superfluous syllable.

Bontate sat on the other side of him, a dark figure amid the scarlet, and watched her. He smoked. He drank—wine, she noticed. Occasionally he ate canapés. His amber eyes were slightly heavy but never dull, never anything but shrewd and calm, as calm as they had been when he had held his lover's hands in Palermo.

Eventually Wei finished. He picked up a fresh snifter of brandy just delivered by a dark maid.

"When will you be able to deliver this to him?" Bontate asked Irina.

"I haven't any idea. He said he would contact me."

"Well, this elaborate secrecy seems a bit theatrical to me," Wei said, piqued at the inconvenience and ignoring the irony of such a complaint coming from him. He glanced at Bontate and then back at Irina. "Remind him of the four days."

"I will," she said. "When I have a response, how will I contact you?"

Bontate answered. "An American named Bob Davis checked into the suite across the hall from you shortly after you registered. You must communicate through him. Just knock on his door. Do not call him. A man staying with him is an electronics specialist. We have spent a very large sum of money on various members of the hotel staff for access to various rooms and for information." He lighted a cigarette. "For instance, we know that the FBI is watching all of you."

Irina was stunned, and it must have showed in her face.

"But it is all right," Bontate added with a dismissive wave of his cigarette. "We know who they are. We imagine that by now they have bugged Stepanov's and Izvarin's suites. As for yours, nothing yet, because when you checked into a different suite from the one reserved for you, they were caught off guard, and you have been in there since you arrived. They don't know you're out now. But they will probably get around to it, so be aware of that."

"Do they—Izvarin and Volkov—know about the FBI?"

Bontate shook his head. "We don't think so. Did you know they flew in here in disguise, like a couple of clowns?"

"No."

"The FBI also has directional microphones in the dining rooms," Bontate went on. "You can't discuss anything in those places. Just forget the hotel."

"And you think you can get me in and out of there without the FBI knowing?" she asked. She was seething, but refused to let it show. What in God's name had Sergei done to her?

Carlo Bontate nodded. "Believe me, we are not surprised at the FBI's presence. We expected it, so there is some comfort in knowing we were right. And we were prepared for it, so there's comfort in that too." He drank from his glass of wine, keeping his eyes on her just as he had done at Marineo. "However, we do not believe the FBI knows that Wei and I are here. And that is the way we want to keep it."

"So they were expecting Sergei?"

Wei Tsing nodded. "So it seems. Or, to be more accurate, we think they had some information that he might be coming and so they alerted their customs people. It didn't require much to flag them when they applied for visas. They still watch all the Russians anyway."

"Do you think he knows about the FBI?"

Wei nodded, studying her. "As you said to me one time, Irina, Sergei probably knows exactly what he is doing."

"The FBI is not infallible," Bontate added. "They are a vain organization—excellent, without a doubt—but they hide their failures almost as well as they publicize their successes. We are used to having our way with the FBI more often than the public knows."

She caught the sexual allusion, but it hardly mattered to her. The fact that she was already under surveillance by the FBI was now her paramount concern, second even to the business she still had to do with these two men.

"Actually," Wei said, "we don't really disapprove of Sergei's, ah, extreme precautions regarding himself. We much prefer him to keep his distance from us, considering his personal liabilities. But you are his only connection to us, and we are disappointed that he didn't take more care in keeping you clean."

"But we have that covered," Bontate assured her. "If you can safely communicate with Sergei, we can safely communicate with you. It's just that everyone needs to be . . . aware."

A maid entered through the red doors, a black-and-white shape seen from the corner of Irina's preoccupied eyes. She handed something to Wei, and as she turned Irina absently glanced at her. The woman had looked at Irina too, but was already turning her face away when Irina recognized her. In an instant she remembered the exact movements of the small Asian hands and the fragrance of her skin in the Paris night.

"The laser disk," Wei said, standing and handing the small clear plastic container to her. Moirés of rainbow light reflected off the tiny platinum disk inside.

Without any visible summons, the two young Sicilians came through the mandarin doors and stopped just inside. As before,

Wei took Irina's hand, and then led her up from the large scarlet well of the room.

"I would like you to join me tomorrow evening," he said softly.

She stopped. "You know that can be arranged under the circumstances?"

"Of course." He hesitated. "I know you are in a strange city, but . . . if you wanted to bring a friend . . ."

She nodded and managed to smile. "I think that can be arranged. I will be looking forward to it."

"So will I." He smiled too. "Very much."

Just as she turned to leave, she glanced back at Carlo Bontate, who was standing and waiting for just this brief moment. He nodded at her, his amber eyes curious, searching.

Thirty-six

IRINA SAT in the Mercedes for half an hour, the silence broken only by intermittent bursts from the Sicilians' radios. The transmissions were in Sicilian; she could not understand them. She had no idea how long she would have to wait, nor did she know Bontate's reaction to her message.

It had been a bold step, but she knew that if she were to accomplish anything at all, it only could be done by taking bold steps. Coming out of Wei's house, she literally had trembled as she turned to one of the young men and whispered to him to tell Don Carlo that she needed to speak to him alone tonight. As soon as possible. The young man was very cool. He nodded but made no other gesture. After he had ushered her to the car and closed the door, he said something to the driver, and they waited while he ran back up the steps and reentered the house. He was gone only a few minutes. When he returned, they drove away, straight to the park where they were sitting now, waiting.

Was Bontate telling Wei of her message? Was he discussing it with the Chinese? Would the two men ally against her, or would Bontate keep her request to himself, hear her out first?

She had no way of knowing.

Finally the Sicilians reacted to one of the transmissions. The driver started the car, and they pulled out onto the road once again.

The restaurant they drove to was on a quiet wooded street in an old section of the city that appeared to be residential, with large two- and three-story homes that had the architectural styles of another century. The restaurant was shrouded by a canopy of huge trees, and near the gravel path that led to the front door a small pale-green neon sign hovered just off the ground: L'ANGELO.

Two other Mercedes were parked in front of the restaurant— she saw the drivers slumped behind the steering wheels and knew there were guards out of sight in the shadows. Through the lace curtains that covered the tall windows of the old house, Irina could see people dining in the dim lights of large rooms. She was immediately struck by the European feeling of the setting, as though she were arriving at a restaurant in Rome or Vienna. She took this as a good omen and tried to quell the nervousness twitching at the muscles in her stomach.

The young man in the passenger seat got out, opened the door for her, and walked her to the restaurant entry, where one of the Sicilians she had seen at Wei's met her. He escorted her into one of the dining rooms she had seen from the street. Carlo Bontate was there, sitting at a long table covered with white linen. Two glasses and a fresh bottle of wine sat before him. He was smoking, and he was alone.

Bontate stood, and the bodyguard left the room.

"Thank you for coming alone," she said, approaching the table.

Don Carlo tilted his head deferentially and pulled out a chair for her next to his. The two of them sat isolated at one end of the dining table. He picked up the wine bottle and lifted his eyebrows questioningly.

"Please," she said.

He poured. The glasses were crystal and pinged sharply as the green bottle touched the rims. The facets in the cut glass refracted the light through the rich red wine as he placed her glass in front of her. Voices from other rooms were faint, conversational, and the air smelled of cooking spices and old furniture. Bontate sat back in his chair and picked up his cigarette from the ashtray. He smoked, and then mashed it out. He looked at her but said nothing.

"I assume you have a dossier on me," she said, raising her glass and taking a first sip of the wine.

He nodded unhurriedly. Irina had both forearms on the linen-covered table, her hands touching the wineglass.

"It is not much of a dossier, I would guess."

He shook his head slowly. "No, it isn't."

She really hadn't expected him to admit it.

"It is very difficult for people to get good information out of Russia," she conceded. "Secrecy and lies, our historical métier."

Bontate said nothing. She guessed he did not know the word "métier."

"I am going to tell you my real story," she said. "I am not going to lie to you at all, because I want something from you, and before you will consent to give it to me, I know you will have to believe you can trust me."

Bontate had fixed his brassy eyes on her.

"My real name is Irina Ismaylova," she said, "and during the last three years I have killed eight people for Sergei Krupatin."

Bontate did not move a muscle, but he stopped breathing. The only change in his demeanor was an infinitesimal widening of his golden eyes. Then, unhurriedly, he reached for the pack of cigarettes on the table, took out a fresh one, and lighted it.

Irina began with the day when she met Krupatin on her way home from art classes at the Repin Institute. She had been twenty-two years old. During the next half-hour she took Carlo Bontate through the ten years of her life up to the present. Knowing that everything depended on her ability to gain the trust of this innately incredulous man, she was brutally candid about her personal tragedies, about her unhealthy early attraction to Krupatin, about her addiction to drugs, for which she had thrown away her beloved profession, about the humiliations she had suffered as Krupatin's harlot, about the bleak years of self-hatred. And she went on. She told him of running away from Krupatin, of the Swiss drug rehabilitation clinic, of Félia and their constant moving from city to city throughout Europe, of how Krupatin finally tracked them down.

Then she told him of Félia's disappearance and her introduction to her new career as a professional assassin. She went into detail about the deaths, identifying each hit, where it took place, and when. She knew it was highly likely that Bontate would know of some of these hits, for in Eastern Europe the Sicilians had used the Russians for many of their contract killings. For all she knew, some of the hits might have been done for Bontate himself. Regardless, she knew that the details would ring true, that they would have the air of fact about them.

Her story took her up to the hit on Bolshoy Prospekt and then to the house in South Kensington in London. There she stopped. Her wineglass was empty. She reached for the bottle, but Bontate's hand was there first, and he filled her glass.

"Thank you," she said. But she didn't go on with her story.

"And when did you arrive in London?" he asked.

"Several days ago."

Bontate nodded. "And then you spent a few days there. A day in Paris. A day with me. And you arrived here last night."

"Yes."

"Then there is more to tell yet."

She sipped the wine. She could read nothing in his face, nothing in his manner. He telegraphed nothing. Less sophisticated than Wei, more stoic than Krupatin, he was no less cunning than either and more reticent than both. Her chest grew tight, and she had to concentrate on keeping calm. Now it was time to put everything on the table.

"In South Kensington," she said, "Sergei delivered the dossiers of my next two targets." She leveled her gaze at him. "You and Wei."

This time the golden eyes did not widen, they narrowed. Bontate held a chest full of smoke and swallowed. He exhaled slowly. His eyes left her, turning away for the first time, glancing through the small panes of the room's French doors to the front hallway, where his two bodyguards were waiting, unaware that their boss was discussing his own death sentence just a few feet away. He turned his eyes on her again.

"What the fuck is going on here?" Confusion and fear made him angry, like most men. They felt out of control, and they could not understand or envision a world that they did not control. Irina spoke quickly so he would not have to show his anger. Once he did so, he had to commit. It was a visceral law. It made no sense, but she had seen it more than a few times with any number of men. If they showed their anger, it was a commitment to irrationality.

"I want to make a deal."

"What! Not to kill me?"

"No, not that. Of course not. I decided I was not going to do that a long time ago. I am not a fool."

"What is it, then? What are you talking about?"

"I want to make a deal with you to kill Krupatin."

Bontate gaped at her. This time he could not hide his thoughts behind his eyes. This time she saw his mind racing ahead of her, racing to see what was coming but finding nothing ahead but fog and night.

"Have you talked to Wei too?"

"No."

"Why? Why are you bringing this to me?"

Her voice was almost a whisper. "Because of your daughter."

Bontate flinched at the mention of the child. He glared at her, his eyes molten, his face engorged with anger, his round cheeks flushing, swelling. He leaned forward in his chair, about to stand, she thought, perhaps about to fly into a rage. Horror filled her as she realized she had miscalculated, and then suddenly his face froze, the tumescence of passion began to subside, his eyes began to cool. His mind had found an anchor. He sat back in his chair and studied her.

"Your daughter," he said. "You believe I will agree to bring your daughter out of Russia."

She nodded. "For killing Krupatin."

"Christ." He shook his head slowly.

She rushed ahead. "Signor Bontate, I cannot do this anymore. Not anymore. I have to stop—I must. But . . . I want my daughter. I want her desperately. I want her back from this Satan, and I want to see him in hell, where he belongs. I have money in Swiss and Belgian accounts. A lot of money. Irina Ismaylova and her daughter will vanish. I know how to do that, to disappear into a new life."

Bontate studied her, his golden eyes penetrating her, creating veins of gold inside her, permeating her with his understanding. He had to make a decision. This was either an opportunity or a trap—or a disaster in the making. Deciding such questions was the marrow of his existence. This was how he grew rich, how he thrived and how he survived: weighing the risks of doing business with people whose lives extruded into the extremes of human experience.

She watched all of this judgment moving, seeking balance, in the molten ore of his eyes.

"It is impossible," he said.

She felt hot inside. "No."

"How the hell do you expect me to find your daughter in that country?"

"Your people . . . his people . . . I know you have communications, contacts inside Russia. You can do it."

He shook his head. "Even if I could, it would take months."

"I have waited years. A few months is nothing."

"You could help?"

"No. If I do this, I cannot go back to Russia for a long while. This will cause an upheaval in the *mafiya*. There will be killing, a lot of killing, until someone takes Sergei's place. I am too close to Sergei to survive what will happen after his death."

He nodded; he knew she was right. Lighting another cigarette, he studied her through the smoke until it drifted from in front of his eyes.

"What if I refuse to do this?"

She knew he would ask. And she knew exactly how to answer him, but she waited, and with every heartbeat of silence her answer gained credibility. Finally she spoke.

"I don't know," she said. She had to strike the right balance of resourcefulness and desperation, to seem enough of a wild card to betray Krupatin in a scheme she had cooked up in two or three days' time but stable enough to do what she said she would do, to follow through and then disappear.

"But you would figure something out."

"I would, yes. I want my daughter, and when I get her I want to be left alone."

Bontate picked up his glass, the thin, delicate crystal looking even more fragile in his thick suntanned hands. He drank all the wine and put the glass on the white linen with a light touch, placing it precisely, a physical representation of his frame of mind. This was a time to be very careful.

"I was surprised to see Volkov here," Bontate said, pouring himself another glass of wine, squinting through the smoke of the cigarette that burned in the corner of his mouth. He pulled his glass closer in front of him and took the cigarette out of his mouth. "What do you think he is doing here?"

"I don't know," she said for the second time. She did not want to tell him that she suspected that Volkov was there to kill her after she completed her assignment. She did not want him to think her proposition was based on a plan to preempt her own assassination. He had to believe the truth of it, that she wanted Félia out of Russia, that she wanted Krupatin dead.

"It so happens," Bontate said, frowning and staring at a fleck of ash on the tablecloth, "that Valery Volkov has been mentioned very often in my last several intelligence reports. It seems he is very ambitious. He thinks he can do a better job of running the business than Krupatin. He has allies in this. There have been rumors that he might try to move against Krupatin." He looked up. "What do you know of this?"

"Nothing." She shook her head. "Izvarin, Volkov, Stepanov— all of the lieutenants are well aware of my past with Sergei. They do not trust me with rumors. I am very much isolated in that regard."

"Do they know what you have been doing for Krupatin?"

"No. That was the only thing Sergei and I ever agreed on. What I did was an absolute secret. He used me very precisely." She paused. "I always suspected that one day he might want me to get rid of one of them. It was always in the back of my mind."

Bontate nodded, his eyes falling thoughtfully back to the fleck of ash.

"I think we should talk to him," he said. "To Volkov."

She was taken aback, but she was cautious. "Talk to him?"

Bontate looked up. "I am not going to lie to you. I cannot get the child out of Russia. I can't do it. But I have a feeling Volkov can." He shrugged. "It seems we have a lot to offer one another, the three of us."

Thirty-seven

IN ORDER TO KEEP her own gin consumption to manageable proportions, Cate volunteered to mix their drinks. After making two or three trips into the living room and seeing no end in sight, she simply brought the gin and tonic and ice bucket into the bedroom—Stepanov did not want to leave the debugged room—and put them on a table near her chair, continuing to mix his drinks and giving them to him as he asked for them. Stepanov, who remained in his armchair, relished being waited on. It was the least of Cate's concerns.

While her own glass sometimes contained nothing more than water, she mixed Stepanov's to his specifications, which meant that his glass received only a token splash of tonic. A serious drinker, he showed no effects from this prodigious consumption except to grow ever more garrulous. His monologues turned to grousing about the impossible demands made on him by the FBI, about having to run Krupatin's business in such a way that he did not arouse suspicion in Russia while at the same time he did not take advantage of criminal opportunities. Because he was now working for the FBI, he could not promote the actual growth of a criminal enterprise.

Sometimes he sounded like a businessman burdened with the complications of competition and personnel management. The complaints were universal and mundane, the global language of commerce. Cate had to keep reminding herself exactly what it was he traded in and what kind of personnel he managed.

Stepanov stopped, looked at his glass, and drained the last of the gin in it. She wished she had counted the number of times he had done this.

"Maybe one more," he said, the same words he had used the last three times.

Once more Cate stood, took his empty glass, refilled it, added ice, and stepped back to his chair to give it to him. So this was what an evening with a *mafiya* boss was like. She recalled the accounts she had read of life in Hitler's Bavarian hideaway: hours and hours, days and days of monumental boredom.

But this time when she handed Stepanov his drink, he took the glass with his right hand, and his left arm reached out and encircled her hips. Lulled by the monotony of the last hour, she was caught off guard. He held her there, looking at her, not smiling, his big hand on her backside, the amount of warmth coming from it surprising her. Since he was seated, his face was on a level with her stomach. She stared down at him. Was he testing her, or had the volumes of gin convinced him he could charm her? She didn't move. How did she handle this? How much liberty did her role require her to give him? She froze, trying to remember her objectives, trying to remember the advice.

Sliding his hand around her hips to the front of her robe, he took the edge between his second and third fingers and pulled it back until he had revealed her naked stomach and shaved crotch. She remained frozen, her disconcertion gradually subsiding into a perverse self-control. Let him look.

"Why a poppy?"

"My husband and I were drunk," she said, determined to treat his little investigation with a kind of brassy insouciance. "Considering my condition, I'm lucky it wasn't something grotesque."

Stepanov grinned and nodded. "Well, you were lucky," he said, and she could feel his breath on the tender flesh of her groin. "It's a beautiful poppy."

Then, slowly but deliberately, his face began to move toward the flower.

She reacted quickly, without thinking it through. She sank the fingers of her right hand into his thick hair, gripped it, and pulled back, stopping his face just as he touched her, pulling steadily until his eyes rolled up to her and his head was arched back, his neck taut. He frowned, surprised. She twisted her fingers in his hair, getting a better grip, and she could see his eyes beginning to water.

"I don't think so," she said firmly.

Instantly Stepanov dropped the edge of her robe, and his great hand shot up and grabbed her wrist, his grip violent, threatening. But she didn't let go of his hair. They stared at each other. Her heart pounded as she saw the anger swimming in his eyes. She tightened her fingers in his hair, astonished at her own audacity.

"Let. Go. Of. Me," she said slowly, evenly.

They glared at each other. Her eyes grew dry, but she didn't blink. Stepanov's mouth was rigid, and she knew that the only thing that kept him from knocking her across the room was the fact that she was an FBI agent. Banking on that protection, she twisted his hair until she thought it would come out by its roots. Suddenly he released her wrist, and she opened her fingers as he jerked his head away from her.

He said something in Russian; he spat it out as he ran his fingers through his hair. She didn't give a damn.

Infuriated by her resistance, Stepanov quickly drank the glass of gin she had poured and then sat sullenly in silence. He didn't ask for another drink, and after a while he got up from the armchair and slouched to the bed, where he untied his robe, dropped it on the floor, and crawled between the sheets naked. He never said another word to her. In a moment he was breathing heavily, asleep.

Relieved, Cate now made a strong drink for herself, turned out the light, and took the drink into the living room to be alone. Not bothering to turn on the lights here, she sat on one end of the sofa and looked out at the pale green illumination in the courtyard. The outdoor furniture looked lonely.

Jesus Christ. What a situation. What an incredible, bizarre situation. She thought of Stepanov's sad boredom, and then she thought of Tavio. God, how she missed him. He was a man who could not abide the kind of tedium that Stepanov found so natural. How Tavio hated to be bored. He had been a restless man, and she realized only after he was gone that that was a large part of what she had loved about him. She remembered the time, shortly after they were married, when he was due back from an assignment of several months. She had been anticipating his return with mental images of the two of them lazing by the pool, taking in late movies, sleeping in, eating breakfast at eleven, lunch at three in the afternoon, and dinner whenever they felt like it.

It didn't happen. When Tavio got into town, he already had the week planned out—a surprise, he said. Rising early the very next day, he leased a plane, and the two of them flew down into central Mexico. There, in a small town, they borrowed a jeep from a man Tavio knew from some former and vaguely described experience, and then they drove all day over dirt roads that grew increasingly less passable as they climbed up to a mountain village on the slopes of the Sierra Madre. They stayed one night in a primitive bungalow and early the next morning packed backpacks, picked up two guides, and began hiking. Tavio never told her what they were doing.

After hours of hiking, ascending steeply past ten thousand feet and then descending into a forested valley, they finally rounded a curve in the trail and stepped into yet another valley. A golden valley. The world suddenly became a vibrating, glittering, shuddering landscape of brilliant living gold. They had come to the winter home of the monarch butterflies, billions of them hanging like dripping honey from every botanical surface, even from the towering gray-green *oyamel* trees. It was a scene from a fairy tale. She had a picture in her mind, an idelible image, of Tavio standing amid this incredible assemblage, his arms outspread, covered with monarchs, little of him showing but his white teeth as he smiled. It was an unforgettable sight. It was a gift of inestimable value, a *recuerdo* of a restless man.

The memory faded, leaving her surprised all over again, leaving her longing for him anew, her anger at him confused and tempered and regretful. God, there was nothing comfortable about the man, leaving her with surprises even in his death, keeping her wondering even in memory.

She got up from the armchair and stood with her glass in her hand, not knowing what to do with herself. She thought of the naked Stepanov in the only bed. Where the hell was she going to sleep? A suite with one bed. She shook her head. It didn't matter anyway; sleep was not about to happen to her anytime soon.

She finished her drink and thought about mixing another. Idly she wandered over to the liquor cabinet to see if there was another bottle of gin. She was looking at the assorted bottles in the dim light when she was startled by a knock at the door. She stared at the door, at the thin seam of light at the bottom. She put down her glass and wiped her hands on a towel that was lying there. There was a second knock. Putting down the towel, she stepped over to a lamp and turned it on. Then she went to the door and opened it.

The woman was tall and blond and incredibly striking. Her skin was flawless, her lips were a deep, moist wine color, and her eyes were the exact, precise color of her emerald suit. Cate's only thought was, why in the hell didn't Ometov even mention her beauty?

"My name is Olya Serova," she said. "I am sorry to bother you at this hour, but I would like to speak to Valentin."

She held a small clutch bag of such a deep green as to be almost black. She stood with her weight on one leg, her hips canted slightly.

Cate backed away, opening the door. "He's in the bedroom," she said.

Irina walked into the suite and paused in the middle of the room, turning half around while Cate closed the door. Their eyes met, and in that moment Cate felt the woman take her in, all of her, without ever moving her eyes. She was an extraordinarily handsome woman, having not only the figure but also the graceful manner of someone used to being considered a remarkable beauty.

"You said he is in the bedroom," Irina said.

"That's right." Cate nodded, gesturing with her hand to the room in front of her.

Irina looked at her, hesitated, though not apprehensively, and then walked to the half-open door and stepped in. She stopped, standing a few feet into the room, and looked at Stepanov on the bed. With her back to Cate she remained motionless for a moment, and then turned and came back into the room. She tucked the clutch bag under one arm and laced the fingers of her hands together, her arms hanging down in front of her.

"He has passed out from drinking, hasn't he? How long has he been like that?"

"A couple of hours."

"Were you drinking with him?"

"I was watching him drink," Cate said. "I'm just now starting. Would you care for something?"

Irina shook her head without hesitation, dismissively, and then she stopped. She looked at Cate, changing her mind in a split second.

"Please," she said glancing at the liquor cabinet. "Whatever you are drinking."

Cate returned to the liquor cabinet, a murmur of excitement stirring in her chest. She picked up a bottle of scotch—she didn't want to go into the bedroom for the gin—poured some into two glasses, and turned and gave one to Irina, who had not been looking around the rooms as anyone might but was standing perfectly still, looking at Cate.

She took the glass and slowly held it up. "Prosit."

They each drank.

Irina touched her tongue to her wine-red lips. "Who are you?" she asked.

"Catherine Miles," Cate said, and put out her hand. Irina extended her long arm slowly, exploring Cate's face and eyes for some clue as to the kind of woman she was. They shook hands.

"Have you known him long?" Irina asked.

"I've seen him several times during the past year," Cate said. "I hardly know him."

Irina smiled at this. She nodded and sipped her drink. "Do you mind if I sit down?"

"No, of course not," Cate said, motioning to the sofa nearest the courtyard. "It's good to have someone to talk to. I guess you work with Valentin."

"We are business associates," Irina said with an ironic smile.

"Russians."

"Oh, yes."

"Times have changed, haven't they."

"Oh, yes." Another smile. Irina's long legs were very much a part of her attractiveness. Her suit skirt was just above the knee, and when she sat she crossed her legs in a way that made them seem even longer, entwining them. She laid the clutch bag on the sofa beside her. She looked around. "So what were you doing? Just watching him get drunk?"

Cate managed a smile. "Well, I was listening to him talk."

"Really? But why weren't you drinking too? You were just letting him get drunk without you? That seems odd."

"I don't like getting drunk."

Irina's green eyes widened in mild surprise. "I wouldn't have thought Valentin would keep company with a woman who doesn't like getting drunk."

Cate shrugged and looked down.

"So what kind of things were occupying Valentin's mind?" Irina asked.

"He seems unhappy."

"Unhappy? Recently unhappy or generally unhappy?"

"Recently, I guess," Cate said.

"And what is he unhappy about?"

"His work, I guess. It seems not to be going well."

"Oh."

"But I guess you'd know about that."

Irina shook her head. "No. He lives in New York. I live in Brussels. We travel, see each other in London, Paris, Munich, but we come from different business involvements. I don't know about his troubles. What kind of complaints did he have?"

Cate looked down again, studying her drink, hoping she would convey a feeling of awkwardness with Irina's line of questioning.

Irina was quick to read the signs and changed the subject.

"Do you have a university education?" she asked.

Another surprise question.

"I have a degree in English literature."

"You wanted to teach?"

"No, I didn't get a teaching certificate."

"Really? Why?"

Cate shrugged. "I should have. It was a mistake."

"You studied Russian writers?"

"Some, yeah."

"Who? Dostoevski? Tolstoy?"

"Right. And Gogol and Chekhov. Some others."

"Of course. That's all anybody remembers." Irina looked away to the lighted courtyard and sighed heavily.

Cate could not stop looking at her, marveling that after all the woman had been through, none of her agonies were reflected in her unlined face. It hardly seemed possible that the things Ometov had described could have happened to this person.

But Irina seemed oblivious to Cate's scrutiny. She stared out at the courtyard, the drink balanced on her long thigh, her thoughts seeming to have taken her far away.

"Have you been here before?" Cate asked. "I mean, to the U.S.?" As soon as the words were out they seemed stupid.

Irina turned back to her and smiled, perhaps at the obvious question, perhaps at old memories.

"Actually, yes. A long time ago. During my university days."

"Really? And what did you study?"

"Art history. But like you, I didn't use my degree."

"Why?"

"Because I was a fool," Irina said. "A bloody fool." She drank from her glass.

Cate had been standing, but now she moved to one of the armchairs and sat down, her feet together on the floor, her forearms on her knees as she held her drink.

"You wonder, though," she said, "if you'd really do it any differently if you had it all to do over again. I mean, if you were just as innocent as the first time, if you were still just as inexperienced . . . if nothing was different . . ."

"That is an old, stale line of questioning," Irina said. "You shouldn't waste a moment of your life with it."

"Maybe," Cate said tentatively, "maybe that's easier for you to say than it is for some other people. Look at you. You're beautiful, you travel all over the world. You've probably met a lot of men who could make you happy."

Irina stared at Cate, her immaculate face caught in a moment of apparent quandary, as though she were conflicted as to how to react to Cate's candid, if naive, remark.

"You haven't found a man who could make you happy?" she asked.

"I'm divorced," Cate said, surprising herself at her response.

There was a pause.

"I see." Irina nodded. "And now you find diversions with men like Valentin."

"Something like that."

"Yes, I know."

Neither of them spoke for a moment, and Cate felt a little flustered at the unexpected turn the conversation had taken. Irina seemed immediately to sympathize with her, albeit with a kind of cold, reserved sympathy. Still, there was no denying that a spark of kindred nature had flown between them. And then, just as suddenly, it was gone.

"Is Houston your home?" Irina asked abruptly.

"Yeah, well, it has been for eight years."

"Good. Tomorrow I have to go shopping for clothes. Where do you recommend?"

"For suits like the one you're wearing? I'd suggest Paris, maybe London."

Irina smiled. "Okay, but what about here?"

"I know some very nice places."

There was an awkward pause.

"Fine," Irina said, another small, slow smile crossing her face. "Do you suppose you could spare the time to take me to a few of them?"

"I think so," Cate said. "Sure. I'd love to."

Thirty-eight

I NCREDIBLE," Ann said, taking off her headphones and falling back in her chair. "Incredible luck."

Erika, sitting across the table from her, removed her headphones as well, leaving them hanging around her neck. But she was not so ebullient. Hain and Ometov exchanged glances and waited to get the two women's reactions.

"It was too easy," Erika said.

"Maybe," Ann conceded, rubbing her eyes, "but all the same, I thought Cate handled it like a pro." She leaned forward again and pressed a radio toggle. "Neil, how'd it go?"

As soon as they had picked up Irina's voice at Cate's door, Jernigan's tech team, which had been waiting for such an opportunity, had gone straight to Irina's suite to install listening devices. Jernigan was still there.

"They installed a few," Jernigan said, "dropped a couple in each room. Nothing sophisticated. The Russians'll find them if they try."

"Well, there's nothing we can do about that," Ann said. "It's the best we can do under the circumstances."

"What you really ought to do is install a video camera in the hallway, focused on her door," Jernigan said.

"I don't know," Ann said hesitantly, thinking of the expense, looking over the telephones at Hain.

"It only has to pay off once," Jernigan said.

"Neil," Hain said, changing the subject, "you still don't have an inkling about Krupatin?"

"Nothing."

"What about Izvarin and Volkov?"

"Snoring away."

"It sure as hell makes it more interesting that these two guys don't know what Krupatin's up to either," Hain mused. "I wouldn't have guessed that."

Erika spoke up with prophetic confidence. "You are not going to see Krupatin."

"Well, one of these people is going to see him," Hain said.

"Irina," Ometov said. "I have no doubt about it. If anyone will lead us to Krupatin, it will be Irina."

"Then you definitely want to stick with her?" Hain asked.

"Definitely."

"You want Cate to pull off of Stepanov?" Ann asked. "You want her to stay with Irina?"

"Absolutely." Ometov was adamant. "Irina *will* be in touch with Krupatin. If Cate can stay with her, we will find our man."

"Listen, Hain," Jernigan came in. "We're going to need more people. If Izvarin and Volkov decide to split up, I'm not going to be able to cover both of them. It's going to be tight. And what about Irina? I know we're supposed to stay clear of Cate and Stepanov, but what about when the woman's not with Cate? Seems to me that's when she's most likely to meet with Krupatin."

Hain looked at Ometov, who was already pondering that question. Slowly he began to shake his head.

"No," he said. "Not yet, not yet. If Irina spots anything even suggesting surveillance, that will be the end of it. She has to be given breathing room from the beginning. If she successfully meets with Krupatin, then it will only give her confidence to do it again. We will have other opportunities. We have to put more faith in Cate's position. It will be the safest way to go."

"Okay, then that's it," Hain said. "And Neil, I'll talk to Strey about more people for you."

"Curtis," Ann interrupted, "what about the camera?"

"Neil, have you already looked at the site?"

"Yeah. It can be done. The suite entry is just around a corner, and there's a fur down for air-conditioning ducting on the turn. We could do it when she's gone."

"So her door would be nearest?"

"That's right."

"Okay. Go ahead with it."

"Anything else?"

"What about the suite next to Irina's? What's going on there?"

"Yeah, we've looked at that. Two women from St. Louis. We ran checks on them. Wives of a dentist and a lawyer up there."

"Okay. Fine."

"Anything else?"

"One quick question, Neil," Ann said. "Did you go to Irina's suite yourself?"

"Yeah."

"Did you by any chance look in her closet?"

"I did. I always check the closets."

"Did she have a lot of clothes?"

"Actually, no. In fact there was only one dress there, and only one overnight bag. I went through the bag looking for bugs— sometimes targets will keep one attached to their bags to let them know if anyone's been in the room, prowling around in their stuff. No bugs, but also not much of anything else. One change of underwear, stuff, some personal correspondence, a few other things."

"But you're sure about the one dress."

"I didn't see anything else."

"Okay, great. Thanks."

There was little else to say, and the communication ended.

Ann rubbed her hands over her face. "Okay," she said, "we've got to talk to Cate and let her know what we're thinking, that we want to concentrate on Irina."

She looked around the room, and everyone concurred. Taking a deep breath, she picked up the secure phone and called Stepanov's suite. The others picked up receivers as well. Cate immediately answered.

"We're all on line," Ann said. "Hain, me, Leo, Erika."

"How did that play out?" Cate asked, getting right to the point.

"Oscar nomination stuff," Ann said. "Everybody's pleased."

"What did you think about her?" Erika asked immediately.

"Well, for starters, Leo, you could've told me the woman was an absolute knockout," Cate said. "She's just stunning, there's no other word for it. She almost makes you uncomfortable. Anyway, first impressions? She's intelligent, of course. A little . . . I don't know, harder than I would have expected. She seems to have an edge to her that comes out at unexpected moments. It's almost as though she has to watch herself to keep it under control. It seems her first impulse is to be . . . defensive, sharp. Then, rather as a second thought, she reins it in. She's under control, but at the same time you can see her doing it, which, oddly, gives you the feeling that she's not very *well* under control."

"I think you did a good job of reading her," Ann said. "I mean, she could have walked out of there without your having any hope of seeing her again."

"Yeah, that whole thing surprised me," Cate admitted. "That was lucky. Of course, nothing says she's actually going to call me up in the morning."

"I think she will," Ann said, and told Cate about Jernigan's discovery in her closet.

"I'll be damned." Cate's voice reflected her surprise. "You know, I did notice that although her suit was obviously expensive, it was also not fresh-looking. I mean, it looked like she'd worn it a long time—really wrinkled across the lap, under the arms."

"Yes, yes, I think so," Erika said quickly, as if confirming her own thoughts. "She's been traveling a long time, and in a hurry."

"And maybe this trip was unexpected," Ann added. "Anyway, Cate, Leo has some thoughts about how to handle her."

"Yes, Catherine," Ometov said. "We have talked a good deal about this, about Irina's presence here. This is quite unusual— extraordinary, really. Because of her special relationship to Krupatin, we now believe that she is critical to the situation that is developing here. I have no doubts whatsoever that if Krupatin eventually shows himself, it will be through contact with Irina, not one of the others. So you see, you are now in a very important position for us, a unique position. You have an incredible oppor- tunity."

He paused, but Cate said nothing. Ometov glanced at Ann and Erika and continued.

"Catherine, it sounded to me as though you gained some sympathy with her. Do you feel that is so?"

"I don't know about sympathy . . . I guess. I don't feel she was particularly suspicious of me."

"Yes, very good. But I think you should keep in mind this sympathy. That is exactly the direction you should go. Since we do not know what she is doing here, it is difficult to imagine her frame of mind. But regardless of her situation, she is going to be vulnerable to sympathy."

"Sympathy, Leo? I'm not really clear what you're meaning by that."

"Whatever else she may be, Catherine, she is above all a very lonely woman. Believe me, I know this. It has been a long time since she has felt comfortable with anyone. She has lived in a very hostile world. There has been no one she can trust, no one she can spill her heart to. It is a paradox: although she has been hardened by this kind of life, she is also very vulnerable because of it, because of the isolation. Everyone has limits to loneliness. She is starved for friendship, for simple kindness. But she will be on her guard. Do not let her see you take notice of this. Do not acknowledge it. Just be open with her, not overeager. Be honest with her. She will recognize this. She is very astute."

"This is a most difficult thing we are asking you to do," Erika said. "That is, to get her to come to you. It takes a lot of patience, but I agree with Leo that that is the only way to get to her. We have to remember, she ran away from Krupatin. Now she is traveling with him. Or traveling for him—we don't know, but somehow she is connected to him again, and we know she doesn't want to be. This suggests she is doing it under . . . what, force?"

"Duress," Ann said.

"Yes, duress."

"Her daughter," Cate said. "Stepanov was talking about Krupatin's taking away her daughter. Maybe he's holding the child hostage."

"Yes, I would guess that too," Erika confirmed. "We have not talked about that here, but this is a good possibility. It is a standard *mafiya* form of coercion. Whatever she is doing for, or with, Krupatin, she is doing it against her will."

"Catherine, I agree, definitely," Ometov added. "You might be exactly right about the little girl. You should keep in mind, if this is indeed true, that this can be good or bad as far as you are concerned. It means that she will do anything to keep the child alive. This kind of coercion leads to desperation. She will do radical things. Your assessment that she seems to be conflicted is an excellent psychological reading. You must become a part of that conflict. Let her see a chance to use you."

"This isn't going to be easy to do," Ann said. "This woman's been through a hell of a lot, probably seen all kinds of shit. She's probably paranoid. If her psychology's not royally screwed up, I'd be surprised. It could get a little weird for you."

"Weird, I'll tell who's weird," Cate said. "Izvarin and Volkov. I don't know about those two."

"Cate," Hain said. "Listen, you need to let Stepanov know that those two guys are armed now. A TEC-9 and a Smith & Wesson 659 each."

"Any more about them?"

"No. We're still flying without instruments here. We just don't know what's up."

"So Irina is our top priority now," Cate reconfirmed. "I'm supposed to concentrate on her?"

"Until Krupatin arrives, or until we find out where he is and what he's doing."

"The bedroom will remain safe?"

"Right, we'll sweep it regularly. Jernigan's got guys in the hotel who are going to do that. You can always talk freely in there."

"And the telephone?"

"It'll be safe too. Just the one in the bedroom."

There was a pause, and then Cate said, "These people—Izvarin, Volkov, Irina—they don't have any idea they're being watched?"

"We're being very circumspect," Hain said. "We're waiting for the big guy. We're not going to give ourselves away. They're keeping their eyes open, and they may spot something. These guys are old cold warriors. They expect to be watched when they're in this country."

"There's no one else in the picture here?" Cate asked. "Maybe more of their people we haven't identified yet?"

"Unfortunately, we don't know for sure," Ann said. "But no one else has popped up yet."

"Yet," Cate said.

"How are you feeling about it now?" Erika asked. "Is this going the way you expected?"

"In general, I guess so."

"And in particular?" Ann asked.

"Nothing in particular, really. I'm just ready to get on with it."

"Don't be too eager," Erika said. "Let it all come to you."

"You're doing great," Ann said. "Just keep it up."

"Cate," Erika said, "you will be okay. Have faith in your instincts."

Thirty-nine

IRINA LAY AWAKE, staring across the room which disappeared through gray into darkness, waiting for the sleeping pills to take effect. Not much of the night was left, but even though she was physically exhausted, she was almost giddy with nerves, her skin atingle, her mind racing. Her thoughts were a moil of possibilities, creating what-ifs, abloom with omens and intimations.

For the past hour she had been going over and over the meeting at Wei's house, his well-rehearsed recitation of planned cooperative projects, and her subsequent meeting with Carlo Bontate, who, though he had been as cautious as she had expected, had been immediately receptive to her proposal and had even made the surprising suggestion of enlisting the help of Valery Volkov. This was the wildest set of circumstances in which she had ever been involved. Krupatin, she knew, favored complicated operations involving numerous persons and schedules and contingencies; his people did not find fast-breaking changes unnerving, or if they did, at least they knew change was characteristic of his way of doing business. But she, having worked in self-imposed isolation for the past few years, found the situation appallingly uncertain.

Now, in addition to Krupatin's signature complexity, she had added her own conspiracy and created a maze within a maze within a labyrinth.

But of course it was not lost on her that the principals in this operational ordeal were well in the background. A lot of people were involved, it was true, but the only ones who weren't seriously exposed were the three men deep behind the scenes. And that was at the heart of her sleeplessness. It made her nauseous to contemplate what she knew of similar occasions in other countries. True, the United States was different from other countries, but these men were the same wherever they were. In Munich, in Moscow, and once in Prague, a string of deaths had followed similar convocations. They were surgical deaths, deaths intended to eliminate cutouts, leaving no chance of a connection to the men at the top. She saw no reason to believe this time would be different. Especially since Krupatin was intending to end the lives of Wei and Bontate. Few intermediaries would survive this. If they didn't die immediately in Houston, they would die in a week, in ten days, in another country.

She put a hand flat on her abdomen and tried to think of something other than these gaseous fears. She thought of the woman she had just met. Catherine. Irina had met many *mafiya* women, but this one was a bit of a surprise. Irina didn't know whether to be suspicious of her or simply to accept her singularity as the attribute of cultural differences. All the other women had been Russian or at least European. Were Americans all that different? She would have thought that Russian men would seek out similar women everywhere, especially Stepanov, who was so aggressively licentious.

But this woman seemed actually to have a personality. She was even—she seemed to be—contemplative. Irina would describe her as vulnerable if she didn't know that such a person would not be appreciated in Stepanov's company. Their paths might cross, but they would never converge. Vulnerable women did not survive in Stepanov's environment.

And yet—it was unmistakable—she did not appear to be a woman who was letting Stepanov between her legs merely for money and good times. She did not have the manner of a *mafiya* woman, self-occupied, opportunistic, intellectually shallow. So what was Stepanov doing with her?

It could be that this woman had not seen enough of him yet. She had said that she had been with him only a few times, and tonight she seemed genuinely disappointed at his boorish drunkenness. Some women would have welcomed it so they could be done with him and turn on the television or entertain a younger man after he passed out. But this woman had been sitting there alone, in silence. Maybe she had been wondering what in the hell she was doing there.

Irina did not have the typical personality of the *mafiya* woman either, and she knew how Catherine must have felt because her own early days with Krupatin were still repulsively fresh in her memory. Perhaps such women were taken in because these men made it so easy to become profligate. No physical desire was too expensive or outrageous to be out of reach. Luxury was a daily companion, a moment-by-moment enticement that became a habit, just as much as the sex and drink and drugs became habits. You hated yourself, yet it was curiously difficult to break away from it all.

But Irina had been younger when she first caught Krupatin's attention, a decade younger than this woman, and Krupatin was more handsome than Stepanov. Also, she had to admit, he was a charismatic figure, and could be as charming as a prince. Stepanov, however, was neither handsome nor charming. It didn't make any sense at all that a woman of such obvious intelligence and beauty would freely choose to spend even one evening with such a man.

Unless she was desperate for money. Irina knew many women who had done far worse things than selling their sex because they were desperate for money. Or—unless she found herself in the same situation as Irina. It made no sense, unless she had no choice.

Now, coming into the verge of drugged sleep, this last idea seized her fading consciousness like a sudden spark and ignited her approaching dream. It was a torturous dream from the beginning, filled with treachery and betrayal and violence, a woman and a crying child. In the manner of dreams it was discordant and illogical and riddled with discontinuities, yet it possessed symbols and circumstances familiar to her from other fitful nights. The desperate woman tries to save the child from a myriad of minacious crises, but success is always just beyond her grasp. Though the child's ruin is never confirmed before her eyes, the woman is aware that she has failed. The child is doomed.

Sometimes in these oneiric horrorscapes the woman bore Irina's own face, though she did not understand the woman to be herself, and the child was faceless. At other times the child's face was that of her tiny daughter Félia, but the woman never quite turned her head enough for Irina to see who she was. But now, in this restless, medicated vision, Irina was startled to see that the woman was Catherine—her face stricken and anguished at being unable to save the child. The threat to the toddler was vague, a menacing darkness where death, or worse, waited for her and toward which she was being drawn. The child was so frightened that her crying was hysterical. She gasped for breath, her eyes wild with terror, her small body stretched tautly toward the woman with Catherine's face.

Forty

SHE COULDN'T HAVE SLEPT more than three hours before she began to wake, coming to the surface in a steady glide, her dreams streaming past her face like spiderwebs. And even as she surfaced she knew that she was waking before she should, before the medicine had run its course. When she tried to open her eyes, her lids labored as though tiny weights were dangling from them, gray leaden baubles left behind by sleep's creatures, who had scattered in fright.

Struggling against unconsciousness, she twisted and rolled to the side, and when she opened her eyes, she faced the windows and the pewter light of predawn. Exhausted, she stared at the slaty panes of the French doors. From the corner of her eye she caught a drifting movement. Flinching, she twisted and fell back and looked up at Krupatin staring at her from the foot of the bed.

"Oh . . . damn," she said, her voice thick with sleep and the dregs of medication.

He moved around to the side of the bed, to the dark side away from the windows, and she felt the bed move as he leaned on it.

Suddenly he flung back the covers. She lay there naked. But he didn't touch her. Struggling to bring herself around, she rolled the other way again, away from him, and managed to swing her feet off the bed and sit up on the edge, facing the wan light from the French doors.

"Where's the CD?" he said from behind her.

She leaned sideways and reached across to the nightstand. Picking up the address book, she opened it. Earlier she had taken a razor blade and cut the leather along the inside seam. The thin slit made a perfect pocket for the CD, which fit snugly and securely. Lifting the leather lip slightly, she pulled out the CD and turned and tossed the shiny disk onto the bed.

Without speaking, Krupatin picked it up and sat down in a chair nearby. She could hear the clicking sounds as he put it into a player, put on the headphones. Then everything grew quiet as he listened.

She stared at the gray light. She didn't know how he got into her suite, but she wasn't surprised that he had managed to do so. Probably he had bribed someone on the staff. He did that everywhere. No matter how big his finances got, no matter how much of his time was taken up with accountants and bankers, he never forgot that the only reason the world still functioned at all was that there was always a working class. A king did not carry out his own chamber pot; he hired a menial to do it for him. The important thing about this mundane fact was that for x number of minutes every day, that menial had access to the most powerful figure in the kingdom, and often with uncommon freedom. Sergei understood the resentments of the menials who carried the world's shit, and he adroitly took advantage of them. If they were willing to do him favors, he didn't mind paying them as if they were kings themselves.

Irina didn't move. Her body seemed to possess an elephant's density. She stared at the waking sky, at the huge ashen clouds that she could just now see looming in the lifting darkness, massive clouds from the gulf, moving inland like great drifting mountains.

"Shit."

She flinched again. Krupatin clicked off the player.

"That goddamn Chinese is an impertinent bastard," he said from the darkness of the room behind her. "Ticking off his 'proposals' in his phony British accent. I can just see him sitting there, cool and prissy in his stupid clothes. Always dressed like he's attending a perpetual dinner party. Christ!"

His voice moved. She guessed he was getting up out of the chair.

"And Bontate. Well, at least he's a practical man. I guess he tolerated this pompous Chinese as a gesture of deference. But Carlo, he's smart enough to know I would never go for these absurd arrangements. Did Wei really think I would concede to these things? Did they think the Colombians were going to go for this? He says their accountants told them this would be to their advantage. Of course! Imbecile!"

Krupatin moved to the foot of the bed again.

"What could he be thinking? I have a very profitable arrangement with the Mexicans and the Colombians already. Why would I want to give it all up for this Chinese pipe dream? Volkov is already running a fortune in the Pakistani heroin routes—that will someday rival the Latin business, maybe overtake it. Wei knows that. The fucker is greedy for it. He's trying to get to me with this fairy-tale megashit of his."

Krupatin was wound up. She guessed he had been awake all night. She wanted to stand but couldn't bring her muscles to respond.

He came around the end of the bed to the side where she was sitting. He kicked a chair around with his foot and sat down by the French doors, looking at her in the pale light coming from behind his shoulder. She was slumping on the edge of the bed and felt ugly. He stared at her.

"Sleeping pills," he said.

She nodded and ran her fingers into her hair, sweeping it back out of her face.

"Let me wash my face," she said. "If we're going to talk, I might as well try to understand what you are saying."

In the bathroom she ran cold water and splashed her face. She splashed her chest and under her arms and her stomach. She washed out her mouth and brushed her teeth. After drying off, she ran a brush through her hair and took one of the chateau's robes off a hook on the wall and wrapped it around her. Then she went back into the bedroom, where Krupatin was still sitting in the chair by the French doors. He was smoking. She came around and got onto the bed, moved the pillows out of her way, and sat upright against the headboard.

"So how is it going so far?" he asked.

"Okay. So far."

"What does that mean?"

"It means that so far everything is okay."

Krupatin smoked. Tolerant, for the moment.

"Do you think you can do this?" he asked.

"I can do it. How do you *want* me to do it?"

He tilted his head at the nightstand.

"I saw how you used the address book for the CD," he said. "Very clever." He nodded. "Actually, I have used it for my purposes also. Pick it up."

Puzzled, Irina reached again for the book on the nightstand.

"It is a very expensive address book," he said, relishing this fact. "You will see that it has a small brass rod that forms a rigid spine. Though it is wrapped in leather, the rod has been left revealed at top and bottom, a decorative touch. And a practical touch. The top of the rod is threaded, manufactured with the precision of a surgical instrument. German. Turn on the lamp."

Irina switched on the lamp. A warm glow flooded the stand, washed over the covers of the bed, and burnished Krupatin's face. She saw the heavy swags of flesh under his eyes. He had indeed lost a lot of sleep.

He stood and stepped over to the bed and took the address book from her. Bending over the nightstand, he carefully unscrewed the top end of the brass rod and tilted it down in front of the digital clock. Four small, elliptical, honey-colored capsules spilled out onto the wood and rolled about in wobbly circles. With his forefinger Krupatin touched one of them, demonstrating its soft, slightly sticky texture. He touched another and watched it wobble.

Then he picked them up with the tips of his fingers, returned them one at a time to the tube, and screwed the brass cap back in place. He turned out the lamp, tossed the address book in her lap, and returned to his chair. Sitting down again, he lighted another cigarette.

"Those four capsules," he said, "contain powerful bacteria in gel form. The gel is not water-soluble. It dissolves only when it comes in contact with certain gastric fluids. It has to be swallowed. Symptoms do not appear for three days. They are irreversible. Death usually occurs within five days."

Irina stared at Krupatin's face in the gray light. Bacteria. She had heard rumors of his efforts to buy from the Soviet Union's chemical and germ warfare stockpiles. But those rumors circulated everywhere about everyone. She should not have discounted them.

"Therefore," he went on, "you have in your possession the solution to problem number one, how to kill Wei—he is going to be first—and not be put at immediate risk. With these," he said, nodding at the address book, "you can kill him, and he himself will not even know he's dead."

So Krupatin had indeed come up with a method of assassination that would enable her to be safely away from the man before there could be any possible suspicion that anything had happened. The only difficult part would be the cunning required to administer it.

Now Irina was truly puzzled. She had assumed that Sergei was sending her on a suicide mission, that he intended for her to be killed in the process of assassinating her targets. It seemed now that she might have been wrong. There was still risk, to be sure, but there always had been. Also, there was still Carlo Bontate. Had Krupatin planned for her to die while she was taking care of him? How could he have planned that?

"That's very clever," she conceded. "What about Carlo Bontate?"

Krupatin sucked on his cigarette and blew the smoke into the still air, where it whorled and loitered above them. The room was growing lighter by the moment, though it changed with such subtlety it was hardly discernible.

"All in good time," he said. "Tell me, is Wei still in rut for you?"

"He has asked me to come to his place tonight."

"Oh." Krupatin grinned, his teeth showing in the gray gloom. "The greedy slope. I hope he has a good appetite. Don't let him hump you. I would like to know that he *didn't* get what was coming to him before he died."

He laughed, and his laughter sounded dry in the pearly light of dawn.

"And what about Carlo? How did he seem when you met him last night?"

Irina tensed. Did Krupatin know about the second meeting? Was he testing her?

"The same way he seemed when I saw him in Marineo," she said. "Quiet. Skeptical. Like a man who knows so much more than he is saying."

"He doesn't know anything," Krupatin scoffed. "Have you spoken to Izvarin and Volkov?"

"No. There hasn't been time."

"Do it this morning."

She paused. "Sergei, I don't like all these people here. Those two, Stepanov. I have never had to do my work with others around. What are you doing?"

"Are you nervous?"

"Very."

"Have you talked to Stepanov?"

"I tried to," she said. She told him about going to Stepanov's suite, finding him asleep. She told him about talking to the woman.

"He brought this woman with him?" Krupatin asked.

"No. She lives here."

"Well, that's no surprise, is it?"

She looked at him. "So he has been coming here on business?"

Krupatin nodded. "We are trying to expand beyond the Northeast. Nothing big right now, but it's promising."

"Then there are others here as well?"

"We have people here, yes. Valentin comes down here from New York to work with them."

This was chilling information. Her own assassin could come from anywhere, not just from these few men she knew but from faces she would never recognize.

"You want me to talk to Izvarin and Volkov," she said. "What am I supposed to say to them? I don't know why they are here."

"*They* don't know why they are here." Krupatin smirked. "Tell them I will be in touch with them soon."

"And Stepanov?"

"The same."

Irina didn't know why, but Krupatin was clearly stalling. Nothing could be done about it. It was his game, his rules. But she definitely did not like being the pivotal element in his deadly charade, the point around which the plot turned, and the only onstage character to whom all the actors looked for their cues.

"And what kind of response do I give Wei and Bontate?"

"You have my response to Wei," he said, gesturing with his cigarette to the address book.

"I have to tell them something."

"If they press you, tell them I am working on a response. Otherwise, don't tell them anything."

She said nothing for a moment, and Krupatin simply stared at her, smoking.

"And you are just going to show up in my suite like this?" she asked.

"Something like this." He ground out his cigarette. "Keep the address book with you at all times. Under the K's there is a name, Walter Kralik. If you have to get in touch with me, use that number, leaving off the country and city codes and reversing the first three digits. Call me. Leave a number and a time you want me to call it."

"Walter Kralik."

"Yes."

"Otherwise, you want me to go ahead tonight"—she held up the address book—"with this?"

"Absolutely." He ground out his cigarette. "I have to go. It's getting light."

Forty-one

AFTER KRUPATIN LEFT, Irina remained on her bed staring out at the armada of clouds still sailing into the city from the coast. With the rising light they had changed from ash to pale blue, their edges tinged with peach from the sun, which was still on the far side of them.

Her first impulse was to run. That was her first, primitive, gut reaction to her situation. Flight. But it had been a long time, a very long time, since Irina had acted on her first impulses. She had learned to suppress them, learned to disobey them, to defy them. Everything had been subordinated to necessity, to Félia's survival. It was amazing what you could accomplish when faced with calamity. You began to think seriously about achieving the impossible; you began planning for the absurd as though it were an expected commonplace. You began to believe in miracles as regular occurrences.

So it was with her now. Everything in her was screaming that the circumstances surrounding this operation had gotten out of hand. Every time she turned around, another person, another contact entered the picture. But she thought of Félia and adjusted her plans once again. Where caution and creativity had served her well in the past, she now would have to rely almost entirely on creativity.

After bathing and drying her hair, she wrapped herself in the robe again, ordered breakfast, and ate it in her bedroom overlooking the city. When she had finished her pastries and black coffee, she unfolded an ironing board and began pressing one of the two outfits she had worn alternately each day since she had left London for Paris and Palermo. Then the doorbell chimed. She knew exactly who it was. She walked through to the living room, went to the front door, and looked out the peephole, confirming her guess. Tucking her robe more tightly around her waist, she opened the door.

"I'm surprised it took you this long," she said.

Izvarin's smile, fluffed to its most charming in anticipation of meeting this mystery woman of Krupatin's, imploded the instant he recognized Irina. He gaped at her, speechless, too stunned even to recover.

"Close your mouth and come in," Irina said with weary insolence as she backed away from the door.

Izvarin recovered enough to move forward into the room, and as Volkov followed him in, his eyes lingered on her, she thought, a little longer than might have been expected. He did not seem so shocked to see her. But then, Volkov was not given to Izvarin's emotional displays.

"It's been a long time since I've seen you," Izvarin said, turning around in the middle of the living room, still in the process of recovery. He managed to begin another smile. "I didn't know you . . . that it was you who was coming. Sergei didn't say."

"Are you feeling a little in the dark?" she asked.

Izvarin's brave new smile crumpled. He didn't know precisely how to respond. If he said no, she would ask him to explain what was going on, and since he didn't know and she might know, he would be a fool to try to finesse a response. If he said yes, he would be admitting he didn't have a clue what was going on.

"What do you mean?" he asked. His situation was pitiful.

"Sergei is not going to join us here at this hotel," she said flatly. "He is going to remain inaccessible."

"Inaccessible!" Izvarin was stunned, even alarmed.

"He is going to communicate with you only through me," she added, "and he said to tell you that you might have to wait several days before he will have any instructions for you."

"When did you speak with him?" Izvarin stammered.

"I spoke with him this morning."

"By telephone?"

"Personally."

"Here?"

"It does not matter," she said. "That is all I am supposed to tell you."

Izvarin stared at her. Volkov said nothing.

"I find this impossible to believe," Izvarin said. "Impossible—that he would communicate with us solely through you . . . Shit!"

"Why?"

"Why! You're a damn junkie, that's why!"

She settled her eyes on him, her calm demeanor calculated to make him uneasy. She said nothing. Silence was always difficult for Izvarin.

"Two things," she said finally. "One, we need to talk elsewhere. Two, I have to buy clothes. That's where I'm going right now. I am taking Valentin's girlfriend with me. Why don't you follow us around? At a distance. When I want to talk to you, I will let you know. I will beckon to you, and you can come trotting over."

"You can't be serious."

"I am serious."

Izvarin's face reddened with indignation. He didn't know whether she was toying with him or Krupatin had indeed arranged this. He gambled. At great cost he managed yet another smile, an uncomfortable one that he must have hoped would portray a confidence he clearly was not feeling.

"Irina, I hope you know what you are doing," he said. "If you want to talk to me, leave a message." With as much assurance as he could muster, he walked out of the suite.

Volkov did not follow Izvarin. His stolid frame seemed rooted to the Persian rug in front of the fireplace. His thin lips and gray complexion accorded with his somber expression. He studied her with his round black eyes.

"You did speak with Sergei?" he asked.

She nodded. "This morning."

"We are to wait to hear from him—through you."

"That was what he told me to tell you."

"And Stepanov?"

"The same."

Volkov nodded, seeming to want to hear more.

"Frankly," Irina said, "I know nothing more than you. This is Sergei's forte, you know."

"Yes," Volkov said without expression, "I know." He looked at her for another moment, and she wondered with a slight flutter in her stomach if Bontate had already spoken to him. Was he trying to decide if he should say something to her now? Then the moment passed, and he turned and walked out the door too, pulling it closed behind him without looking back.

Irina stood in the middle of the room with her arms crossed. Then, stepping over to the telephone, she called Stepanov's room.

Stepanov answered.

"This is Olya Serova," she said.

There was a long pause. Then he said, "Hello. I recognize your voice, even though it's been a long time. I'm surprised to hear from you."

"I just spoke to Nakhimov and Bykov," she said. "Nakhimov is upset."

"Really."

She couldn't read him very well. In many ways he was more difficult to deal with than Izvarin. Stepanov had been running the American enterprise a long time. That kind of independence, away from Krupatin, had instilled a lot of confidence in him. His paranoia was in much better control than Izvarin's.

"The main office is going to be sending instructions to you through me. I will pass them on as soon as I know what they are."

"Mmmm. More surprises."

She didn't respond to that. "Did your friend Catherine tell you that we talked last night?"

"She did."

"I would like to speak to her."

Stepanov hesitated. "When do you expect to hear from the main office?"

"It may be a couple of days."

"Really? That long?" He paused. "Okay."

She heard him lay down the telephone and say, "It's Olya Serova."

The fact that none of them knew what they were doing there was working on each of them in different ways. Blind operations were not unheard of, but none of them had ever been involved in blind operations in America. That was different. America's law enforcement agencies were second to none, except for Israel's, and no one liked going against them blind.

Krupatin had put them all in a very precarious position, and the way he was handling his information did nothing but foster suspicions among them. And as always he knew exactly what he was doing. That, as much as anything, was what worried all of them the most.

Forty-two

T HEY TOOK A TAXI and went straight to the Galleria and
began shopping. Cate watched Irina with fascination. With
no hesitation she quickly identified the most exclusive shops, and
with little contemplation she selected the fabrics, colors, and
styles that suited her best. The first thing she did was buy a new
suit to wear, asking the clerk to throw away the one she had worn
in. When she asked for alterations, she told the seamstress why
she wanted them made and exactly where and how to make them.
She agreed to pay outrageous fees to have the alterations made
within a few hours. It was clear she was used to having no financial restrictions whatsoever.

They went from shop to shop, making what seemed to Cate to
be quite specific purchases. Often Irina would walk in and mention a style or a designer name or a color, and if the store had
nothing along those lines she would walk out. Yet even though
she shopped with precise preconceptions of what she wanted, she
seemed to do this in an offhand manner, not looking in the windows, never stopping to examine something that might catch her

eye unexpectedly, never browsing with a vague yearning for something to surprise her. And she never asked Cate's opinion, as other women often did, either out of curiosity or from a desire for confirmation. Rather, she shopped as though she were completing an assignment, an assignment that she was repeating from other times, other cities, other countries. This was simply a variation on a theme with which she was intimately familiar.

Cate noticed something else as well. None of the fabulous clothes she was buying ever seemed to delight her on purely aesthetic grounds. Though she chose her clothes with an artistic eye, she seemed to take none of the artist's pleasure in what she was doing. Her taste was unfailingly accurate—even the women who waited on her were clearly delighted to find someone with such sure and correct opinions about what was best for her particular features. But there was no satisfaction in the process, no appreciation of the beauty of the clothes she was acquiring. She knew they were beautiful, but it was a cognitive recognition, not an emotional one.

When they finished in the Galleria, around two o'clock, they had not yet stopped for lunch. Cate suggested Cafe Annie, near the Palm Court, where there were even more exclusive shops if Irina wished to continue shopping.

Even though they arrived well after the height of the lunch hour, the trendy restaurant was still quite full. Irina's striking appearance demanded the instant attention of the maitre d', and when she asked for a table with as much privacy as possible, she got it without question. Heads turned as they made their way to their table, and though Cate had been feeling increasingly dowdy as the morning progressed, she now realized she no longer had to worry that anyone would notice. Irina was the one who made the herd raise their heads from grazing as she made her way across the restaurant.

Irina refused the chair the maitre d' offered her, the one from which it was easiest to see the others in the room and that best allowed the others to see her. Instead she politely sat where a column would obscure not only her view but her face. The maitre d' was crestfallen. Irina and Cate ordered wine and a light lunch, and for the first time since they had left the hotel, Irina allowed her green eyes to settle on her companion. Her face softened.

"These shopping frenzies happen to me more frequently than I like," she said, seeming to want to explain the unusual morning. "My business often requires quick trips for which I have no opportunity to pack or plan. I've shopped so often in unfamiliar cities that I seem to have developed a . . . a method of concentration that tunes out everything but the task at hand." She sipped her water and sighed. "I do appreciate that you saved me the time of hunting down the shops."

"I don't think I've ever seen anyone buy so much in so short a time," Cate said. "It looked fun."

Irina tilted her head to the side and shrugged. "Not fun," she said.

The wine arrived, and Irina asked the waiter to please open the bottle and leave it on the table without pouring. He did so and left. She poured for both of them.

"I've got to get these shoes off," she said, and slipped her feet out of her heels and crossed her legs. "Prosit."

They drank. The white wine was cold and dry. Irina studied Cate.

"You have very good taste in clothes," she said. "That color is perfect for you. Auburn hair and your complexion are beautiful to work with. Soft colors, strong colors—both work if you know how to use them."

"That's nice of you to say." Cate glanced away, suddenly uneasy at having the attention brought around to her. "I wish my budget allowed me to shop in the places we've been in today."

Irina shrugged indifferently. "Well," she said, "beautiful clothes are small comfort. In fact, they are no comfort at all. There are other things I would much rather have. These things, they are what I can have . . . so I have them."

"What would you rather have?" Cate asked.

Irina looked up at her. Her face portrayed nothing at all of what she was thinking.

"A peaceful night's sleep," she said. "With no dreams. That would be a good beginning."

Cate frowned quizzically.

"An odd thing to say?" Irina asked. "Yes, of course." She sipped her wine, her eyes looking at the glass as she set it down on the table. "We know so little of each other—strangers. I almost have forgotten what it is like to have . . . well, a circle of friends." She looked up. " 'Circle,' is that what you say?"

"Yes," Cate said. "A circle of friends." There was a moment's hesitation before she asked, "Why don't you have a circle of friends?" Instantly she remembered she had been cautioned about asking questions and tried to negate the gaffe by offering her own benign answer. "You travel too much, I suppose."

"Yes," Irina agreed, nodding. "Too much travel. That is exactly the reason, much too much travel."

Their lunch arrived very quickly, and they conversed about inconsequential things while they ate. At least, they seemed inconsequential at first blush. It was nonetheless curious. If Cate had been cautioned against asking too many questions, Irina evidently had no such reservations. She kept up a steady string of queries throughout the meal. At first Cate was tense, cautious, thinking that Irina was testing her, fishing to catch her up or hoping to hear a false note in her responses. Then after a while it seemed that Irina's questions were merely one woman's interest in another woman's life. She seemed to be searching for a similarity of experience, some grounds of commonality. Once Cate realized this, Irina's questioning actually took on an unexpected poignancy. Suddenly it struck Cate as a revelation: this woman was, as Ometov had claimed, simply lonely.

Irina pushed away her plate before her food was half eaten, losing interest in it. She poured another glass of wine.

"Tell me," she said, leaning forward, forearms on the table, her hands resting lightly on the stem of the wineglass, "what is your interest in Stepanov? If that is not too rude a question. Excuse me when I say that . . . Really, you are so attractive, this is your city, where you must have many friends—how can you be interested in Valentin, who it is clear to see is no romance idol?"

The question could have stopped with the first terse sentence. And if it had, Cate's response might well have betrayed an uncertainty. But Irina's elaboration gave her a moment to gather her wits.

"You are a beautiful woman yourself," she said, "and yet you tell me you are lonely. How do you explain that?"

"I told you, I travel too much."

"And I don't travel enough. There's not so much difference when you think about it."

Irina looked at her for a moment. She was not about to be stopped with a clever riposte.

"No." She shook her head. "I don't understand that. I don't see it as the same thing at all."

Cate was preparing to make another run at it when Irina spoke again.

"Do you have a child?"

A child? Wouldn't one normally ask, do you have children? Or do you have any children? The singular noun gave Cate her clue. She wiped her mouth with her napkin, taking her time, and picked up her own wineglass and drank before she answered, hoping to portray reluctance.

"I have a daughter," she said.

Irina's eyes reflected a spark of excitement, which she immediately brought under control.

"A daughter? Really? How old is she?"

Cate was grateful that their conversation had not turned to this earlier, when Irina might have revealed the existence of her own daughter. This "coincidence" of daughters would work only if it came from Cate's direction first.

"She's three."

Irina stared at her, unable to hide her excitement now. "Three . . . oh God, so young. Does she live with you?"

"Yes, she does. She's with my parents right now, of course, for a few days."

"Yes?" Irina was still staring. "*I* have a daughter too," she said eagerly, bringing one hand up and placing it flat on her chest. "She is five years old. Not so much different from yours. I remember so well when she was three."

Cate smiled. "You must miss her when you travel."

The animation subsided from Irina's face. "Yes, I miss her terribly." She shook her head. "But she does not live with me anymore."

"I'm sorry," Cate said. "You're divorced too, then?"

Irina shrugged. "Something like that." She grew serious and turned and looked at the few tables she could see from where she was sitting. Her manner seemed to indicate that she wanted to change the conversation almost as abruptly as she had seized upon it.

"Listen," she said, turning suddenly back to Cate. "You don't know what you are doing with this Stepanov."

"What?"

"You haven't known him long, you said."

"That's right."

"Well, you don't know what it is you are getting into with him."

"I'm not getting into anything," Cate said.

"Oh, yes, you are." Irina leaned forward again. "I can guess. You probably met him at a club, a hotel bar, wherever business people go for drinks after work. You struck up a conversation. He was a foreigner. That is interesting. Russian? Really? Even more interesting. He buys you several drinks. Why not? After a few, he offers to take you out to dinner. Well . . . okay, why not? During the meal, maybe over more drinks, he makes a polite pass at you. Very polite. You laughingly brush him off. He drops the subject. A few more drinks. Again he brings up the subject. What if you slept with him just this once? What harm could come of it? He knows you are not a prostitute, but he is lonely, so very lonely. He travels so much. No, you say. Sorry, really. Look, he says, what about . . . what if you slept with him just this one time, and he gave you two thousand dollars. No, three thousand dollars. You laugh. Cash, he says. That's ridiculous, you say. No, please, he says. He understands. What about four thousand dollars?" Irina paused and looked at Cate. "It was something like that, I would guess."

Cate studied her. Jesus. She looked down at her drink again.

"Look," Cate said. "This is the only time in my life I've ever done something like this. I'm not a prostitute, for God's sake."

"No, no," Irina protested, and she reached out and placed one of her long hands on Cate's. "I understand all too well. He probably pays you more money for one night than you can make in one or two months. And after all, what is going to bed with someone? It's not like you are selling your soul. People do that, even with people they have just met. A fling."

Cate looked at her and shook her head. "I can't turn down that kind of money. It's a hell of a lot of money. No one knows. This guy's a total stranger. I can make fifteen thousand dollars the five days he's in town. I don't care where the money comes from. I don't have a dime in savings. My ex-husband hasn't sent me a single dollar in over a year."

Irina squeezed Cate's hand, leaning forward over her glass of wine. From a distance they were two well-heeled Houston wives, gossiping.

"Listen to me," Irina said, almost pleading. "I know what you are saying. This man is experienced with women such as yourself. He seeks out and understands vulnerability. If he were blind and could not see it, he could smell it on your breath. But I am telling you . . ." She looked at Cate, her words stopping just behind her teeth, her face betraying her temptation to say more than she knew she should. She let go of Cate's hand and sat back, looking at her.

"Look, let's drop the subject," Cate said. She smiled a little. "I appreciate . . . what you've said. I appreciate that you don't judge me because of it. It's good to have someone who understands, who knows what it's like—to be alone, to have the responsibility . . ."

She let her voice trail off, allowing Irina to fill in the rest with her own imagination. The conversation had taken a dramatically different turn from what Cate had expected, though it had been very much to her advantage. She did not want to deflect Irina from pursuing her own thoughts and interests, which so far had been advantageously revealing.

"How long has Valentin told you he will be in the city?" Irina asked.

"Up to five days, I think he said."

Irina nodded, thinking.

"How long will you be here?" Cate asked.

"Two or three days, no more." She rotated her wineglass by its stem. "What did he think about your going with me today?"

"He didn't seem to mind. He thought it was odd."

"Odd? He is such a fool." She had grown sober, thoughtful. Silence.

"Well, I'm not with him all the time," Cate said. "Maybe . . . maybe we could have lunch again, or dinner."

"I will be keeping very strange hours while I am here," Irina said offhandedly. "That might be hard to do."

"Well, won't he be keeping strange hours too?"

"I don't know. This trade commission business is . . . Well, it is not a routine situation. We don't work together, I mean, directly together." She sipped from her glass. "I have to go to the ladies' room. Excuse me."

She took her purse and left, making her way through the dining room, again causing heads to turn. Tall, blond, expensively dressed, and having a body every woman would envy, she possessed an aura that people were most likely to associate with a famous model or actress. You could almost see people trying to decide where they might have seen her.

Knowing that she would be alone for probably ten minutes or more, Cate was tempted to talk to Hain and the others. Then she realized there was nothing she could say that would clarify what they had been hearing. They knew what she was doing. If they didn't like it, they could get a message to her. It seemed to her to be going all right. Her only concern was the time frame. If Irina's reference to her schedule was not a fabrication, they didn't have a lot of time. And still no sign of Krupatin. Still no indication that these people—Irina, Izvarin, Volkov—were making contact with anyone else. Everyone seemed to be waiting. Krupatin was still the center of attention, even in his absence.

Forty-three

W ELL," Ometov said, shifting the headphones away from his ears but not taking them off his head, "if we can read between the lines and separate the fact and fiction of her story, I think we can be sure that our first guess was right about her. Krupatin has taken her daughter away from her. That is why she is doing whatever it is she is doing for him."

Curtis Hain nodded and pulled away his headphones as well, putting down his pencil on the pad next to him. The folding metal tables were now so crowded with electronic equipment they were almost sagging. The cables snaked all over the floor of the living room.

"Cate was beautiful with that," Ann said, nodding at the radio receiver. "She saw the opening and took it."

"And Irina seemed to accept this," Erika added, chewing a bite of apple. She and Ann were sitting on the opposite side of the tables, their backs to the courtyard. They had to peer around computer screens to see Hain and Ometov. "I was surprised at the sound of her voice, the way it changed when they were talking about their daughters."

Ometov stared at the table, tapping a computer screen with the back of his fingernails. "I am going to guess that Sergei is planning on remaining out of the picture. Whatever he is up to here, I think he is going to do it through these people he has sent. He wants to stay hidden."

"If he's even here."

"True."

"We still haven't any proof he's left London."

"True. But I think he is here. With all of these people . . . He is here."

"Irina mentioned three days or so," Ometov said, almost to himself. "I think that has significance. If this operation has a limit, everything is going to move fast."

One of the telephones at Hain's elbow rang, and he picked it up.

"Curtis, this is Jernigan. Listen, we've got an interesting development. About an hour ago Izvarin decided he'd go out to the pool and hang around and look at the babes. Volkov took off in another direction. He went down to the lobby and wandered around a bit. He got his shoes shined. He wandered into the tobacco shop, looked around, got a few cigars, killing time. Two guys walked into the shop. One of them started looking around too, but the other one walked up to Volkov and said something. Volkov was caught off guard, but the guy had a lot to say and Volkov listened. After about ten minutes Volkov pays for his cigars and leaves the shop with the two guys. They walk to the elevators and the three of them get into one of them. You could see them punching all the buttons as the doors closed. There was no way we could tell where they went."

"Son of a bitch," Hain said.

"We got photographs of the guys, though. They're Italian, Curt. Way Italian."

"No shit." Hain raised his eyebrows at Ometov and motioned to everyone to pick up the other phones. "Everyone's getting on the line."

"If they're not from Sicily, I'll lose a ten-dollar bet," Jernigan continued. "We've got Strey's people running the photographs through the ID section."

"Did you have people outside?"

"Yeah. They didn't leave the hotel. And that's not all. Early this morning, before dawn, someone, I guess it was Irina, found all the bugs in her place. They're out. We got the camera in place about midmorning and forty minutes later someone spray-painted the lens."

"Jesus."

"So I guess we've got Italians in the hotel here somewhere, but we've been in the business office for the past hour trying to find out where they might be and can't. Someone's fronting for them. We'd have to physically walk into every room."

"Italians contacting Russians?" Ann asked rhetorically. "Curt, you think this is Bontate?"

"The Camorra has a very healthy presence here," Jernigan said. "We have good records on these guys. It could be they're just checking, heard the Russians were coming in and thought they'd pay them a visit, let them know who's got a grip on things around here."

"Who painted the lens of the camera?" Erika asked.

Ometov wrinkled his brow. "I don't know. Why would the Italians care who got their picture taken going into Irina's suite? Unless *they* were going in."

Hain thought a moment. "When Irina checked in, she deliberately avoided the room Izvarin had reserved and took another one at random."

"Seemingly at random."

"She couldn't have known before arriving that it was going to be empty."

Ometov shrugged. "Then Sergei has other people there?"

"Or maybe it was the Italians," Hain offered. "Maybe they're making passes through Irina's suite too, planting bugs, just like us."

"And they want you to know they know you are there."

"Yeah," Hain said, disgusted.

"So there are questions. Are they guests in the hotel, registered guests? Or are they just coming and going, some of the anonymous transients who occupy busy hotel lobbies and dining rooms?"

"I don't think someone passing through would have found that camera or seen it installed. Someone's watching."

"Then you think it was someone on that floor, observing her room, or observing everything that takes place in the hallway."

"Someone's sure as hell watching her door," Hain said. "The question is, from what vantage point?"

For a moment none of them spoke, all of them thinking through the maze of possible scenarios, the possible rationales of possible adversaries.

"Krupatin is like Satan," Ometov mused. "Everybody is Jesus to him. He takes them up on the mountain and shows them the world. He promises them everything they want in exchange for a little favor, a little service."

"Someone in the hotel," Hain said. "Staff."

"I think that is a good possibility."

"Neil, can you check that out?"

"Sure."

"Wait," Hain shot back. "Second thoughts—I'm not thinking right. We don't know how high up on the staff he might have made payoffs. If we go after them like that, there's a good chance they'll hear of it immediately. We could run them off, scatter them all the hell over the place. Let us put our heads together, Neil. We'll get back to you."

Hain broke the connection, and they all looked at one another.

"Maybe Sergei has other people there besides Izvarin and Volkov," Ometov said. "In other rooms. Maybe that is how he will communicate with Irina. Maybe they are others your people have not identified yet."

"Jesus, Leo. You make it sound like they're swarming," Ann said.

"Oh," Ometov said, nodding emphatically, "I think they are indeed swarming. I think you will be surprised when this little episode is over. You are working against people who used to be with Soviet intelligence. Some of them used to *be* Soviet intelligence. Do you want to think about that? How did your country fare in that little contest? These are the people who turned Aldrich Ames and assassinated ten of your agents. We bankrupted an entire society to train these people. The social system did not survive, but these people got the best education imaginable in deception, and they *did* survive. These are not just gangsters you are dealing with here, my friend. These are the people who used to manipulate a nation. And now, as criminals, they still do."

"Okay, Leo," Hain said, sitting back and making his chair creak as he massaged his right thigh with both beefy hands. "What do you suggest?"

Ometov crossed his legs, dropped his head, and began nodding, his rounded shoulders looking for all the world as though they were carrying a burden that would cripple him. As he pondered Hain's question, he absently tore a piece of paper off the notepad on which he had been doodling and began rolling it between his fingers, mashing it, kneading it, working it into a tiny, hard little pellet.

"It is my feeling," he said, his head still down, "that Sergei Krupatin has outmaneuvered us already."

"What?"

Ometov looked up and put the little pellet into the breast pocket of his rumpled suit coat.

"These little games of bugs and cameras," he said, "—they are, you might say, a diversion. I think your instinct not to try to root out who might have been bought off at the chateau was a good one. I think Izvarin and Volkov are decoys to keep us busy in the old cold war ways, to preoccupy us with bugs and cameras and teams of agents conducting surveillance, even the gambit about the disguises. This is humbuggery to convince us that these men mean serious business. And then Irina arrives. The girlfriend. Not terribly important with all these other men around, these big boys."

"The trip Izvarin and Volkov took to pick up the guns."

"Just busywork for us. Old games."

"So what's the new game?"

"I don't know." Ometov shook his shaggy head and sat up straight for a moment, looking at the screen savers, which were taking him through starfields into deep space. He slumped again. "What I do know, what I feel in the marrow of my bones, is that Irina Ismaylova is at the very center of this. And by simple, stupid luck, Cate has found herself in exactly the right place. We thought of her as an enticement for Krupatin—we instructed her as a concubine, a Mata Hari, a bait of flesh for Sergei. But as it turns out, her real value to us is simply to be a sympathetic woman, a friend to another woman."

"So how the hell are we going to keep them together?"

"We cannot keep them together. Irina will have to get away

from her to communicate with Krupatin. But we can make them closer."

"And how do you propose to do that, Leo?"

Ometov looked at Hain with a sober, almost forlorn expression. "Sympathy," he said.

Forty-four

FROM THE FOYER of the women's room in Cafe Annie, Irina called the hotel and asked for messages. There was only one. Irina looked at her watch. She had a little over an hour.

When she got back to the table, Catherine smiled at her as she sat down. It had been a long time since she had seen a smile that she thought was genuine, a smile meant for her only with kindness and without an undercurrent of lechery or brutality. It was difficult to accept it just as it was offered, difficult not to dissect it, not to pick it apart for its real meanings.

During the nightmares of the last few years, one of Irina's great secret concerns had been what she would be like if she survived this hell into which Krupatin had shoved her. If she ever was able to escape him, to escape this unimaginable intercourse with death in which he had buried her, what was she going to be like? He had initiated her into a world of deception and menace and taken away her innocence, just as if she had been a child on whom he had forced himself, bringing into her life all the ugliness and sickness of his own putrid world. Would she ever be able to accept innocence again? Would she even be able to recognize it except in a child—in another adult, a good person who might come her way and help her restore all that Krupatin had taken from her?

She poured what was left of their wine, a little bit into each glass. She made a small toasting gesture, and each of them drank.

"I have to go back now," she said. "I have things to do." It was difficult. She wanted to smile too but couldn't.

Cate nodded. "Well, I enjoyed it. I've never seen anyone shop like that," she said, laughing easily.

Irina looked at her mouth as she laughed, her clean, bright smile. It disguised the unpleasantness of Stepanov, perhaps even made it disappear—the triumph of good over evil. For that moment the woman was free of Stepanov's corrupting taint, and Irina could almost sense, almost remember, what that was like, as if the waft of an old fragrance had for an instant transported her back to a dear and former time.

"Maybe . . . it would be good to do something together," Irina said. Her heartbeat actually accelerated. Could she really allow herself to believe that this woman was what she appeared to be? Was she, Irina, going to act on pure faith? Suppressing her suspicion of this person was like anticipating losing her virginity: it made her nervous and created a giddy quiver deep in her abdomen, as though she could not imagine the experience, its sensations, its possibilities.

"Sure," Cate said. "I'd like that."

Irina stared into her and through her, her suspicion as irrepressible as Catherine's apparent honesty.

During the brief ride back to the hotel, they agreed that Irina would call Catherine as soon as she had the time. They didn't have to have anything specific to do. It would just be good to visit. But it wasn't lost on Irina either that this unallied woman might be more than a friend; she might prove to be a useful friend as well.

When they arrived at Chateau Touraine, Irina reached out and impulsively squeezed Catherine's hand just before the doors were opened by overzealous attendants. For an instant their eyes met, and Irina believed in that sudden moment that she and this woman were more than acquaintances, more than friends, that their lives had become intimate in a complex but genuine way.

□ □ □ □

In her suite, Irina went to the liquor cabinet in her living room and selected a single-malt scotch. She poured some over a tumbler of ice and swirled the liquor to cool it. She looked at the scattered boxes and bags of new dresses and underclothes and perfumes and cosmetics. How many times had she done this, traveling fast, buying what she needed—more than she needed—on the way? Twelve years ago, when she was a student at the Repin Institute, her eyes firmly fixed on a career filled with the smells of paints and lacquers and canvas, of musty old storage rooms and chemically fragrant laboratories, how could she have foreseen this? Impossible. She held the cool glass to her temple. Impossible.

The doorbell chimed. She did not move. She drank from her glass and put the glass to her other temple. The doorbell chimed again.

Still holding the glass, with her long arm hanging down at her side, she walked to the door and opened it. One of the young Sicilians she had seen before stood there. He jerked his head slightly to the side, a cocky gesture that came as naturally to him as his black eyes. She was to go with him.

Forty-five

WHEN CATE OPENED the door to Stepanov's suite, the late afternoon sun was falling obliquely over the garden wall and throwing sharp shadows across one side of the living room. As she turned to close the door, she saw the two men behind it, too late to react before one of them spun her around, pinned one arm to her side, and wrenched the other hard up between her shoulder blades. The second man clamped one hand over her mouth and pressed the barrel of a handgun to her forehead.

Cate and the gunman stared at each other for a moment as he raised his eyebrows in query. She nodded. The gunman then produced a foam ball, which he roughly crammed into her mouth. Both men were wearing surgical gloves. Handcuffs clamped her wrists together behind her, and the man behind her threw her onto the sofa.

The gunman laid down his gun on the coffee table and produced a notepad and felt-tip pen. "The room is bugged," he wrote.

She stared at him. He was Anglo, about her age, wearing jeans, sneakers, a polo shirt, and a navy blue sport coat. His partner was about the same age and wore dress slacks with a navy silk shirt and a linen sport coat.

The gunman turned the notepad to a clean sheet and wrote, "We want Izvarin's list."

She frowned at him.

He gave an exasperated look, reached into his coat pocket, took out a square of sandpaper. He wrapped the paper around his fist and hit her. The blow so astonished her that she didn't even feel any pain with it, except the searing scrape left by the sandpaper.

He raised his eyebrows again and jutted his face forward.

She frowned, shook her head, trying as best she could to portray her consternation.

He picked up the pad and wrote the word "Names!"

She shook her head.

He hit her again, on the side of the head, scraping a swatch of skin just to the right of her left eyebrow. He hit her a third time, scraping her chin. Again she was stunned, not by the blows, which really weren't hurting all that much, but by the fact that this was actually happening to her. He hit her again on the cheek. Her eyes were watering profusely.

He picked up the notepad again and wrote, "We know about Volkov. We know what you are doing. We know you had the list."

She was shaking her head now, her eyes streaming, the raw scrapes from the sandpaper beginning to sting sharply. She shook her head again and looked at the other man. Through her tears she saw that he was wearing tiny headphones, and occasionally he would put his fingers to the earphones as if to hear more clearly.

Suddenly he reached out and slapped his partner on the shoulder and quickly tapped on one side of the earphones.

The hitter grimaced and his mouth formed the word "Shit" without making a sound. He reached into his pocket, took out the key to the handcuffs, tossed it on the coffee table, and the two of them opened the door to the suite and stepped outside, closing the door behind them. It was over.

Cate immediately fell onto the floor and rolled over on her stomach. She got on her knees, put her mouth to the corner of the sofa, and began using the piping on the edge of the upholstery to rake at the foam gag. Working her jaws as she dragged her mouth back and forth over the piping, she began to loosen the ball, and in a few seconds it popped out onto the floor. She walked on her knees to the coffee table, turned around backward, felt around with her fingers until she got the key, and struggled to her feet. Then, staggering into the bedroom, she slammed the door closed with her foot.

"Goddamnit, Ann," she muttered, coughing and working frantically to get the key into the handcuffs. "A couple of guys were waiting for me in here at Stepanov's when I got in just now. They cuffed my hands behind me and slapped me around." She made one wrench of the key and one of the cuffs sprang open. "I'm pissed," she said, "really pissed. If you know something about this, I want to hear from you right now."

She sat on the edge of the bed and held a cold, damp washcloth to her head. She was furious, a little shaken, maybe even a little embarrassed at her frantic call. She was holding the telephone receiver to her ear with her other hand, and everyone at the off-site was on the line.

"This doesn't make much goddamn sense," Ann was saying.

"They were *American?*" Erika asked.

"I guess. Well, I don't know that. They were white," Cate said. She was looking at herself in a mirror she was balancing on her lap. There were a lot of scrapes. The punches hadn't been hard enough to cause any bruises, but the sandpaper had produced a sensational effect, making her injuries look far more substantial than they were. She was going to have little scabby places all over her face. Shit.

Ann Loder had already been through a gush of apologies for having allowed this to happen, and Cate had quickly regained her composure and said she was sorry she had overreacted. She really was shamefaced about having panicked, and was regretting it, hoping it hadn't made her look too bad in their eyes. It wasn't anything they could have helped, under the circumstances. As soon as all of them realized she really wasn't seriously hurt, they began putting the attack into perspective, or at least trying to figure it out.

"So someone was watching the hallway for them?" Ann asked.

"Watching—I don't know where they were watching," Cate said. "Just a lookout, I guess."

"And they never said a word," Erika mused. "So you don't know if they really were Americans or just dressed like Americans."

"That's right," Cate said. "But they sure as hell looked like Americans."

"The list?" Ann said, the confusion apparent in her voice. "Shit, what a goofy deal. This doesn't fit in anywhere. I guess the sons of bitches have criminal records, didn't want to leave any fingerprints. So maybe they are American."

"And they thought *Cate* had the list?" Erika said. "No one knows about Cate. And what damn list?"

"Okay." Ann took a deep breath. "So where does this put us?"

"Somebody has some screwed-up information," Cate said, wiping her forehead, leaning over the mirror more closely to see if the cut on her lip was going to cause it to swell. She dabbed the spot with the washcloth. "They said that they knew I had the list, that they knew what I was doing."

"Maybe they thought they were working on Irina," Erika volunteered. "They said, 'We know what you are doing.' They just got the wrong woman."

"That's the best I can figure it, too," Ann said. "But that's a pretty big screw-up. I mean, how could they have done that?"

"So where is Valentin?" Cate asked.

They told her the situation with Volkov. Cate sighed hugely, still feeling her muscles loosening.

"Then where does this put us?" she asked.

"Excuse me, Catherine," Ometov said. At the beginning of this conversation, when they had called in response to her news, both Ometov and Hain had offered their commiseration immediately, as was appropriate. But now that the three women had had their discussion, it seemed the men were ready to press on to new matters.

"I have a proposal for you," he continued, his voice steady, calming. "Everyone is pushing hard to find out what this is all about, of course, as you might imagine, but I think—and this is my idea, I have talked it over with Curtis—I think this unfortunate incident can work to our advantage."

"To our advantage," Cate said.

"Yes, yes indeed. Let me explain. As we already have told you, we think you have done a remarkable job in befriending Irina. You practically read my mind when you told her you had a child nearly the same age as her little daughter. This was a brilliant decision. If in fact Krupatin is holding Irina's child as a hostage, as a means of coercing her to do certain things—and we believe that you were right about that—then we need to know what those things are. We need for you to remain as close to her as you can, to get even closer to her, if possible. These bruises, these scratches you have received, could be used . . ." He stumbled only a little but was clearly hesitant, tentative. "I think Irina is somewhat taken with you. Perhaps she sees in you the friend she has not had for a long time . . . If she can sympathize with you, see in you some of the pain she feels within herself, if she can more closely identify with you, I think it will increase your bond to her."

"The point being . . ." Ann urged.

"I think you should tell Irina that Stepanov has abused you, Catherine," Ometov concluded. "That he has threatened your child if you do not agree to help him in some way to set up a new operation he wants to establish here in Houston. Irina must know about Stepanov's operations here. Perhaps he wants you to sleep with certain people to help him gain some kind of advantage. Irina is all too aware of the coercive tactics I have already told you about." He paused. "If we are right about what is happening to her, this could be a crucial time for her. She seems to us to be highly stressed, under a lot of pressure. And we think we see a crack in her emotional armor. Perhaps you, Catherine, can open that crack a little wider, maybe wide enough for us to break her."

There was moment of silence. Cate knew in an instant that the proposal was a good one. She also knew that this was going to be an emotional stretch for her. The personal stakes would increase dramatically.

"What do you think, Cate?" Ann asked.

It was a moment before Cate said, "It sounds right, doesn't it?"

"Yeah. I have to say it does. This sounds good."

"But what about Irina?" Cate asked. "What if she knows about these men? She's going to know I'm lying, that Stepanov didn't do it."

"No," Ometov said. "She can't have known about the beating. I cannot imagine how she could have known."

Erika spoke up. "Cate, it does sound right. But—and I want Leo to note this—"

"Yes, go ahead," Ometov said.

"If Cate goes on with this," Erika continued, "everyone needs to be aware that we are playing with the emotions of a woman who not only is under a great deal of stress but probably has been for a very long time. Irina may be at a breaking point, yes, but when she breaks she may do so in a radical way, very crazy, irrational. Cate might well be in the middle of that. This one is going to be difficult, even dangerous, to stop once it gets going."

There was another pause. Erika had brought out in the open what everyone else was allowing to remain implied. Cate was grateful to her for that.

"Yes, okay, Erika is right." Ometov had little choice but to acknowledge this now. "Yes, that is very true. If we are right about Irina's situation, about her state of mind, she might be unpredictable. We do not know what she is doing. If we knew, it would help us assess the situation. But we don't. What Erika says is very true."

"And what about the two guys who just left here?" Cate tossed the washcloth on the floor. "I don't want to go through that again."

"Okay," Hain said. "I'm going to get on that. Just be satisfied that we're on it." He paused. "Just a minute, Cate. Strey's patching through. Everybody stay on. Ennis, go ahead."

"Cate?"

"Yeah, I hear you, Ennis."

"Listen, kid, this thing is getting a little crazier than I had expected. This is dicey, no doubt about it. You're not obligated to this level of play. I want you to know that flat out."

"Your confidence slipping, Ennis?" Cate asked.

"Not even a scintilla," he said. "But I'm a by-the-book man, Cate, and the book says an undercover agent has to go in with her eyes wide open, of her own free will. I know you know that. I'm just reminding you. When the game changes this much, it's a whole new game."

That bit of advice, Cate knew, took some professional courage. Hain was Strey's superior, and it took some fortitude to warn an agent about an operation initiated by a superior, an operation that clearly meant as much to that superior as this one meant to

Hain. But Hain said nothing on his end of the line. He wouldn't. Recordings of these conversations were going down in the great, vast storehouse of FBI operations records. When this operation was over and people were assessing the results—whatever they might be—they were going to judge everyone by everything they said here, even by the tone of voice they used when they said it. Cate could imagine Hain and Ometov grimacing and holding their breath.

"Ennis, I appreciate that," Cate said. "More than I can tell you." She paused. "But I'm committed to this. It's not even an issue. I want to finish it."

"I know you can do it," Strey said. "If we'd known all this up front, from the beginning, I still would've picked you. You've got my confidence, kid."

"Then I guess we'd better decide where to go from here," Cate said.

"One last thing, Cate," Ann added, glancing at Hain. "We've contacted you twice now, and you've called us once. It wasn't our original intention to do it this way, to be talking to you this often. Irina's arrival called for some fine-tuning, and of course this was a blindside. But listen, we're going to pull back now. If we keep up with this kind of communication, we're going to get caught. So all of this has got to stop. You won't be hearing from us again unless there's something critical or we're wrapping this up. You're going to have to fend for yourself, make your own decisions when the unexpected happens. You're on your own now."

There was no hesitation. "I understand," Cate said.

"Good luck."

It was Cate who broke the connection.

Forty-six

CARLO BONTATE had set up residence in a darkly wooded section of the city several miles away from the airy domicile of his associate Wei. Unlike his country house on the bright Marineo hillside, the enclave he established in Houston was overshadowed by tall straight pines and heavy-limbed water oaks and was embraced on two sides by the sinuous loops of a muddy bayou which sluggishly flowed southward through the city between weedy, insect-infested banks. It was a sun-dappled world, and the young Sicilians who secured the two-story house and its walled environs for their don were not happy about the coastal summer humidity, which caused them to perspire profusely through their baggy silk shirts.

Irina walked along a brick path behind two dark *palermitani*, the pine needles crunching under her feet as they negotiated between cascades of azaleas to a large courtyard behind the Georgian mansion. Bontate was sitting under a cabana watching several young women swimming in the pool, dusky, lean Italian bodies in the glittery azure water.

He stood as Irina approached and offered her a seat at the table with him. He was in short sleeves, off-the-rack dress slacks, and sandals. He looked like a young man already habituated to an old man's ways, destined to become a watcher of slow afternoons from a café table on the main piazza in Marineo.

The two young men said something in Sicilian to the three girls, who, without protest, undulated to the edge of the pool and climbed out, dripping and glistening, rearranging their olive buttocks and bosoms to fit strategically beneath the few square inches of bright bikinis.

"I apologize for sitting out here in this goddamn heat," Bontate said, gesturing with his beefy arm to the hazy lawn, "but I've had enough of that shitty air conditioning. It reminds me of morgue air. I'd rather sweat out here with the mosquitoes."

Two telephones sat on the wrought-iron table near him, and a third one, a portable one, sat beside a little flowerpot on a stand to one side. An ice bucket and a pitcher of icewater sat on the table, along with what appeared to be a pitcher of lemonade and a tray crowded with various liquor bottles and a few bottles of wine. The pool was surrounded by lush flowerbeds and a thick emerald lawn. Tropical flowers and bromeliads rested in colorful clusters among the lower branches of the trees.

"Would you care for something to drink?"

"Just water," she said.

He poured her a tall glass of water, ice falling into it from the pitcher. She took it and drank.

"Volkov is inside," Bontate said, lifting his chin toward the house. "He is making some calls to St. Petersburg."

"Then you have already told him my proposition?"

"Of course."

"And his reaction?"

"Skepticism."

"But he was interested."

Bontate smiled, surprising her. "Of course."

"And why is he calling St. Petersburg?"

Bontate shrugged. " 'Preliminary inquiries,' he said."

Irina felt an adrenaline rush; her abdominal muscles quivered, though she could not be sure whether this was from fear or excited hope. Already perspiration was gathering on the surface of her skin beneath her clothes.

"Here he comes," Bontate said, his amber eyes narrowed to slits as he looked toward the house through the dappled summer sunlight.

Valery Volkov, stocky, built low to the ground, was walking briskly along a path, with one of Bontate's young men not far behind. He was carrying his suit coat draped over one arm, and his voluminous trousers, with their long crotch and full-cut legs, bagged limply in the humid heat. His shirt was white, short-sleeved. By the time he got to them, his putty-colored skin was stippled with sweat.

He spoke to Irina as he approached but did not extend his hand. Bontate let him pull out his own chair, throw his suit coat over the back of another, and sit down. Irina noticed that Bontate poured him a lemonade with ice without asking him what he wanted. They must have been talking some time before she arrived.

Volkov drank the lemonade greedily and then put the glass in front of him and crossed his arms on the table. He looked across them at Irina.

"Carlo told me about your proposition. I have doubts," he said bluntly.

"About what?"

"That you can do it."

"Why?"

"Have you even talked to him yet?"

"I told you when you came to the suite with Izvarin, I saw him this morning."

"I thought you were lying."

"No, it's true."

"And what did you talk about?"

She wanted to glance at Bontate but didn't. The only way this was going to work was if she went all out, didn't appear to be holding something back from one and not the other. Volkov was probably testing for this.

"He gave me instructions on how to kill Wei. He wants Wei to be first."

Bontate didn't move a muscle.

"When?"

"Tonight. I am supposed to meet him at his home."

"Oh, really? Why?"

"He likes to talk about art," Irina said pointedly.

Volkov nodded. "And how are you supposed to do it?" he asked.

She told them.

Volkov snorted, a kind of laugh at Krupatin's ingenuity. "Crazy fucker. And that gives you plenty of time to be somewhere else when the Chinese actually dies."

She nodded.

"And when are you supposed to hit Carlo?"

"He didn't tell me. He said he would let me know."

"But you don't know how?"

"He said he would tell me."

"And when will he do that?"

"He said he would get in touch with me."

"He didn't set up any system for contacting you?" Volkov asked skeptically.

"No."

"In other words, you cannot contact him."

"No, I cannot." She was not about to give up everything to this man. Not at this point. She had worked alone too long not to hold something back. A secret was only a secret as long as it remained solely within your mind. There it had inestimable value. If you set it loose, it turned to dust in an instant.

Irina took a drink of her water. Volkov studied her.

"How are you going to kill Sergei?"

"I don't know. How are you going to get my daughter?"

"I'm checking into it."

He continued to study her. This did not bother her. She knew enough about Volkov not to be intimidated by his aggressiveness. She found it interesting that Bontate was silent. While Volkov was testing her, Bontate was reassuring himself about her by watching her closely. She could feel his brassy eyes.

"Did Sergei tell you why we are all here—Valentin, Izvarin, and myself?"

"No. As a matter of fact, I didn't even know anyone was going to be here besides myself until after I arrived."

Volkov wiped his gray forehead with his hand and looked at his sweaty fingers. "How did you come here?"

She told them of how Krupatin had picked her up at Wei's house in Paris, of the flight to Mexico and the drive north.

"Now," she said, "I have done most of the answering. I want you to tell me how you are going to get my daughter out of Russia."

Volkov drank some of his lemonade. He smacked his lips and then drank some more. By now she knew he and Bontate had checked out some of the assassinations she had related to Bontate. She knew that some of them could be confirmed quickly, to a degree at least, enough for the men to know that she was either extraordinarily connected—or she had done them herself, as she claimed.

"I must confess," Volkov said, wiping his mouth with his fingers, "that I did not know you were hitting for Sergei. I personally knew two of your targets. I suspected Sergei was responsible for them, but I could never prove it. I did know too that Sergei had your daughter. I did not know why, naturally. You have been an exceptionally well-guarded secret. This part of your life, I mean. Anyway, to answer your question," he went on, "I have made inquiries. At this moment I cannot tell you exactly where your daughter is, but I know people who know. The trick for now is to be sure of her location without alerting the wrong people that we are inquiring."

"How soon can you do it?"

"Quickly." He flicked his eyes at Bontate and then back to her. "You realize that you cannot make a mistake here. If you try and fail, I will never be able to sleep another night peacefully for the rest of my life."

As always, she noted, Volkov was thinking only of himself. He would not be the only one who would never be able to sleep again.

"It is true," she said, "that you don't have any assurances. But then, neither do I. I have heard nothing but lies since the day I met Sergei Krupatin. However, if I do accomplish this—when I do—I expect you to do as you promise."

This was not a threat, only a reminder that she was not without resources. She could not be duped or disregarded without consequences. She knew this was not lost on Volkov.

Volkov nodded. "Sometimes determination can achieve the impossible."

"I don't worry about its being impossible."

"No, I suppose not."

A bead of perspiration ran down the small of her back.

Volkov wiped his mouth with his bare fingers to remove the sweat that was forming rapidly on his upper lip and chin. His pasty coloring was even less appealing when bathed in perspiration.

He said, "Also, something has to be done about Izvarin—and Stepanov."

Irina returned his gaze and slowly shook her head. He was fishing. She wasn't going to take the bait.

"We'll talk about it," he said. "They have to be dealt with."

Irina realized that all the calls Volkov had made to Russia on Bontate's telephones in the past few hours had probably had more to do with his own coup plans than with locating Félia. After all, he was contemplating the elimination of the top of Krupatin's huge organization—and she guessed he was planning assassinations in the European cells as well—and he had to put his own people into place immediately to secure his control.

Volkov studied her, but it was Bontate who spoke next.

"What about Wei?" he asked her.

"Sergei told me it would take three days for the bacteria to produce symptoms," she said. "In five days he would be dead. I don't think Sergei will want to wait to see the symptoms before he gives me the other instructions. So he will never know that I didn't administer the bacteria."

Both men looked at her in silence, and she felt something new. Again it was Bontate who spoke.

"We want you to go ahead with it."

Jesus. She was caught off-guard, but she didn't let it show. "You want me to give the bacteria to Wei?"

"We see no reason to interrupt Krupatin's plans—at this point."

Irina nodded. Inside she was stunned, and frightened. She had offered them a small opening, an opportunity, and in the blink of an eye they had hacked it into a chasm, their eyes glazed red, greedy for the leverage of death. Like hyenas quick to take advantage of even the slightest wound, they already had their snouts buried deep in the entrails. How could she trust people like this? How could she ever hope they would honor this agreement? The answer was a bleak one. She had no choice.

"Then consider it done," she said.

Forty-seven

WHEN IRINA WALKED into her suite, she immediately saw the red light blinking on her telephone. Unbuttoning her blouse as she picked up the receiver, she punched the button and waited for the voice mail. There were three messages. All three of them were from Catherine.

The first one was urgent, frantic; she sounded like she was crying. Something had happened, she said. Please call as soon as Irina got in. The second one was terse. Please call. The third one, not ten minutes before, was soberer but had an edge of fear about it. Please, please call as soon as possible.

Irina stood by the telephone and looked at the light, blinking, blinking, blinking. She punched the button to erase the messages and put down the receiver. She was growing numb. How many emergencies could she deal with? But why would this woman want to talk to her? What kind of an emergency could she possibly have that would suggest that Irina could be of help? She was suspicious, and now questioned her optimistic feelings that Catherine was exactly who she appeared to be. Should she call her?

No, not until she bathed. Her hair was wet with perspiration, and her entire body felt as if it had been in a steambath. She looked at her watch. There wasn't a lot of time.

She stripped out of her clothes, left them lying in a pile near the foot of her bed, and went directly to the shower. Leaving the hot water off entirely, she took a cold shower, lathering every inch of her body, shampooing her hair twice. She felt as if she might never wash off the sticky residue of the muggy bayou air.

She was rinsing her hair for the last time when the telephone rang. She turned off the water, opened the glass door to the shower, stepped onto a thick bathmat, and reached for a towel with one hand and the telephone on the wall with the other.

"Irina?"

"Yes, Catherine. I got your messages."

"Can I come up?"

"Are you all right?"

"Yes—I'm okay. Something's happened. I'm afraid to talk here."

"Okay. Yes, come up."

Irina wrapped one towel around her hair and dried her body with the other. She had barely finished taking the towel off her head and wrapping it around her body when she heard the door chimes.

She went to the door and opened it. Catherine was standing there, her auburn hair falling generously around her face but failing entirely to hide the marks there.

"My God, what has happened to you?" Irina took her arm and pulled her into the room.

Catherine shook her head, unable to speak. It was obvious that she had been distraught, had recovered, and was now holding on as best as she could.

"Could I get something to drink?"

Irina quickly mixed something for both of them, and they sat on the edge of the sofa, holding their drinks in their laps.

"Stepanov did this?" Irina asked. The expression on Catherine's face was a familiar one. *Mafiya* girlfriends were always being beaten. They were sexual chattel, the recipients of a brutal tradition.

Catherine nodded, dropping her eyes. She wasn't crying, but there was something else. It was a reaction Irina had often seen.

Though the beating was no fault of their own, women were often embarrassed by what had happened to them. It was a demeaning emotion, shame for what another person had done to them, shame at being a victim. But Catherine seemed furious too, both furious and frightened. The complexity of her emotions was conveyed by small details: the set of her eyes and mouth, the way she held her shoulders, her hands, the way she swallowed.

"He got rough with me before, but never anything like this," Catherine began to explain after swallowing a mouthful of her drink. "Not often, but he's been . . . close to it." She drank again.

Irina listened attentively to her unsteady syllables and noted her hesitation. The woman was still very agitated.

"He wanted me to sleep with others, men, a man he said was crazy about my type. I said no. He said it would be more money. I said no, that wasn't the point. He began swearing . . . and then he hit me. Twice, very fast. I was stunned . . . I've never been hit before. I fell down. He picked me up and threw me against the dresser and . . . had sex with me, standing there."

She stopped, resorting again to her drink. Irina did not flinch. She became very calm.

"He said I damn well would do what he wanted," Catherine went on, swallowing. "He said . . . he said I didn't know what I was mixed up in. He said that he knew who was taking care of my daughter, and if I wanted her to stay safe, I would do what I was told to do."

She stopped, her face crumpling momentarily, but she gained control of herself, and her eyes welled with tears as she stared straight at Irina.

"What is going on here?" she demanded. Her voice was determined but wobbly. "Who the hell is that man?"

"He is a beast," Irina said steadily. "He always has been a beast."

"What's going *on* here?" Catherine insisted again. "This doesn't feel like . . . I don't know. He's not just a businessman, is he?"

Irina didn't answer. She stared at Catherine, noting that the scratches on her face were still raw and painful, though no bruises showed. Still, to a woman unaccustomed to this, being slapped around could be just as horrifying as a real beating.

"Why do you ask that?"

Catherine glared at her. "He threatened my daughter. That's not an ordinary kind of thing. How did he know where she was? Why would a businessman look into something like that?" Her tears welled, and she had to stop. Again she recovered. She swallowed. "And this afternoon . . . You said, you tried to warn me about him."

"I told you, the man is a beast," Irina said stoically. She paused. "Why don't you go to the police?"

Catherine shook her head emphatically.

"What's the matter?"

"I can't do that. No, definitely not the police. Stepanov would tell everything, that he paid me to sleep with him. He would say that I was only a prostitute. My ex-husband's family—they'd have my daughter taken away from me. It's an impossible situation. I'm afraid they'll find out anyway." She grew agitated. "It's impossible. I may have ruined everything. I'm afraid Stepanov is going to hold this over my head. He's clever enough. He knows I could lose my daughter because of this. He knows that."

Irina watched this woman who sat only an arm's reach from her. A mother. How many times had she seen this kind of agony? These men had taken the purest bond in the world and time and time again had wrenched it into a relationship of hopelessness, plunging their hands into the heart of it and pulling it inside out. Having discovered that a mother would make soul-threatening sacrifices to protect or save her child, they realized that such a fierce love was at the same time a woman's greatest vulnerability. This knowledge became a dependable weapon, and with it they committed unspeakable cruelties, profaning this, the most tender of all affections.

Cate was rendered almost limp by this performance. Not only was she frightened that she might not be convincing and that Irina would see right through her, but she was shaken when she saw by the expression on Irina's face that her portrayal had been successful. The look of empathy that slowly grew like a tragic mask on this beautiful woman's countenance was unnerving. And it was also frightening as Cate realized that she had wrought this—or rather, her story had—and the story was evidently causing Irina genuine anxiety, no doubt recreating in her mind the distancing of her own daughter and the circumstances of that separation, which obviously had been so painful.

"What are you going to do?" Irina asked.

Cate put down her glass, pressed her cool fingers to her forehead, and looked away. She did not doubt that she conveyed perplexity, for in fact she had no idea what to say. Suddenly again she was frightened.

"Maybe you should leave the city," Irina suggested. "He is not going to come after you."

"How do you know that?"

"I think I can assure he won't."

"But I can't—he knows my name. He's looked into my private life."

"You should run, believe me."

Cate paused. "He hasn't paid me."

Irina shook her head, exasperated. "God, you have no idea how insignificant that is. What you risk by staying overwhelms the value of the money he would pay you."

"Look, I literally don't have enough money for that. And my ex-husband's family has visiting rights with my daughter. If I take her away, they'll charge me with kidnapping." She looked at Irina. "The laws here—they're complicated. Leaving is not an option."

She averted her eyes again, but she could feel Irina's stare. She couldn't bring herself to look her in the face. She had no idea what her expression might convey to the woman, but she just couldn't do it at that moment.

"Why did you come to me?" Irina asked. "This city is your home. You have friends who can help you."

Cate was already shaking her head.

"No," she said, "you're the only one who knows about this . . . this . . . No one knows—I told you that. They can't know about this. Really, you have no idea how . . . how unacceptable this is, what I've done. It . . . it's stepping way over the line. I've made a tragic mistake doing this." She began to blink; in fact, she was surprised to find herself actually feeling these emotions, as if she had this daughter, as if she had done this shameful thing with Stepanov. The image of Stepanov's face only inches away from her bared genitals as she let him look at her tattoo burst into her mind. "This is . . . this is a nightmare."

A sob surprised her, caught in her throat. She felt odd, hot, almost as if she were about to be swept up in an out-of-body experience. She almost believed what she was saying. She could feel herself actually waiting for Irina to come up with some kind of solution to rescue her.

"Can you get your clothes out of Stepanov's room?"

Cate hesitated. "I could, I guess. He's gone right now."

Irina nodded. She was holding her iced drink, with her wet hair stringing down, water seeping from it and here and there causing small rivulets to trace down her bare shoulders and into the bathtowel tucked tightly over her breasts. Her green eyes appeared softer now that the emerald dress was gone, jade instead of emerald. Her mouth tended to have a slight pucker at one corner, giving her a pensive air. And she was sexy, with her long legs smooth and shapely, the towel riding high on her thighs, her breasts significant even beneath the cotton towel.

"I can help you, I think," she said. "But you will have to leave Stepanov and come with me."

"Go with you? Where? No, definitely not, I can't leave the city. I—"

"I am not leaving the city." Irina's voice was deliberate, unemotional.

Cate looked at her.

Irina set her glass on the coffee table in front of the sofa and ran her fingers through her hair. She sighed heavily.

"Let me tell you something, Catherine." She paused and spread one of her long-fingered hands out on her thigh, then looked at it as though she were thinking about what she was going to say. "You have become involved in something that is very complicated."

She paused again, and Cate could almost hear the wheels spinning in her mind. Irina reached out and took one of Cate's hands and put it on her bare thigh. Her skin was smooth and cool. She covered Cate's hand with her own and looked at her.

"I am going to tell you things that will change your life," she said. "Actually, your life has already changed, only you do not yet realize this. It changed when Valentin Stepanov made a request you refused, and when he mentioned your daughter. You are right to fear his long reach. You are wrong if you think there is anything you can do about it . . . short of killing him."

Cate flinched and gaped at her.

"No, wait," Irina said and held her hand, not letting her withdraw it. "Listen to me. You will not have to do that. Of course not. But maybe there is in fact another way." She smoothed her hand over Cate's, caressing it. "I think I can help you, but I will need your help in return. Where is your daughter?"

"With my parents. They're keeping her for a few days—I said I had a business trip. They like to keep her."

"Then you do not have to see her for a few days?"

"No, I don't."

"You are free to be with me."

Cate nodded tentatively.

"Valentin Stepanov lives in New York, but he is from St. Petersburg. He is not with the Russian trade commission but is an important figure in organized crime in Europe. He is a member of Russia's *mafiya,* a very dangerous man."

"Jesus, what have I done?"

Irina gripped Cate's hand and held it. "The other men, Nakhimov and Bykov, are also Russian *mafiya.* They have all come to Houston for a meeting with the man who is the head of their organization."

"And you," Cate interrupted her, slowly but firmly pulling her hand away from Irina's thigh. "Why do you know this?"

Irina nodded patiently. "Yes," she said, "I will tell you my story too, but first we have to get you away from Valentin."

Forty-eight

OF COURSE it was no trouble at all to move her things out of Stepanov's suite. Irina quickly slipped on a dress and the two women went downstairs, gathered Cate's toiletries and clothes, and took them up by the stairwell in order to encounter as few people as possible. When they got back to Irina's suite, the long summer day was ending and the evening light was turning sapphire through the French windows in the bedroom, where they put Cate's clothes away. Her department store fare looked colorless alongside Irina's French and Italian labels.

"Would you care for another drink?" Irina asked as they were closing the closet door.

"Sure," Cate said. "That would be nice."

"Okay, good. Why don't you wait here, then? I will get it for us."

Cate went to the French windows and looked out at the city lights emerging from the falling dusk. She had never felt so unstable in her life, as though absolutely anything could happen, as though the only things that *could* happen would be unexpected things. From this moment on, everything was going to be a surprise. With her eyes wide open, she had walked straight into the darkness.

She heard Irina come into the bedroom behind her but continued looking at the nightscape, taking one moment more to enjoy a view of the city that was real and beautiful. It was not a mirage or a hallucination. It was simply the city at dusk.

When she turned around, Irina was standing beside her bed, slipping out of the simple shift she had put on to go downstairs. She was completely naked except for a locket on a chain around her neck, and Cate was struck anew by her extraordinary physical beauty. Her body was flawless.

"I have to change clothes," she said, tossing the dress on the bed. Then, without making a sound, she formed a shushing gesture with her lips and opened her hands palms outward to Cate, cautioning her to be quiet.

Cate frowned, and a warm dread swept through her. It must have shown on her face, for Irina quickly made a pacifying gesture and approached her.

Reaching out, she put her fingers on the buttons of Cate's blouse and began undoing them, her face close enough to Cate's for Cate to see the fine downy hairs on the side of her jaw below her ears. Cate started to protest, but Irina gestured quickly again, raising one hand, stopping her, her eyes saying it was all right, placating, calming.

Cate was genuinely confused. What in the hell was she supposed to do about this? In fact, what *was* this? Irina's green eyes looked into Cate's as she opened the unbuttoned blouse and leaned in so that their cheeks actually brushed, and Cate could smell the soft fragrance of sachet as Irina slipped the blouse off her shoulders.

Tossing the blouse on the bed, Irina moved her hands to the waistband of Cate's skirt and undid the buttons there, still with her eyes fixed on Cate's. The material fell to the floor. They were very close. Cate hesitated and then stepped out of the skirt. She could feel a curious humming begin in her body as she stood breast to breast with this beautiful woman, still unsure of where the next moment would take them.

Irina reached up and put her long fingers into the center of Cate's bra and found the hook. She undid it and slowly pulled the material away from Cate's breasts, the backs of her fingers tracing across the surface of Cate's skin.

Cate was petrified. She was. But she was also finding the encounter unmistakably erotic. Her senses were alert to every slight brush of flesh on flesh, aware even of Irina's breath on her nipples as Irina drew the bra straps off her shoulders.

Then Irina stepped back. Holding Cate with her eyes, she began feeling along the seams of Cate's bra, tracing the seams of the cups, then the straps, feeling the snap in the center. Satisfied, she dropped the bra on the floor, bent her knees slightly, and picked up Cate's skirt. Again she began going over the seams, drawing the hem through her fingers and then doing the same to the waistband.

It was only when she dropped the skirt too and picked up the blouse that Cate realized what was happening. Irina was searching for a wire. The thought jump-started her heart and almost caused her to stagger. As she stood there naked except for her panties, the implants in her arms seemed to swell to manifest dimensions. Feeling that she had to speak or she would faint, she managed to find her response in Catherine's personality.

"What . . . what are you doing? What is this?"

"I apologize," Irina said, dropping the blouse also. "But I have known these people a long time. I have learned to distrust everyone. Suspicion is second nature to me. I hope you understand that. You must not think of it as a personal insult."

Would Catherine take it personally? Would Catherine know *what* she shouldn't take personally?

"I don't think I understand what's going on here," Cate said. "What are you doing, feeling my clothes?"

"I have discovered, Catherine, that sometimes people put electronic devices in their clothes. Listening devices." Her eyes didn't move from Cate's.

"Oh," Cate said. "I see."

"And there is one other thing," Irina said. "I will explain first. In Russia, in Eastern Europe, and I suppose everywhere, there are all the time assassinations among those in the crime world. Some of these assassins can be very clever. Some are women. Women have been known to hide many things—cyanide capsules, razors, piano wires . . ."

As she said this, she put her hands on Cate's hips and slid her fingers into the sides of her panties. Pushing her hands downward over Cate's hips, she crouched slowly and peeled the panties down her thighs, pausing at the appearance of the poppy tattoo, then continuing down to Cate's ankles. As she rose to stand, she paused again at the red flower, put her finger on it, felt it. Then she stood.

"Will you turn around, please?"

Cate obliged, haltingly, and turned to the French windows and the dusk, which was deepening from purple to black. She felt Irina's body press up against her backside as the woman reached around in front of her with her right arm, her hand skirting downward over the flat of Cate's stomach and between her legs.

The complex of emotions Cate felt was impossible to unravel: panic because Irina's arm was inches away from the implants, excitement at the sensation of Irina's breath on her neck, confusion at the erogenous sensations of Irina's fingers inside her, and finally, fear at the sudden realization that this woman was more dangerous than she had been led to believe. Again a wash of warmth spread over her, and she felt perspiration pop to the surface of her flesh. For a moment she thought her legs were going to fail her, and indeed she must have bobbled, because immediately she felt Irina's left arm encircle her waist and hold her firmly until she finished with her right hand.

When Irina moved away, Cate immediately felt the coolness on her damp skin where their two bodies had been together for those few brief moments. She didn't turn around; she didn't know what to do. She wasn't sure what she had done. If anything. The intense combination of unexpected eroticism and sudden fear had actually weakened her, and when Irina spoke, the sound of her voice had the effect of startling Cate to her senses, almost as if she had been snapped out of a trance.

"Catherine," Irina said, "I am sorry if that embarrassed you. Are you all right?"

Cate nodded.

"I am sorry, but it was necessary for me to know for sure."

Cate nodded again—she couldn't speak—and turned around. Irina was standing at the side of the bed, still naked, holding both glasses. She handed Cate her drink, the ice in the glass rattling softly. They had not turned on the lights, so the room was suffused with a deepening cobalt blue coming from the large windows. Cate was grateful for the failing light. It obscured her bare arms, where she feared Irina would detect the telltale ripples of the implants, and it obscured her face, where she was sure her confusion was clearly written. Somehow even though she had told herself over and over that she was Catherine, not Cate, she had not been able to protect herself from the surprise of her own reactions to what had just happened.

She was relieved to have the drink Irina had given her and eagerly swallowed several large mouthfuls of gin and tonic.

Aside from her pummeled emotions, there was another disconcerting result of what had just happened. Regardless of what Ometov had told her about Irina, it was now clear to Cate that she was dealing with a woman who was far more sinister than Ometov had led her to believe. Either Ometov had been naive about her—which Cate found difficult to believe—or he had withheld information. This woman was intimately familiar with the Russian *mafiya*'s darker side. The strip search had been chillingly thorough, but the more sobering aspect of it was that Irina had felt it necessary to search Cate not only for a wire but also for a possible assassination weapon. Did she fear assassination, then? From whom? Certainly not from Krupatin. She was supposedly on an errand for him. Then from whom? And how long had she had to live with this particular suspicion? And why?

Cate took another drink of gin and tried to calm herself. She tried to put everything into a proper perspective. She tried to maintain her emotional equilibrium. Most of all, she tried to tell herself to be analytical. She had to remember to play the role of someone emotionally rattled while maintaining a calm, critical inner balance. This was the beginning of the "stretch," the challenge that she knew had been lying in wait for her.

Irina pushed her clothes off onto the floor and crawled onto the bed, reclining on her side on the damask cover, facing the French windows. Her long limbs were hazily visible in the dim light. Her voice was low, and her accent seemed, in an odd way, soothing to Cate.

"Come on, Catherine, get on the bed," Irina said. "I want to talk to you. There is much you need to understand before we can do what we have to do."

Forty-nine

THEY LAY on their stomachs, propped on their elbows, holding their drinks, and looked out the French doors at the last hour of evening. The room was lighted only by the pale castoff light of the city, which, visible through the ornate iron railings of the balcony, seemed in a far other country. Irina's husky accented voice completed the sense that Cate had been transported out of place, out of time, to an elsewhere she had never imagined.

In a matter-of-fact voice, Irina began telling Cate how she came to be where she was. Her story was essentially the same story that Leo Ometov had told Cate and the others only a few days before. Had it been only a few days? But Irina's version was full of details, memories of a college student, of a young woman flattered by the sophisticated attentions of an older man, of a promising career in a prestigious profession, of a love turned to obsession, of hopes soured, of dreams denied, of a life spiraling out of control.

Sometimes Irina would pause to remember; sometimes she would pause to take a drink and press the cold glass to her temple. At one point her long bare leg drifted over to Cate's and her foot absently rubbed the side of Cate's foot, a gesture that seemed to reflect a desire not to be alone with her memories.

Then suddenly Irina's story took a turn that caused the hair to prickle on Cate's arms. Actually, it wasn't a turn away from Ometov's account, it was rather a refraction of it.

"So, after two years of running," she said, "of being free of Sergei and recovering my self-respect, I was once again dragged back into his life. But now everything was different. Sergei loved me still, but he also hated me. This is not a contradiction but a paradox. A person can feel both emotions toward another. I know this. Sergei could not tolerate what I had done. It was not the money I had stolen. No, that was so little money to him. It was the fact that I wanted so badly to be away from him. He could not bear to think that I found him revolting."

She reached down and put her empty glass on the floor beside the bed and hung her head, letting her long buttery hair stream down over her head, almost touching the floor. She stayed that way, rocking her head from side to side, her hair swaying, stretching the tendons in her neck, which must have begun to ache. Then she slung her head up and back, swinging her hair out of her face. She looked at Cate.

"Then he made sure I never again would leave him," she said. She reached over and took one of Cate's hands and brought it to the locket that dangled around her neck.

"Hold this," she said, wrapping Cate's fingers around the oval locket. "It is too dark for you to see the picture I carry here, but I think you can feel the innocence of the face inside, the face of my daughter, Félia."

She was quiet a moment, holding Cate's hand, which held her daughter. Then she released her grip, and Cate did too, and the locket swung from Irina's neck, throwing off a pale glint in the blue light.

"He took my baby," Irina said, "my little Félia, and gave her to a family I did not know. She would be safe, he said, as long as I did what he wanted."

She stared out at the city, at the lost light of night.

"I cannot tell you how this happened," she continued. "I mean, of course, I could, I remember it as vividly as I remember—" She caught herself. "But I cannot say the words to describe it. It would kill me. I can only think these words. I cannot say them.

Even thinking them causes me to die a little every time. I die every day. Every day."

Cate turned her head slightly to see Irina's pale profile in the soft light. Her cheeks glistened. But she went on.

"Sergei's behavior toward me was schizophrenic. One moment he wanted me above all else, the next he could not bear to have me around him. And even when he wanted me—and he always wanted me in a sexual way—he was cruel. But through all this, one thing remained the same: he trusted me. Because of Félia. He knew I would do whatever I was told to do because I would never jeopardize her.

"So I became a messenger for him, a courier. There were many, many times when he needed someone to travel for him, to deliver this or that, to receive something, to confirm that something was true. I became his black angel, messenger to all the other devils in his empire. For a while I traveled constantly, and I got to know many of his lieutenants. I kept my mouth shut. I did what I was told. But I kept my eyes open, too. I learned where all the skeletons were hidden. I learned everything about his organization— who was discontented, who was happy, who was on the way up, who was on the way out. Sergei ran his empire like Caligula. He could cause someone to die simply by frowning." She sighed. "And that is still what I am doing now."

She stopped and rolled over on her side, propped her head on her hand, elbow on the bed, and looked at Cate.

"But that is not all I am doing," she said, pausing, regarding Cate a moment. Then she went on.

"A little more than a year ago I was in the Caffè Florian in Venice. Have you ever been to Venice? No? Such a beautiful city. So beautiful. Anyway, I remember this morning perfectly, the way one does with hopeful moments that later turn into great disappointments. I had one of the small alcoves all to myself—*il cinese*. It was the off-season, cold and wet outside, with a heavy mist drifting across St. Mark's Square. I was half dreaming, lingering over a cup of espresso near a window, watching people here and there lean into the mist as they hurried across the square.

"A man came down the corridor and stopped. I was aware of him but paid no attention. " 'Excuse me,' he said. 'May I join you?' This was Leonid Ometov, a very high official in Russia's Ministry of the Interior. Years ago he was a dear friend of my parents', before they died, which happened a few years before this took place. At the time we knew him he was in Soviet military intelligence, but I had not seen him in years, and it took me a moment to recognize him. In fact, he had to introduce himself."

Ometov! Cate felt a momentary disequilibrium. For an instant she imagined what must be going on in the off-site. The silence. The stunned silence. Suddenly the options were wide open again. It was possible, just possible, that everything had changed. Uncertainty became an ever larger part of the mix. She swallowed, and clung to every word as Irina continued.

"Of course he could join me, I said. I was delighted to see him, but secretly I was mortified. First, it is difficult for Russians to relax around anyone who is in any form of intelligence work, whether it is in the Soviet Union or in the present Republic of Russia. We suffered too much from these people in the past fifty years. But more important, I guessed immediately what he was doing there. It was no coincidence. Russians do not believe in coincidence. I knew this meeting was the culmination of a long, intricate intelligence operation. For him to be able to walk casually into the Florian and sit down with me like this meant that his agents were all over the place, in the square, in the café . . . I knew Ometov was surrounded by an invisible circle of agents who made sure it was safe for him. And I knew that they knew that I was alone, and that my business for this trip already was behind me. I was taking a day of relaxation just for myself."

Irina paused, remembering. Now and again Cate could see the moist glint of her eye reflected in the oblique light from the French doors.

"To give him credit," Irina went on, "he read all of this passing over my face in that first moment and did not insult me by trying to pretend he did not have business with me. We chatted for a moment, waiting for his coffee to arrive, and when it did and the waiter left, he did not toy with me.

"He said he knew what I had been doing for the last two years. His people had got onto me about that long ago, and by now they had a detailed dossier on me. The proposition was very simple. They wanted me to inform on Sergei. They wanted a long-term relationship so they could create a detailed picture of his organization, of his international contacts, of his plans for the future. They knew I was his main communications conduit and wanted everything that passed through me. They wanted to know everything I knew.

"If I agreed to cooperate, he said, after six months they would rescue my daughter, give her back to me, and provide me with a new identity, and I could disappear. I could go where I wished.

"I was ecstatic. Frightened, to be sure, but here was hope, real hope, from an unexpected source. Ometov told me that I would have the rest of the day to think it over. If I wished to go ahead with it, I should call a certain number. He would then meet me that night at the hotel where I was staying, and we would talk about the details.

"That evening I called the number as directed, and he appeared at my hotel as promised. We talked about how this operation could work. We went over all the possibilities. By this time I already had developed considerable undercover skills on my own, and it was their awareness of this that encouraged his people to believe that I might actually be able to operate successfully as a double agent."

Irina sighed hugely and rolled onto her back, one foot on the bed, knee in the air, her hands resting on the flat of her stomach. She stared up into the darkness of the high ceiling.

"Before he left that night, of course, he began to intimate other interests. His hand found a delicate position on my leg, here, and an innocuous touch became a caress. I had nothing to gain by denying him. I let him have what he wanted. It was nothing to me. I was full of hope. What was his greedy appetite compared to what I had to gain?"

She paused, her eyes wide open, looking up into a space without light where there was nothing to see.

"Even then," she said, "with all I had been through, I was capable of hoping. I should have known. I should have been more cynical. As I looked back on it later, I realized that it must have been Félia. A child does that to you. Even when the dark is blackest, when it is the most impenetrable and hopeless, a child can make you imagine a glimmer of light."

A pall fell over Cate in the silence that followed. Good God. How much of this was she supposed to believe? Why would Irina lie about any of this? If, as they all were wanting to believe, she had in fact gained Irina's confidence, why would Irina lie to her at all? Rather, why would she lie to Catherine?

If she was telling the truth, why had Ometov withheld this information from the FBI? Or had he? Maybe they had simply withheld it from her? If they had, why would they? And could Cate believe what Irina said about Ometov, that he had taken sexual advantage of her? Cate could not reconcile this portrayal with the kind, if shrewd, man she had gotten to know in the past few days. There was truth here, to be sure, but could it *all* be true? What could she believe? What *should* she believe, and what should she reject?

Cate put her own glass on the floor also and turned on her side to face Irina. She looked at Irina's handsome profile once more, at the line of her long, fine body. To possess such beauty and not be destroyed by it, a woman had to be wiser than a philosopher. Irina was intelligent, without a doubt, but she had not always been wise. Wisdom, Cate guessed, was a very rare thing anyway, and most of mankind, including herself, probably would not recognize it in another person if they saw it. But intelligence was recognizable, and Irina was intelligent. Unfortunately, it had not saved her from the serpents attracted to the accident of her loveliness.

"What happened?" Cate asked. Her own voice sounded oddly out of place in the context of this space and this story, which belonged so entirely to Irina. "You didn't get your daughter, but you said that you were still working for this man, this Krupatin. And you're still a double agent?"

"A triple agent, a quadruple agent—I don't know anymore," Irina said dismissively. She turned her head and looked at Cate. "After six months Ometov said, oh, it is impossible to stop at this point. You will have to work with us a little longer. We are at a crucial point in understanding Krupatin's German operations, just a little longer. Later he would say, you are too valuable to us. We are too close to understanding important facts about the Asian connection to stop now. Later, when I was desperate, near a nervous breakdown from worrying about my daughter and the pressures of my new responsibilities, he told me they had tried to locate her but Krupatin had moved her. They had begun an intensive search to find her. They were doing their best. They wanted very much to help me."

"And what happened?"

"Nothing." Irina turned her face toward the ceiling and the

darkness again. "I now believe he never intended to rescue Félia. Of necessity, as you can imagine, our meetings always have been very secret. He tells me the information he wants regarding Krupatin. He makes more promises to me. Spins more lies. Then, of course, he wants between my legs. I have never refused him. There is too much at stake. I think only of Félia. Always."

"Didn't Krupatin ever allow you to see her?"

"Yes. About every four or five months he allows me to see her." Irina stopped. "The last time, oh, it was so sad." Her voice grew hoarse. "The child, I think, is beginning to forget who I am. I am like, I think, a vague friend, someone whose face and smell comes into her little life so seldom that she finds it difficult to remember me from one time to the other. I tell her stories about when we were together, before Sergei found us, of what it was like for us. She was too young then actually to remember, I know, but if she remembers me at all, it will be from these stories, which perhaps she will remember like fairy tales. The last time I talked to her, I looked into her eyes very deeply, saying to her never to forget me, to remember my eyes, my mouth, the sound of my voice, my smell. But I think she was puzzled by my passionate manner. Maybe I even frightened her a little." She paused. "It breaks my heart."

Cate could think of nothing to say to this. She lay very still and watched the tears trailing down the side of Irina's face and running into her hair. Though her expression did not change from its passive beauty, the tears ran in frightening abundance.

Cate reached out and put her hand on Irina's arm. She felt the other woman's cool flesh. She reached up and touched the tears at Irina's temples with the back of her fingers, wiping them away, feeling their warmth, feeling even, it seemed, their salty heaviness.

"You see," Irina went on, "they are swine, these men. Boars who eat their own young, who snuffle and feed on the little bodies of their own offspring."

She lifted her hand from her stomach and wiped the tears away from the other side of her face. She cleared her throat and then turned to Cate.

"But Catherine, for the first time I have real hope now." She raised herself on her elbow. "I have a few more things to do for Sergei, a few things to do for this Ometov . . ." She paused, her eyes on Cate, and Cate imagined she could see the green in them even through the lightless space.

"I have a simple request to make of you," Irina said. "It is not difficult, not dangerous. You might be frightened, but you have no need to be. You must believe that."

She stopped and waited for Cate to answer. Cate nodded.

"If I can."

"Oh, you can. It is so simple." She reached out and laid her hand on Cate's hip. "If you do this for me, Catherine, in return I will promise to rid you of Valentin. I know how to do that. You can forget the man ever touched you. Neither you nor your daughter will have to fear him again."

"How are you going to do that?"

"I know things about him."

"Blackmail?"

"Let me take care of it."

Cate looked at her. "Okay." She nodded. "I'll help you."

"Good. It is done, then."

Fifty

THE TRANSMISSION stopped, or rather the voices ceased. Everyone waited. Jernigan and John Parmley sat in the main surveillance van with the red digital readout on their receiver registering a flat line. Ennis Strey waited, hunched over a notepad in the field office tech room, the voice-activated reels in front of him motionless. Ann and Erika sat across the table from Ometov, their eyes focused on him in anticipation. All waited and wondered.

Hain said nothing for a moment. Then he reached up and began flipping off toggle switches. He shut down all outgoing radio communication, took off his headphones, and turned to Leo Ometov. He looked at him a moment. Ometov slowly removed his own headphones as well and turned around in his chair.

"I suppose you would like some explanation," Ometov said, sighing heavily. He shook his head and rubbed his eyes. "I swear to God, I am too worn out for this business. It is going to kill me."

Ann and Erika both removed their headphones too. Their confusion and suspicion were clearly visible in their behavior; they were averting their eyes now, as they began to absorb the shock of what they had just heard.

Hain said nothing. He had been in the business a long time, and he knew he didn't have to say anything in order to get the answers Ometov knew he owed him.

Ometov looked as if the energy had been sucked out of him in one breath, and he stood wearily and walked slowly over to the glass doors to the courtyard.

Now he will turn on the light, Hain said to himself.

Ometov reached up to the light switch and turned on the light.

Hain had never seen a guy so in love with the sight of palms and bougainvillea. Ometov stood with his hands in the pockets of his frumpy suit, his hair needing a touchup with a comb. Hain thought of the pictures he had seen of the nattily groomed Krupatin. The two men did not seem to have come from the same culture.

Ometov turned around.

"It is true," he said. "I have been her case officer for over a year—almost two years, actually." He looked at Ann, who had turned in her chair to watch him as he spoke. "Much of what I have been able to pass on to you has come from her. She has been a gold mine. It is true that I contacted her in exactly the way she related, at the Caffè Florian in Venice, in the Chinese room, on a rainy day." He smiled. "She forgot to say it was November. I did promise her we would get her child away from Sergei in exchange for her cooperation. It is not true that I used the child as a carrot on a stick, a prize that Irina never would be able to obtain. The sad fact is that Sergei knows what an asset he has in that little girl. She has proved to be impossible to find. Irina thinks we are not trying, that we are deceiving her." He shook his head. "We are simply . . . inept. Unequal to the task."

He turned and regarded the palms. He talked into the glass, his reflection echoing his words back to him, his voice muted by the closeness of his face to his reflected face.

"It is not true that I have been sleeping with her." His hesitation was slight and almost went unnoticed. "I have never touched her, though she must know how much I have wanted to."

Hain couldn't believe it. The man was in love with her. He couldn't believe it because it was hackneyed and predictable and an old story in the spy business, with only slight variations from incident to incident—an old story that always surprised, always saddened, always repeated itself. When he was dead and gone, some case officer of the future would sit in another chair in another city in another century and listen to a colleague or an asset confess that he was in love with someone he shouldn't be in love with. And the case officer would be surprised, perhaps even shocked. The fact that this would happen again and again to unknown agents in the future was already a certainty, foretold by the enduring frailties of human nature.

"I know what you are thinking, my friend," Ometov went on, addressing Hain now, though his back was still turned to them. "I too have been where you are sitting now, listening to this kind of story. But you know, the odd thing is, I am not ashamed of it, as I thought men were who confessed such things to me. Not a bit. I think it is because . . . well, probably because this business has stolen everything from me, even shame." He stopped. "No, that is not the truth at all." He seemed to be talking to himself in his reflection. "This business has not stolen from me—I have whored away everything willingly. This game of secrets and lies has been a game I have played with all eagerness, wagering away anything it asked of me. Somewhere along the way I must have laid shame on the table too. Anyway, it's gone."

Ometov moved along the glass wall, keeping his face and his reflection near the clear smooth surface.

"But I never touched her, Curtis," he said, "not even when I risked her life and mine to set up meetings in impossible cities at impossible hours, not even when we were alone and only one or two people in the world knew where we were. Not even then, when we were nearly lost to the universe. I never touched her. It wasn't my integrity. I don't know what it was. But it never happened." He stopped. His breath made a wavering ghost beneath his nose. "It was surpassing strange to hear her talk of the things that I have so often imagined doing with her as though I had actually done them. It was as if it had indeed happened, but so long ago that I had forgotten how to remember it, forgotten the details of it. I felt a strange regret, for something I had lost but never had."

He continued to gaze out past himself. Beyond the pane the palms hung still in the hot, breathless night. He turned around.

"I fell in love with her long before Sergei Krupatin even knew she existed. I knew her parents, as I said before, and I knew her as a girl. I am eighteen years older than she. Sergei is ten years older than she. The summer that Sergei and I watched his father and brother die on the sand of the Black Sea, she was eight. Incredible. A dozen years later Sergei and I were well into our opposing careers and she was attending the Repin Institute to study art. Not long after that, Sergei saw her on the sidewalk." He stopped. "That," he said, "was a piece of black luck."

Ometov shoved his shoulders away from the glass wall where he had been leaning and returned to the folding metal tables laden with computers and cables and telephones. He pulled out the chair he had been sitting in and sat down again. Ann was looking away, her own gaze fixed on the palms outside. Erika was staring at Ometov with a fixed, almost catatonic expression.

"The irony," Ometov said, "is that Irina is really a very cerebral woman. Her extraordinary beauty belies her intellect. She was attracted to cerebral men. I cannot say we had begun a real affair. I would be flattering myself. But we had made a beginning. And then Sergei . . . well, he simply overwhelmed her. It couldn't be helped. It was one of those things."

Hain studied Ometov. He didn't know what made this guy tick, but he did know he was looking at a man who had had shitty luck. It made him wonder about the ancient concept of fate.

"As for Irina's showing up here yesterday," Ometov said, sighing again, turning to the situation at hand, "I had no idea. I was genuinely shocked. I don't know why she is here. To tell you the truth, I have not had any communication with her for nearly three months. I was stunned to see her here. She has given up on the idea that I will ever be able to do anything about her daughter. There is nothing I can do about it. This is one agent I have no power over whatsoever. I was lucky to have had her access to Krupatin for as long as I did."

"But when you did recognize her," Hain interrupted, "you had no hesitation in trying to attach Cate to her?"

"None. Why should I? Irina may have become a stale asset, but only because I have not held up my end of the agreement. She still is Krupatin's trusted messenger. She still has the best access to him of anyone available to us. I know she is here because Sergei wants to use her here." He stopped and looked squarely at Hain. "But that is all I know."

Hain stared back at him. Christ. Maybe he too was too worn out for this business.

"What about her reference to having a few more things to do for Ometov?"

Ometov was shaking his head before Hain even finished the question.

"I don't know. I don't know why she was saying that. I told you, I had assumed she was through with me. Our last few meetings were little more than altercations. Nothing was really accomplished because of her anger at our failure to free the child. And then—again—I have not seen her for nearly three months, until yesterday. I have no idea what she has to do for Ometov."

"But still you feel we should let Cate go on with this."

"I see no reason why not. We should consider ourselves fortunate to be in the position we are in."

"So what you're saying," Hain responded evenly, "is that this doesn't change anything, the fact that you had already turned her."

"Exactly, it changes nothing. She would not work for us now if we asked her. We know she is still working for Sergei. We want to get our hands on Sergei. She is the best way to do that."

"Then for Irina it's just business as usual. Krupatin still has her daughter, and she is continuing to pay the price."

Ometov nodded. "I am afraid so."

Hain thought a moment. "What does it look like to you, Leo? How does this thing end for her?"

"Tragically," Ometov said honestly and without hesitation. "And she knows it. Especially now, since she has failed with me. That was an extraordinary risk for her, extraordinary. And I think it demonstrates how desperate she was that she even tried it. If Krupatin had found out, he would have killed the girl, out of fury. Irina risked her daughter's life to save it. She didn't lose. It was a draw. The child still lives, but she lives in Krupatin's fouled nest."

Again silence fell over the room. The lights on the incoming lines were blinking furiously. Hain had been ignoring them. He couldn't much longer. Everyone wanted to know what the hell was going on. What was next.

"Tell me something, Leo," Hain said. "The little girl—she's Krupatin's child, isn't she?"

Ometov's face sagged, weariness and dejection lining his face like seams of erosion.

"It is almost a certainty."

"You don't know for sure?"

"No. Irina will not speak of it."

"But she loves the child."

"Fiercely. Irrationally."

"And Krupatin, he doesn't claim her."

Ometov looked down. "He refers to the child as 'that feces of a rape.' " He shook his head with grim resignation. "It is an insane story of Dostoevskian depths. For most people, it would be a difficult situation even to imagine. For Irina, it is only too real. It is her life."

He had nothing else to say, and neither did Hain. The two women did not speak. The silence lingered, the four of them lost momentarily in their own thoughts. Finally Hain turned around, picked up the headset and put it on, and began flipping toggle switches, opening up the lines.

During extended undercover operations, when surveillance was unrelenting and could accurately be described as an ordeal, food was degraded to a common necessity like sleep and going to the bathroom and coffee. It kept your blood sugar up, kept the acid of too much coffee from eating a hole in your stomach, kept you from fainting. But otherwise, it was a momentary pleasure at best. Its importance was easily displaced by an unexpected transmission, which could jerk your thoughts away from food in an instant and keep them diverted for abnormal lengths of time. In the short term, food was no competition for adrenaline.

But within an hour of Ometov's confession, no one could ignore the need for it any longer. It was Ann Loder's turn to go out and get it. She took a list of wants and left, heading for the nearest fast-food strip, not far away.

Ometov went out to the courtyard to smoke, leaving Hain and Erika on the radios. But Hain's eyes kept drifting to Ometov's solitary figure roaming among the palms. After a few minutes he took off the headphones, glanced at Erika, who nodded, acknowledging he was leaving, and got up stiffly and walked to the courtyard door. He slid back the glass and stepped outside. The muggy night air instantly wrapped around him.

Ometov nodded at him and kept walking as Hain made his way over to him. Neither of them said anything for a while, and then Hain sat down on one of the stone benches to relieve his knees.

"Leo," he said, grabbing the front of his own shirt and fanning it, "I've got to say some things."

Ometov stopped his pacing and came over. He continued to stand, finishing his cigarette.

"Okay."

Hain looked at him. "After we talked to Cate late this afternoon," he said, starting slowly, "after she had been slapped around by these two unknowns, two things stuck in my mind. One, when Cate expressed some hesitation at your proposal that she tell Irina that Stepanov had beat her up, because she was afraid that Irina herself might have had been behind it somehow and would know she was lying, you assured her that that wouldn't be the case. You said, 'I cannot imagine how she could have known.'" Hain paused. "Now, that's an interesting statement, Leo. How could you be so sure of that? It seems like a damned impossibility to me that you *could* have known that Irina *couldn't* have known.

"Two, those two guys used sandpaper on Cate. By her own account she wasn't really bruised, not really pounded on. Just scraped up." He paused again. "That's an old trick, Leo. It makes it look like there's been a lot of damage done when actually there hasn't been." Hain shook his head. "Shit, Leo, you set her up, didn't you?"

Ometov stared at him. He lifted his cigarette and pulled on it, continuing to stare at Hain as he exhaled, expelling a stream of white breath.

"Yes," he said, "I did. Early this morning, when I went out to breakfast with you, I called Valentin from a telephone in the men's toilet. He arranged it."

"Good God, man. You can't do shit like that."

Ometov dropped his cigarette and ground it out on the stones with the toe of his shoe.

"Tell me honestly, Curtis, that you wish I had not done it," he said. His eyes were flat. When Hain did not respond, he went on.

"It had to be done. They didn't hurt her. She had to be shaken, genuinely shaken. So I did it."

"It may have worked, Leo, but you're not the one who's going to get busted if this ever gets out."

"I am not going to tell anyone," Ometov said coldly.

Hain shook his head. He knew Ometov was right about the effect of Cate's pummeling. It was an inspired maneuver. It worked for Cate. It worked on Irina. It moved their relationship farther along faster than would have been possible otherwise in the short time available to them. And it was entirely unethical. It was even risky. It had been a gamble that paid off.

But it was done. And yes, Hain couldn't say he was disappointed with the results.

"This is not a time to be squeamish," Ometov said. "I already have seen too many people die because I could not stop Krupatin. I lost my faith in proper conduct a long time ago. What we have gained by having Cate knocked around was worth it. I would not hesitate to do it again. I am sorry. But I would not hesitate a moment."

He took out his cigarettes, shook one up from the pack, and put it in his mouth. He lighted it.

"My friend," Ometov said, "you will not get your hands on Sergei Krupatin by drawing a line on the ground and saying, 'I will not step over this.' No. Impossible. If the line is there, well then, eventually you will have to make the decision to step over it. Do you know why? Because that is where he lives—and kills. On the other side of the line."

Fifty-one

THE CONFUSION Cate felt in regard to Irina, the inherent eroticism in the strip search, the compassion that it seemed anyone would feel for a woman who had been through what Irina had been through, the intuitive fear of her that Cate felt—all these conflicting emotions were only compounded by the events that immediately followed. Not only did her feelings grow more complex, but the imaginary tightrope she walked as an undercover agent metamorphosed into something entirely unrecognizable. Rather than a hard thin line, the tightrope changed by the minute, broadening, flattening out, until the demarcation formed by the sharp line of the wire blended with the territories on either side of it and Cate no longer could tell what was the wire and what were the two spaces it divided. The colors to the left and right faded and intermingled, depth perception flattened out, dimensions flowed together; everything became so much a part of everything else that variations were indistinguishable, and the only discernible element was an immense barren plain with no differentiating features with which to establish orientation.

Having suspended her own reality, she was finding it difficult to locate another to take its place. Irina's reality was unacceptable. Cate's old reality was forfeit. And that which lay between was ill-defined and amorphous.

Once Cate agreed to help, Irina's melancholy vanished, and she was immediately buoyant.

"Look," she said, "we don't have much time. If you want to bathe before we dress why don't you go ahead. I'll pour us another drink."

Cate stood under the shower and tried to calm her nerves. She could not imagine what she might have just agreed to do but somehow she felt incapable of coming up with a logical scenario for finding out. In fact, she was afraid to ask, afraid that what she learned would be more than she could handle. Somehow she wanted to believe what this woman promised, that it wouldn't be difficult, that it wouldn't be dangerous, that Cate could trust her. She wanted to believe her, but the emptiness in her stomach carried a stronger warning than Irina's assurances could overcome.

When she got out of the shower Irina was already in the dressing room with their drinks. As Cate dried her hair Irina chatted animatedly, one woman to another, as though across a backyard fence. She talked about the cities she had seen and what she liked about them and what she didn't, where there was the best Turkish bath in the world, the best coffee, the best pastries, the best spas, the best shopping. She talked of art galleries and museums, of the burgeoning market in East European and Baltic icons, of the latent market for Latin American art, of the slippery, changing scene in contemporary art.

They stood in front of the long vanity mirror in their underwear and did their hair together, Irina continuing to talk as though she did not realize that this was the strangest of circumstances, while Cate tried not to succumb to a grim and growing sense of foreboding. When they were finished, Irina helped Cate select the right dress for the evening, and then they slipped them on, each helping the other with her zipper. Then Irina helped Cate apply just the right amount of makeup to cover her scrapes, which in truth had proved minimal once the redness had faded. Again Cate found herself all too aware of the difference in quality of their clothes. Irina appeared oblivious to this, oblivious even to the luxury that surrounded her, taking everything for granted: the outrageously priced suite of rooms, the lavishly costly clothes, the once-in-a-lifetime jewelry, the ridiculously expensive perfume. She took it all for granted, or—and Cate found it difficult to determine which—she didn't really care one way or the other. Something told Cate that a simple cotton summer dress would have satisfied Irina just as well. It was an attitude that she wore with the same grace with which she wore her beauty. Perhaps it was not that she took it for granted after all. Rather, it seemed that she long ago had put it all into a larger perspective and had assigned it to an inferior place in her own secret world of valuable intangibles.

But all of this quickly came to an end. Irina stood in front of the full-length mirror in the bedroom of the suite. Her thick and slightly wavy golden hair was pulled back from her face and fastened in a chignon at the nape of her neck. A large smoky black pearl adorned each ear. Her evening dress, also black, was cut low over her breasts, with only spaghetti straps scoring her otherwise bare shoulders; the material hugged her rib cage and waist, then fell over her stomach and hips to just below her knees in a loose and liquid intimacy. She was drop-dead beautiful.

She turned from the mirror, looked at her bracelet watch, picked up her black clutch purse, and squared her shoulders. Then she formed the same shushing shape with her lips as she had done before and held up the long fingers of one hand in a cautioning gesture, and the sudden hollow feeling sucked at Cate's stomach once again.

She motioned for Cate to follow her, and they walked out of the bedroom, into the sitting room, and then to the living room. Throwing a look back at Cate, Irina opened the door of the suite carefully, and they walked out into the hallway, where Irina cautiously closed the door behind them. Then, to Cate's surprise, she walked across the broad corridor and down a few steps to the next suite on the other side. She knocked twice. The door quickly opened, and they went inside.

They stood in the middle of the living room of yet another elegant suite and listened to four fashionably dressed young men carry on a sober, soft-spoken dialogue in Sicilian. They did not argue; they did not engage in the mannerisms of cinematic stereotype; they did not appear confused or indecisive. Their discussion seemed to deal with strategic concerns, with logistics; it did not seem to be about making choices but about timing. There was cautionary head-tilting, watch-checking. Dark eyes bored into dark eyes to confirm issues, and finally there were nods of consensus all around.

Irina said nothing during all this. In fact, she seemed hardly concerned. There were two men in the room besides the Italians and themselves, both Americans. One, in his thirties, wore head-phones on his crewcut head and sat at a bank of electronic equipment not unlike the one set up at the FBI's off-site. The other man was middle-aged and sat in an armchair, smoking, a notepad resting on his lap. He was flanked by two telephones, one balanced on either arm of his chair. He didn't listen to the Sicilians either, but his eyes never stopped slithering over every square inch of Irina's thinly covered body. Irina ignored him, as though he were part of the chair in which he was sitting. Her concentration was interior, and Cate doubted if this man's silent lechery would matter to her even if she were aware of it.

Cate's senses worked greedily, trying to take in as much as possible, as many details as possible: the faces, the nationalities, the equipment, the appearances, the mannerisms, the attitudes, the overriding tenor of the moment. It couldn't have been more than three or four minutes before she saw Irina looking at her. When their eyes met, Irina took her by the arm and the two of them moved aside, farther away from the lecher, of whom Irina obviously had been aware all along. There was very little of which Irina was unaware.

"Listen to me, Catherine," Irina said, their arms interlaced. "You must be very clever tonight. You must be an actress. You must go along with everything I do as naturally as if you had known in advance what was going to happen. I cannot tell you ahead of time what that will be. I don't even know everything myself, but you must put your total faith in me and do as I say. This is absolutely essential. Do you understand what I am saying?"

"Yes, I do," Cate said. And she did understand. She understood that she was on the lip of a maelstrom, looking down into its constricting coil, feeling the sinister drag of its dark gravity.

"Signora," said one of the young Sicilians, who had come up behind them, "we have to go now."

□ □ □ □

The Sicilians didn't use an evasive departure as they had earlier, but merely took both women out through the discreet route of interior stairs and back doors to a large Mercedes in one of the chateau's rear drives. Apparently they were going to rely entirely on their dry-cleaning talents to protect their route and destination.

"Okay, this is what we wanted," Hain said, the strain discernible in his voice, though he was forcing a calm manner. Ometov, Ann, and Erika were all hunched over their notepads around the tables laden with technology, their eyes fixed on an invisible spot, their concentration welded to the audio of Cate's transmissions.

"Jernigan," he added, "do not leave the hotel with these people. Stay clear. Let 'em go. We don't want to throw this away."

"Yeah, I got it," Jernigan said. "That's Sicilian. They're talking Sicilian, that's for sure. You get any kind of ID on these guys?"

"We're pretty sure they're Carlo Bontate's people, but the computers didn't give us any hits on the photographs, so we're not sure about it. Strey, you getting some of your agents who speak Sicilian? We don't know shit here."

"I'm already on it," Strey said.

"She's not saying much," Ann said. "She's not talking . . ."

"Hell, she can't talk," Hain said impatiently. "Think about it."

"What about Stepanov and the other two?" Erika asked.

"We've got them," Jernigan said. "They're busy dry-cleaning."

Two hours earlier Valery Volkov had suddenly appeared back at the hotel. After half an hour, both Volkov and Izvarin had appeared at Stepanov's suite and told him they had to go check on some friends—a lame excuse to get him out of bugged territory—and they had all left together. This brief conversation had been picked up on the FBI bug in the living room of Stepanov's suite. The three men had immediately left the hotel, so that Stepanov had not been able to contact Hain.

"What if they end up going to the same place?" Jernigan asked. "What do you want us to do then?"

"Drop back. Stay the hell away. Cate and Irina are priority. We do not want to spook Irina."

"What if Krupatin shows up?"

"We'll get back to you."

During the next hour there was minimal transmission from Cate's implants, which indicated that the Sicilians were probably still intensely involved with their dry-cleaning duties. In the meantime Jernigan's team stayed with the Russians, who seemed to be taking their own dry-cleaning efforts to extremes.

Fifty-two

DESPITE THE BALD FEAR she felt at her situation, Cate sat in silence and tried to take in as much of what was happening to her as she could. The Sicilians were utilizing a surprising amount of state-of-the-art electronic technology in their countersurveillance, and their evasion techniques, as far as she could tell, were much the same as the ones practiced by the FBI.

For the first forty-five minutes, they remained in the huge Mercedes, working a pattern of routes around Houston. The driver was clearly familiar with the city. The front seat of the car was equipped with a console of electronic technology manned by a thin young man who was very intent on his work. They had a police scanner with some electronic devices attached to it, which the young Sicilian was playing with the virtuosity of a musician, managing after fifteen minutes to find—incredibly—secure channels. They had countersurveillance cars on the street spotting for them.

A crucial juncture came at the forty-five-minute mark. They drove downtown and entered one of the countless parking garages. They descended several floors underground and pulled up beside a dark Lincoln. Cate and Irina and their escorts got out of the Mercedes, and two women from another car got into the Mercedes with the same number of escorts. A couple of the automatic windows came down in the Lincoln so the men could talk among themselves, and Cate saw two women in the back seat of that car as well. An exchange of vehicles, or a feigned exchange of vehicles, was a routine evasion action, so one car was a decoy. But in this case two cars were going to be decoys. Cate and Irina did not enter a car at all.

Together with their escorts, they walked to the elevators, which took them up several floors to the underground tunnel system that honeycombed beneath the streets and buildings of downtown Houston. When they entered the first tunnel juncture, two electric carts were waiting for them. There were miles and miles of tunnels, and walking would have been impractical. With their young escorts wearing earpieces and keeping in constant communication with someone, they moved through the tunnel system, passing silently through the nether regions of several skyscrapers. The tunnels were bright and silent and empty at this hour of the night. Finally they arrived at another elevator stop. This elevator took them to another parking level and another Lincoln, which was as electronically well equipped as the Mercedes. They got into the Lincoln and the driver coiled up to the street level, emerging into the city a mile from where they had entered.

If they had been under surveillance, this maneuver would have been a difficult one to follow. It would have been, that is, if not for the crucial fact of Cate's presence.

After the downtown maneuvering, the dark Lincoln began cruising the hundreds of miles of freeways and tollways that threaded through and encircled the city. They followed these arteries west out of the city and then back in again. They followed them south and back in, then north and back in. The radios crackled; sapphire, ruby, and emerald lights winked on the console in the front seat, with one bank of lights undulating in a glittering pattern, drifting waves like sonar.

Once, as they were coming back into the city from Galveston Bay, they pulled onto a dirt road that ran out into the flat plains of coastal grasses and turned off their lights. In the distance all around them the lights of the city and the suburbs glittered on the black horizon. Two of the men took a small box the size of a car battery out of the trunk of the car, attached a convex, disk-shaped antenna to it, and set it on the hood of the car. As the antenna rotated, they studied an instrument panel, occasionally looking up to the night sky.

They left the Lincoln running for the air conditioning, but even so, when they opened the doors the rich, verdant smell of damp grasses invaded the car. All of this time Irina sat in silence. Occasionally she glanced at her watch or looked out at the darkness on the black stretches of gulf grass, lost in her thoughts.

The back door of the car opened, and one of the young Italians looked in.

"Signora," he said, speaking to Irina, "we think it is okay to go to the meeting."

"Good. Very good," Irina said.

The man closed the door. He and his partner disassembled the device on the roof of the car and put it in the trunk, and they drove away, the low, dark Lincoln creeping through the tall grasses like a heavy feral cat.

"Anything on the Russians?"

Jernigan's voice could not disguise his chagrin. "We lost them."

"Oh, shit. For Christ's sake, Neil—"

"Listen," Jernigan snapped back. "You want airtight coverage, give me the manpower. That's pretty much common sense, you know that."

"Okay, okay," Hain apologized.

"They went to a goddamn Rockets game at the Summit," Jernigan explained. "Parked in one of the garages and split up. That's the last we saw of them."

"These guys are from out of town, Neil. How the hell do they know how to get around—"

"Yeah, right, well, we think they're each hooking up with one of the Aulovs or Semenyakos who've been working with Stepanov here. Must've had it worked out beforehand. We have all the registrations for their vehicles and we're watching for them. We're monitoring all the cab calls for this area. We've contacted all the security operations in a five-block area, so they're watching all the entrances and exits with their security cameras. I mean, we're on it, but . . ."

"But what?"

"Well, shit, when they split up like that, Curtis, they're just too damn spread out."

Stepanov and Pavel Aulov were the first to arrive at the Global Maritime wharves east of the Turning Basin on the Houston Ship Channel, a muddy, odorous waterway that ran fifty miles inland from Galveston Bay and terminated in the eastern end of the city. The flat bayou bottoms that flanked the Ship Channel were the equivalent of the dirt underneath the fingernails of international mercantilism, which presented a much prettier face a few miles away in the glittering skyscrapers downtown. Here the paper-shuffling and the billions of bits of data zipping through bright, sterile fiber optics turned into sober reality amid miles and miles of shipyards and railyards, acres and acres of petroleum storage terminals, city-size refineries, chemical plants, industrial storage yards, and worlds of wharves.

Global Maritime consisted of a warren of warehouses on the south side of the channel, where a collection of tankers always berthed, leviathan hulks lying up against the wharves pissing rusty bilge into the soupy water of the channel while gantries groaned in the wharf-lighted night, tending to unknown cargoes.

Valentin Stepanov stood on the grimy cement floor and looked into the cavernous bowels of a warehouse leased by TransEuro Shipping Ltd. The stench in this particular depot was overwhelming, because it was the holding platform for hundreds of pallets of animal hides shipped in from Brazil and destined for Europe. The hides, shipped raw from freshly slaughtered cattle, were stacked flat one on top of another, each one generously salted to prevent it from rotting. Blood serum and adipocere oozed from each hide and mixed with the salt to create an unctuous seepage that soaked into the hair of the hide beneath it, leaked to the edges of the hide "cake," and dripped off in a thick, syrupy exudate that threw off a nauseating smell. It was this stench that made the hide pallets valuable to Stepanov's drug trafficking operations. This particular operation was one he had managed to keep hidden from his new FBI partners.

He stood with Aulov, hands in pockets, and looked at hundreds of pallets of hides stacked five feet high and arranged in long rows forming narrow aisles a hundred yards long.

"So the cavities were larger this time," he said.

"Oh, yes, two thirds of a meter deep, nearly two meters long, and well over a meter wide." Aulov grinned. "Almost like a coffin." Aulov could be described by two words that rhymed in English: crude and shrewd. "These were loaded in Maracaibo, Venezuela. I was there myself when it was loaded on. They removed about a dozen hides, cut out the center of the stack in those dimensions, and laid in the plastic bags of cocaine. They are using thicker plastic bags, too. We kept having punctures. We fill the void to the top, make it good and solid, replace the dozen hides, and fasten the lot to the pallet with metal bands, like lumber. It makes a tight package."

"And still no problem with the dogs?"

"Shit." Aulov laughed. "They don't even bother anymore. A dog's nose is ruined before he finishes half a row. This is one of the safest means of shipping we have ever used."

"That's 1.36 cubic meters of cocaine," Stepanov said, quickly calculating the street value and savoring the results.

"Per pallet," Aulov said. "There are over two hundred pallets here, and twenty-five of them, scattered throughout the warehouse, are carrying cocaine."

"And how much cash are you able to put into the holes after you remove the cocaine here?"

"Well, we are disappointed in this. Oddly enough, the portion of hides we remove to make the hole weighs almost as much as the cocaine we put in. This causes only a slight variation in the customs weighing. They allow a fifteen percent variation per pallet, because of the varying weights of the hides. So we have a little wiggling room there. But cash is heavier, meter for meter. We can only get three million per pallet. So . . . only seventy-five million here now, headed for Europoort, the Netherlands."

"How long has it been here?"

"The hides arrived two weeks ago. We can unpack the cocaine and repack with cash at the rate of just two pallets a night, so we only finished two nights ago."

"When does it sail?"

"In three days. The day after tomorrow they will load the pallets on that ship sitting right out there. It's a French freighter."

Hearing voices near the front doors of the warehouse, they

turned and walked back a few aisles to meet Izvarin and Volkov, who were arriving with their separate escorts.

"Good God." Izvarin gasped, standing in the wide opening of the wharfside doorway and covering his nose with his hand. His dapper clothes made him look like a pale flower against the drab hull of the freighter behind him.

Volkov walked up behind him. "Jesus." He frowned.

Izvarin turned. "This is your brilliant idea, Valery. I'll wait out here."

"I want to see how it's done," Volkov said. "I'm the one who's got to move it at the other end. And you're bloody well going to see it too."

Stepanov turned to Aulov. "We want to see inside one."

Aulov nodded at one of the escorts who had come with Volkov. He was carrying a pair of long-handled band cutters and was slipping on work gloves.

"Let's go to a pallet at the back, away from the doorway," Aulov said.

In single file they followed the man with the band cutters down a series of cross aisles to the farthest part of the warehouse. They slowed as the man checked the pallet numbers and then stopped.

"This one," he said, looking at Stepanov.

"Okay."

The man wedged the jaws of the snippers under the first flat metal band and pressed the handles closed, snapping the tight metal band with a sharp ping. He walked around the pallet and snapped the second band, and then, together with another of Aulov's men, who was also wearing work gloves, he grabbed the first several hides, pulled them off the pallet, and laid them on top of an adjacent pallet. The stench suddenly intensified as the long-stored raw flesh was exposed, ropy strings of exudate running from the lifted hides.

Izvarin gasped, coughed, and almost gagged.

They grabbed another handful of hides and pulled them, sliding them off to expose a rectilinear cavity cut into the center of the pallet of hides.

Stepanov and Volkov moved forward and peered into the cavity.

"What the hell is this?" Stepanov said, straightening up and turning. "It's empty."

There were two quick spits from Volkov's silenced Smith & Wesson, fired pointblank. They struck Stepanov in the bridge of the nose and blew out the back of his head. Izvarin didn't even have time to take his hand down from his nose before Aulov's two shots blasted into his right ear, removing the left side of his skull.

"Stepanov is big," Volkov said to one of the men with gloves as he backstepped to avoid the dark pool of blood spreading on the concrete floor under Stepanov's deformed head. "You may have to make the hole in the hides a little bigger."

The Lincoln nosed around the corner of the Global Maritime warehouse and paused. There was some radio communication in Sicilian, and then the Lincoln pulled out onto the quayside and moved to the doorway of the warehouse. When it stopped again, the front passenger door flew open and one of the young Sicilians got out and opened Irina's door.

Irina turned to Cate. "Wait here," she said and swung her legs out the door. Then she paused. She turned back and looked at Cate. "On second thought, Catherine, I think you should come with me. I want to show you something so you will understand what is going to happen later."

Cate nodded. Immediately her own door was opened, and she got out under the lee side of the huge freighter, which loomed high above her, fifty feet away. She could hear the bilge splashing into the channel, falling from high up on the filthy bow of the ship. Suddenly, silently, out of nowhere, half a dozen Sicilians were standing around, their weapons much in evidence but not flourished.

The smells of the channel side were thick with petroleum and mud and garbage, enough to induce an involuntary grimace, but were nothing compared to the much stronger stench that assailed their nostrils as they stepped into the musty and cavernous warehouse. Volkov was waiting for them just inside the door, smoking. He cast a quick disapproving eye at Cate.

"This is my decision, Valery," Irina said.

He offered no further protest before he turned and headed into the warehouse. Cate felt her gorge rise at the hideous odor and could not stop herself from clamping her hand over her mouth and nose. Immediately she recognized what was strapped down on the pallets, and for some reason it struck her as nightmarish. This was not leather, it was piles and piles, acres, of flesh stripped from animals whose deaths seemed to have occurred only moments earlier, their still liquid blood seeping from living cells, their bawling deaths still reverberating in the upper regions of the fetid warehouse.

Cate fixed her eyes on Irina, just ahead of her. Her long striding legs and sensuous hips created a graceful rhythmic sway in the hem of the black dress—black, clean black. Her blond chignon was immaculate, her head held straight and proud. Beauty and symmetry suitable for paradise were taking a strange, deliberate walk into corridors of leaching tissue.

Finally they all stopped a few yards from a partially disassembled pallet of hides. Irina walked alone to the edge of the pallet and stared into the center of it. Cate noticed that she had no expression of distaste on her face. She didn't seem to shrink from the filth of the oozing pallet of hides, though she never touched them. Everyone held back, waiting for her.

Irina turned. "Catherine."

One of the Italians took her arm and went forward with her. Irina turned the other way and reached out her hand and said, "Valery."

As Cate stopped at the edge of the pallet, she saw the hole in which a body was curled on its side, not quite in a fetal position, its head bent forward. There was blood everywhere. Cate's heart deserted its natural rhythm and began slamming against her sternum. She recognized Stepanov, sleeping in his own blood, asleep in a cocoon of alien flesh.

"He's already dead," Irina said. "At least, he looks dead, doesn't he?" She raised her hand and fired the gun. *Phut! Phut! Phut!* Stepanov's body shrugged one, two, three times.

Cate's knees almost buckled, and she felt the Sicilian's arm around her waist.

"You are now free of Valentin Stepanov," Irina said. "Over here," she said, stepping over to another pallet, "is Grigori Izvarin."

She raised the gun again, and again fired three times, the silencer sputtering quickly, abruptly.

"It is done, then," she said, and she turned and handed the gun back to Volkov.

Fifty-three

J ERNIGAN!" Hain yelled over the radio. "Where the hell are they? Quick!"

"Looks like the signal's coming from the vicinity of the Ship Channel . . . the wharves . . . uh, somewhere between the Turning Basin and Brady Island—closer to the Turning Basin."

"Curtis," Ann said steadily, trying to control her rage as she glared at Hain over the top of the equipment in the center of the table, "you want to tell me what in the *hell* I just heard? Did my man just get nailed in that warehouse? Is that what happened?"

"I don't know," Hain said. "It sounded like he's been killed, yeah, but I don't think she did it—"

"She said, 'He's already dead,' " Jernigan said, cutting in. "She was making sure—that's what it sounded like to me, that she was making sure."

"Jesus, Leo." Ann shook her head as she turned to Ometov. "That was damned cold-blooded. Leo?"

"Yes, yes, I know." Ometov's face was grim. "I don't know what is happening here. No, I do not under—"

"She said 'Valery,' " Erika snapped. "She and Volkov are in this together."

"Is that what you read?" Hain asked. "I heard his name too, but I don't know what in the hell she meant by saying it. You sure she was speaking *to* him?"

"Well, what the hell else?" Ann was furious. "It was like a command. She said 'Valery,' you know, like a command."

"I heard the shots," Hain said. "And Izvarin—him too. They killed him just then, or before."

"She wanted Cate to see what she was doing," Erika said. "She called her over to watch."

"I don't know . . ." Ometov equivocated.

"That's what it sounded like to me, too," Ann said.

"What does that mean?" Hain asked. It wasn't clear whom he was talking to or what he was talking about.

"They're back in the cars," Jernigan said. "They're moving."

"What is it? Is she crying—is that it?" Ann's voice jumped around the intermittent transmissions from the Lincoln.

"Goddamn Sicilians again," Jernigan muttered. "They're moving . . ."

"Jernigan," Hain barked, "where the hell are you?"

"Navigation Boulevard."

"You're not moving pickets in . . ."

"No, do you want me to?"

"No—no, definitely not," Hain confirmed quickly. "We don't want to spook them now, not now. The burst transmitter's doing its job. Let them go. That's what we wanted. We don't want them jumpy. They gotta calm down."

"Damn, I sure as hell didn't hear anybody upset in that warehouse, except maybe Cate," Jernigan said. "They sounded like a pretty damn cold bunch to me."

Hain turned on Ometov. "What is this, Leo?" he snapped. "It sounded like Volkov hit these two before Cate got there. He was there when Irina arrived. They were dead already, but she knew the hit was coming, didn't she? What is it—is she working for Krupatin, or is she turning against him? And Volkov?"

"And Bontate?" Erika said. "Leo, these are *Carlo's* men with Irina."

"We don't know that," Ometov said.

"Oh, come *on*." Ann groaned.

"These are Carlo's men," Erika pressed, "and they were involved in these hits. Carlo is moving against Krupatin, I think. They have been working together in Europe for five years. Now this . . ."

"I don't know, I don't know," Ometov was muttering. The others could almost hear his mind racing, stumbling on the heels of his words.

"Izvarin was Krupatin's senior lieutenant in Europe," Erika persisted. "Stepanov was his senior man here in the States. Either they have done something to make him think they needed to be eliminated—"

"Jesus," Ann interrupted, her eyes widening, "do you think Krupatin found out that Stepanov was working with us?"

"—or Carlo is moving in on him," Erika finished.

"If Bontate is moving against him, it looks like Valery Volkov is in on it with the Sicilians," Hain said.

"Or maybe Volkov is maneuvering his own coup," Ann said. "Everybody always wants to be at the top. What I want to know is, where in the hell did this innocent little art student get such a bloody cold streak? Leo, I don't believe this is a surprise to you."

"Okay, people," Jernigan said. "They're out of the port authority grounds now and heading back into the city. What about the men back at the warehouse, Curtis? You want to pick them up? Volkov, whoever's with him?"

"Volkov didn't come out?"

"No. Only car that came out was the dark Lincoln. The Sicilians."

"No!" Ometov interjected. "This is obviously very closely coordinated. The moment you pick them up, Carlo, and perhaps Krupatin, will know of it instantly." He paused in a moment of frustration. "Remember, remember—we want Sergei Krupatin. That is what all of this has been set in motion to do. We must not be distracted by these unexpected events."

"Curtis, this is Strey. One of our agents who speaks Sicilian just got into the tech room here. He'll have to play catchup from the tapes, but he'll start monitoring live transmissions in about twenty minutes."

"Better late than never," somebody muttered.

"Thanks, Ennis," Jernigan said. "Okay, people, we're headed into the city on Navigation."

□ □ □ □

As they frantically tried to sort out what was happening, sporadic transmissions were coming from Cate's implant. There was more Sicilian dialect, calm, precise, and infuriatingly unintelligible, and then there were softer words, whispers that prompted everyone to lean forward in concentration.

"Listen to me—listen to me, Catherine." Irina's voice was hoarse, low. "Come here to me." Now the volume was intimate, close, hushed. Cate was absolutely silent.

"Catherine. That must have seemed brutal to you, what I did back there. But I had to do it. The two men were dead, but I had to make sure. *My* life, and yours, depended on my being sure they were dead. Listen to me. Shhhh . . . shhhh." Comforting sounds. "Listen." Whispers, barely audible. "You are in the middle of a dangerous situation. Through no fault of your own, only your misjudgment. A simple misjudgment should not have such grave consequences, but that cannot be helped now. What is important is that we make no mistakes from here on."

"From here on . . ."

"No, no, please—listen. Catherine!"

"What is going *on* here?" Cate's voice was impatient, frightened.

Silence. Then Irina's voice, calm, careful: "I am in the process of extricating myself from a very long slavery. I will let nothing get in the way of my deliverance. Nothing." Pause. "Not even you, Catherine."

Silence.

"Do you understand what I am saying?" Irina asked.

There was another moment of silence, and then Cate said, "Yes." Her voice was steady. "I do understand."

"Good," Irina said. "Now listen to me, Catherine. You must know that everything I do now is to save our lives. We have fallen into a well of serpents. You have to understand serpents, how they think and what they want, if you expect to have any hope of surviving."

"Why did you get me into this?" Cate asked evenly. She did not know herself whether it was Catherine or Cate speaking.

"What?"

"We haven't fallen into this well. You took my hand and jumped in. You said I made mistakes, you said 'misjudgments'—

that that's why I am where I am. But that's not strictly true, is it? I didn't have to be involved in this—you brought me in."

"You wanted to save your daughter."

"I did, yes. But I'm not stupid. What happened to Stepanov back there, and to the other one, the fact that they were killed, wasn't done in order to save my daughter. There's a hell of a lot of other stuff going on here. He was going to be killed anyway, wasn't he? And you've brought me along tonight for some other reason, haven't you? It has nothing to do with my daughter."

In the silence that followed, the voices of the young Sicilians skittered over the airwaves like the conversation of ghosts, sibilants hissing through the aural nightscape, as elusive as an audible ignis fatuus.

"No, Catherine, you are right," Irina said after a long time. Her voice was flat and hard. "I will not lie to you about this anymore, because our lives depend on your doing as I ask you to do. It is true, I have used you for my own purposes. I am not ashamed of that. And I would do it again. My life, all that I am—all that is left of me—is at stake here. And now, so is yours."

"Are you really with Russian intelligence?"

"Yes."

"Then what on earth are you doing? Why aren't law enforcement people involved here, people from the government—somebody?"

"Listen to me. I told you my story. I tried to make it clear to you that my situation is more personal than professional. Russian intelligence was useful to me as long as it was useful to me. My only concern here is personal. The government be damned, as far as I am concerned. The truth is, if you are human, everything you do is personal. It does not matter whether you are a peasant or a prime minister. Everything is personal. What I am doing here now is entirely personal."

"To save your life."

"And Félia's."

"Even if you have to sacrifice mine."

"No. If I die, you must live. Under the circumstances . . . I have to make sure of that, above all."

Cate shook her head in frustration. "I don't understand this."

"No, you do not yet, but you will. But what you *must* understand now is that your life is tied to mine, even your body. Perhaps right now, especially your body."

"My *body?*"

"The man we are going to see now is an associate of Sergei Krupatin's. He is Asian, a man of enormous wealth. I am taking messages to him. But that is not all. I am taking my body to him as well. It is part of the deal." She paused. "He prefers the ménage à trois."

"What?"

"I have made promises to him."

"About me!"

"About someone like you. It happens to be you."

"You expect me to do this because *you* promised?"

"If you were willing to give your body to Stepanov for money, you should not find it so difficult to give it to this man to save your life."

"To save my life?"

"That is the situation we are facing now. Anything less than what I have promised would bring suspicion on both of us. And with these people, whatever causes suspicion is treated like gangrenous flesh—it is quickly cut out wherever it is found, as soon as it is found."

"I don't know if I can do this . . . God, really, I don't know."

"Yes, I counted on that," Irina said. "This man is predatory. He will quickly sense that your timidity, your natural anxiety and reluctance, are genuine. It will be like catnip to him."

"My God, this is incredible. Don't you . . . don't you have any conscience at all?"

"Conscience?" Irina spoke the word with a gentle gasp, a softened inflection that carried an unmistakable note of longing. "Dear Catherine, you have no idea what you are saying. My heart is made of glass. You have no idea."

"Jesus Christ, Curtis." Ann's voice was tight. "Jesus."

"Wei Tsing," Erika snapped. "She's talking about Wei Tsing."

"Yes, I think so," Ometov agreed, nodding, turning to look at Hain. "I think this is who it will be. I have no doubt about that."

Cate remembered Ann Loder's last remarks: you won't be hearing from us again unless there's something critical. Good God, what was their definition of critical? She could hardly believe what was happening to her. It seemed almost too naive of her to think it, but she was only now realizing how serious her situation was. Suddenly Hain, all of them, seemed mercenary beyond belief. She wasn't on the front line in this theater of the war on crime; she was underneath it, down in the sinkhole where none of the trappings of legitimate battle were allowed, things like uniforms and codes of conduct and guidelines and rules of order, the kinds of symbols and structures of empowerment that gave her confidence and made her believe she was doing the right things for the right reasons. None of these elements was present in this part of the war. The intensity of the battle, the unorthodox nature of its course, were such that she quickly—surprisingly quickly—found herself in imminent danger of losing sight of all the reasons, and therefore justifications, for being in the sinkhole in the first place. In fact, she began to lose sight of just about everything—except survival.

Automatically, without even having to make a conscious commitment, Cate began to think instinctively. Even now, as she absorbed this new, dark revelation from Irina, as she realized that she was not going to be getting any help from her superiors in this subterranean theater of battle, she was able to reach down inside herself and drag up from her guts a kind of resolve that she did not recognize, a unique thing, a new and radical creation. It was the resolve of dire necessity, a calculation born of the elemental will to live that had lain dormant inside her, heretofore unneeded and therefore unbidden. Even in the midst of her fear, she felt the burgeoning instincts of a harried animal. Mentally crouching, her eyes and ears quickened to the possibilities of threat, she weighed her odds, trying to determine whether her next move should rely on claws or cunning.

Fifty-four

S ON OF A BITCH," Hain said in dismay. He flipped off the toggle switch on his microphone and turned to Ometov. "This is finally it. These guys are negotiating to put together an American co-op."

Ometov nodded, wearily rubbing his face with his hands. "We are sitting here listening to all of our dire predictions coming to life. They are building the monster we all have feared. Who knows how far they've already gone with it?"

"But it's falling apart, Leo," Hain said, perplexed. "Major people are dead here, and they're all in one camp. Krupatin is losing important men. And he's the only one."

"No, no, no. We cannot jump to conclusions," Ometov argued, tilting his head skeptically. "We do not know if Sergei was aware of Stepanov's betrayal, though it would not surprise me in the least if he was. Perhaps Carlo and Wei learned of it, and perhaps getting rid of Stepanov was one of their stipulations for agreeing to organize with Sergei here in the U.S. Maybe it was they who discovered Stepanov's betrayal and told Sergei. Who knows?"

"And Izvarin?"

"His ambition was well known. He was always crowding Sergei, stepping on his heels. He was too eager. Sergei may have gotten tired of it or come to distrust it. Paranoia is a Krupatin trademark. Sometimes it saves his life. Sometimes others lose theirs because of it."

"No," Hain said. "I'm not buying that. I think they're moving against Krupatin. Maybe he knew it was coming, or suspected it, and that's why he hasn't shown his face."

"How do you explain Irina, then?"

"Shit, I don't explain her," Hain said. "That's your job."

"Okay, then," Ometov said, resting his elbow on the metal table and raising a thumb. "Let us consider some possibilities. One, Irina was overseeing the killings for Sergei, who, for whatever reasons, wanted Stepanov and Izvarin eliminated. With help from Volkov, his trusted lieutenant from his eastern operations, who will now undoubtedly hold a higher position, and with the help of Bontate. This suggests too that Sergei and Carlo may have a closer alliance than we thought. It is not common for two organizations to cooperate in such a manner. But we see it happening here, with the Sicilians consistently acting as Irina's escorts."

"Maybe Wei is in on it too," Erika suggested, "only we do not know this yet."

"Okay, yes, that could be true," Ometov conceded. He went on, "Two, Irina is working for Bontate, and perhaps Wei, and is indeed moving against Sergei. Three, Irina has allied with Bontate and has agreed to help him remove both Krupatin and Wei, his chief competitors. It would be easier to get rid of them here, away from their better-organized situations in Europe. If that is true, Carlo's men are probably moving simultaneously against their operations in Europe. We should contact our counterparts there and see if they are experiencing a rash of assassinations."

"But neither Carlo nor Wei is dead, Leo," Ann argued. She was studying the Russian across the table. Her face was stiff with growing impatience.

"That is true," Ometov acknowledged, looking at his watch. "But it is relatively early in the evening," he said with a sarcastic smile. "And it promises to be a long night."

"There is another possibility," Hain said.

"What is that?"

"That Irina is still working for you—and only for you."

Ometov was not intimidated.

"I wish it were true, Curtis. I will not lie to you. I wish it were true. I think then we would have a chance of getting our hands on Sergei Krupatin. But honestly, I would have no reason to kill Stepanov and Izvarin. They would be much more valuable to me alive—and talking."

Hain looked at Ometov. It was difficult to decide whether the Russian was being devious or simply straightforward.

"Irina is all over the board, Leo. First she says one thing, then she says something else. What is this? Is this typical? Is this what she's like to work with?"

Ometov shook his head. "No. She sounds distracted. I think she is saying whatever she thinks she has to say to keep Cate with her, to keep her from running."

"Then this business about their being in danger—how much of that is manipulation?"

Ometov looked away, pulling down the corners of his mouth in an unconvincing gesture of dismissal. "Who knows? I don't know how much drama to believe anymore." He looked back at Hain. "You have your own files on this Asian, don't you? What is your judgment?"

"I don't know either," Hain admitted. "Yeah, it's hard to say."

Silence followed as both men set about rationalizing a tacit decision to let the situation proceed. They were close, very close, to three men who were causing havoc for international police agencies. Were they going to jeopardize this unique opportunity by being overly cautious about one of their agents? What kind of danger would justify forfeiting such an unexpected advantage? They were going to have to justify losing Stepanov, explain why they hadn't had a better handle on their double agent's safety. But in the end, Stepanov had been a double agent, after all, and such people led precarious lives. It was disappointing to lose them, but you couldn't always say it was a surprise.

But Cate's safety was something else altogether. Her loss was not something Hain would want to have to explain. Still, neither man really wished to examine the question of her safety openly. Privately, each of them was actually engaged in the question, and privately each was making a decision to defer serious scrutiny of the issue. The situation in which Cate and Irina now found themselves was unforeseen and incredibly fortuitous. The hunt for the Russian fox had unexpectedly brought them near the lairs of the Sicilian leopard and the Asian tiger as well. This astonishing circumstance had the same effect on Hain's and Ometov's moral compasses as greed or lust often had on other men. Their judgment was affected. Wisdom withered in the face of such temptation. Suddenly it did not seem like such an unreasonable thing not to intervene.

Ann Loder abruptly jerked the headphones off her head and stood up, raking both her hands quickly through her dark hair.

"This is making me sick to my stomach," she hissed, looking down at the two men on the other side of the table, "watching you two silently equivocating about Cate's safety." She paused, trying to get control of her voice. "But not only that. Tell me the truth—don't either of you feel just a little bit sleazy?"

Both men gaped at her, honestly puzzled by her outburst. But it was Erika who responded.

"You mean Cate's situation with Wei?"

"Yes, goddamnit." Ann snapped her head around at Erika. "That's exactly what I mean."

Erika regarded her calmly. "You have run undercover agents before," she said. "You have never been bothered before?"

"Not like this."

"Why is this different?"

"Well . . . Shit, we're pimping her out to these people."

"You knew this was a possibility when we were planning this. Why didn't you say something then?"

"To tell you the truth, I didn't really think it would come to this."

"Tell me something," Erika said, turning to face Ann squarely. "You have put men in dangerous situations before, haven't you?"

"Yes, sure." Ann nodded. She knew what was coming.

"And there was the possibility that these agents might have to shoot someone, kill someone."

"Yes."

"And you have put men into situations in which the best tactic they could use to get information from a woman was to have sex with her?"

"Of course."

"Did you feel sleazy then?"

"No," Ann answered honestly.

"Killing, then, it is not so bad as having sex? Or a man having sex to obtain information is not so bad as a woman having sex to obtain information?"

"For God's sake, Erika, we're asking her to allow herself to be raped."

"It would be better if we asked her to kill someone?"

Ann looked at her without answering.

"You Americans," Erika said, answering her own question, "still have this strange sense of moral imperatives. What is the moral difference between a man and a woman? None. We are all human beings. If something is beneath the human dignity of one, it should be beneath the human dignity of the other; if something is permitted or prohibited for one, it should be permitted or prohibited for the other. We are *all* human beings, aren't we? But Americans, my God, you always are creating new moral imperatives that separate the sexes. I don't know why. Men can kill in organized groups on behalf of governments, but women may not. Men routinely use sex in the course of gathering state intelligence, but for women it is somehow an unseemly offense, a degradation. I am sorry, but this kind of thinking doesn't make any sense to me," she added flatly. "And frankly, it makes me angry to hear Americans always whining about it."

"A female agent's rape is hardly equivalent to a male agent's seduction strategy," Ann shot back.

"Listen, Ann, if Cate is consenting to this sex, then it is not rape, you know that. And so far, I haven't heard her use her code signals for calling this off. Cate is making her own decisions here, and I seriously doubt if she is deciding to be raped."

"So it isn't going to bother you to hear this encounter broadcast over the radio?"

"That, yes, that will make me uncomfortable," Erika admitted. "It is a cruel twist, I must say. But I do not believe that she is committing any greater offense, or that she is being offended against in any greater way, than a man doing the same thing." She hesitated. "I do regret that the first agent to use this device is a woman. I regret it on Cate's behalf—as a matter of privacy, not on moral grounds."

"Jesus." Ann was still angry—angry at herself and at the two men across from her, whose sexist assumptions were so deeply buried they could only give her puzzled looks. She was also frustrated. Erika's argument held water. It was harsh, but it held water. It was a shitty situation any way you looked at it.

"Do you know anything about Wei's taste in sex? Is this going to get dicey?" she finally asked.

"That depends on what you consider dicey."

"Is she going to be in danger of getting hurt here! Christ!" Ann couldn't keep her temper in check. "This whole thing is getting way out of line. I don't give a damn what you think about *my* double standards. It still feels sleazy to me. And it *ought* to feel sleazy to them," she spat, her right arm shooting out and pointing across the table.

"I have read the BKA file on him," Erika said. "He has a fondness for Caucasian women."

"In pairs?"

"If he can get them in pairs."

"Well, he's got them now."

"It seems so."

"What about the rest of it?"

"Just about everything, I would say."

"Shit!" Ann jerked her head and grimaced. "Shit, shit, shit." She looked up at the ceiling, feeling trapped by circumstances and, she hated to admit it, afraid. "How in God's name is she going to live with herself?"

"If Cate believes we do not know what she has done, it will be bearable," Erika said. "She can live with herself so long as she does not know that we heard everything."

"That's a hell of a secret for us to have to keep."

"That's the reason for the bandages."

"Those goddamn Band-Aids," Ann said. "That's a lie *I'll* have a hard time living with."

"Your problem is that you are too selfish, Ann. We have to hear everything. Cate's safety is the main concern here, not your conscience."

"Shit. Tell me a lie," Ann said, rolling her eyes. "The fact is, we're so damned greedy for information that we don't really give a damn how we get it, even if it rides on the sounds of Cate's sacrificial rape. And we don't even have the decency to turn our heads while she does this for us. As to the question of her safety, that's bullshit. You know—we all know—that the way this is shaping up, we don't have a chance in hell of getting to her in time if things start to go bad. This is not about her safety."

"It was merciful to lie to her about the bandages," Erika insisted, choosing not to address the other issue. "It gives her a psychological way out."

"That's neat." Ann seethed. *"We're* giving *her* a psychological out. The lie was a sleazy thing to do to her. But more than that, this whole thing is beginning to smell a little sick to me. We want this so bad we're willing to put Cate in a whorehouse to get it. Okay, I know, 'she didn't have to do it.' But she didn't know, really, did she, what she was dealing with here. She didn't know when she tacitly agreed to fuck for law and order that we were going to be right there inside her, listening."

Her words hung in the air, lingering amid the crackling sounds of the radios, the background buzzes and beeps of electronics.

"I appreciate your sentiments," Hain said, his voice sober, controlled. "But you're not calling the shots here."

"Fine," Ann snapped, glaring at each of them in turn. "I hope this haunts every one of us, all the way to the grave."

Fifty-five

FROM THE INTERIOR of the Lincoln, the transition from Sicilian to Asian oversight was hardly noticeable until a large Mercedes sedan passed the car on a thickly wooded lane as another pulled up close behind them. The three cars slowed, their tires crunching reassuringly on the gravel shoulder of the lane.

The Lincoln was immediately surrounded by Asian men wearing headphones with thermometer-size mouthpieces, in the manner of rock stars on stage. Two of these men opened the back doors of the Lincoln, and without exchanging a single word, the Sicilians nodded at the two women. Irina and Cate got out of the back seat and were escorted to the second Mercedes, which Cate now saw was a limousine. Again the doors were opened for them, and they stepped into the spacious interior, which was cold and fragrant, smelling faintly of flowers. Two Asian women were waiting there for them, dressed in scorching mandarin red silk dresses cut in a revealing modern fashion, with high hemlines and low necklines.

As the doors closed and the Lincoln pulled out from between

the two Mercedes and disappeared, the two Asian women, moving slowly, produced silk blindfolds, wrapped them around Cate's and Irina's eyes, and tied them gently. Then Cate's escort sat very close to her and took her hand in a comforting manner, holding it between her own small ones. Cate could smell her perfume, as soft as sachet. The limousine's stereo played Chopin—at least Cate thought it was Chopin—soft piano notes falling like drops of dripping water into the otherwise silent compartment.

In this way they drove for a period of time that Cate found difficult to calculate. Always poor at gauging the passage of time, she nevertheless guessed that they had driven for something close to half an hour. She could feel the motion of the car and occasionally the gentle pull of gravity as the limousine turned ever so subtly one way or the other. At such moments, she could feel the body of the woman beside her shift slightly, and from time to time, when the woman moved one or the other of her hands, cool air came into the warmth created by their touch, a sensation that for some reason surprised Cate because of the degree of heat generated by the other woman's skin. She was surprised too at being aware of the preciseness of the woman's hands, her delicate fingers, her softly shaped nails. Now and then Cate could feel the woman's long hair brush against her bare shoulder, and, curiously, she could feel the quiver of her breath too, as light as a fleeting thought.

The fact that she noticed such detailed sensations, Cate thought, must be the result of being blindfolded, of having one sense taken from her and thereby stimulating the others to compensate. Whatever the reason for her heightened sensitivity, it was there, surprising and distracting her from the fear that gnawed at her unrelentingly. With her left hand she ran her fingers over the bandage she had surreptitiously put over the implants in her right arm while they were still in the Lincoln. Whatever was going to happen from here on, she was not likely to forget. She could tell Hain and the others what they needed to know and keep the rest—whatever the hell that might be—to herself.

The limousine slowed and began a gentle turn up a slight incline. Immediately Cate's companion released her hand and reached up and untied the blindfold. As the cloth came away from her eyes, she reflexively looked at Irina, who was already returning her gaze. Cate could tell nothing from the expression on her face.

As soon as she looked out the window of the limousine, Cate felt her heart, which had calmed some during the ride, begin to pound again. The house was large and modern, built on a slight rise with terraced landscaping, its cantilevered rooms curiously and sophisticatedly lighted, with an attention to dramatic detail that was seldom seen and never achieved without an enormous financial expenditure. Cate looked back briefly as they started up the first tier of stone steps and saw that the grounds were completely surrounded by high walls, the curving drive lighted by soft firefly lights leading to the lane below.

Cate could not help noticing the extraordinary architecture as the four of them entered and started up a flight of red steps between black granite waterfalls, which whispered on either side of them as they ascended to the second level. They proceeded in silence down a spare corridor, its sole illumination being ribbons of glowworm trails along both sides of the ceiling, so that they were guided by the merest suggestion of luminescence.

Midway along this passage a doorway appeared on their left, and they were ushered into a room that was not large, though its furnishings and design made it feel spacious. The floors were white marble, the windowless walls a rich ochre, and the ceiling once again floated in its own sourceless light. The room was empty except for a dozen glass cases positioned at random, each resting at about waist height on a cylindrical carved stone pedestal. In each spotless case an abundance of gold artifacts were displayed, as in a museum.

Irina went straight to the nearest case. Bending over it, she looked at the artifact, gasped softly, and put a hand flat on her chest.

"Good God," she said. "I do not believe my eyes."

Cate stepped up beside her, and Irina moved eagerly to the next case, continuing to exclaim softly. After a few moments she turned to Cate, who had followed her to yet another case.

"These are ancient pieces of jewelry," Irina explained, "mostly, perhaps entirely, Greek. They are quite likely beyond value." She looked into another case. "Earrings, ear reels, rings, bracelets, fibulae, necklets . . . settings of garnet and emerald, crystal, sard, colored glass . . ."

"A remarkable collection, isn't it?" a man said.

Cate flinched and turned to see the Chinese standing in the doorway. He was wearing a white dinner jacket, formal black trousers, and opera slippers. His white shirt had a high wingtip collar set off with a black silk bow tie.

"Incredible, yes," Irina said, but stopped. The man was looking at Cate. "This is Catherine Miles," she said. But she did not mention the Asian's name.

The man approached Cate, took her hand, and smiled, bowing slightly from the waist. He held her hand and brought it to his face as though he were going to kiss it, but he did not, though he did, she believed, smell it.

"I am delighted to meet you," he said.

Cate nodded, unable to speak. He was much more handsome than she had expected, though she couldn't have said exactly what she had expected. There was something about his appearance that made her think he was of mixed blood, not entirely Asian.

Continuing to hold Cate's hand, he took a couple of steps farther into the room, taking her along.

"Of course, Irina, you are right," he said. "Greek. Some items came from the Crimea, some from the Greek colonies in Italy and the eastern Mediterranean."

"I am familiar with the collection of similar artifacts in the Hermitage," Irina said. "This rivals it. It is quite enviable."

"I wouldn't have it if it weren't enviable." The Asian smiled, glancing at Cate. "My favorites are the pendants of Ganymedes and the female pendants," he said, leading them to another case. "The figures of Eros, sirens, Aphrodite . . ."

The case he stopped in front of was dedicated solely to these nude figures, the ornaments executed in such extraordinary detail that in some cases the nipples on the breasts were clearly visible even though the object itself was no more than four centimeters in height. One object, the pendant of a necklace, was even mounted on a stand behind a magnifying glass to enable the viewer to see this particular detail.

As they were bending to look at this, a maid dressed in a black uniform with black stockings silently entered the room and offered them tall glasses of champagne. They each took a glass, and the Asian continued to narrate a description of his collection.

There was a display case of finger rings, many with erotic depictions, and sheets of what he called appliqués, also with erotic scenes. Even with her unpracticed eye, Cate could see the dazzling craftsmanship for herself. The collection was breathtaking.

"When did you acquire most of these?" Irina asked. "Recently?"

"Within the past five years," he said.

"And you are still adding to the collection?"

"When I can find the right pieces."

He looked at Cate and smiled, his glittering black eyes falling to her breasts, which he regarded with frank appreciation. She did not find his gaze offensive, though at this point her emotions were so chaotic that she wasn't quite sure what she was feeling. Nor could she imagine how she was going to feel as the night progressed. Already the events of the evening had created an aura of unreality, and somehow the Asian's admiration of her breasts seemed trivial by comparison.

She glanced at Irina, whose face showed nothing.

The champagne was very good, and they all finished the first drink rather quickly. Without being summoned, the maid returned with fresh ones. The Asian and Irina continued to talk about Greek gold while the three of them circled the glass cases, admiring the displays. The man continued to hold Cate's hand. Sometimes in his answers to Irina's questions he spoke directly to Cate, as if she had been the one to ask. Sometimes as they moved from one case to another he released Cate's hand and put his arm around her waist, letting his hand rest lightly there, now and again letting it fall lower, to the crest of her buttocks, where she felt his fingers explore the curve and cleavage of her body.

Cate wondered whether she should drink the champagne quickly to dull her inhibitions or whether she should barely drink any at all in order to stay in full control. How in hell could she bring herself to do what she thought she was going to have to do? She had put this moment out of her mind, telling herself that it might not happen, and if it did happen, something would come to her to enable her to avoid it. Well, it *was* happening, and suddenly she was at a loss; she had no frame of mind within which to play her role. She didn't feel panic; she didn't know what she felt, aside from a sense of absurdity tinged with anxiety.

What did come to her was a sudden decision not to drink any

more champagne. She would be nuts to sedate herself for this. She *wanted* her inhibitions. She wanted to do this with her eyes open, her senses alive, her mind engaged, her will tightened down by a tenacious discipline. Whatever was going to play out here, she wanted to be responsible for it. She didn't want to forfeit anything.

The Asian turned to her. He smiled. "This is enough about gold, isn't it?" His teeth were very white and absolutely perfect. In fact, the man himself was immaculate. He had no physical flaws, no scars, no moles, no feature slightly out of balance or distracting. He was like a carefully manufactured man, lacking any imperfections that humans normally consider faults. He seemed to be made of porcelain, all blemishes carefully eliminated by repeated inspections.

Smiling, he bent toward her and put his face to her neck, his lips lightly touching her hairline at the nape of her neck. She managed to breathe normally. Then his lips traced around, over the hollow in her neck, across her collarbone, down, down to the tops of her breasts, where she unmistakably felt his tongue dart toward her cleavage. She felt a ridge of goosebumps ripple down toward her navel.

He lifted his head, still smiling. Perfectly.

"I want you to see something upstairs," he said, taking each woman by a hand. "There's a beautiful room there. I think you both will like it."

He walked to the far corner of the room, where a spiral staircase of white marble was embedded in the wall. Since it was narrow, they started up one at a time, the Asian first, then Irina. Cate followed, her eyes fixed on the softly lighted treads, her heart failing to provide all the oxygen she needed.

When they emerged from the stairwell, she thought they had stepped out onto the roof of the house. In fact, they were standing in the corner of a spacious room. The two walls that converged where they were standing were of deep jade-green polished marble, as was the floor. The other two walls, the corner of which was opposite them, were of glass. Through these two walls the city lay before them, glittering in the vast darkness like the glitter in the darkness of the Asian's eyes. Immediately Cate smelled the fragrance of flowers again, and heard music, a woman's voice singing in German, accompanied by a slow, solitary, clear-noted piano.

In the center of the triangle created by the two glass walls—a space that seemed to be cantilevered out into the night sky—was a raised oval of polished scarlet stone the size of a bed, with a collection of dark red damask pillows scattered about on it. The sides of the stone were decorated with a bas-relief, and as they approached, Cate recognized the imagery and saw that the figures represented there were finely and delicately carved. Though she didn't know the names of the sites, she knew that these were reproductions of erotic stone carvings from ancient temples in India.

On three sides of the elliptical stone dais and within arm's reach of it were three smaller cylindrical stone pillars, the height and size of small tables. On the flat top of one of these was a stack of thick mandarin red towels. The second pillar consisted of two basins cut into the stone, one higher than the other and with water flowing over its edge into the lower basin. The third pillar held an enormous jade bowl of brightly colored fruit.

It took a moment for Cate to absorb these ceremonial elements, the colors, the architecture, the textures of the polished stone and glass, the fragrance of flowers, the clear voice of the German lyric soprano—was she singing Schubert? Schumann?—the piano's notes, clean, sharp, sad. It was an extraordinary orchestration of sensations that surprised and captivated her.

When the inevitable happened, when she felt the Asian undressing her from behind, she remembered what Irina had said about Cate's nervousness being an enticement to him. She would not pretend to be other than she was. When the Asian turned her around, he was already undressed and was speaking Chinese to her, softly.

As he removed her clothes she looked at him—she couldn't help it—and saw that his body was as flawless as his face. Even his erection, which she had dreaded confronting, was startlingly attractive in its proportions. It was in no way offensive, and, to her even greater consternation, was in fact wonderfully and appealingly erotic.

He dealt with her gently, surprised and intrigued by her tattoo and absence of hair. When they turned around again, Irina was lying on the elliptical red stone, her naked, extraordinary body reflected in its highly polished surface, her buttery hair undone. Her beauty was displayed in this imaginative setting as though it had been designed exactly for her, and the visual composition of what Cate saw caused her to take a quick breath.

In this moment she realized how she had deluded herself. This was no place for reason, no place for control, no place for discipline or restraint. Nor was this a moment that could sustain convention. Though Cate did not understand it, though she had never sought or experienced it, she could not refuse the attraction that she felt for what she saw on the scarlet stone. Irina was irresistible—to man or woman.

If Cate had resolved to be responsible for her own actions, she realized now, then she had no one to blame for her abandon. Time condensed. It expanded. At times a single sensation—a fragrance, a taste, a tactile experience—seemed to last endlessly and be of such intensity that it engulfed her, and she became entirely, wholly that sensation, to the exclusion of all others. At other times she was overwhelmed by an engagement of all her senses at once, tasting, hearing, smelling, feeling, seeing, so many sensations in so short a time that she could think of the experience only as an explosion—perhaps an implosion—of heightened erotic sensibility. She was helplessly aware of her unraveling emotions, of a profound spiritual havoc.

The soprano's voice was limpid and melancholy, as though coming from the distant ether.

The piano notes fell gracefully, dreamily, like diamonds through leagues of clear water.

The grapes in the bowl of fruit were large and purple and dusted with bloom, and it was only because of Wei's complete pleasure in Catherine's body that Irina had the time to utilize them for one of Wei's favorite gratifications.

She had taken the bacteria capsules from the address book back at the chateau and wrapped them in a small piece of nylon she had cut from a pair of pantyhose. While she and Catherine were dressing, she had surreptitiously pinned the small packet into her hair as she wound her chignon. Now, as Wei grew glassy-eyed with Catherine, Irina turned away and used a hairpin to puncture four of the grapes, then she inserted a capsule into each one. It took only moments.

Now, turning toward him so that Wei could see what she was doing, she artfully slipped each of the large grapes into her vagina. Five minutes later she looked down at him and watched with a smile as he greedily retrieved them with his tongue, one by one. He ate them all.

Fifty-six

AS SOON as they could tell from the conversation that Irina and Cate had arrived at Wei's house, Hain spoke up.

"Jernigan," he said, "you have a fix on that?"

"1511 Mousset."

"Incredible," Hain enthused, throwing himself back in his chair. "Christ! An hour ago we didn't even know this guy was on the continent. Now we know his address. *And* Bontate. I don't *believe* this implant. It's goddamn incredible."

"Curtis." Ann Loder's voice was all business this time, her emotions well under control. "What's our response time if we have to send people in there?"

"I don't know. Not quick. We're not going to have to go in there," Hain said.

"But if we did," Ann persisted.

"Then we would," Hain snapped. "There's no way to back out of it now. She's in. We're learning shit we didn't know before and it's all happened in the last twelve hours, for Christ's sake. Through Cate—it's all been through Cate. So we're in this up to our eyeballs, people. We're *not* calling in the cavalry now, not yet."

"I wasn't suggesting that we do that," Ann said, keeping her voice calm. "It was a contingency question."

"Okay, well, you've got my answer, then."

Everyone listening to Hain was thinking the same thing. At this point, Cate was on the short end of a triage decision. They were all acting as though she was not going to find herself in a life-threatening situation and then praying to God she wasn't. They were going to sit tight for what Hain called "the big sweat"— when an agent was strung out farther than anyone could reach to help. There wasn't anything anyone could do about it. They were lucky, and they were unlucky. Sometimes it happened that way. They just had to wait and listen and hope to God they didn't hear the kinds of sounds that would give them nightmares for the rest of their lives.

For the next fifty minutes they listened to Cate's transmissions in taut silence. It was the silence of concentration, fascination, embarrassment, natural human curiosity, discomfort, voyeurism, and trepidation. Except for the voice of the soprano, the transmissions were rarely articulate. They were only sounds. Occasionally Wei spoke in Chinese. There was labored breathing. There was moaning. The women's voices—the sounds they made—were not always distinguishable. There were long pauses when only the piano could be heard.

Cate lay on her back on the red stone bed, the polished surface cool against her naked back and buttocks, her head resting on one of the damask pillows. She had just washed herself at the stone basins, and as her damp skin dried in the cool air, it prickled lightly, as though covered with a thin film of effervescence.

At the foot of the oval bed, the Asian sat alone with his bare feet on the jade floor, his naked back to her, smoking hashish, lost in his own thoughts as he stared out at the city lights and listened to the solitary notes of the piano that came from nowhere and everywhere, slow and soft and timeless.

Irina was standing at the stone basins, where she too had just finished washing. She was combing her hair, and Cate could feel her green eyes studying her.

When Cate had committed to this assignment, at the very moment when she knew there was no turning back, she also had made up her mind not to torture herself afterward over what she might have to do. And yet in the quiet aftermath of her abandonment she found herself struggling, despite her brave convictions, with a web of shame. Her conscience already had begun to spin the fine threads of guilt's cocoon about her.

But an extraordinary thing had happened during the past hour, during which she had experienced a welter of conflicting emotions. Cate had never had sexual intercourse with another woman, and now she doubted if it would ever have happened at all if the other woman had been anyone other than Irina. Irina's beauty was simply undeniable, and sex with her had been as good as it had ever been with a man. If Cate felt ashamed of what she had just done, it applied only to the Chinese. She felt no shame about what had happened with Irina. She acknowledged the inconsistency of this. She didn't understand it. That's just the way it was.

But that wasn't all. Something else had happened that was just as disturbing, and it brought to mind the sight of Irina standing over Stepanov and Izvarin curled up in the mucus-filled cavities of the piles of raw hides and firing into them. She had been willful about it, passionless. That side of Irina, Cate feared, was a very large part of her, a larger part than Cate wanted to let herself admit.

She turned her head and looked at Irina, who was still looking at her as she folded her red towel. Dropping the towel onto the jade floor, she sat down on the stone, lay down, and turned over to Cate. She nudged herself a place on the damask pillow and laid her long, graceful arm across Cate's stomach.

"Are you all right?" she asked softly, her face next to Cate's, her breath warm against Cate's ear.

"I'm fine," Cate said. They were almost whispering. The Asian ignored them or didn't hear them. "I need to talk to you."

"All right. What about?"

Cate moved her head slightly and looked toward the foot of the stone dais.

"Oh, forget him," Irina said. She leaned against Cate until their bodies touched along their full length and her breast lay against Cate's. She bent her right knee and her long thigh moved across Cate's, and Cate could feel the mound of damp hair between

Irina's legs pressing against her own hip. Irina's lips touched the lobe of Cate's ear as she spoke. "Right now he hears nothing, cares about nothing. He smokes a special kind of hashish. Very strong. He is lost to us now, adrift in a green Asian haze."

Cate could feel her heart pounding. But she had to know.

"Did you drug him?" she asked. "Is that why he is like that?"

"No, why do you ask?" Irina snuggled up against her like a sister—no, like a lover. The scent of flowers had given way to the sweet resinous smoke of hashish. It hung above them in a still, coiling ribbon, like a river of incense.

"I saw you do something to the grapes."

Irina didn't move. There was a long pause before she spoke. "I killed him," she said, her voice a husky whisper.

"What?" Cate could not help herself; she looked again at the Asian. "What are you talking about?"

"I killed him."

They could feel each other breathing. Cate didn't know what to say.

"It was one of the last things I had to do, Catherine," Irina said. "I did not have a choice."

"Jesus Christ. What are you talking about?"

"I poisoned him," she whispered. "A very slow poison—it will take a few days."

"Oh, God . . ."

Irina's arm tightened over Cate's stomach. Her face moved closer. "Do not be seduced by any moment of kindness, any thing of beauty that you might experience when you are with these people," she said. "The truth is, they live ugly, cruel lives. Never, never forget that."

"But why—"

"Shhhh . . . whisper, softly. Why? I told you, I have things to do for people."

"You did this *for* someone?"

"For someone, yes. But ultimately for me—for Félia. You lose sight too easily, Catherine. There are many twists and turns between what we desire and what we accomplish. I had to do it."

"Ometov . . ."

"Ometov?"

"You said you had a few things to do for Ometov."

"No, of course not. Not Ometov. It doesn't matter who it was for. After tonight I won't have to do it ever again. This is the last of them."

Cate was stunned. *This is the last of them.* Them? Again she saw Irina firing into Stepanov and Izvarin. She smelled the exudate of skinned hides. Good God.

"Catherine, I know . . . no, I can only imagine how this must seem to you." Her lips skimmed Cate's ear as she breathed these words into her. "Or perhaps I cannot even imagine. There is much of me that is gone now, lost in the confusion of my sins. There are innocent ways of thinking that I can no longer remember, nor will I ever again." She paused. Her hand moved against Cate's hip. "But do not think that I am evil. Only try to understand that you cannot understand. If God had put your soul into another heart . . . Who knows? Be careful that you do not find too much comfort in your own righteousness."

Dumbfounded, Cate grew clammy in Irina's embrace. She saw the Asian on his knees between Irina's spread thighs, eating his own death while Irina leaned back and smiled down at him. Cate's stomach turned; her mouth grew dry. She wanted to take a deep gulp of air but couldn't.

"Now I have to go to Sergei's," Irina said.

"Now?"

"Soon." She moved her hand up along Cate's rib cage and lightly cupped the underside of her left breast. "I want you to come with me."

"What?" Cate was startled. She fought to remember her role as if she were fighting to keep her head above water in a powerful undertow. Catherine. She was Catherine. How would Catherine react? What would Catherine do? Now there was little difference between Catherine and Cate. Both of them were astonished. Afraid. Trying to understand how to behave in the face of such unbelievable developments. "Why, what do you want with me?"

"What do I want with you?"

Cate remembered Ometov's insistence on the importance of Irina's loneliness. It was a point of leverage, an opening that Cate could use to her advantage. But Cate couldn't use it. Not now. If she had thought of it earlier, if she had made use of it earlier, maybe. But now, how could she now? She finally gathered enough saliva to swallow, just as she realized that Irina had suddenly stiffened. Had she sensed something?

"Irina, please . . . understand. I'm scared. I don't understand this. I'm afraid . . . I don't even know what to say. I've done this—for you. I don't know what else I can do."

"It is very simple," Irina said. "I have to pick up a package from Sergei. Money. A lot of money. Usually he gives it to me in one or two small bags. I could use help in carrying it." She paused. "And I will pay you for this evening. More than Stepanov would ever have given you. Much more than that."

This caught Cate by surprise. Catherine could hardly turn down the money. She probably would even think she had it coming to her. She had been through a lot.

"Is it going to be safe?" Cate asked hesitantly. She dropped her hand down and found the inside of Irina's thigh and let it rest there. "I mean, what about Stepanov . . . and the other one?"

"He does not know that they have been killed."

"How do you know?"

"It does not matter. Take my word for it. There have been arrangements for communications. He believes I have done what he wanted me to do. All he has left to do is pay me."

"But what about me? He doesn't know me—what's he going to do when he sees me?"

"I am taking care of that."

"How?"

"I cannot tell you, Catherine."

Cate shook her head skeptically. "I don't know—this scares me. All of this is crazy. I want to help you . . . I do, and God knows I need the money, but I don't know how much of this I can handle."

"No, there is nothing to be afraid of," Irina said soothingly. "This is routine. I pick up my money. This is all."

Cate moved her hand on the inside of Irina's thigh. "How long will it take?" she asked.

"I have to call him to get directions. I don't know—not more than an hour, I would think."

Cate waited a moment, thinking it over. "We're just going to pick up the money and that's all. Just get the money and go."

"That is all," Irina said. "And then I am through."

"And what about your daughter?"

"Sergei will give me instructions about her when we see him. I have fulfilled my obligations to him."

Cate was silent a moment. She realized now that not much of what Irina had been telling her had been adding up. She had said she had messages to deliver for Krupatin and things to do for Ometov. So far Cate hadn't seen any of this happen. Irina had said she had a message to deliver to the Asian, in addition to the sex. Cate had seen what had become of that. It seemed that Irina was making up all of this as she went along. There was more unseen than seen here, volumes more.

"Irina," Cate said, and she pressed her hand into the inside of Irina's thigh, unsure of what exactly this gesture might convey, "I . . . I don't want to die in this . . . nightmare. Don't do that to me."

Irina dropped her hand from Cate's breast and hugged her. "No, no, no—never. I would never put you in that kind of danger."

Cate breathed the breath that carried Irina's words, she felt anew her lovely, seductive nakedness, and she wondered which of them was telling the other the greatest lies.

Fifty-seven

JESUS CHRIST ALMIGHTY!" Hain moaned and slumped back in his chair, rubbing his eyes with the palms of his hands, his head tilted back. "Oh, shit!"

Ometov said nothing. He shook his head and stared intently at the lights on the electronic console in front of them. He had been sitting very still, listening silently.

Hain was a restless waiter; his huge frame and athletic energies were a poor combination for stakeouts, despite the fact that he did this sort of thing for a living. When he listened to wire transmissions, he chewed dozens of sticks of gum, one after the other, spitting them out as soon as the sugar was gone, and moved his arms and legs, stretched, drank coffee, grunted as he twisted his back muscles, shifted positions in his chair hundreds of times.

Ometov, in contrast, listened to the transmissions like a stone. When he needed a break, he calmly would take off the headphones and walk to the windows and look out at the courtyard. Sometimes he would step outside and smoke several cigarettes, walking along the paths, one hand in his pocket, his head down.

Ann Loder said nothing and did nothing. She and Erika had been drinking diet soft drinks, making regular trips back and forth to the refrigerator in the kitchen and to the bathroom. Erika had both forearms on the table. She was looking at Ometov.

Hain turned off his microphone and raised his right arm in the air and began massaging his shoulder with his left hand. He too was studying Ometov, who had grown noticeably quiet during the last few minutes. Hain reached out and pulled over a chair and propped his feet up on the seat. He picked up his coffee mug and rested it on his stomach and regarded his Russian counterpart. Both of them were drinking coffee; Hain's was black, Ometov's thick with cream.

"You knew this, didn't you?" Hain said. For the first time his voice could not hide his anger.

Ometov studied the blinking lights and sipped his coffee. His rounded shoulders seemed weighed down by the lateness of the hour, by the tension, and by the heft of his own personal history with the woman they were discussing. He pushed his chair away from the table, wiped his forehead with his hand, and shook his head.

"I do not know if she is killing for Krupatin," he said. "I have no proof. But yes, I suspect she has been doing that, yes."

"How long have you suspected it?"

"Even before I recruited her in Venice."

"Jesus God." Hain was furious. "And you could never confirm it?"

"No. But I am sure that Krupatin used her for strategic killings. Not for killing others who were in the killing business. He used ex-KGB for that. Her targets were civilians, people whose lives had become entangled with Krupatin's, people who used him as much as he used them—bankers, lawyers, businessmen, politicians, powerful people who were willing to look the other way in order to have access to his money, to make a quick fortune off his illegitimate involvements by bringing him into legitimate enterprises."

"Then why is he hitting them?"

"Things change." Ometov shrugged. "They use up their usefulness. Somehow, for countless reasons, they become a liability. Sergei decides he would be much better off without them, then he gets rid of them. Rather, Irina does."

"Damn."

"She must have started out as one of his 'surgeons,' " Ometov mused, looking into his cup, "taking a life to spare another. But he never let her go. If you kill once in order to save the life of someone who is held hostage, then it is a horrible thing. You do it. It's over. But then he comes to you again. Incredible. A nightmare. But your choice is the same. And you make the same decision. Then he comes again. And again. Then one day you wake up, and it has become a way of life. Your life is now beyond horrible. It is unbelievable. You have become an assassin. But the hostage is still alive."

"Félia."

Ometov nodded. "Yes, Félia."

"She's going to kill him," Ann said bluntly.

"Krupatin?" Ometov shook his head without looking at her. He started to say something, then seemed to change his mind. "I don't know."

Ann snorted in disgust. "*I* know," she said. "She's going to blow his face off."

"Wait a minute." Erika looked around at each of them. "Stepanov. Izvarin. Wei. And perhaps Krupatin." She tilted her head. "Who is out of the picture here?"

"Bontate," Hain said quickly. "She's turned to the Sicilians."

"And who else?"

"Volkov," Ometov said, nodding slowly, looking at Erika and realizing what she was thinking. "You are right . . . yes, exactly. Irina is bringing Krupatin down. She is Volkov's opportunity."

"Jees-us!" Hain hissed. "This is an incredible thing here."

"And what are we going to do about it, Curt?" Ann asked. "Are we going to let her do it?"

"Who believes her story about Wei?" Ometov asked. "About the poison?"

"Shit, I believe it," Hain said.

"Why?" Ometov pressed his point. "Why would she reveal something like that to Cate? This is something that bothers me. Why would she tell her?"

"Maybe we are underestimating how well Cate has done her job," Erika said. "Maybe she really has managed to gain Irina's confidence. The woman cannot be perfect all the time. She is human, after all. Maybe you were right, Leo. Loneliness is her weakness. She sees something in Cate that makes her open up. She talks to her, she tells her too much. A fatal mistake in her business. But these people don't live forever, do they?"

"It seems to me the question is not, why did she tell?" Ann offered. "It could be that Erika is right. But if Erika is wrong, then the question we should be asking is, why would she lie about it?"

"You mean you think Irina suspects Cate is undercover?" Hain asked.

"No, I'm not saying that." Ann shook her head. "I'm just saying this is a question we need to answer. If we can't, then we have to assume that Irina did in fact give Wei a lethal dose of poison."

"I cannot think of any reason why she would lie about it," Ometov said. "I don't know what she would gain by it."

"The only reason she would lie about it," Hain said, "is if she thought Cate was a plant of some kind—for us, for one of the other organizations—and she wanted the people Cate works for, or who she thinks Cate works for, to believe she's killed him."

"That doesn't make any sense at all," Erika said firmly. "What kind of scenario would accommodate a situation in which it would be a benefit to someone to have someone else think Wei was dead when he wasn't?" She looked around at everyone. "No, I think we are trying too hard to find conspiracies. We are going to outsmart ourselves and miss the obvious point. The woman is lonely. She talked too much. Her mistake. Our gain. It is that simple."

"I think she's right," Ann said.

Ometov raised his hand tentatively as he took a sip of coffee.

"Okay," he said, wiping his mouth, "I have a question. What if Irina is not going to kill Krupatin? What if . . . I don't know, what if she has to create this one last deception before Krupatin will free her daughter? What if all of this is an effort by Krupatin to flush out traitors? Stepanov. Izvarin. And now, because he was willing to plot with Irina, Volkov."

"So where does that leave Wei?" Hain asked.

Erika nodded. "And Bontate?"

"I don't give a damn where it leaves them." Ann couldn't contain her impatience any longer. "We're not discussing the questions we ought to be discussing here."

Hain looked at her. "Okay."

"Are we going to let this rock on as a collection effort only?"

she asked. "Are we going to intervene? What are we going to do about Cate?"

"Last question first," Hain said. "Is she safe?" He looked around the room. No one answered immediately. Then Ometov nodded slowly.

"Yes. I don't know whether anyone around her is safe, but I think she is."

Erika did not answer immediately, and when she did, she began shaking her head slowly.

"I'm sorry," she said, "I disagree again. As we have seen, we have a lot of unanswered questions here. We do not know what any of this means for Cate. What if she *has* been discovered? Or if not, after all she has seen, what if she is considered a risk that cannot be ignored? If not by Irina, then what about Volkov? What about Bontate? These men only have to give the word and she is gone."

"And one possibility we haven't mentioned," Ann interjected. "What if there is someone in Wei's camp who is in essentially the same position as Volkov in Krupatin's camp, an ambitious Judas? Maybe Irina's in collusion with a faction of the Chinese too, in some way we haven't figured out."

"I thought you were tired of theories," Hain said.

"The fact is, Curtis," Ann said evenly, "this thing has gotten out of control. Wei, Bontate—we didn't know they were in the mix. Krupatin's inexplicable behavior. We thought he was coming down here for a straightforward meeting with his people. Our agent's been killed. Our undercover operative is—shit—having sex with his killer. Her 'best friend.' Does this sound under control to you? Does this sound stable to you?" She paused. "What are you going to say to the guys in Washington if we lose her?" She looked at him. "What are you going to say to Ennis Strey?"

There was a long silence as Hain and Ann stared at each other. Then Hain took his big feet out of the chair where he had been resting them and said, "This is a fucking undercover bonanza. I want to hear Krupatin's voice. I want to hear him breathing on those goddamn implants. As long as we don't have anything but a bunch of bullshit theories, we don't have anything. Where is Bontate? Who's goddamn conspiracy is this, anyway? Who's in charge here? If Krupatin's being squeezed out, who's squeezing? If all these guys—Wei Tsing, Carlo Bontate, Sergei Krupatin—if all of them end up dead at the end of the day, who the hell's taking their places? Somebody always does, and you know damn well that if we don't know who the new players are, we are back at square one. We're starting from scratch. We've *got* to know who's giving the orders to these organizations when the dust clears here, or we're worse off than when we went into this."

He stopped and fixed his eyes on Ann Loder.

"And Cate is our only hope of finding out the answers to these questions." He shook his head. "No way am I going to pull the plug on this thing at this point. We've got to have the guts to stick it out. I mean, these organizations are going through a sea change right here before our eyes. If Cate hadn't been inside this thing, not only would we not know that these people had had a meeting here, we wouldn't know that, apparently, some new people will be taking over. God knows how long it would have taken us to figure this out. And in the meantime they'd be growing, spreading out. Way ahead of us."

Hain had grown red in the face. He was tired of Ann's second-guessing him; he was tired of having to justify his decisions to his own people. He slammed his coffee mug down on the table beside his headphones.

"We are intelligence, not operations," he added. "So we are going to gather intelligence. We are not going to call in operations and risk having those damn cowboys blow this thing wide open. I don't even want the damn *wind* to shift right now. Cate is about to walk into the same room as Sergei Krupatin, and I don't want *anything* to screw that up. Especially some kind of weak-kneed, bullshit theory that we can't take the risk. We sure as hell fucking can! That's what we're all about. That's what our undercover people *do*." He was still glaring at Ann. "We sit tight, and we *listen*."

He swung around in his chair, snatched up his headphones, slapped them on his head, and flipped the toggle switch on the radio.

"Jernigan. Give me an update."

Cate would remain on her own.

Fifty-eight

THEY DRESSED QUICKLY, Irina suddenly moving with an urgency that seemed to have been born of nothing other than Cate's agreement to go with her. It took only minutes to slip on their dresses, and then Irina, carrying her shoes in her hand, walked over to the Asian.

She crouched down beside him, looking at him on his level, at his profile as he stared out at the city lights. He was no longer smoking, only staring.

"We are leaving," she said.

He didn't react. She looked at him a moment. He was oblivious. She reached out and put her hand on his bare leg, still looking at him, both of them silent. Then she stood, and she and Cate walked out of the green marble and glass room, away from the scarlet stone bed suspended above the city, away from the small universe where Cate had experienced the most startling sensations of her life.

When they emerged from the gold room downstairs, the two Asian women who had ridden with them in the limousine met them in the long, lunar-lighted corridor and ushered them out the rear of the house and into the back seat of a silver Jaguar. One of the women drove the car while the other sat beside her in the front seat. Both wore earpieces and microphones similar to those worn by the men who had intercepted the Sicilians' Mercedes earlier in the evening, and both kept up a constant soft-spoken communication with others through their headgear.

Cate and Irina both looked out their windows and rode in silence. After a while Irina reached over and took Cate's hand, though she continued to gaze out at the city. It was not so much a gesture of affection as one of comfort, or one of seeking comfort. Her grip on Cate's hand was firm, almost too firm, more like a grip of desperation than anything else. It was extraordinarily odd, and Cate found herself being frightened by the fierceness of it, as though it were the gesture of someone *in extremis.*

Cate lost track of time, staring out the window, her mind racing. She wondered if Hain and the others had panicked when she had blacked out her transmissions—she secretly had removed the bandage while she dressed—and whether she should say something now to reorient them.

Suddenly the car pulled over to the side of the street and stopped under a long canopy of trees. She hadn't been paying attention, but she thought they must be in Memorial Park. She shot a quick glance at Irina.

"Everything is all right," Irina said without explanation.

Within moments a taxi drove up and parked just in front of them. The woman in the passenger seat turned to them.

"The taxi will take you back to your hotel," she said, and then both Asian women got out of the Jaguar and opened the back doors for them.

Within moments they were in the taxi and traveling back to the main streets. In less than ten minutes Cate realized they were nearing the Chateau Touraine again. Just then Irina asked the driver to pull into a convenience store.

"I have to make a call," she said, looking into her purse. She took out a card. "I will take only a moment."

"Okay. I'm going to see if they have a bathroom."

Irina didn't even hesitate at that, and the two got out of the taxi and asked the driver to wait. Irina went straight to a telephone kiosk while Cate went inside, asked for the restrooms, and headed toward the back of the store, past boxes of stock and cleaning supplies to a tiny restroom. She flipped on the light and went inside and closed the door. The place stank; the floor was gummy.

"Okay," she began, speaking quickly, softly. "I've spent the last hour at the home of a Chinese national. You heard Irina tell me about him so you know he works with Krupatin. Only one thing happened you should know—I saw Irina do something to some grapes which this guy later ate. I asked about it. She claims she poisoned him. A slow-acting poison. I don't know if this . . . Also, I think she hits professionally for Krupatin."

Someone knocked on the door.

"God." Cate jerked her dress up, shoved down her panties, and sat down on the toilet just as another knock followed and the door was pushed open. It was Irina.

"We have to hurry. Come on."

"Okay, okay, I'm coming."

Irina closed the door, and Cate stood quickly, pulling up her panties. It was only then that she noticed the toilet was stopped up, toilet paper and urine floating in its bowl. She stood back from it, straightened her panties, and dropped her dress, her heart hammering.

After they returned to the taxi, it was not more than ten minutes before they were turning into the curving drive that led to the hotel, where the doorman was waiting in the softly lighted portico. He smiled pleasantly at them, as though they had been out to a quiet dinner.

Once they were upstairs and safely in Irina's suite, Irina looked at her watch and went straight to the fireplace in the living room. Crouching down in front of the opening, she reached up into the flue and worked a few moments with something she had obviously hidden there. When she finally succeeded in detaching it from its niche, she pulled out a small package wrapped in brown butcher paper. Kneeling on the rug between the sofas in front of the fireplace, she began unwrapping it.

With surprising dexterity, she proceeded to assemble a SIG-Sauer P220, a 9mm autoloading pistol with a chrome silencer, which she screwed into place and tightened with a final firm grip.

"What do you need a gun for?" Cate asked anxiously. "I thought we were just going to pick up some money."

"We are," Irina said. "But it is going to be a lot of money, and I do not want it taken away from us." She stood up and looked down at her black evening dress. "Come on, let's get out of these things." Holding the P220 in one hand and a box of cartridges in the other, she looked at her watch and headed for the bedroom, where she tossed the pistol and cartridges onto the bed and began taking off her dress.

When they both had finished changing clothes, Irina was dressed in a long-skirted shirtdress of navy silk with pale ivory moonflowers. Her hair was pulled back in a freshly and smoothly combed chignon, and she looked for all the world like an indulged society wife from one of the Villages in west Houston. She was innocent and gorgeous, a magnolia blossom with a brown recluse spider hidden in the creamy center of her beauty.

Bending over the bed, she opened the box of cartridges, picked up the spring-loaded magazine of the P220, and pressed nine rounds into it. Ramming the magazine home into the butt of the pistol, she slammed back the slide, putting one bullet into the chamber, and flicked on the safety with her thumb. Her efficiency was disconcerting, and Cate noticed that her manner had significantly changed. Her concentration was so intense she even moved differently, with economy of motion, with more purpose than grace.

Again she checked her watch. Quickly pulling the covers from her bed, she stripped off one of the sheets and folded it as small as she could, to purse size, and put it under her arm.

"Now we have to go," she said.

"What's the sheet for?" Cate asked. But Irina didn't answer. She was already striding out of the bedroom.

They went down in the elevator and into the cavernous lobby. Cate suddenly was stricken with a panicky desire not to leave the hotel. That which so often in the past had seemed impersonal to her—hotel lobbies, no matter how ingratiatingly they might be decorated, always struck her as unfriendly—that which had seemed so lacking in warmth, suddenly became the very epitome of comfort and security. For a moment she feared an overpowering impulse to break and run. Then she thought she was going to hyperventilate. She did neither. Within moments they were outside under the porte cochere, getting into a waiting taxi that had just arrived.

"Well, hello there," the driver said with surprise, beaming at them over the back of the seat. "I'll be damned. You must've saved my card after all."

"Of course I did," Irina said, smiling sweetly. "Did you think I would not save it?"

The taxi driver, a woman in her mid-thirties, shrugged. "Hey, you never, never know." Obviously gay, she wore her hair in a severe masculine cut, had a cigarette tucked behind one ear, and wore a faded blue denim work shirt with jeans. The sleeves of the shirt were rolled back on the forearms. She was a thin woman, but rather buxom.

"Well, so where do you girls want to go?" She was grinning as if they all shared a secret, clearly delighted to have them in her car.

"We have a small, special problem," Irina said. "We thought you might be just the person to help us."

"I'll give it my best shot," the woman said. Cate saw her license on the dashboard but couldn't read the name from the back seat.

"It will take maybe twenty minutes," Irina said, "and we will be very generous with you."

"Twenty minutes, huh?" She paused. "And how generous might that be, honey?" She cut her eyes at Cate, her grin brightening even more.

"We would be happy to pay you five hundred dollars."

Her eyebrows shot up. "Whoa! That's a pretty good rate for half an hour." She hesitated and wrinkled her brow. "I don't have to break any laws, do I?"

"Oh, no, of course not."

"Hey, I'm in," the woman said.

"Good. I will explain to you while we are driving."

The driver radioed her fare in to the dispatcher. She was picking up a couple of riders at the Chateau Touraine and taking them to the Burlewood condominiums, just off Westheimer. The ride was not a long one, and all the while Irina kept up a chatty conversation with the driver; she was coy, almost seductive, and her effect on the driver was nothing less than captivating.

When they arrived at the Burlewood, the driver took them down into the underground parking area and found an isolated spot at the far end of one of the rows. Irina and Cate got out of the back seat and the driver opened the trunk. Irina spread the sheet out on the floor of the trunk, which was, luckily, large and clean, since the taxi was a new one. Then they crawled inside and arranged themselves as comfortably as possible. When they were ready, the driver gently closed the lid, tapping on the top twice when it clicked shut. Cate was curled into the curve of Irina's body like a sleeping lover, but the dark, confining space made her tense.

"You will be all right," Irina said. "You will be safe," and she embraced her gently. Cate could smell her fragrance briefly, and then the driver started the car.

As they drove out of the Burlewood garage, the driver radioed that she had just dropped off her two fares and that she was going to a nearby diner for a cup of coffee. At the diner she bought a cup of coffee and a doughnut and chatted a little while with the waitress. Then she went back out to her car.

She drove back into traffic and after five minutes radioed to her dispatcher that she was picking up a fare at a certain address on Fountainview and would then be headed to an address in Park West. Then she turned around and pointed her taxi in the opposite direction.

The Amberson Towers were three twenty-five-story condominium buildings sitting at angles to each other like the legs of a tripod. The buildings were about a block apart, separated by heavily wooded grounds. After cruising along the serpentine lane that laced together the front grounds of the three towers, the taxi approached the parking garage entrance of Amberson II, the center building. The driver stopped at a keypad at the entrance and punched in the appropriate code, and the horizontal tubular rod gate rose up slowly, allowing them to descend the ramp into the garage.

The garage took up three stories deep in the ground, but the taxi driver pulled into one of the second-level aisles and found a parking space. She cut the motor and quickly got out and went around and opened the trunk.

"You okay?" she asked, helping first Cate and then Irina out of the trunk. "Shit, I knew it'd be hot in there. And it's not a hell of a lot better down here."

Cate was indeed perspiring, but mostly because of the tension of her confinement, not the heat. The car trunk had made her even more claustrophobic than she had feared.

"You okay?" the driver asked again. Cate saw that she was wearing cowboy boots.

"Yes, we are all right," Irina answered for both of them, straightening her dress. "Did you see anyone following you?"

"I don't know. There may have been this one car at first, a Mercedes. It showed up at the doughnut shop, cruised by, and then left. But I didn't see it again after I left the Burlewood. I know nobody came into the Amberson gates after me."

"Excellent." Irina opened her purse and counted out seven hundred dollars and handed it to the driver.

"Seven!" The driver fanned out the one-hundred-dollar bills in her hands.

"Two more to forget us if anyone should ask you later," Irina said. She leaned over and kissed the driver on the mouth. The woman looked as if she were going to melt.

"You still got my card?" she stammered.

"Oh, yes." Irina smiled. "I am keeping it."

The woman beamed. "Listen, anytime you need me, honey, I'm your woman." She hesitated, not wanting to go, her curiosity elevated to absolute fascination. She was clearly fearful she would never see this gorgeous woman again. "You two take care," she said finally, stuffing the money into her tight jeans pocket. Then she turned, got back into her taxi, and drove out of the garage.

Fifty-nine

AS SOON as the taxi turned the corner out of sight, Irina
headed for the nearest stairwell without saying a word.
Cate followed. But instead of going up, they headed down, their
footsteps gritty on the cement stairs, every move or bump against
the welded pipe railing echoing off the hard surfaces of the concrete stairwell.

The stairwell ended at the next door they came to. This was the
bottom of the garage. Irina opened the door cautiously and
looked out. It was just another parking level, with residents' cars
lined up against the walls. When she was satisfied, she stepped
out, and Cate followed her straight down the first aisle behind the
bumpers of all the cars. Irina went the full length of the aisle to
the very rear of the garage, where an area was closed off by a cage
of chainlink fencing.

It was, Cate guessed, some kind of electrical transformer, a
power station or relay station. Irina stood directly in front of the
door-size gate, then turned around and faced the last row of cars
in the garage. Walking straight to a red car opposite them—Cate

noted its rental agency sticker—she knelt down at the back bumper, reached under the license plate, and took out a small packet. It was a plastic security card and four keys wrapped together with masking tape. She studied the keys as she returned to the gate and then used one of them to unlock the padlock that secured the gate latch.

Inside the cage the floor was damp and dirty, and the entire area smelled of heated electrical wiring. The wind washing through the cage from a huge fan with blades as tall as Cate was hot and dry. Once they were inside, Irina reached through and locked the gate behind them, and then headed around the far end of the roaring equipment to the back side of the cage, where they came to a metal door. Irina used another key to unlock this. She pulled it open, paused, reached down to the floor, felt about for a moment, and then picked up a flashlight that was standing upright just behind the doorframe.

"Sergei is always so precise with his planning," she said. "He never forgets even the smallest detail." She didn't say it to Cate. She just said it.

"What the hell are we doing this for?" Cate asked. "The driver said we weren't followed."

"You cannot depend on taxi drivers to tell you about surveillance," Irina said.

"Then you know we are being followed?"

"We do not know. We assume."

"Who? Who's following us?"

"It does not matter who. Everyone is equally unwelcome."

But Irina didn't turn on the flashlight. Instead, she felt around on the wall until she located a light switch, which she flipped on.

Stretching out before them was a long, narrow tunnel illuminated by low-wattage bulbs, their discrete illuminations throwing a series of pale highlights on an endless drapery of electrical cables, which stretched far away into a dim infinity.

"Where does this go?" Cate asked.

Irina stood looking into the long tunnel.

"To Sergei," she said. "And beyond."

Irina made sure the door was closed behind them and then turned and started walking, with Cate following close behind. The tunnel was clearly a service access for the universe of cabling that was necessary to provide electricity to the three condominium buildings. The air in the narrow corridor was musty and smelled of concrete, and as they proceeded into the tunnel, the trajectory of a curve was clearly visible. They obviously were going to one of the adjacent buildings, but since they had gone around and around as they had descended into the parking garage in the taxi, and then gone around and around again in the stairwell, Cate had no idea which direction they were traveling in now, whether they were going to Amberson I or Amberson III.

The walk through the narrow service tunnel to the next building, whichever one it was, did not take more than fifteen minutes, though to Cate it seemed excruciatingly long. The echo of their footsteps on the grit, the dark night above them, the jaundiced glow in this subterranean passage through which they traveled, the SIG-Sauer in Irina's purse, Irina's cryptic answer to Cate's question—all conspired to contribute to the eerie feel of this strange journey. And the symbolism of Cate's situation did not escape her. If she was lost, in how many ways was she lost?

Staring at Irina's back, Cate tried to ignore the swags of electrical cable all around her. The moment Irina had flipped on the dull lights, the festoons of black wiring had reminded her of a monstrous gnarl of intestines, and now, as she and Irina negotiated their way along this hot, moist passage, she could not avoid the thought that they were pushing their way through the entrails of death.

But the melodrama vanished in an instant when she heard Irina chink the keys together and realized they were approaching another door. Irina stood looking down for a moment, locating the right key. Cate waited.

"Don't open the door."

Both women reflexively spun around to the voice, but neither could immediately see its source. Then, momentarily, the smutty shadows gave up the partial figure of a man standing about ten feet away against a backdrop of a black cobweb of wires and cables. The weak light above them caught him just below the waist, so that only his legs were visible, beginning with the skirt of his suit coat.

"Sergei!" Irina's voice was unsure. "What's the matter? Why are you here?"

"This is the woman?"

"You told me to come up."

"I changed my mind." His hands were not visible. "What is your name?"

Cate was lightheaded. "Catherine."

"And who do you know who knows me?"

Cate's mind was lurching. His voice was more sophisticated than she had imagined, which somehow intimidated her. His English was accented but precise.

"Valentin Stepanov," she said.

"And you know something that concerns me?"

Cate stared into the dark above the trousers of the suit. What in God's name was he talking about? What had Irina told him? Her mind was as dry as her mouth.

"You cannot expect her to talk about a traitor in the dark like this," Irina said with a note of indignation. She had recovered her footing. "Who else is here? Do you have the money to pay her for her information? She doesn't know. I don't know. This is not what you said would happen. We do not have all night. Valentin will miss her. She will have to explain. If you want to work out something with her, we have to make the most of the time. This is a stupid thing you are doing."

Irina spoke urgently, hoarsely, her stage whisper echoing, dying away along the cement walls in the sickly light.

Krupatin said nothing. He shifted his weight on his feet, the grit on the floor grinding against the leather soles of his shoes.

Cate's mind was working like a shuttlecock, back and forth, back and forth, trying to weave together the tapestry of Irina's hints. It seemed that Irina had told Krupatin that Cate had information to sell him about Stepanov's betrayal, but something had gone wrong here. If Irina ever had intended for Cate to relate such a story, she would have prepared her. If Irina had expected Cate to have sex on cue, with little preparation, surely she would have had no problem rehearsing her to tell a tale of intrigue—which, by eerie coincidence, just happened to be true. But she had not. No, Irina clearly had not intended for this meeting to happen. Not like this, anyway.

"Give me your purse," Krupatin said to Irina.

To Cate's surprise, Irina handed it to him immediately. He put the strap over his shoulder without looking inside.

"And yours." Cate handed it over, and he did the same with hers. "Okay," he said. "Go ahead. I'll follow."

Irina unlocked the door. They stepped out of the tunnel into a mirror image of the electrical equipment they had seen on the way in—the same huge fan blowing hot air, the same chainlink wire cage, the same low-ceilinged twilight of a garage. As if they were retracing their steps—they might have been; Cate was beginning to feel severely disoriented—they eventually reached the garage elevator. They rode up to ground level, which was as far as these elevators went, and when the doors opened, they found themselves forty feet from a set of double doors made of glass, through which Cate could see the lobby of the building.

Irina stepped out of the elevator, walked straight to the doors, and ran the magnetic security card through the track on a panel mounted on the wall. The electronic lock on the doors popped open.

They pushed their way inside and walked to the center of the lobby, where Cate noticed that the security guard's desk was unoccupied. She doubted that a building of this class would ever have a time when no guard was on duty. His absence set off an alarm in her nervous system.

The three of them rounded the corner of the desk, a curved marble affair sitting two steps above the lobby floor and having three television monitors on which colored surveillance shots flickered for no one to see. When they got to the elevator, all three of them stepped inside.

"Turn around and face the wall," Krupatin said.

They did as they were told, the doors closed, and Krupatin pushed a button. The elevator began its ascent. When the doors opened again, Krupatin told them to look down as they exited in front of him. Behind her, Cate could hear him punching five or six buttons before he let the doors close behind them.

Only three condominiums had entries from this small anteroom, each one at the end of its own narrow, barrel-vaulted corridor. Krupatin's front door was at the end of the passage directly in front of them. It had no number on the door. Cate had no idea where she was.

Krupatin opened the door.

"Just a minute," he said, and stepped inside ahead of them. He walked to a panel on the wall in the foyer and turned a dial. A screen lighted up. "Irina, you first," he said.

She walked through as Krupatin studied the screen in front of him.

"Now you," he said to Cate. She followed Irina through the doorframe, which was obviously wired with some kind of scanner. Satisfied, Krupatin turned off the screen and closed the door himself. Cate heard an electronic lock fasten in the wall behind them.

Telling Irina where to go, he followed them into a living room that looked out over the city. For some reason, all the rooms— Cate could see a hallway opening off the living room, a dining room on the opposite side, a kitchen beyond—were submerged in near darkness, though there was enough light to enable the three of them to move about quite easily without bumping into furniture. No one suggested turning on the lights.

Unlike the vast open spaces viewed from Wei's strange room, Krupatin's view was ornamented with a forest of tall buildings punching up out of the darkness like satellite planets, floating illuminations, slowly turning in the night space. Beyond, a sea of glittering lights stretched to the horizon, all the way out to the warm, swift waters of the Gulf of Mexico.

Krupatin moved past them farther into the room, nearer the glass walls, his gray silhouette visible against an ocean of sequins. As far as Cate could tell, the room was filled with modern furniture, low-profile bone white sofas and armchairs, glass coffee tables, sleek, expensive furnishings. He took the purses off his shoulder and dropped them in an armchair and then turned to a cabinet nearby. Cate heard the clacking of ice scooped into a glass, the chinking of the crystal stopper in a decanter as Krupatin poured himself a drink. He offered them nothing.

"What is all this about?" he asked, taking a drink from his glass before setting it on an end table next to the chair. He clicked on a lamp, creating a pool of light and illuminating his face. Cate was surprised again. He was handsome. His carefully barbered salt-and-pepper hair and trim mustache were flattering to his oval face and straight nose. He was wearing a charcoal double-breasted suit and a dress shirt with blue stripes, but no tie.

Bending down into the light, Krupatin picked up Irina's purse and opened it. He took out the SIG-Sauer and laid it on the table with his drink. Then he checked Cate's purse, and when he found no gun he tossed it back into the chair with a lack of interest.

"First of all," Irina said, "Wei is finished."

"I know," Krupatin said, picking up his drink again.

Irina was silent, and Cate sensed her body stiffening. It was clear that she was surprised by this.

"You know?"

"Yes, dammit, of course I know."

Irina stared at him. "Who?"

Krupatin took another drink and looked at her over the rim of the glass, relishing the fact that this was a surprise to her but seeming to consider whether or not to answer her.

"One of his Chinese maids," he finally said, smirking. "The one you found so comforting in Paris. And you saw her here too, the first time you met with Wei and Bontate in the red room. She watched the . . . spectacle tonight. She said you were a good little whore, Irina." He turned slightly to Cate. "Both of you were."

Cate's face burned. Jesus Christ.

"Did she tell you about Valentin Stepanov?" Irina asked. "Did she tell you about Grigori Izvarin?"

"No," Krupatin said, "she did not."

"You are surrounded by traitors, Sergei. You are rotting from the inside."

Sixty

JERNIGAN! Jernigan!" Hain was shouting into the radio. Everyone in the off-site was gaping at him. All of them had stood up instinctively, unable to remain in their seats when Cate's signal blacked out.

"I don't know . . . I don't know," Jernigan was saying.

"She was in the elevator," Hain was shouting. "They were walking into Krupatin's place. What happened?"

"Man, I've got a flat line on her signal. That's all." Jernigan's voice was not calm.

"Both of them? Nothing from the transmitter?"

"Nothing—just nothing."

"What does that mean, Curtis?" It was Ennis Strey, in the field office tech room.

"Jesus, I don't know. Neil, get Geller on the telephone, find out what this could be."

"We've got to get somebody over there," Ann snapped, one hand on her hip, one nervously combing back her thick, wiry hair. "We—Strey, you have people you can get over there?"

"That's Jernigan's call, but sure, we've got them."

"Just a goddamn minute," Hain barked. "We don't know what's going down here—"

"Exactly the damn point," Ann said.

"—and I'm not going to shove people in there before I can tell if the signal's glitched for some electronic reason that hasn't got anything to do with—"

"Curtis," Erika said, walking around the end of the table, "she's right. It sounded to me as if Irina had been lying to Krupatin about Cate. Cate did not know this. I think Ann is right, was right before. I think Irina is going to kill him."

"Well, I don't read it that way!" Hain shouted. "He took the goddamn gun away from her."

"Anything could happen," Erika persisted.

"We're going to *wait*"—Hain pointed his finger at Ann across the table, furious—"until we hear from Geller." There was a sudden silence. "You people aren't being professional here—get a grip!" His face was livid.

"How many stories are in the building?" Ometov asked calmly. He was rubbing his forehead, looking down, thinking.

"Twenty-five," someone said. "This is Parmley. Neil's on another line, trying to get Geller. The computer tells us it's a condominium complex, three separate buildings called the Amberson Towers. There's twenty-five floors in each of the towers."

"And if I remember what Mr. Geller said, your computer cannot tell us what floor she is on."

"That's right."

Everyone knew what he was getting at. Even if they sent a SWAT team over there now, there was going to be a frustrating delay while they located Krupatin's residence. Everyone was making the assumption that the condo was not listed under his name, that he had not made it easy for them to find him.

There was another silence while everyone looked at Curtis Hain, who was fuming, standing facing the others like an old lion backed up against a rock.

"Curt." It was Ennis Strey. He wanted an answer. The right answer.

It was another moment before Hain began to shake his head in defeat.

"Okay, Parmley, dammit. Tell Jernigan to go ahead with the

SWAT team. But you tell him, by God, that I . . . want . . . it
. . . *quiet.* And if it's not, tell him I'll dedicate the rest of my
fucking career to memorizing the names of the jerks who screwed
this up."

Nobody had ever forgotten that Curtis Hain worked out of the
Washington office. And he had been there a long time. There were
three beats of silence before Parmley responded.

"I'll tell him that, sir."

Sixty-one

ROTTING from the inside . . ." Krupatin nodded, looking down, frowning as if pondering the gravity of this news. But his manner was disingenuous and patently obvious. He was mocking her. Cate glanced at Irina, who was well aware of Krupatin's contemptuous game; she was staring at him, rigid with humiliation and animus.

Krupatin looked up. "Irina, you can be such a fucking stupid cow," he said. "I really do not know how you have survived all these years, mooing your way from one death to another. How have you avoided your own for so long?"

Irina seemed speechless. She stood with her arms hanging down at her side like a schoolgirl before the headmaster, frozen with embarrassment and resentment.

Krupatin took a step toward her, one hand stuffed casually into his pocket as though he were at a cocktail party, the other holding his drink. His arrogance was insulting and provocative.

"Have you yet to puzzle out this episode in America?" He looked at Cate, then returned his eyes to Irina. "Valentin Stepanov is an informer for the FBI. I know this. Grigori Izvarin has been stabbing me in the back for too long. He has nasty ambitions. I know this too." He sipped his drink. "You did not mention Valery Volkov." He raised his eyebrows in mock surprise. "No?"

Irina said nothing.

Krupatin took another step forward but turned his attention to Cate.

"What happened?" he asked. "Did Valentin moan his traitorous dreams while he was squirming on your belly? And you squealed to your girlfriend here? Money? You want money? You open your legs, and you want money. You open your mouth, and you want money."

"Sergei, please."

Krupatin spun around angrily, his teeth bared, prepared to unleash his fury on Irina. But even while he was still in the motion of turning he saw her outstretched arm, saw what was about to happen, and shouted, flinging up his arms to his face, twisting himself away and backward, gasping, coughing, roaring.

Irina was in motion too, lunging for the table where her SIG-Sauer lay, snatching it up without stopping, pursuing Krupatin's retreat like a spider scuttling to take advantage of an entangled fly.

"Goddamn! Goddamn . . . damn . . ." Krupatin was rolling on the floor, getting to his knees, fumbling his way past the liquor cabinet, knocking off bottles, flinging open a closet door to a wet-bar sink, plunging his face under the tall faucet as he turned on the gushing water. He was grunting, swearing, coughing, spitting.

Irina was suddenly against him, the silencer of the pistol pressed into the side of his head, water splashing all over both of them. She was trembling, grimacing. Krupatin froze, realizing what she was pushing into his temple. Cate braced herself for the shot. Nothing happened. The sound of the water was the only sound. No one moved. Krupatin was bent over, his head turned sideways, his eyes blinking wildly to get the water and whatever it was she had sprayed out of them.

All of them realized at the same moment that the spray had not gotten into his eyes, that he had blinked and ducked in time and most of the spray had hit his arms and head.

Unexpectedly, Irina shoved herself away from him, as if he

were a leper, and backed away, out of his reach. He was gasping for breath as she felt behind her without turning around, not wanting to take her eyes off him for an instant. Krupatin, still bent over the sink, seemed to be taking refuge under the rush of water, gathering his thoughts.

"Stay away from him," Irina said to Cate. "Get over here by me."

Both women backed away from the broken bottles near the liquor cabinet, moving into the middle of the room.

"I'm burning up," Cate said. "I feel like I'm on fire. I'm hot, burning up."

"Relax," Irina said. She was panting. "Take deep breaths."

Nothing was said for a moment as the two women watched Krupatin as if he were a stunned wolf, expecting him at any moment to wail and turn and lunge at them. But he didn't. Finally he turned off the water, groped around on the cabinet until he found a hand towel, and put it to his face. Slowly he turned around and leaned back against the sink.

"I want to sit down," he said through the towel.

Irina hesitated. "Go," she said.

Krupatin, dabbing at his face, made his way past the broken bottles to one of two sofas that sat at right angles to the view of the city, a coffee table between them. He sat down heavily and took a moment to catch his breath. Irina moved over behind the opposite sofa, keeping it and the coffee table between her and Krupatin.

"You stupid cow," he said, sniffling, looking up at her. "You have made the biggest mistake of your life."

Irina was more collected now. And she was focused.

"No, Sergei. I am a fortunate woman."

He shook his head. "You live a fucked-up life. You always have, and that will never change. It's your fate."

"I am fortunate because I have lived long enough to see the end of you. This fate of mine, Sergei, is also yours. We have come to this together. You have made me what I am, and in doing so you have created your own death."

"Look," Krupatin said wearily, "if you are going to shoot me, then go ahead and do it. I don't want to hang around to hear your philosophy."

Irina shook her head. "First you are going to get a short education."

"Wonderful," he said sourly. His hair was in disarray, his suit splashed with water and rumpled.

"I'm burning up," Cate said. "Jesus, it's hot in here."

"What the hell is she babbling about?" Krupatin glared at her. He ran his fingers through his hair and tugged at his suit coat to straighten it.

"Earlier tonight, Valery Volkov killed Stepanov and Izvarin."

"Well, then something has gone right, hasn't it?"

"But it wasn't for you that he killed them."

"Well, I don't give a damn why he killed them. I wanted them dead, and they're dead."

"He killed them for us."

Krupatin nodded monotonously, indicating yes, yes, he was sure she had a story.

"Volkov. Me. Bontate."

"Carlo Bontate." He paused. "Goddamn greasy fucking Sicilian." He paused again. "What about the silly Chinese?"

"I gave him the capsules."

Krupatin snorted with amusement. "No kidding?"

"I killed him for Volkov and Bontate."

This time Krupatin was less dismissive of what he was hearing. He held the towel in his lap and looked at her.

"There's been a coup, Sergei," Irina said, almost with kindness in her voice, as though she were breaking bad news to a simpleminded man. "You are a dead man. Now Valery Volkov is the new man everyone has to fear. Night passes into a new day—without you."

"How am I supposed to believe this came about?"

"I made a deal with Volkov and Bontate. I knew you were going to have me killed when this was over."

"You knew?" Krupatin scoffed. "My God, you stupid bitch. You have a useless imagination." In spite of his mockery, he was clearly finding it more difficult to be cavalier about what he was hearing.

"I went to Bontate. We made a deal. He wanted to bring in Volkov."

"Why? What made him think Valery would go for this deal?"

"His intelligence had informed him that Volkov was wanting you out of the way. Volkov was just waiting for the right time."

"I don't believe it."

"And Ometov told me that as well. That is how I knew that Bontate was telling the truth."

Krupatin was silent. He looked at the floor. "Shit. Leo Ometov."

"Yes, Leo."

Krupatin shook his head. "I don't know who hates me more, you or Leo." He made a disgusted face. "I really don't know why I didn't have him killed a long time ago. It made sense. I just didn't do it. I don't know why I didn't do it." He looked up. "So you agreed to kill me."

"No, I did not 'agree' to kill you, Sergei. I begged to do it. I consider it an act of human kindness, a gesture without any moral ambiguity."

"Oh, God, listen to you—'moral ambiguity.' How can you talk about morals? The word ought to stick in your throat. You are just like me, Irina, only I don't pretend to be righteous. You whine and moan and suffer, but you never change your life, do you? Look at you. You are disgusting, a scab on the ass of society, and you want to talk about morals."

For a man who was staring at his executioner, Krupatin seemed completely lacking in any desire to ingratiate himself, to curry any measure of mercy. In fact, he seemed to be goading her.

He sneered. "Tell me, damn you. What are you getting out of this, Irina?"

"What am I *getting?*" The question seemed to amaze her.

"Yes. What? A promotion? Instead of killing people now, you will advance up the ladder to whore? What? A house in the country? I don't know."

"My *daughter!*" she yelled. "You *know* why I have lived like this—you *know!*"

"Oh, God," Krupatin groaned, cutting her off. "Not again, whining about that—"

"Shut up!" Irina screamed. "Do not even speak of her." She stormed around the sofa, the SIG-Sauer leveled at Krupatin's face as she shoved aside the coffee table, sending a crystal vase flying into the glass wall. Without stopping, her fury displacing her common sense, she climbed onto the sofa, straddled him on her knees, grabbed his hair with her left hand, and put the silencer to his mouth.

"Open it!"

He refused.

"God*damn* your soul!" she screamed. She pulled back the gun and rammed the silencer into Krupatin's mouth, shattering his teeth, bloodying his lips as he yelled in pain.

Cate heard the snick of the safety on the pistol.

"No! Irina!" Cate didn't think; she spoke without forethought, only impulse. "Listen to me—listen to me." She quickly moved closer to them, until she knew she was in Irina's peripheral vision. "Irina, listen to what I am going to say. I'm an FBI agent. I am working undercover."

Irina and Krupatin were frozen in a timeless, weightless instant, their eyes as dead as stone upon each other, and all the confused and distorted passions that had tied them together throughout the endless years were condensed into this slender moment between what was and what was to be.

"Krupatin is right." Cate spoke rapidly, fighting to deflect the direction of the impending action. "Stepanov was working for the FBI as an informant. I was working with him. They knew Krupatin was coming to Houston. Stepanov was going to lead them to him. Irina, don't do this."

Irina's eyes were locked wide open. She was wild with adrenaline. Krupatin swallowed, trying to keep from gagging on his own blood, which drooled down his chin under the barrel of the silencer.

"Irina!" Cate was frantic to be heard. "Listen to me . . . The FBI, they're listening to us right now—they're on their way. Leave me the gun; leave me Krupatin. Get out of here. They only want him. If you stay, you'll be killed, or they'll put you in prison. Either way, it will be a disaster for Félia. Don't you understand that? You have money. You can take her away. The two of you can disappear. You know how to do that."

Nothing happened. No one moved.

"No." Irina shook her head. "Impossible. They . . . The agreement is . . . This is the condition."

Krupatin's eyes were frozen on Irina, his head arched back, blood stringing from his mouth onto his suit.

Cate could hear her own heart. She could hear time slipping

away like a sigh. She could hear her thoughts moving through her mind like rain.

Krupatin suddenly brought his hand out from under the cushion on the sofa and rammed it up between Irina's spread legs. There were two explosions as he fired into her pelvis, and Cate saw a spray of blood and tissue lift up the back of her dress and blow out from between her buttocks.

Sixty-two

UNBELIEVABLY, Irina's SIG-Sauer did not go off in Krupatin's mouth. Simultaneously with firing his own gun, he twisted his head back and away, so that Irina's reflex shot blew past his face, taking away part of his ear and searing his jaw. Leaping to his feet, Krupatin sent the shocked Irina sprawling, which launched the SIG-Sauer into the air, end over end toward Cate, past her. It landed on the parquet floor and skittered away from her toward the far curve of the glass wall.

Without even thinking, Cate lunged across the room, scrambled for the gun, and in an instant was dropping down on one knee, both hands gripping it as her arms swung up. Looking down the length of her outstretched arms, she found Krupatin halfway to the front door, whirling around as he raised his wobbling arm to fire.

His gun had no silencer, and the bursts of his gunfire were deafening. They both fired. Cate felt the SIG recoil but didn't hear her own silenced shots against Krupatin's cannon blasts. She saw his muzzle flashes, heard the sizzling rounds splitting the air around her, heard the shattering glass.

Krupatin was down but picked himself up and scrambled for the door, turned again, fired again. He was out into the foyer. Cate floundered toward him. She managed to get to the front door herself and got a glimpse of him fumbling with the elevator button. She fired twice, wildly, her slugs hitting the elevator door above his head. As he whirled she fell back, anticipating the *boom!* that followed, and then she stuck her head around the corner again and heard the stairwell door open and slam.

"JesusChristJesusChrist you people hear me? He's going down the stairs—the stairwell, going down the stairwell!" she screamed. "We've got casualties up here, you hear me—casualties!"

She checked the barrel of the SIG. There was one round in the barrel, but she didn't think it was the only one left. She counted her rounds, tried to count them, but gave up. There was no way in the excitement.

Standing in the doorway, she turned to look at Irina, who was trying to get up. Jesus God. Her gestures, her expression of shock, dehumanized her. She was not a woman but a gravely wounded animal that did not understand what was happening to it.

Cate grabbed a picture from the wall and a small chair sitting in the entry. She wedged the chair in the apartment door, ran to the stairwell, opened the door, went inside, and put the picture frame in the jamb to keep it from closing and locking behind her. Then she paused and listened. She could hear Krupatin going down.

She started down, stumbling five or six steps and then jumping the last ones to the next landing. She did the same with the next flight, and the next, and the next, before she stopped to listen. Nothing. But she saw blood on the cement stairs. Then she heard him moving. Closer now. Two flights down.

Again she ran, stumbled, jumped. And again. And again she stopped. There was a lot of blood on the stairs, and there were long drags of it smeared along the wall. She must have hit him. Maybe in the side or the stomach. But he was definitely slowing.

Silence.

She waited. She heard him move, just around the corner on the next turn.

"Come on," he said, his voice weak but amplified in the empty stairwell. "I'll kill you."

She moved down one step at a time until she saw him, sitting in the corner of the next turn, the two walls holding him up. He was aiming at her, but didn't fire as she darted her head around the corner. He was too weak to risk an uncertain shot at a small target.

"Throw the gun out where I can see it," she said.

"Go to hell."

"You'll die there. I can get you an ambulance."

"I'm going to kill you," he said. "Goddamn you."

Cate thought of Irina upstairs, dying alone. Oh God, she thought, don't let her die alone. Cate was furious. She remembered a small plastic trash bucket that had been set outside the door on the landing behind her. She took off her shoes.

"I'm going to ask you one more time," she said and hurried up the steps to the trash bucket. Krupatin shouted something at her, but she couldn't understand him. The plastic bucket had some twisted wire coat hangers in it, which she dumped out on the floor. Then she retraced her steps. Staying out of Krupatin's sight, she began unbuttoning her dress. After stepping out of it, she put the bucket in the top and buttoned it up to hold the plastic bucket in. She cinched up the belt to hold it in on the bottom.

"Krupatin," she said. "Your last chance."

He did not respond. She leaned slightly forward and saw his knee doubled up on the floor. He hadn't moved.

"Okay," she said. "If you want to make this . . ."

She threw the dress onto the landing, the bucket giving it body for an instant, the skirt flying, a big target—something he could hit. And he did. There were three *booms*. The bucket flew back, slammed against the wall by the slugs fired at point-blank range. Then she heard a sound: *clickclickclick, click.*

Cate came around the corner and stepped down onto the landing with Krupatin. He was slumped, bleeding from the stomach, from the mouth, drenched in sweat. They stared at each other, and then he threw the gun at her, startling her, thwacking her in the side.

They stared at each other.

"You had better think about this," he said. "Do you have any idea how much money I could give you? Untraceable. A Belgian account."

Cate walked up to him and put the SIG-Sauer to his forehead.

Krupatin said nothing, swallowed, and began involuntarily urinating.

"Goddamn you!" He swung his arm at her, a sloppy, wobbly swing. His gut was hemorrhaging a lot of blood.

She gave it a second thought. She would have to explain the contact wound. She took the gun away from his head. She picked up her dress, unbuttoned it, and dumped out the trash can. Carrying it across her arm, she walked back up five steps, turned, aimed, and fired. One, two, three times.

She had thought she had four shots left.

But three was enough.

Sixty-three

AFTER SLIPPING into her dress—Krupatin's three shots had ripped three tears, one each in the midriff, the left breast, and the skirt—she hurried as fast as she could up the stairwell, stopping at each landing door to try the doorknob, even though she knew all of them would be locked. She was exhausted, out of shape, dizzy. She had come down farther than she had guessed. All the turns looked the same. Had someone removed the picture? Had she passed it already? Then she rounded a corner and saw it.

When she jerked open Krupatin's door, which was still propped ajar with the chair, the whole place was dark again. They must have knocked out the lamp. She could not find any light switches and finally located another table lamp near the sofas where she had left Irina. Putting down the gun, she fumbled hastily at the lamp switch, and when it came on she was stunned at the amount of blood and how it glistened in the feeble light. The furniture was scattered and knocked over, but Irina was not there.

Then she saw the trail of blood on the carpet leading around the corner to a hallway. Her heart sank as she noted the volume of it. Suddenly the place gave her the creeps.

"Irina!"

She was taut inside, dreading what she would find, sick at what she had done, horrified at what the night had been like.

"Irina!" She was running now, down the corridor, which was wide and curved gently past a kind of office and after that opened into a bedroom. Just as she entered, something fell on a tile floor in the bathroom around the corner.

She ran past large windows that looked onto the city and skirted a round bed—Krupatin's idea of luxury, a round bed with rumpled sheets—to reach the bathroom. It was an enormous room that was reached through double doors of glass. Deep cobalt tile glittered with cleanliness, and full-length mirrors were placed at angles to expand its size. There was a large vanity, and a large shower without walls in the center of the room, with a shallowly sloped, disk-shaped marble floor to catch the water for the drain.

Close up against the windows was a long bathtub made of tiny brilliant gold tiles, a construction of such richness that it seemed as if it had been made of fine, sheet-thin gold foil. A sludge of blood trailed across the tile floor to the tub. Irina was inside.

"Oh, God . . . God . . ." Cate ran over and knelt down.

Irina reclined in the tub, still dressed, her skirt pulled up to her waist and a pile of white towels, dark with grume, jammed between her legs. She held them in place with both hands. She was as pale as a mannequin and was sweating profusely.

"Did you get him?" Her voice was frail.

"I killed him," Cate said. She jumped up and ran to the vanity and grabbed another towel. Where the fuck *was* everybody? On her way back to the tub she folded the towel, then she put it under Irina's head, which was lying back on the sloping gold tile. She knelt beside the tub. She realized she was crying, in frustration and horror and exhaustion.

Irina tensed the corners of her mouth briefly. "It is my fault. We were so close. I should have shot him while he was bending over the sink. It would have been so easy. And it would have been over . . . We were so close."

"Jesus, Irina." Cate was sobbing. Whatever small threads of her emotions had held together up to this point, they were now long past their ability to hold. There was nothing left.

For a while there was only the sound of her weeping.

"I do not think this is going to stop," Irina said, lifting her head, looking at the pile of towels between her legs. Blood was running from the saturated pile into the drain. Cate could actually hear it trickling into the pipe.

"You're going to be okay," Cate said, a stupid, silly statement in the face of what both of them could see. She had put her hands on top of Irina's. The situation was pitiful. Horrible and pitiful.

Irina smiled. It was a dry, parched smile, her lips stiff with the dehydration of shock.

"I had no idea you were with the FBI," she said. "You were very . . . very good, Catherine." She paused. "Your name is Catherine."

"Yes," Cate said. The admission almost stuck in her throat.

"You were very good, yes, but . . . Tell me, I believed you had real . . . affection for me. You did, didn't you? It wasn't all just an act. We were friends, real friends."

"I . . . Of course. More than that. I learned to love you," Cate said, not knowing whether she was lying or telling the truth or what it meant exactly. She could feel the tears actually falling out of her eyes.

"Yes, we had that." Irina nodded. Her chignon was coming loose, and buttery blond hair was falling down her neck.

Oh, God, dear God. Cate could hardly stand it.

"There is a little time," Irina said. "I would like to talk." She swallowed, tried to find some moisture in her mouth.

Cate jumped up and got a glass of water and helped her drink it. Irina kept both her hands on the scarlet towels.

"I have killed eight people, Catherine," Irina said. "I want you to know that because . . . because . . ." She sighed and swallowed. "You know . . . when I could, when I was able to do it, I would go to the Alexander Nevsky Monastery, to the Trinity Cathedral there, and pray. I wouldn't pray for my soul, for my sins. No, not for that. I would pray that I would be able to kill the people I was supposed to kill. I prayed to God: please take the man in Prague. Please take the man in Rome, the man in Milan, the woman in Bern. Take them, please, God, and spare my Félia from this devil Krupatin. That sounds horrible, I know." She swallowed. "And it was horrible. But it was not as horrible to me as what would have happened if I had failed. Every prayer for death was also a prayer for life." She paused. "So what am I to think? Could God answer such prayers with a yes?" She looked down at her legs. "Ah, well, it is confusing if he did, isn't it? But it seems to me that that is what he has done, and for that I am grateful."

She studied the blood rolling out between her knees. Cate couldn't look down. Her attention was on Irina; her eyes were fixed on her face. She was fearful of turning them anywhere else.

"Blood from my veins," Irina mused, still looking at her legs. "Red against gold. In an icon that is one of the most beautiful combinations of colors." She was thoughtful, the expression on her face serene. "There is an icon in Venice, a fifteenth-century one from Crete, I think, and it is the most beautiful use of scarlet and gold I have ever seen. Mary Magdalene is kneeling before the risen Christ. Christ's robes are dark, highlighted with golden folds, and Mary . . . is wearing a scarlet cape. *Noli me tangere,* he is saying—'Touch me not.' "

She raised her head, then once again looked down between her legs. Her expression was grim. "Dear God—this is very bad, I think." She laid her head back on the towel and closed her eyes. After a moment she opened her eyes again and went on.

"Do you believe in God, Catherine?"

Cate supposed she did. She nodded.

"He gave me a glass heart," Irina said matter-of-factly. "Do you remember I told this to you before? I did not ask for it, the glass heart. It was a gift." She waited as if to let something subside—a pain, perhaps; a dizziness. "Hard is the glass heart. Nothing moves through it. It has no fragrance or softness. Cold to the touch. It hears no music, sees no light . . ."

She stopped again. Phlegm was accumulating in her throat, and she had to cough. Her eyes were growing heavy. Her breath jerked in her chest, and then she went on.

"And yet it is fragile too, so very fragile. When Félia smiled . . . my heart crazed. When she laughed, it shivered almost to breaking. When she kissed my cheek, it shattered into powder." She paused. "A glass heart. Hard . . . and fragile. I needed both—to survive. And, in the end, to be redeemed. God is grace, even to the damned. One of his endless paradoxes."

Cate was heaving with sobs. In her mind she could hear the blood trickling over each tiny gold tile, like the sound of tongues moving just below a whisper.

In a little while Irina opened her eyes one last time, just barely, so that Cate saw only a thin gleam of green.

"After I die," she said, her tongue searching for moisture, "take the locket."

In the silence that followed, Irina grew paler against the gold. As the night moved steadily into the thinness of its time, her beautiful face grew still and slack. And then, just moments before the eastern sky pulled away from the weakening grasp of darkness, Cate felt a sudden stillness in the room, and she knew that she was very much alone.

Epilogue

Rome, early May, ten months later

S HE SAT in the anteroom of the office of Documentos Uf-
ficiales on the third floor of the Palazzo di Giustizia. Func-
tionaries came in and out of the anteroom, which was as huge as a
house, with terrazzo floors, a twenty-foot ceiling, wood paneling
along the walls, and twelve-foot wooden doors leading to all the
offices. The hard leather soles of Italian shoes echoed in the voluminous room, and voices hung in the slightly chilled air. The
cavernous old travertine building had not yet absorbed enough of
the bright spring sun to warm its winter-cooled stones.

She had been waiting for over half an hour, she and two men,
the three of them clustered together, sharing the space of a few
square feet to one side of this grand space. One man unwrapped a
piece of candy, the cellophane crackling like birds scratching
through dry winter leaves. But winter was gone and it was now
spring, and from where she sat she could see through the tall
windows across the room the canopies of the chestnuts and stone
pines that stood on the opposite bank of the Tiber, just outside.
The azaleas were in full bloom on the Spanish Steps, and the trees

were still trying to decide which shade of green suited them the best.

Nearly a week in Rome with nothing to do other than enjoy the city's beauty had done little to calm her uneasiness, though that was precisely why she had come five days before the appointed date. She had strolled along the Via dei Condotti, staring into the windows of the expensive shops at fashionable clothes she could not afford and did not need. She had lingered around the fountains and sidewalk cafés, watching the effects of the Roman spring on the Romans and tourists alike. It was beautiful to watch, but she felt no connection with it whatsoever. Perhaps it was an inevitable nervousness, considering what she was about to do, but it was also the uneasiness of association. It was not that far down the highway south of the city that she had come twenty-four months ago to collect Tavio's body from the small, grim morgue in Salerno.

"Signora Cuevas."

The sound of her own name startled her. She looked around, and a young man wearing a loose-fitting Italian suit was standing in one of the huge wooden doorways, a sheaf of papers tucked under his arm. He was looking at her, and the two men who had been her companions in this hollow chamber for three quarters of an hour were also looking at her.

"Yes," she said, standing.

"This way, please," the young man said.

They entered another, but much smaller, anteroom and then walked into a long, grand room which was sparsely furnished except for a few straight-backed chairs along the walls. The walls themselves were a pale canary yellow and were hung with enormous paintings, portraits of forgotten men from other centuries. At the far end of the room sat an enormous solitary Baroque desk with gilt scrolling on its face and legs, papers stacked about in an organized if not entirely neat fashion, and two gilt lamps that glowed in the shady vastness. Behind the desk sat a small balding man with a precise black mustache.

"Signora Cuevas," he said, standing as she approached his desk. He introduced himself. "Please sit down."

Cate watched him closely, wondering how all this had been worked out, wondering if he was nervous about it, or if he was glad to be of service, or if he was doing this against his will but had no choice, or if he was a sycophant and only too eager to please. None of this showed on his round forehead or in his beautiful eyes or on his generous mouth, which he tended to purse.

"I have all of the papers for you right here," he said, getting straight to the point. Perhaps he was eager to be done with it. He picked up a packet of documents, which were in a large folder tied with a bright scarlet ribbon, and handed the packet across the desk to her. "Please feel free to look at them and make sure that they are prepared to your satisfaction."

"I can't read Italian," she said, putting the packet in her lap, "and besides, I wouldn't be able to understand the complex legal points. I trust that you have done all the proper things for me. I'll make sure that the right people hear of your efficiency."

He smiled with a little bow, but the mention of the "right people" put an edge to his smile. He was probably hoping to God he hadn't screwed up anything.

Cate stood and shook his hand. "Again, thank you," she said.

"If I can be of any further service to you," he added quickly, "please contact me immediately. I am more than happy to be able to help you. *Arrivederci.*"

It was a long walk back to her little hotel not far from the Piazza di Spagna, but she didn't mind. Now that she had the documents, her mind turned to the meeting in the afternoon. The long walk would help settle her butterflies. Perhaps it would even give her an appetite.

She ate a light lunch in the hotel garden, under the dappled shade of an arbor. Afterward she had an extra glass of wine. When her watch told her it was two o'clock, she paid, walked out of the hotel, and stood at the entrance—still holding the documents—in front of the vine-covered stucco walls facing the piazza.

A dark Mercedes entered the opposite side of the piazza and made its way around to the front of the hotel and stopped. A young man got out and approached her.

"Perhaps you are Signora Cuevas?"

She nodded, and he opened the back door of the Mercedes and she got in. She didn't even try to keep track of where they were going, but simply sat back and watched the streets and piazzas of Rome pass by outside her window. The car left the heart of the city and climbed up narrow lanes into the wooded hillsides, where the homes grew grander and villas stood back from the lanes behind walls or on beautifully landscaped grounds. Eventually she felt the car slowing and saw that they were turning into a high-walled compound. A brass plaque on the pillars of the gates said CONVENTO SANTA CECELIA DEL MONTI. Cypresses grew along the gravel road that led up to the main building, which was as fine an example of a Renaissance villa as she could imagine.

The Mercedes stopped in front of the convent, and the young man got out and opened the door for her. As she was getting out of the back seat, a nun came down the front steps of the villa, smiling, her entirely white robes and wimple brilliant in the afternoon sun.

"Ms. Cuevas? I am Sister Sabina," she said in very good but heavily accented English. "Please come inside. We are so happy to have you."

Sister Sabina was in her thirties, Cate guessed, and she was nothing less than charming. Together they walked through the great rooms of the old convent, meeting other nuns in groups and alone as they passed through corridors, across courtyards, and along loggias. Finally they went through an open gallery and out the other side to a large and beautifully tended garden. There were lime trees and azaleas, cypresses and palms and chestnut trees, paths with privet hedges and flowerbeds and garden benches.

Cate could not get used to the idea that she was expected and welcomed everywhere she went. The way had been prepared to perfection for her. All was arranged.

"Your friend arrived just ahead of you," Sister Sabina said, and then she slowed and stopped and motioned with her hand to a secluded corner of the garden, where a man was sitting on a bench alone, staring at the water splashing in a fountain on the other side of the path from him.

"Thank you very much," Cate said, and Sister Sabina turned and left her.

The man glanced up and saw her and stood as she approached him. He was wearing a suit and tie, which she had not expected, and he was a little taller than she had guessed from his photographs, his complexion a little ruddier, his face a little kinder. But none of the pictures she had seen had prepared her for his eyes. They were stunning, bright amber, like chunks of pyrite shaded by long sable lashes. He was smoking a cigarette but switched it to his left hand to greet her. They shook hands without actually introducing themselves.

"Please sit down," he said, and together they sat on the bench facing the fountain and a flowerbed of cerise flowers. He nodded at the folder with the bright scarlet ribbon. "Everything is arranged, I hope."

"I don't know," Cate said. "I told the man that I was taking his word for it."

"Oh, don't worry," he smiled. "The Italian government won't give you any trouble about this, and neither will the Americans. But before you leave, the sisters inside will have to put a bunch of seals and things all over the documents to make them legal from their standpoint, since the convent is the registering agency for this." He smoked. He glanced at her. "This is very amusing to me. Me helping the FBI."

"No," Cate said. "You are helping me, not the FBI."

"Oh, yes, okay." He smiled again. "I guess they didn't make this easy for you."

"No, you're right. They didn't."

"You can imagine," he said, blowing smoke away into the afternoon heat, "how surprised I was to receive these . . . overtures from you. After all that."

"Yes. As a matter of fact, I was a little surprised to be doing it."

They were both silent for a moment, and the convent garden was silent too, except for the droning of cicadas.

"Well, anyway, the world is better off without Sergei Krupatin," he said, dropping his cigarette and mashing it out in the gravel. Cate thought how out of place a cigarette butt was in this immaculate setting. There were already several on the ground at his end of the bench. "But I am sorry about Irina."

Cate said nothing.

"He was a real bastard," the man said.

"Is Volkov any better?" she asked.

"Better?" he shrugged. "It all depends on what you mean by better. He is different, at least."

"How is he different?"

"Well, he's not crazy. That's something. And he kept his end of the bargain with Irina, even though she was dead. That's something."

Another pause.

"Then you're still working with him?" Cate asked.

The man kept his eyes on the fountain and smiled slowly. "We really should not talk about this."

"What's happened with the Chinese organization? They still don't have a clue about what happened?"

"Well, it took him so long to die. That was very clever. People get sick. There is not much you can say about that. I think some of Wei's lieutenants are suspicious and very angry. But he had very good doctors. You know what, he had been in Thailand. That's where the doctors think he got it. I really didn't know Sergei was that clever."

He continued looking at the fountain. The sounds of its splashing accompanied the drone of the cicadas.

"I want to thank you," Cate said. "I know this was not easy to do."

"I promised her too," he said. "Some of us are honest guys. We have morals." He paused. "And you know, I don't care how he died, exactly—the details. I still owed her a debt. She could have killed all three of us."

Cate did not look at him, so she didn't know whether he was fishing for the real story or actually knew it. She had managed to convince the FBI to keep the facts, as they appeared in the media, vague enough for Volkov and Bontate to believe that all the rules had been followed—just in case there was no honor among thieves. But apparently there was.

Cate didn't even know what to think. She had just received a lot of help from the Russian *mafiya* and the Sicilian Mafia, all of it illegal, and yet she thought it was the right thing to do. She knew it was. It had to be.

They heard voices through the trees in the garden, and Cate looked around.

"A couple of the sisters took them walking," he explained.

"Them?"

Just then the voices came closer, and from around the corner between two palms on the sun-dappled pathway appeared two nuns in dazzling white and in between them two little girls about six years old, wearing very similar white lace dresses with spotless white stockings and black shoes. One of the girls was as dark as a Gypsy, with long jet hair. She was leading a speckled hen on a string.

"This is my daughter, Stefania," he said affectionately.

The other little girl made Cate's heart stop. As pale as a gardenia, she had thick, long flaxen hair pulled back from her face and falling over her tiny shoulders like spun gold. She looked at Cate with curious sea-green eyes and almost smiled.

"And this . . . is Félia."

Cate almost lost her grip on the folder of documents that made this child her adopted daughter. Tears sprang to her eyes so suddenly it frightened her. As she knelt slowly on the gravel path and put down the packet, Félia stepped toward her hesitantly, as if she understood what was impossible to understand. Cate smiled, and at that moment she knew that she had done the right thing. As long as this child breathed, she would be a living reminder of her mother's love. Surely in the scales of eternal judgment the love that Irina so fervently had nurtured for this tiny child would weigh heavily against all the evil and sadness that had been so large a part of her life. Félia would be a living requiem for her mother, a constant prayer, and a reminder that of all the many passions that gripped and compelled the human heart in the course of a lifetime, the greatest of them was love.